The Atlas of Middle-earth

KAREN WYNN FONSTAD

Revised Edition

HOUGHTON MIFFLIN COMPANY   BOSTON

To

Todd, Mark, and Kristi

— (still pieless) —

who have shared ten years of trials
and triumphs from Middle-earth,
and to Kit Keefe, my cheery and
courageous friend who first
lent me *The Lord of the Rings*

Also by Karen Wynn Fonstad

The Atlas of Pern
The Atlas of the Land
The Atlas of the Dragonlance™ World
The Forgotten Realms® Atlas

The compass rose on the cover was modified from the heraldic device of Eärendil the Mariner, a design by J. R. R. Tolkien.

The runes shown were those used on all maps in Middle-earth, regardless of language. Note that the chief compass point was west, toward Valinor.

númen (west) formen (north)

hyarmen (south) rómen (east)

Library of Congress Cataloging-in-Publication Data

Fonstad, Karen Wynn.
The atlas of Middle-earth / Karen Wynn Fonstad. — Rev. ed.
p. cm.
Includes bibliographical references and index.
ISBN 0-395-53516-6
1. Tolkien, J. R. R. (John Ronald Reuel), 1892–1973 — Settings.
2. Middle Earth (Imaginary place) — Maps. I. Title.
G3122.M5F6 1991 ⟨G&M⟩
823'.912—dc20 91-25932
CIP MAP

Printed in the United States of America

CRW 10 9 8 7 6 5 4 3 2 1

Acknowledgments

Although the quality and accuracy (or inaccuracy) of the product within these pages rests entirely with the author, the work could never have been completed without the encouragement and assistance of many people:

My husband, Todd, an associate professor of geography, who not only lent emotional support, but also provided references and guidance during the critical initial evaluations of the physical geography for the regional and thematic maps.

My mother, Estis Wynn, who painstakingly typed much of the original manuscript, and my sister Marsa Crissup, who retyped it all on a computer.

My husband's parents, Fay and the late Ward Fonstad, my good friends Lea Meeker and Zenda Gutierrez, and others of my family and friends who listened to my woes, watched the children, ran errands, and forgave me for being too busy to return their good will.

The many readers who have shared their enthusiasm, questions and suggestions during the ten years the *Atlas* has been available.

Numerous University of Wisconsin–Oshkosh faculty members who answered my questions, including Paul Johnson, William and Doris Hodge, Andrew Bodman, Nils Meland, the late Donald Netzer, Neil Harriman, Donald Bruyere, Herbert Gaede, Ronald Crane, and Marvin Mengeling.

Lisa Richardson, who introduced me to Liquid Eraser™ ink remover!

James M. Goodman, my major professor at the University of Oklahoma, who instructed me in cartography and directed my thesis, giving me the invaluable knowledge of how to organize a long paper.

The staff of Marquette University's Department of Special Collections and University Archives, who cheerfully gave access to the Tolkien Manuscript Collection, notably Chuck Elston and Taum Santoski. Without the drawings made available at Marquette, this *Atlas* would have required much more work in the beginning, and would have required far more extensive revision.

The University of Wisconsin–Oshkosh Department of Geography, Cartographic Services, Learning Resources Center, and the Oshkosh Public Library, from which many of my references were drawn.

Houghton Mifflin's editors and other personnel, who were enthusiastic and supportive from the outset. Special thanks go to my editors on the two editions, Stella Easland on the original, and Ruth Hapgood on the revision, and to Anne Barrett, my delightful first contact.

Robert Foster, without whose excellent glossary the original atlas would have taken much longer to complete.

Christopher Tolkien, whose release of *The Silmarillion* supplied the spark that began my work, and who has performed a monumental task in organizing *The History* series.

And especially J. R. R. Tolkien, who wrote not only enthralling books, but also meticulous ones. Only such breadth of knowledge and attention to detail could provide the data for an entire atlas — *and* a revision!

Contents

REGIONAL MAPS

THE HOBBIT

THE LORD OF THE RINGS

THEMATIC MAPS

Foreword

In the summer of 1988, a reader (who due to the inadequacy of my 'non-filing' system must remain unknown) asked a question which has frequently been posed since the release of *The Atlas of Middle-earth* in 1981: "Are there any plans to publish a paperback edition?" Of more importance, however, was the reader's second question: "Will the atlas be revised based on the *History of Middle-earth* series?" This edition is the direct response to both of those queries.

Even before the original atlas went to press, it required revision when Houghton Mifflin sent the typescript of *Unfinished Tales*, which was not expected to arrive until after the atlas was in print. Christopher Tolkien apparently began immediately on *The History*, with the first volume copyrighted in 1983.

Volumes one through five of *The History* covered the period through the downfall of Númenor, while volumes six through nine expanded on *The Lord of the Rings*.[1] *The History* thus far has two notable omissions. Except for *Unfinished Tales*, there is no publication expanding on *The Hobbit* or the appendices relating the history of the early Third Age, and there may not be.[2]

> The importance of *The Hobbit* in *the history of the evolution* of Middle-earth lies then, at this time, in the fact that it was published, and that a sequel to it was demanded . . . Its significance for Middle-earth lies in what it would do, not in what it was.[3]

Early in the process, the decision was reluctantly made to use *The History* simply as a reference to confirm and/or elaborate on the original atlas, rather than to add maps and discussion comparing various forms of the stories *The History* relates. The wealth of information simply could not be incorporated into the atlas without complete redesign, which would double the length, and, most important, produce possible confusion to the thousands of readers who had read only the original (finalized) version of the Middle-earth tales. Also, to avoid simple duplication, *History* references are listed only when they are correct or if they add extra insight or information to the existing text.

Within the role of correcting the original atlas, *The History* had an impact in three areas: additional drawings and maps not previously available; more detailed discussions in early versions which were absent (but not necessarily replaced) in the final published accounts; and additional names for many locations. The revision also incorporates suggestions from readers. There has been no attempt to standardize the atlas with maps, drawings, and writings of non-Tolkien sources.

The maps detailing the lands of the earlier ages, especially those in volume four, *The Shaping of Middle-earth*, were especially helpful in remapping the whole of Arda. In the original atlas the world maps were based strictly on analysis of the written text.

In the volumes covering *The Lord of the Rings*, one crucial role of *The History* was the assignment of the various drawings and maps to the appropriate version of the text. This information immediately clarified why some of the sketches that had been available from Marquette University archives during the initial writing and design of the atlas differed in some details from the published descriptions, notably Isengard, Dunharrow, and Minas Tirith.

While Christopher Tolkien states that *The Lord of the Rings* was created "in waves"[4] (the author writing a section of the tale, then recommencing several chapters back), the striking impression is often of the similarities rather than the differences — although it is more intriguing to analyze the latter! Tempting as it was to trace Tolkien's visions through the various stages, those interested must be referred to *The History*. The same was true of the many changes of the pathways and chronology. "The Tale of Years" continued to stand as the authority for the quest of the ring, as well as the Elder Days.[5]

Introduction

LIKE BILBO, I have always loved maps. I was first introduced to *The Lord of the Rings* in 1969 as a graduate assistant in cartography, when one of the students in my class chose to redraft the map of Middle-earth as her term project. She did not complete her map by the semester's end. I do not know if she ever did, but the work and the idea stuck with me.

Two years later I finally read *The Lord of the Rings* and *The Hobbit*. Immediately I developed an explorer's need to map and classify this (to me) newfound world. The complexity of history, diversity of landscapes, and proliferation of places were so overwhelming that I longed to clarify them with pen and ink for my own satisfaction. I wished for one gigantic indexed map, showing every place-name and all the pathways. Rereadings, so numerous that I have ceased to count them, only reinforced this need. Finally, I tackled the project. With no schedule except my own, the work went slowly. The publication of *The Silmarillion* filled so many gaps, and added so many new complexities, that I finally realized no one map could ever be sufficient; and from that realization came this atlas.

Tolkien warned us not to ask to see the "bones" boiled to make the "soup,"[6] but in the preface to *The History* Christopher Tolkien stated: 'Such inquiries are in no way illegitimate in principle; they arise from an acceptance of the imagined world as an object of contemplation or study valid as many other objects of contemplation or study in the all too unimaginary world.'[7] In accord with this attitude many of us have such an insatiable desire to look into every corner of Middle-earth that we seem unable to follow Tolkien's advice. So, properly warned, I shall attempt to show you some of the "bones."

Tolkien's "Sub-Creation"

In "On Fairy-Stories" Tolkien explained that in order to make an imaginary land (and the story that takes place within it) believable, the Secondary World must have the "inner consistency of reality."[8] The more a Secondary World differs from our Primary one, the more difficult it becomes to keep it credible. It demands "a kind of elvish craft."[9]

Tolkien did not wish to create a totally new Secondary World. In an interview he once responded, "If you really want to know what Middle-earth is based on, it's my wonder and delight in the Earth as it is, particularly the natural earth."[10] He also wanted to provide a new mythology from the English viewpoint.[11] So he took our world, with its processes, and infused it with just enough changes to make it "faerie." This was the basis of all the decisions necessary for the atlas: (1) What would it be like in our Primary World? (2) How was it affected by the Secondary World?

Round Versus Flat

Although Kocher suggested that we should not look too closely into a question that Tolkien chose to ignore,[12] the consideration of whether this world was round or flat is inescapable for the cartographer attempting to map a world. One reference strongly indicated that Arda was originally flat: At the time of the fall of Númenor, Valinor was removed from Arda; then "the world was indeed made round," although those permitted could still find the "Straight Road" to Valinor.[13] Prior to the change, the usage of the phrase "Circles of the World"[14] referred not to a planetary spherical shape, but rather to the physical outer limits or "confines."[15] The maps and diagrams in *The Shaping of Middle-Earth*, "The Ambarkanta," all confirm this interpretation.

Tolkien was envisioning his world much as our me-

Figure 1

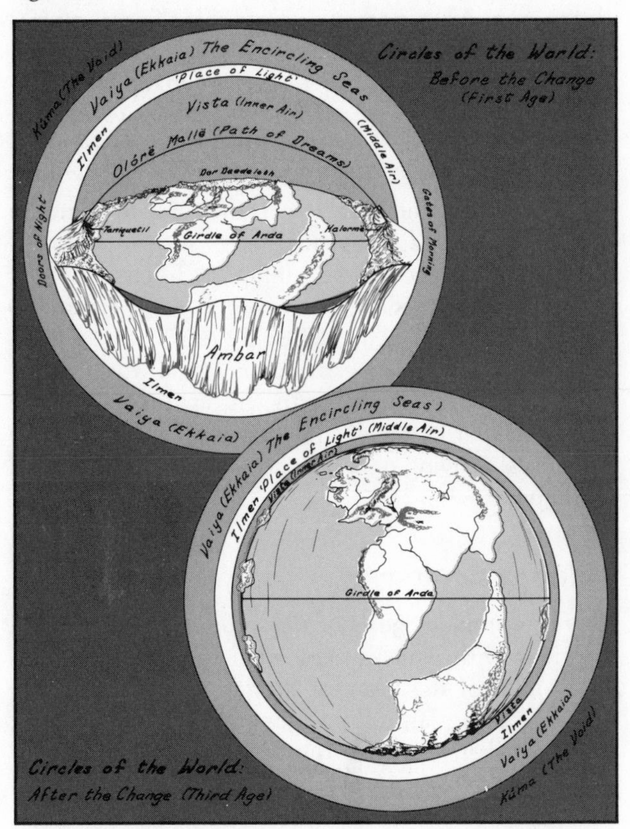

dieval cartographers viewed our own.[16] They showed the earth as a disk, with oceans around the circumference. The top was oriented toward "Paradise" in the east. Conversely, Tolkien stated that in Middle-earth the compass points began with and faced west[17] — apparently toward Valinor, *their Paradise.* In spite of Tolkien's comment, however, all *his* maps were oriented for his readers rather than for inhabitants of Middle-earth. They show *north* at the top, and those in this *Atlas* do the same.

From the edge of the disk, however, the reader sees the 'Vista' (inner airs) domed above the land surface, and the solid 'Ambar' (earth) below; with 'Vaiya' (the encircling 'seas' — but obviously not used in the usual sense of seas) separating the whole from 'Kúma' (the Void).[18] There is no contradiction in the statement "it was globed amid the Void,"[19] for the diagrams clearly demonstrate that Middle-earth could be both round *and* flat! So we can safely consider Middle-earth as flat — at least until the Fall of Númenor . . .

After the fashion of the world was changed, and Arda was made round, there were cartographic difficulties. The maps of Middle-earth included in *The Lord of the Rings* showed both a north arrow and a bar scale. This means that both distance *and* direction were considered to be accurate — an impossibility in mapping a round world. One of the biggest mapping problems through the centuries has been putting a round world on a flat piece of paper. It is impossible for all distances to be correct in any case. If the direction is consistent, then the shapes and areas are distorted. Maps of small areas can ignore the variations as negligible, but continent and world-sized maps cannot. Accuracy of any of these properties can only result in inaccuracy of the others. How many of us once thought Greenland was larger than South America thanks to wall maps at school!

So we return to the beginning — Tolkien's world, at least after the Change, was round; yet it appears to have been mapped as flat. The only reasonable solution is to map his maps — treating his round world as if it were flat. Then Middle-earth will appear to us as it did to Tolkien. After all, how few of us really perceive ourselves as living on a rounded surface, even though we know it is!

Indexing Locations

One of the major goals of this project was to provide an index with which places could be readily located. In an atlas of the Primary World, coordinates would be listed using latitude and longitude. We have been given neither. Latitude can be roughly guessed by climatic clues — seasons and wind patterns. These alone indicate that the familiar lands of the northwest must have lain in roughly the locale of Europe. Tolkien, upon questioning, was even reported to have said that Middle-earth *is* Europe,[20] but later denied it.[21]

Using real coordinates from our real world not only brings us back to the flat earth problems but seems presumptuous and unnecessary. Instead, all location maps have been based upon a worldwide grid that extends from Valinor to the mounts of Orocarni, and from the Grinding Ice to Far Harad. Each square is 100 miles on a side, as are those used on Tolkien's working maps.[22] Each location, including all language variations, has been indexed using this grid; and all regional location maps include the coordinates on the margins.

How Long Is a League?

In these days of the kilometer, when even the English mile is fast disappearing, Tolkien's usage of leagues, furlongs, fathoms, and ells added to the mystique and feeling of history — and to the bewilderment of the mapmaker. A fathom equals six feet; an ell, 27 to 45 inches; a furlong, 220 yards or one eighth of a mile. These smaller units are relatively unimportant to the cartographer's calculations, but a league — how long is a league? Its distance has varied in different times and countries from 2.4 to 4.6 miles.[23] Multiplying such variance by a hundred or more resulted in unacceptable, unusable data; but at last, with the release of *Unfinished Tales,* a definitive figure was given. A league "in Númenórean reckoning . . . was very nearly three of our miles."[24]

To assure that the distances were uniform, meticulous map measurements were done by road and "as the crow flies" for every reference to distance in leagues given in *The Lord of the Rings* (the only work whose maps included a scale). The usage ranged from 2.9 miles per league (up the Anduin between Pelargir and the landings at Harlond) to 17.5 miles per league (the straight-line distance from Helm's Deep to the Fords of Isen). Most of the measurements were reasonably close if the leagues in the text were considered as straight-line measurements, whether or not that was specifically stated. Applying the constant of 3.0 miles per league to the map and distances given in *The Silmarillion* produced a marvelous result: The curvature of the Blue Mountains — the only feature common to maps of both the First and Third Ages — matched exactly even before the maps in *The History* were available! For those who wish to compare these values on all the large regional maps (except Valinor, Númenor, and The Shire), use the accompanying scale.

Pathways created another dilemma. They were the basis of most original distance calculations for the base maps, as well as being used in their own right for

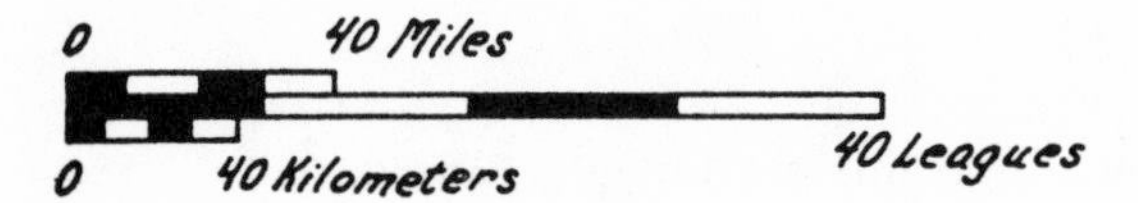

Figure 2

campsite locations. Many mileages had to be estimated, based on our Primary World. How many miles per hour could be sustained for more than a day — by a Man on foot (with an Elf and a Dwarf)? Armored cavalry on horseback? Halflings on short rations? Ponies on mountain paths? Finally, the daily distances were calculated using known location of campsites and times of arrival, interpolating the mileage covered since the last known site, with adjustments for change of travel speed (e.g., being chased by wolves). The mileage charts in *The History* have been checked against the original paths, but due to the constant restructuring of the tale the originals have not been altered, with one exception, and then both versions are shown.

The Physical Base Map

None of the cultural geography and history of the Free Peoples could have been traced without first establishing the physical base. Tolkien's marvelous descriptions were invaluable here, and his breadth of knowledge is evident; yet it was difficult to interpret some features in terms of our Primary World. Usually the alterations were an intrusion of the Secondary World, but occasionally the differences may have been unintentional. Some writers have suggested that his maps were heavily influenced by Europe.[25] Similarities are apparent, but I prefer to think of Tolkien's landscape as having resulted from vivid mental images based upon specific areas with which he was familiar.

In illustrating the landform features, I have applied an almost pictorial style, commonly used in physiographic and block diagrams. This method is capable of giving only a general impression of the distribution and type of relief features. It certainly cannot be construed as showing every hill. Tolkien's original maps and illustrations have been utilized as general references for location and elevation; but if differences arose, the final drawings were usually based upon the text and inferences drawn from its passages.

On some cross sections, the phrase "Vertical exaggeration 3:1" (or some other number) occasionally appears. Anyone who has ever flown over a mountain range can verify that topographic features appear much more flattened than they seem when viewing them from an earthbound perspective. The reverse is also true. Vertical exaggeration means that the feature is shown as proportionately higher than it actually is.

The Cultural Overlays

The atlas, then, is a composite of the physical surface with the imprint of the Free Peoples upon it. Six basic map types have been included: (1) physical (including landforms, minerals, and climate), with place names; (2) political (or spheres of influence); (3) battles; (4) migrations (closely tied with linguistics); (5) the travellers' pathways; and (6) site maps (towns, dwellings). These have been arranged roughly in sequence. The place names included on the maps may vary from one Age to the next, depending upon which language was prevalent at a given time and location. All spellings from *The Silmarillion*, *The Hobbit*, and *The Lord of the Rings* agree with Robert Foster's excellent glossary, *The Complete Guide to Middle-Earth*, while those selected from *The History* are those which seemed most often used. Dates from the First Age also are based on Foster, for 'The Later Annals of Beleriand' were not used in preparation of *The Silmarillion*, for they had not yet been found, and thus are off by a year or two.[26]

Symbols used to represent various physical and cultural phenomena were kept fairly constant, although some variations were necessary as the same elements were not present throughout. Whenever good and evil were mixed, evil was represented by black, and good by gray and/or brown. A legend has been included with most maps for easier reference, but the symbols usually fit one of the categories shown on the following page.

Conclusion

An almost endless series of questions, assumptions, and interpretations was necessary in producing the maps on the following pages. Differences of opinion have and will almost certainly continue to arise on many points. Each line has been drawn with a reason behind it, and much of the justification has been given in the respective explanations; yet space has not begun to allow inclusion of the entire reasoning process. Among various alternatives, I have chosen those that seem most reasonable to me, as I was unable to go to "Old Barliman" for further information — although the availability of *The History* is a close second! I hope the reader will learn as much in questioning the drawings, as I have in drafting them.

PHYSICAL:

- Low Hills
- Downs
- Snowcapped Mountains
- Submerged Land
- Ice Floes, Bergs
- Ocean
- Lake
- Perennial Stream
- Intermittent Stream
- Rapids
- Falls
- Forest
- Marsh

CULTURAL:

- Political Boundary
- Walled City
- Town
- Watch Tower
- Ruin
- Temporary Abode or Camp
- Road
- Bridge
- Ford

BATTLE FLOW:

- Attacking Force
- Continuing Action
- Retreat

TROOPS:

- Servants of Morgoth, Sauron
- Evil Men
- Other — Dragons, Balrogs
- Elves (or joint forces)
- Good Men
- Dwarves
- Other — Eagles, Ents

PATHWAYS:

- Main Character's Path
- Secondary Character's Path
- Joint or Consecutive Paths
- Daytime Campsite
- Night Campsite
- Encounter

SITE MAPS:

- Dike
- Fortified Wall
- Gate
- Courtyard
- Assorted Buildings
- Large Hall with Pillars
- Ascending Stairs
- Descending Stairs
- Doorway
- Pier
- Tree

The First Age

— THE ELDER DAYS —

The First Age

"In the beginning . . ." (Genesis 1:1)

ILÚVATAR SENT THE VALAR to order the world, preparing Arda for the coming of his Children — Elves and Men. Melkor, brother of Manwë, being arrogant in his own strength and power, sought to mar all the works of the other Vala. Thus, Arda began in battle and turmoil: the Valar, building; Melkor, destroying. In this first of the Great Battles, only the might of Tulkas routed Melkor, who fled to the Outer Darkness.

The Spring of Arda and the Settling of Aman

With Melkor gone, the Valar were at last left free to quiet the tumults of the world and order things as they wished. The Valar dwelt originally on the Isle of Almaren, which lay in the Great Lake in the midst of the land.[1] To the north they set the lantern of Illuin, and to the south, Ormal. The pillars of the lights were mountains taller than any of later times.[2]

Far in the north, where Illuin's light failed, the Iron Mountains stretched in an unbroken curve from east to west.[3] It is unclear when these great mountains were raised. At one point Tolkien stated that Melkor had reared them "as a fence to his citadel of Utumno,"[4] which seems to imply that they were uplifted at the time Utumno was built. Yet elsewhere it was told that Melkor returned in stealth over the Walls of Night and delved the fortress beneath the Ered Engrin[5] — evidence that the mountains might have already been formed in the earlier turmoils of Arda. Although the Valar knew Melkor had returned, they could not locate his hiding place. From Utumno he struck the lights of Illuin and Ormal, casting down their pillars. So great was their fall that the lands were broken and Almaren destroyed.[6] In one version of these ancient days, the Valar were said to be on one of the Twilit Isles, and the meltwaters from the fall swamped most of the islands. Then Ossë ferried the Valar to the West, upon the same isle which he later used to carry the Elves![7] It is possible that these islands were the lands seen by Eärendil, who, sailing west to Valinor, passed over "foundered shores that drowned before the Days began."[8] Whatever the mechanism, the Valar left Middle-earth, and passed over the sundering seas of Belegaer, which were more narrow at that time than ever after. They settled Aman — "the westernmost of all lands upon the borders of the world. . . ."[9] As a defense against Melkor they lifted the Pelóri — east, north, and south — and these stood as the highest mountains of Arda.[10] Behind them the Valar established the Blessed Realm of Valinor. The Valar continued their works, returning seldom to Middle-earth. In their absence, Melkor's power spread south from Utumno, and from his fortress of Angband, which lay in the northwest, facing Aman.[11] Only Oromë and Yavanna ventured into the Outer Lands. To hinder Oromë's travels Melkor raised a new mountain chain — the Hithaeglir, Mountains of Mist.[12]

The Awakening of the Elves and the Second Great Battle

Uncounted time passed. Yavanna had grown the trees of light, and Varda had kindled the last of the stars when the Elves — firstborn of the Children of Ilúvatar — awoke by the waters of Cuiviénen. They dwelt in the Wild Wood by its shores and delighted in the music of the streams falling from the Orocarni, Mountains of the East.[13] Cuiviénen was an eastern bay of the Inland Sea of Helcar, formed by the meltwaters of the pillar of Illuin.[14] Cuiviénen could not have been very far east of Utumno, for later, during the Siege, the Elves could see the light of battle in the north — not the west.

The Siege of Utumno occurred after Oromë discovered the Eldar had at last appeared. The Valar wished to free the Elves from Melkor's evil domination, for he had already captured some, using them to breed the twisted race of Orcs. Thus began the Second of the Great Battles. The Valar quickly routed Sauron's forces at Angband, breaking the lands of the northwest. Then they passed east to Utumno. There the strength of evil was so great that a siege was mounted.

In every confrontation between Melkor and the Valar the lands of Arda were much changed, and the Siege was no exception.[15] Belegaer grew wide and deep. The coastlines were much broken, forming many bays, including the Bay of Balar and the Great Gulf. A map in "The Ambarkanta" shows 'the Great Gulf', called also Beleglo[rn?].[16] The map is "a very rapid pencil sketch . . . many features are absent."[17] In the turmoils at the end of the First Age the shape of the gulf probably changed, joining the eastern end of the

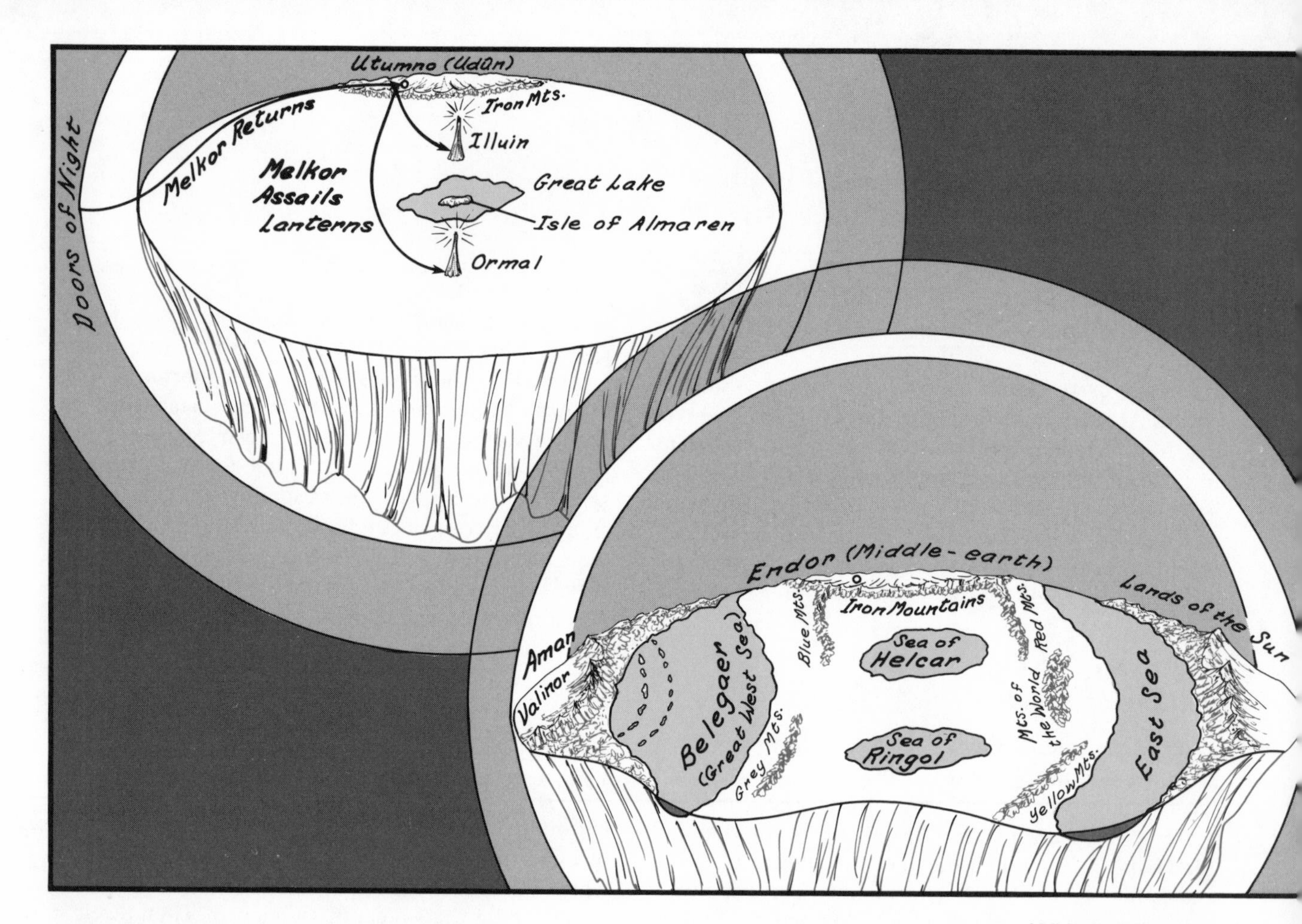

SPRING OF ARDA

gulf with the inland Sea of Helcar, forming the later Bay of Belfalas.

Not only were the seas changed during the Siege of Utumno, but also, the lands. The central highlands of Dorthonion and Hithlum were said to have been raised — specifically, the "Iron Mountains 'were broken and distorted at their western end . . . made the Eredwethrin and Eredlómin, and that the Iron Mountains bent back northward.' "[18] The Echoriath probably also appeared during these great turmoils — as a gigantic active volcano. New rivers (such as Sirion) were formed.

The Westward Road

The Valar at last defeated Utumno, and unroofed its halls — but only partially. The mighty Ered Engrin, which once had towered as a predominant wall across northern Middle-earth, were neither mentioned nor mapped by Tolkien after the First Age. The western portion near Angband stood until the Third Great Battle (the War of Wrath), at the end of the Age. It is not known whether the rest of the range was destroyed during the Siege, or during the fall of Beleriand, or whether they still existed in the Third Age. The accompanying map (drawn at this point of the First Age) assumed that the mountains were only partially changed during the unroofing of Utumno,[19] and that the final destruction of all but a few remnants must have occurred later, possibly in the War of Wrath.

Melkor was chained in the Halls of Mandos for three ages, and the Quendi were free to take the westward road toward Valinor. The leagues from Cuiviénen were uncounted, yet using the Ambarkanta map one may estimate the journey to have been in excess of 2000 miles. Nothing was told of these travels until the Elves reached the great forest, later called the Greenwood. Their route would have been fairly straight west once they had journeyed to the northern shore of the Sea of Helcar from Cuiviénen. It is possible that Oromë led them along the very path that eventually became the Great East Road and the forest path. Oromë probably did not lead them south, because another, greater barrier existed there — dense forests. Treebeard said that woods had once extended from the Mountains of Lune to the east end in Fangorn.[20]

West of Greenwood they crossed the Great River, then faced the towering Mountains of Mist. These were even "taller and more terrible in those days."[21] This alone reveals how vast an expanse of time passed between the westward migration to Valinor and the return of the Noldor to Middle-earth during the Sleep of Yavanna before the Sun Years. Half a million years would hardly be sufficient for the gradual processes of erosion to noticeably lower the peaks. Nothing else was told of the lands east of the Ered Luin, except that the Ered Nimrais (the White Mountains) had been raised.[22] As those did not appear on the Ambarkanta map, they were probably lifted at the same time as the Towers of Mist when Melkor sought to hinder the riding of Oromë.[23] Notably absent from both map and text are the mountains of Mordor. That land would later lie in what now was the Sea of Helcar.

At last the wanderers crossed the Ered Luin, which must have been lower than the Hithaeglir, for they seem to have formed less of a barrier. The pass lay in the upper vales of the River Ascar — where later the mountains broke apart and formed the Gulf of Lune. West of the lands of Beleriand were the Sundering Seas. The Elves could go no farther.

The Noontide of Valinor and the Return to Endor

To provide passage for the great host, Ulmo uprooted an island that stood in the midst of Belegaer. On it he carried the Quendi — first the Vanyar and the Noldor, and then the Teleri. Being driven on the shoals, the point of the island remained in the Bay of Balar.[24] Ossë anchored the greater portion in the Bay of Eldamar — Tol Eressëa, the Lonely Isle.[25]

This was the Noontide of Valinor. Through the Pelóri the Valar opened a deep chasm (the Calacirya) to light Eressëa. The three kindreds dwelt in the glory of the Blessed Realm — until the pardon of Melkor. Subsequently he poisoned the Two Trees of Light, stole the Silmarils, and escaped to Middle-earth — pursued by the Noldor. There he piled the towers of Thangorodrim at the gates of Angband. When Tilion, guiding the newly made Moon, traversed the sky, Melkor assailed him. The Valar then, remembering the fall of Almaren, raised the Pelóri to even more unassailable heights, with sheer outward faces and no passes except the Calacirya. Beyond Aman were set the Enchanted Isles.[26] No help went forth from the Guarded Land until the end of the Age. The Noldor and the Sindar were left to their own devices and strength.

The Elves gained assistance, however, from Men; for with the rising of the Sun, the Younger Children of Ilúvatar awoke in Hildórien. That land, too, lay in eastern Middle-earth.[27] From Hildórien Men spread west, north, and south,[28] with many taking the road west toward the place where the sun had first risen. Some eventually came to Beleriand, and their destinies, with those of the Elves, were intertwined in all the tales that passed until the end of the Age and the fall of the lands beneath the wave.

Beleriand

To produce a detailed world map it was necessary to piece together the mapped and unmapped portions of Arda. While the map from the Ambarkanta provided a rough world-wide view, the crucial locale during the First Age was Beleriand. It was necessary to establish both scale and relationship to the rest of Middle-earth. All the 'Silmarillion' maps excluded both the northern and southern extremes of the area. The original key to the latter was the location of the Dwarf Road to the cities of Belegost and Nogrod, where the Ered Luin were broken asunder in the Great Battle, forming the Gulf of Lune. With the publication of *The History,* however, it became possible to confirm the placement by superimposing the "First Map"[29] designed for *The Lord of the Rings* over the "Second 'Silmarillion' Map"[30] — aligning the locations of Tol Fuin over Dorthonion (Taur-nu-Fuin) and of the isle of Himling with the city of Himring. Although the index grids used on both the maps used squares of the same dimension (100 miles on a side, as are those of the *Atlas*), the lettered axis differed by fifty miles, and neither letters nor numbers coordinated. This difference was merely one of inconvenience, however. With one exception* it was possible to reconfirm the relative size and location of the distances within the area that were mentioned in the text:

1) Menegroth to Thangorodrim	*150 leagues[31]
2) Highlands of Dorthonion E–W	60 leagues[32]
3) Nargothrond to Pools of Ivrin	40 leagues[33]
4) Nargothrond to Falls of Sirion	25 leagues[34]
5) East Beleriand, Sirion to Gelion	100 leagues[35]
6) River Sirion	130 leagues[36]
7) River Narog	80 leagues[37]
8) River Gelion	
a) Confluence Greater and Little to River Ascar	40 leagues[38]
b) Total length, "twice . . . Sirion"	260 leagues[39]

For this atlas, the southern coast was mapped at a point 260 leagues from the sources of River Gelion — based on the assumption that the river continued its southwesterly flow. This brought the coast near that of the Bay of Belfalas. The southwestern tip was extended to emphasize the bayed shape of the Bay of Balar. The area was shown as forested, assuming the circumstances that produced Taur-im-Duinath would have prevailed.

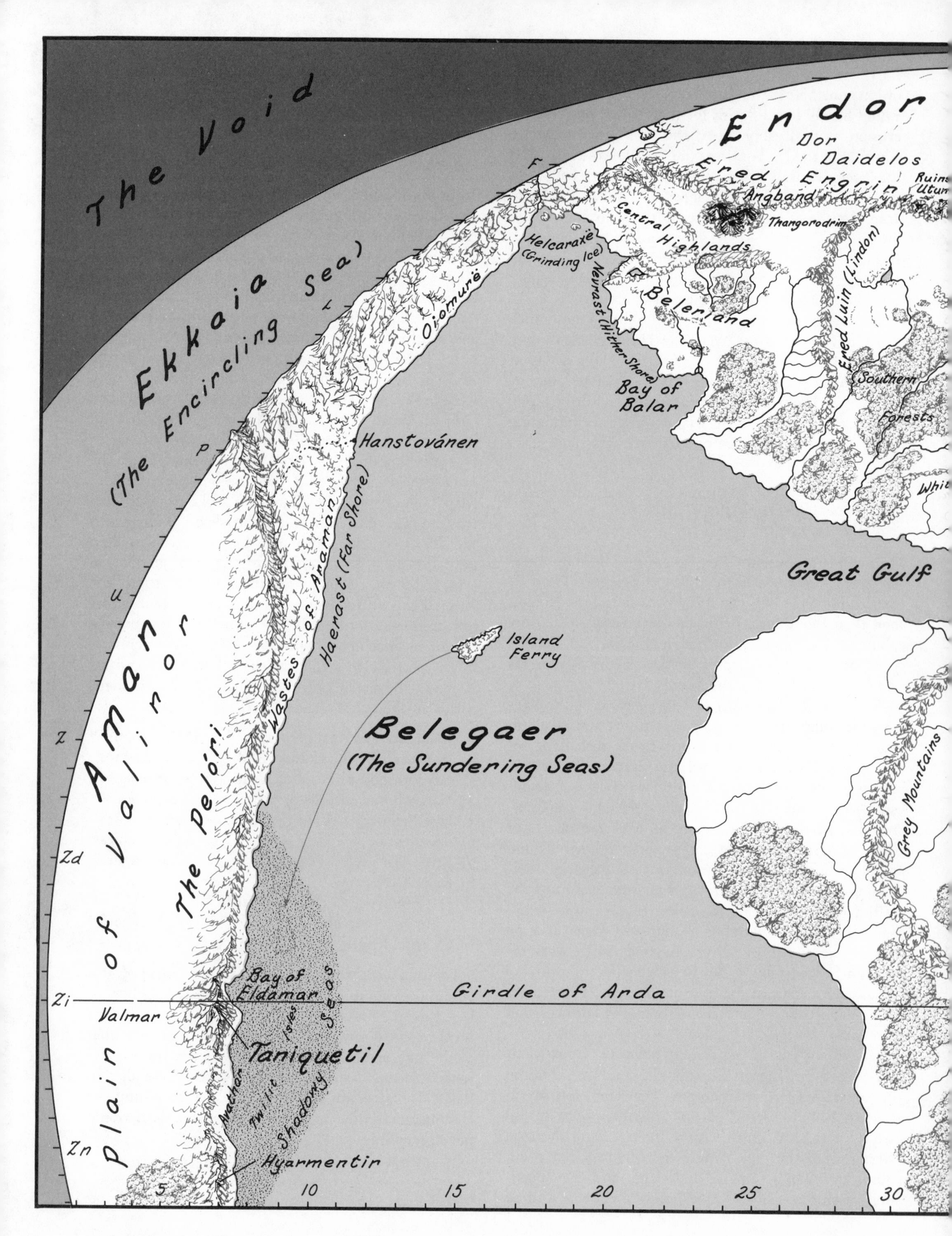
The Void
Ekkaia
(The Encircling Sea)
Endor
Dor Daidelos
Ered Engrin
Angband
Thangorodrim
Central Highlands
Helcaraxë
(Grinding Ice)
Nevrast (Hither Shore)
Beleriand
Ered Luin (Lindon)
Southern Forests
Bay of Balar
Oiomurë
Hanstovánen
Haerast (Far Shore)
Wastes of Araman
Great Gulf
Island Ferry
Belegaer
(The Sundering Seas)
Grey Mountains
Aman
Valinor
The Pelóri
Plain of Valmar
Bay of Eldamar
Girdle of Arda
Valmar
Taniquetil
Isles
Twilit
Shadowy Seas
Avathar
Hyarmentir
F
P
U
Z
Zd
Zi
Zn
5
10
15
20
25
30

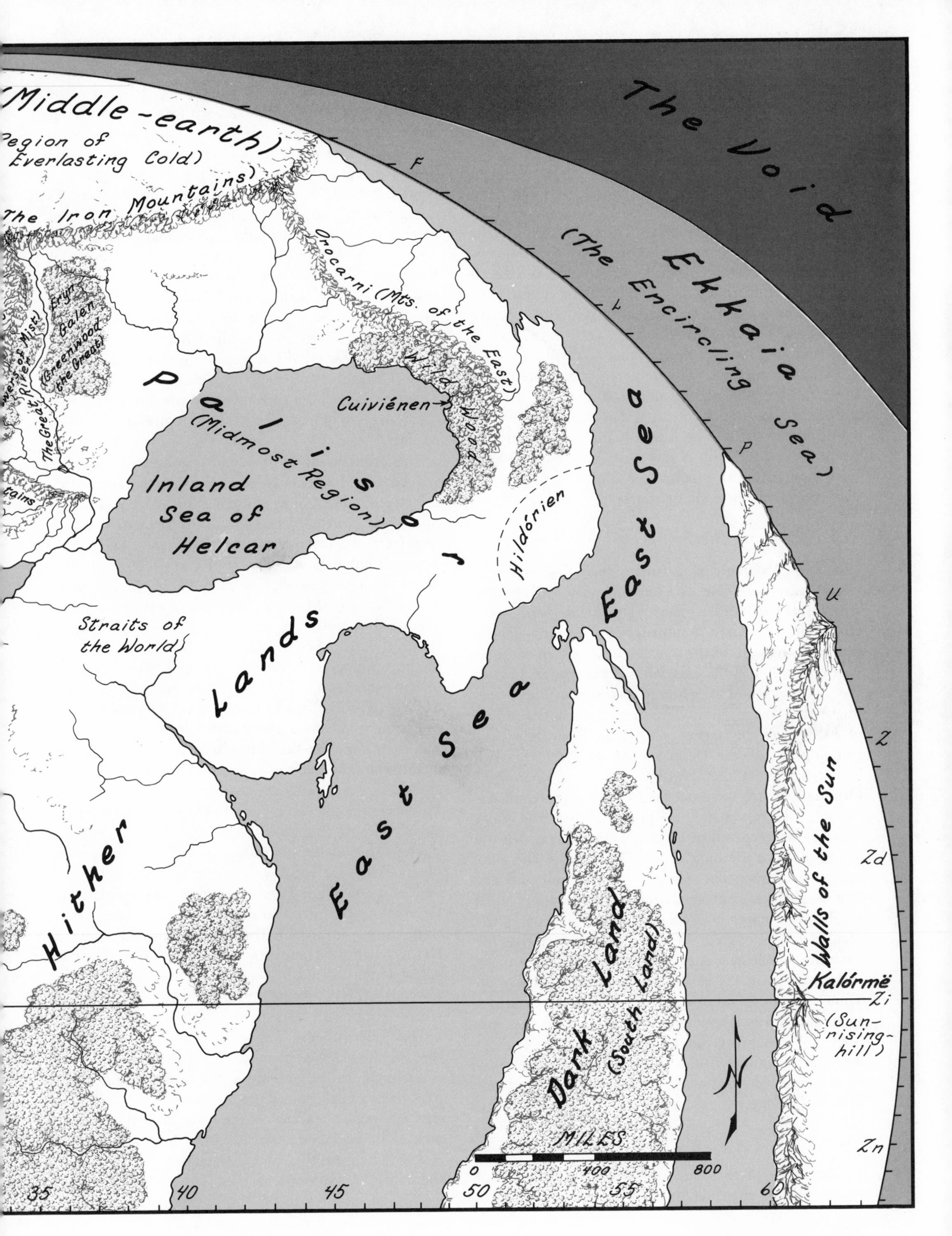
The Void
Ekkaia
(The Encircling Sea)
(Middle-earth)
(Region of Everlasting Cold)
The Iron Mountains)
Orocarni (Mts. of the East)
Wild Wood
Cuiviénen
Eryn Galen (Greenwood the Great)
The Great River
Palisor
(Midmost Region)
Inland Sea of Helcar
Hildórien
Straits of the World
Lands
Hither
East Sea
East Sea
East Sea
Dark Land
(South Land)
Walls of the Sun
Kalórmë
(Sun-nising-hill)
MILES
0
400
800
F
P
U
Z
Zd
Zi
Zn
35
40
45
50
55
60

Valinor

ALTHOUGH AMAN LAY WITHIN THE CIRCLES of the world during the First and Second Ages, it cannot be viewed as having been simply another land area. It held mountains, coasts, lakes, hills, plains, and forests, and it was bordered by the same seas that washed against the shores of Middle-earth; yet it was an ethereal land — a land of the Secondary World.

Distances not only were not given, they were meaningless. The Valar, being spirits, must have had the power to pass any distance at any time. Instead of meticulously calculating leagues, Tolkien left impressions of Valinor with a few swift strokes that have been composited to produce the drawings of parts of east-central Valinor and of scattered locations.

The Coast and the Pelóri

When the Valar occupied Aman, their first endeavor was to raise the Pelóri as a fence against Melkor, who still resided in Middle-earth. The Pelóri were steep facing the sea but had more gentle western slopes,[1] dropping into the fertile plains and meads of Valinor. East of the Pelóri the coastlands lay in the shadow of the mountains and were barren wastelands. The shores of Avathar in the south were more narrow than those of Araman in the north.[2] As Araman approached the grinding ice of the Helcaraxë, it was covered with heavy mists, so that portion was called Oiomúrë.[3] Originally there were no passes, but when Ossë anchored Tol Eressëa in the Bay of Eldamar the Valar opened the steep-walled Calacirya, through which the Teleri received the light of the Two Trees.[4] The glow streamed through the valley and fanned out over the Bay of Eldamar; but north and south the light failed as the mountains blocked the light, producing the Shadowy Seas.[5] While the mountains curved east, the coastline of Belegaer curved west, stretching from the Helcaraxë, past the girdle of Arda near Tirion on Túna,[6] and south out of knowledge. Thus the Calacirya spanned from Bay to Plain at the most narrow point. South of the great canyon was Taniquetil, highest mountain in all of Arda. The next highest peak was Hyarmentir, far to the south, where Ungoliant dwelt in a dark ravine.[7]

Dwellings

In the midst of the plain of Valinor was Valmar of Many Bells — the chief, and possibly the only, city of the Valar. It was filled with imposing structures: the many-storied home of Tulkas, with its great court for physical contests; Oromë's low halls, strewn with skins, and the roof of each room supported by a tree; Ossë's 'temporary quarters' during conclaves, built of pearls; and outside the city bordering the plain, Aulë's "great court," which held some of each of the trees of earth.[8] In spite of this splendor Valmar's features of renown stood outside its golden gates: The Ring of Doom and the Two Trees. In Mahanaxar, the Ring of Doom, the Valar held council and sat in judgment.[9] There, Melkor was sentenced, and later freed. There, Fëanor was sentenced to exile. There, Eärendil gave his plea.[10] Near the Ring stood a green hill, Ezollahar. Atop it Yavanna sang her song, bringing forth the Two Trees of Light. Beneath them Varda set great vats, capturing the light, and scattered it through the skies as stars.[11]

The other areas of the land that were briefly described were given only general locations. Formenos, the stronghold of Fëanor during his exile, was in the hills of the north.[12] The pastures of Yavanna could be seen from Hyarmentir west of the Woods of Oromë.[13] Nienna's lodgings were "west of West" on the borders of Aman, near the abiding place of Namo and Vairë — the Halls of Mandos, whose dark caverns reached even to Hanstovánen, the dark harbor of the north: site of the Prophecy of Mandos.[14] Irmo and Estë dwelt in the Gardens of Lórien, where Estë slept on an isle in the lake Lorellin.[15] There, too, stayed the Maiar Melian (who became Queen of Doriath) and Olórin, the familiar Gandalf. The most spectacular dwelling of the Valar stood on the pinnacle of Taniquetil: the hall of Ilmarin. The marble watchtower was domed with a sparkling web of the airs through which Manwë and Varda viewed all Arda, even to the Gates of Morning beyond the eastern sea.[16]

The other cities mentioned were all those of the Elves. Tirion (as renamed from the original Kôr) was built atop the hill of Túna in the midst of the Calacirya. Crystal stairs climbed to the great gate.[17] Fair houses were raised within by the Noldor and the Vanyar. Higher than all stood the tower Mindon Eldaliéva,[18] whose lantern could be seen far out to sea. Before the tower lay the House of Finwë[19] and the Great Square where Fëanor and his sons swore their terrible oath.[20]

The Teleri, being drawn by the light streaming through the pass, abandoned Eressëa. They built Alqualondë, the fair Haven of the Swans, north of the pass, desiring still to see the bright stars of Varda. The city was walled, and the entrance to its harbor was an arch of living stone.[21] Eressëa was deserted until the end of the First Age, when Elves fleeing Beleriand built the haven of Avalónnë on the south shore.[22]

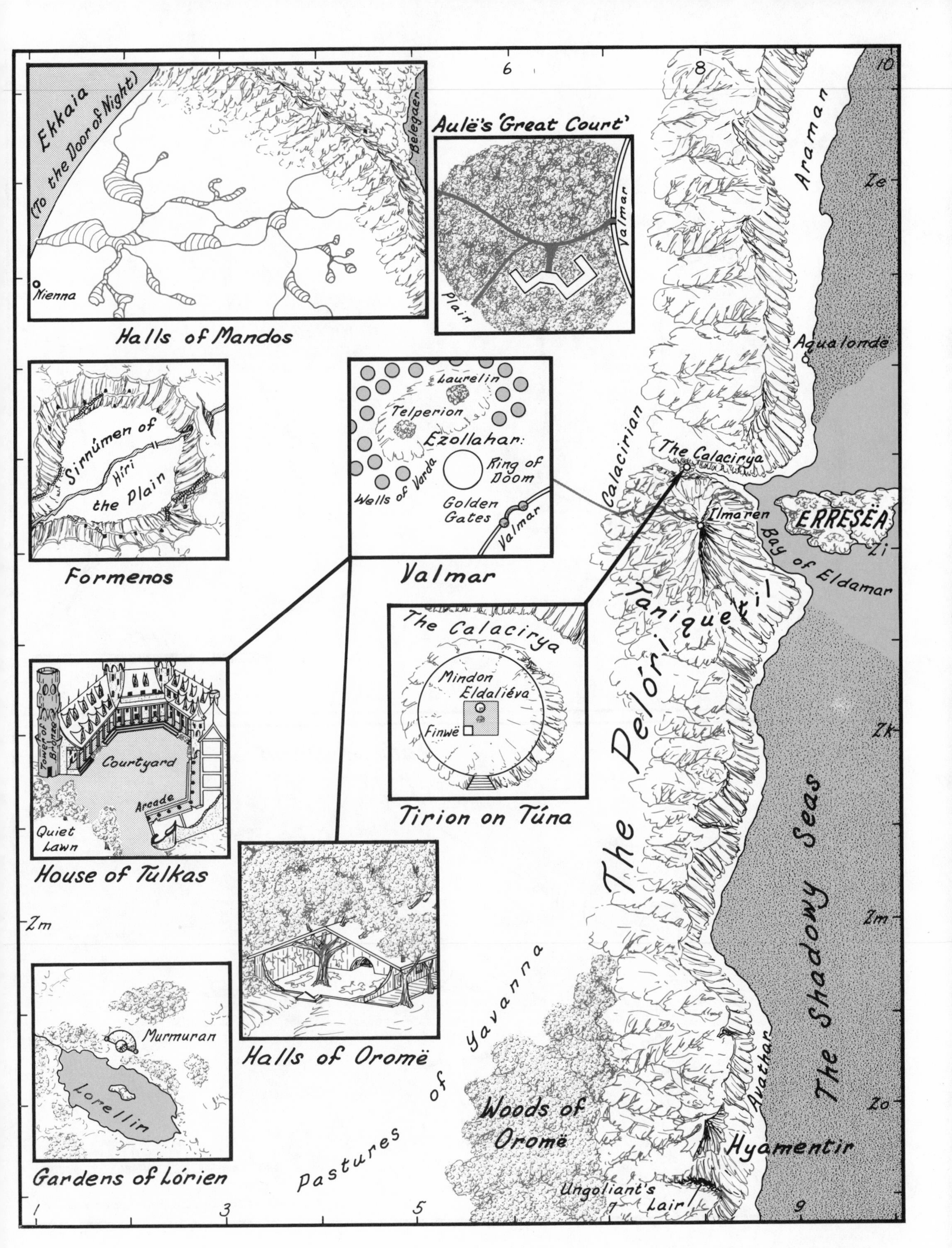
Ekkaia
(To the Door of Night)
Belegaer
Nienna
Halls of Mandos
Aulë's 'Great Court'
Valmar
Plain
Araman
Aqualondë
Sirnúmen of Híri
the Plain
Formenos
Laurelin
Telperion
Ezollahar:
Ring of Doom
Wells of Varda
Golden Gates
Valmar
Calacirian
The Calacirya
Ilmarën
ERRESËA
Bay of Eldamar
Taniquetil
The Pelóri
The Calacirya
Mindon Eldaliéva
Finwë
Tirion on Túna
Tower of Bronze
Courtyard
Arcade
Quiet Lawn
House of Tulkas
Halls of Oromë
Pastures of Yavanna
Woods of Oromë
Murmuran
Lorellin
Gardens of Lórien
Avathar
The Shadowy Seas
Hyamentir
Ungoliant's Lair
1
3
5
6
7
8
9
10
Ze
Zi
Zk
Zm
Zo

VALINOR

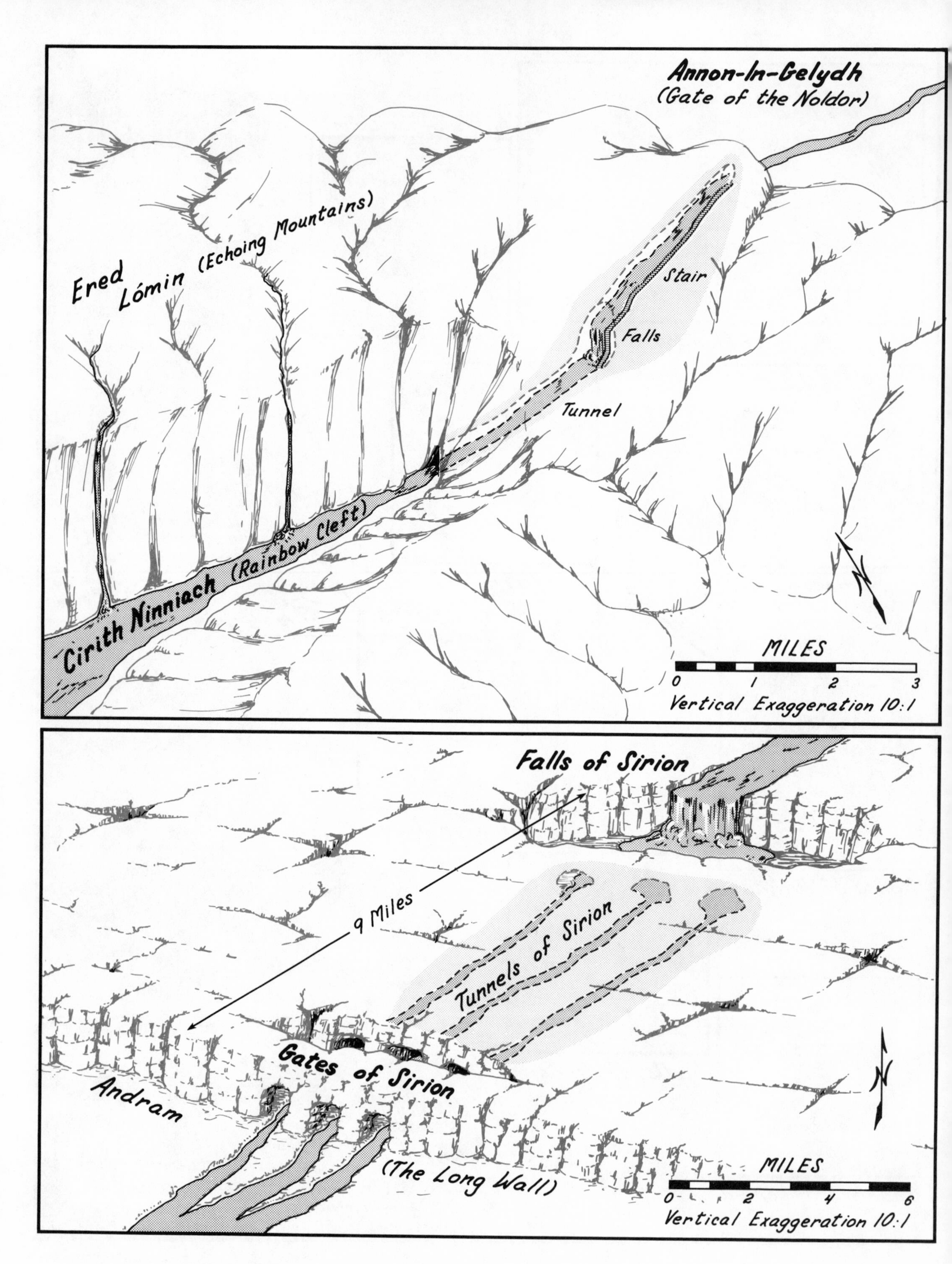

Upper: GATE OF THE NOLDOR Lower: FALLS OF SIRION (Oblique Views)

Beleriand and the Lands to the North

Most of the recorded history of the First Age was set in the lands west of the Ered Luin. In later ages all the lands that went under the wave were sometimes referred to as Beleriand, but originally that term was applied only to the area between the Bay of Balar and the highlands of Hithlum and Dorthonion, and the lands under the wave were much more extensive. The lands could be divided into four regions based on climate, topography, and politics: (1) the northlands of Morgoth, (2) the central highlands, (3) Beleriand, and (4) the Ered Luin.

The Northlands of Morgoth[1]

There were two prominent features of this region — the Iron Mountains and the plain of Ard-galen. Lammoth and Lothlann were also related. Melkor raised the Ered Engrin as a fence to his citadel of Utumno,[2] which he delved during the Spring of Arda.[3] In the west, where the range bent north, he built the fortress of Angband below the Ered Engrin, but the tunnel to its great gates exited below the triple peaks of Thangorodrim.[4]

The location of Angband and Thangorodrim was not shown on the map in *The Silmarillion,* and originally it was mapped beyond the northern borders, in keeping with the statement that Thangorodrim lay 150 leagues from Menegroth — about 450 miles — "far, and yet all too near."[5] It was uncertain if this distance were "as the crow flies" or "as the wolf runs." If it were the latter, the striking arm was brought much closer. Several points support this second interpretation: (1) The heights of Dorthonion necessitated bypassing it in any travel between Thangorodrim and Menegroth. (2) From Eithel Sirion, Thangorodrim could be seen.[6] (3) Tolkien's illustration of Tol Sirion showed Thangorodrim clearly — closer than the more northerly location would have indicated.[7] (4) In the west, Fingolfin's host took only seven days between the Helcaraxë and Mithim.[8] (5) Fëanor, after the second battle,[9] and Fingon, prior to the fourth,[10] passed quickly over the plain. (6) Most important, "Angband was beleaguered from the west, south, and east[11] by forces from Hithlum, Dorthonion, and the hills of Himring — a more northerly latitude of Angband would have placed all these far to the south.

On both the first and second 'Silmarillion' maps, however, Thangorodrim was shown in a location that was empty on the previously published map.[12] Why the location of this vital feature was omitted from the redrafting for the map in *The Silmarillion* was unclear. Perhaps it was due to Christopher Tolkien's apparent unease about (1) the discrepancy on the distance from Menegroth to Thangorodrim, which the southern location would make "scarcely more than seventy," rather than the 150 leagues in the text;[13] (2) the separation of Thangorodrim from the long curving mountain chain (which is not shown);[14] or (3) explaining the inability of Morgoth's troops to 'flank' Hithlum and attack from the coast,[15] as well as Morgoth's path to Angband via the Firth of Drengist upon his return from Valinor.[16] The southern location would have been even more convenient for Morgoth to threaten the Elves, however, and for them to do battle in return.

Topographically, the Ered Engrin have been illustrated as a block-fault range with a south-facing escarpment. This interpretation was based on the idea that a sharp south-facing scarp would have lent maximum protection to Melkor's fortresses. Volcanic activity was evident from the smokes blown over Hithlum during the Noldor's first encampment.[17] During the third battle there were earthquakes and the mountains "vomited flame;"[18] and during the fourth battle Ard-galen perished in rivers of flame.[19] Much of this activity was attributed to Morgoth's gigantic "blast furnaces," but in the mythical setting of Middle-earth, volcanoes may have served as blast furnaces. Thangorodrim itself appeared to be volcanic, for its triple black peaks[20] spued smoke, in spite of their being called "towers" — built of slag and tunnel refuse piled by Morgoth's countless slaves.[21] For a Vala such a feat was not deemed impossible: even the earliest tale of Valinor said the Pelóri were built by quarrying stone from the seaside, leaving flat coastal plains.[22] Although the cliff above the door stood only 1000 feet high,[23] not only was Thangorodrim higher than the main range of the Ered Engrin (as shown in Tolkien's illustration of Tol Sirion[24]), but it was the highest peak in Middle-earth![25]

Climatically, the mountains lay in the borders of everlasting cold and were impassable because of the snow and ice.[26] It may have been due to ice along the coast near the Helcaraxë that Morgoth and his troops could not bypass Hithlum on the north.[27] Bitter winds from the mountains, as well as from the Helcaraxë, made Lammoth a wasteland, with so little vegetation and precipitation that its eastern ravines and barren shores echoed in their emptiness.[28] Winds also howled across the featureless plains of Ard-galen and Lothlann, bringing winter snows to the bordering central highlands. The plains were probably a steppe climate, for they were fairly dry, as well as cold. The moisture of the west and south winds could not reach them, for it fell in the central highlands. Thus, the plains had no streams,[29] although they supported grass, until during Dagor Bragollach, the Battle of Sudden Flame, when Ard-galen was burned. Afterward, the sod could never reestablish itself, due to the poisonous airs of Thangorodrim; and the plain became Angfauglith, the choking dust, a desert with dunes.[30]

The Central Highlands

This region included the mountains of Hithlum, the highlands of Dorthonion (including the Encircling Mountains), and the Hills of Himring, which were all formed during the Siege of Utumno.[31] Nevrast was also associated with the highlands, but its lower elevation and warmer climate allowed it sometimes to be considered with Beleriand.[32] The lands formed an effective buffer — politically and climatically — between the lands of Morgoth and Beleriand. This was the area settled, for the most part, by the Noldor. From its borders they set watch over the northlands of Morgoth.

The lands received warmer south and west winds, and were cool but pleasant, except in the higher elevations. The north winds of Morgoth often assailed them. Hithlum had cold winters.[33] Beren fled from Dorthonion in a time of hard winter and snow.[34] The Hill of Himring, the site of the citadel of Maedhros, was the "ever-cold," and the Pass of Aglon "funneled the north winds."[35]

The highlands might have been formed by folding of the bedrock over a large area. Dorthonion was raised into a high plateau. Portions in the south were steeply folded and possibly faulted, producing the sheer southern precipices of the Ered Gorgoroth. In the east were also higher peaks, and what appeared on the map to be a fault-line valley. "Tarns," in the strictest use, are small, deep lakes left by glacial meltwater. These usually form high on glaciated mountains. The tarns in Dorthonion, however, lay at the feet of the tors. It is more likely that Tolkien applied the term as it is used in the North of England — a generic term meaning *any* lake.[36] Where Barahir and Beren and their eleven faithful companions hid west of Tarn Aeluin, there were moors.[37] On the moors stood "bare tors"[38] — small heaps of rounded boulders, called "corestones," produced by deep penetration of water and frost, which shattered the highly jointed bedrock. These periglacial features usually occur on granite, and less frequently on sandstone.[39] The moors would have had marshy conditions. Few trees could withstand the water, so there the evergreen stands of the gentle north slopes failed.[40]

The Echoriath, the Encircling Mountains, appeared to be a classic example of a volcano that collapsed, built a secondary cone, and then died out. All this was far enough in the distant past for a lake to have formed and drained (through the underground river), leaving its alluvial sediment to stand as the flat green Vale of Tumladen. The volcanic areas of the Iron Mountains were close enough to account for this otherwise isolated volcano to the south — especially since the mountain-building activities would produce weakness in the earth's mantle, allowing extrusions of lava. The heights of the Crissaegrim may have resulted from the residual caldera crest atop the already steep and sheer escarpment of Dorthonion. The ores mined by Maeglin in the north of the mountains might have been either intruded later or might have occurred in rock formations there prior to the vulcanism.

Hithlum was described as ringed by mountains. The Ered Wethrin of the east were the highest portion, yet were lower than the Ered Gorgoroth.[41] Between them and the Echoriath, Sirion had carved a steep-sided vale. The interior of Hithlum appears to have been slightly elevated as well. A low plateau would account for the rapids and falls that Tuor found while passing through the Gate of the Noldor between Dor-lómin and the Firth of Drengist.[42] The Firth may have provided the drainage for western Hithlum and Dor-lómin. The course of Nen Lalaith ("Laughing Water") was not described.[43] Lake Mithrim was illustrated as fed from interior drainage, yet in one version of Tuor's journey he came upon a river from Lake Mithrim which was the source of the river which cut the Rainbow Cleft.[44] Also, the lake may have drained into an aquifer — a porous rock layer that might have carried the water from the interior to the lower mountainsides — producing springs such as those of Ivrin and Sirion. Caves, such as those of Androth where Tuor lodged, could have occurred in many rock types — as do springs.

This map includes an area north of that mapped by Tolkien. The mountains of Tolkien's drawing extend off the edge, leaving the reader ignorant of what lay to the north. The extension of the mountains north was shown for one reason: All travellers from Valinor to Thangorodrim — even Morgoth — passed through Lammoth and Hithlum. If the mountains of Hithlum had extended farther north, they could have been snow-filled and would have created a considerable barrier to passing east from the Helcaraxë to Angband.

In the west of Dor-lómin the hills dropped into the low-lying land of Nevrast. Its land dipped gently east from the black sea cliffs "torn in towers and pinnacles and great arching vaults"[45] to Linaewen with its marshes. The waters gathered from the lands wandered in intermittent rivulets, for there were no permanent streams. Linaewen, with its fluctuating shores, widespread marshes, and reedy beds, must have been quite shallow — probably only about twenty feet in depth.

Beleriand

These were the lands held mostly by the Sindar, with the notable exception of Finrod's realm of Nargothrond (though the Noldor later retreated to Beleriand after the north was overrun). The most noticeable features of the lands south of the central highlands (other than the Wall of Andram) were the rivers that headed from the southern slopes. On the eastern border flowed Gelion, a product of the Ered Luin. For the most part, Sirion's system drained the region, and its channel divided West and East Beleriand. Its original source was Eithel Sirion, where springs emptied from the Ered Wethrin, but the river was fed by many tributaries. Those of the west arose in the Ered Wethrin — most notably Teiglin and Narog. Those of the east were fed in many directions from Dorthonion — Rivil's Well, the Dry River of Gondolin, Mindeb (which had breached one of the few passes into the highland), Esgalduin, and Aros (which arose in the high southeastern portion). Only the River Celon, a tributary of Aros, arose in the Hills of Himring, close to the source of the Little Gelion.

Even clues about the topography of the area were, for the most part, couched in references to the river systems. The rivers flowed south, as the land sloped down from the central highlands; but the flow was not always steady and smooth. At Dimrost, the "rainy stair" (later called Nen Girith, the "shuddering water"), Celebros tumbled toward Teiglin. In about the same area Turgon climbed the cliffwall of the gorge of Teiglin to kill Glauring.[46] East in Doriath, Carcaroth had stopped to drink where Esgalduin had plunged over a steep falls.[47] Evidently all these rivers underwent a sudden drop at that locale. They possibly crossed an outcrop or escarpment of some relatively resistant rock. Between Sirion and Narog moors rose — probably northeast of Talath Dirnen, the Guarded Plain. Amon Rûdh stood on their edge,[48] at their most southern extreme. Farther east, it is possible that fissures along beds and joints in an outcrop of rock may have formed the basis for the delving of Menegroth.[49]

Cutting through central Beleriand was the "Long Wall" of Andram.[50] From the north, the wall may not have even been evident, for the land fell steeply. Approached from the south, it appeared as an endless chain of hills. The rock layer forming this outcrop may have been soluble limestone. There were extensive caverns at Nargothrond in the west. Sirion plunged underground at the north edge of the hills, and reissued from tunnels three leagues south (nine miles), at their feet.[51] Such an occurrence would be extremely rare for a river of that size, even in soluble bedrock, for usually the overlying rock would have collapsed, leaving gorges — such as those of Ringwil and Narog in the west. The process[52] normally involves a surface stream (with rapids), which gradually develops underground channels that disappear at a "swallow hole." If the channel force is sufficiently strong and the rock layer is quite thick, the hole will be enlarged, developing steep falls. If the subterranean stream develops several courses,[53] such as Sirion's tunnels, collapse is less likely. Partial collapse at the point of resurgence of the overlying rock may leave natural arches, such as the Gates of Sirion.

Ered Luin

The Ered Luin were more important as a barrier to westward migration and as the source for the tributaries of Gelion than they were as population centers. In the mountains themselves, only the Dwarves dwelt, carving the cities of Nogrod and Belegost, and mining the iron, copper, and related ores throughout most of the history of Middle-earth.[54] The mountains, as shown in *The Silmarillion* map, seemed to have been folded in places. The appearance of eroded upfolds ("breached anticlines") indicate sedimentary rock, which often holds lodes of iron. Copper, however, is more commonly found in crystalline rock, so the geology was evidently complex, as could be expected in any large range. The area around Mt. Rerir was fairly high and may have supported glaciers in the past. Lake Helevorn was "dark and deep,"[55] and appeared to lie in a trough thrusting into the mountains, similar to a finger lake. The rest of the range must have been fairly worn down, with its former peaks eroded and washed down to form the alluvial plains to the west. The mountains were not snow-capped, and the Elves had far less difficulty crossing them than, for example, they did the Misty Mountains.

The western slopes captured the moist winds of Belegaer and the Bay of Balar and fed the seven rivers. North of Ascar the winds would have been drier (having passed over a larger land area), and there were no tributaries for forty leagues. The lands of Ossiriand were warm and gentle, with the seven rivers flowing rapidly in valleys such as that of the Thalos where Finrod first discovered mortal Men.[56]

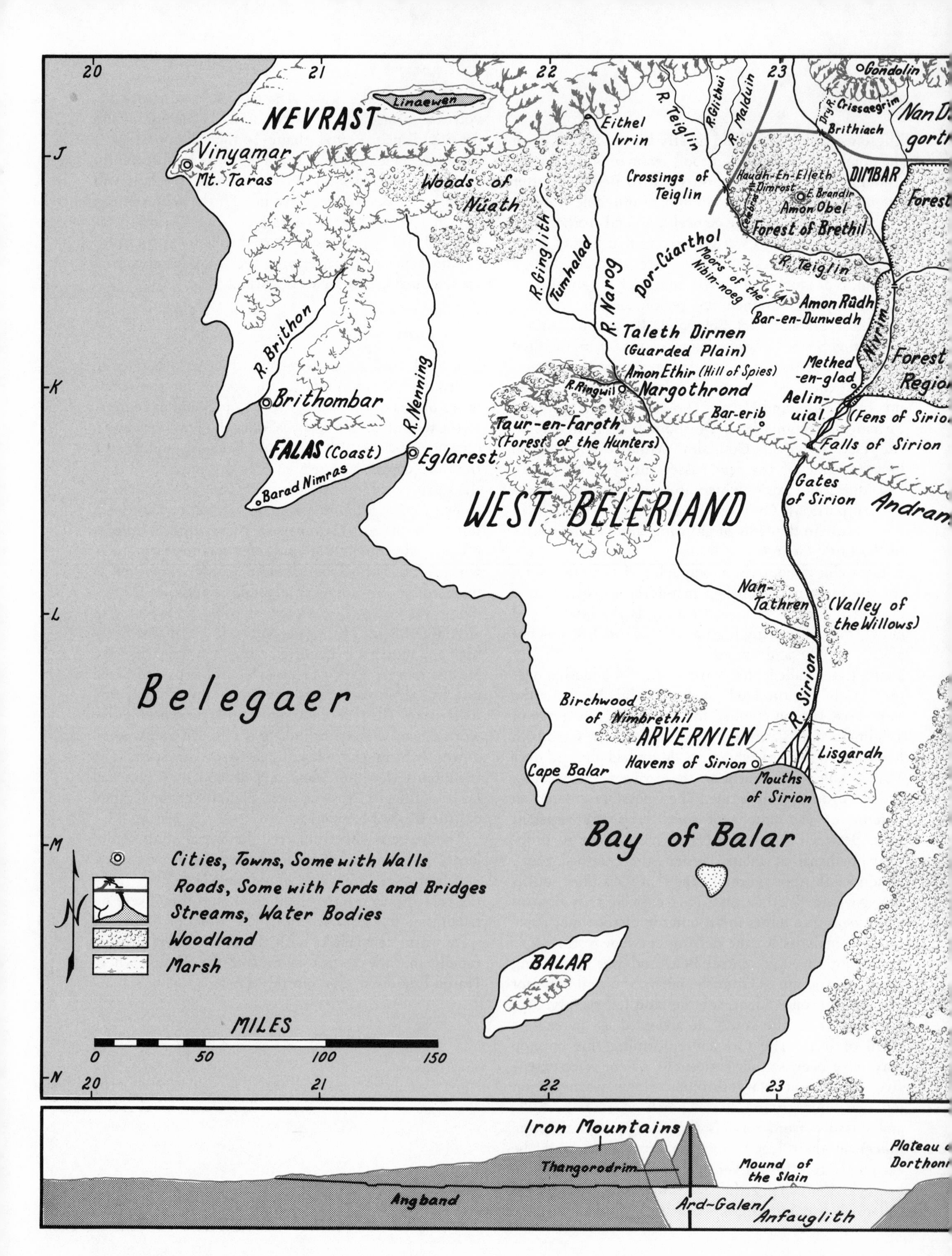

NEVRAST
Linaewen
Vinyamar
Mt. Taras
Woods of Núath
Eithel Ivrin
R. Teiglin
R. Glithui
R. Malduin
Gondolin
Dry R. Crissaegrim
Brithiach
Nan Du gortr
DIMBAR
Crossings of Teiglin
Haudh-En-Elleth
Dimrost
E. Brandir
Amon Obel
Forest of Brethil
R. Ginglith
Tumhalad
R. Narog
Dor-Cúarthol
Moors of the Nibin-noeg
R. Teiglin
Amon Rûdh
Bar-en-Dunwedh
Nivrim
Forest Region
R. Brithon
Taleth Dirnen
(Guarded Plain)
Amon Ethir (Hill of Spies)
R. Ringwil
Nargothrond
Methed -en-glad
Aelin-uial
(Fens of Sirion
Bar-erib
Falls of Sirion
Brithombar
R. Nenning
Taur-en-Faroth
(Forest of the Hunters)
FALAS (Coast)
Barad Nimras
Eglarest
Gates of Sirion
Andram
WEST BELERIAND
Nan-Tathren
(Valley of the Willows)
R. Sirion
Belegaer
Birchwood of Nimbrethil
ARVERNIEN
Lisgardh
Cape Balar
Havens of Sirion
Mouths of Sirion
Bay of Balar
BALAR
Cities, Towns, Some with Walls
Roads, Some with Fords and Bridges
Streams, Water Bodies
Woodland
Marsh
N
MILES
0
50
100
150
20
21
22
23
J
K
L
M
N
Iron Mountains
Thangorodrim
Angband
Mound of the Slain
Ard-Galen/Anfauglith
Plateau of Dorthoni

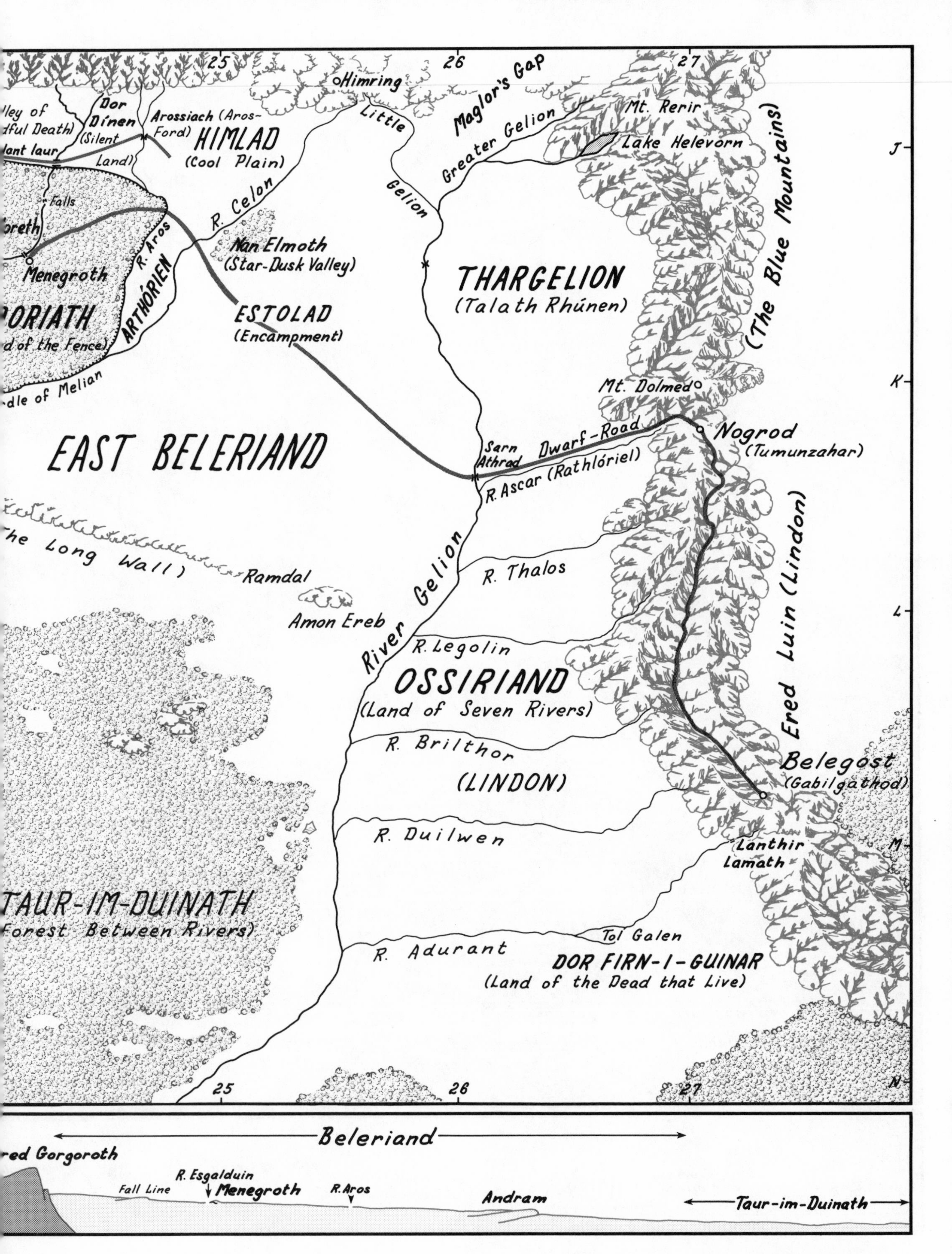
Himring
Maglor's Gap
Little
Gelion
Greater Gelion
Mt. Rerir
Lake Helevorn
(The Blue Mountains)
Dor Dínen (Silent Land)
Arossiach (Aros-Ford)
HIMLAD (Cool Plain)
Falls
Menegroth
R. Aros
ARTHÓRIEN
R. Celon
Nan Elmoth (Star-Dusk Valley)
THARGELION (Talath Rhúnen)
ESTOLAD (Encampment)
Mt. Dolmed
Nogrod (Tumunzahar)
Sarn Athrad
Dwarf-Road
R. Ascar (Rathlóriel)
EAST BELERIAND
The Long Wall)
Ramdal
R. Thalos
River Gelion
Amon Ereb
R. Legolin
OSSIRIAND (Land of Seven Rivers)
Ered Luin (Lindon)
R. Brilthor
(LINDON)
Belegost (Gabilgathod)
R. Duilwen
Lanthir Lamath
TAUR-IM-DUINATH
Forest Between Rivers)
Tol Galen
R. Adurant
DOR FIRN-I-GUINAR (Land of the Dead that Live)
25
26
27
J
K
L
M
N
Beleriand
red Gorgoroth
R. Esgalduin
Fall Line
Menegroth
R. Aros
Andram
Taur-im-Duinath

BELERIAND Cross Section: NORTH–SOUTH

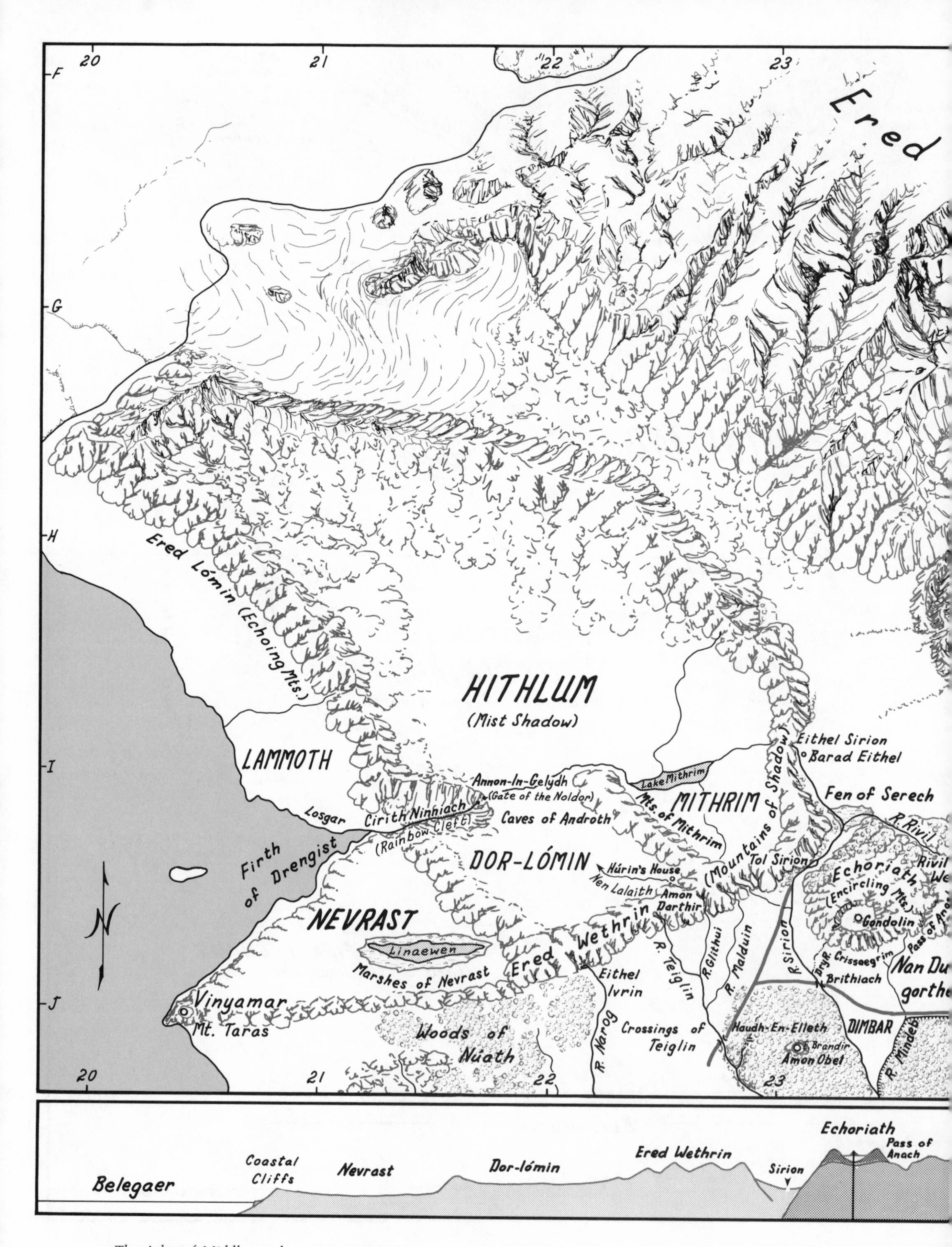
Ered
Ered Lómin (Echoing Mts.)
HITHLUM
(Mist Shadow)
LAMMOTH
Eithel Sirion
Barad Eithel
Lake Mithrim
Annon-In-Gelydh
(Gate of the Noldor)
Fen of Serech
MITHRIM
Mts. of Mithrim
(Mountains of Shadow)
Losgar
Cirith Ninniach
(Rainbow Cleft)
Caves of Androth
R. Rivil
Firth of Drengist
DOR-LÓMIN
Húrin's House
Nen Lalaith
Amon Darthir
Tol Sirion
Echoriath
(Encircling Mts.)
Gondolin
NEVRAST
Ered Wethrin
Linaewen
Marshes of Nevrast
R. Teiglin
R. Glithui
R. Malduin
R. Sirion
Crissaegrim
Brithiach
Pass of Anach
Nan Du
gorthe
Eithel Ivrin
Vinyamar
Mt. Taras
Woods of Núath
R. Narog
Crossings of Teiglin
Haudh-En-Elleth
Brandir
Amon Obel
DIMBAR
R. Mindeb
Belegaer
Coastal Cliffs
Nevrast
Dor-lómin
Ered Wethrin
Sirion
Echoriath
Pass of Anach

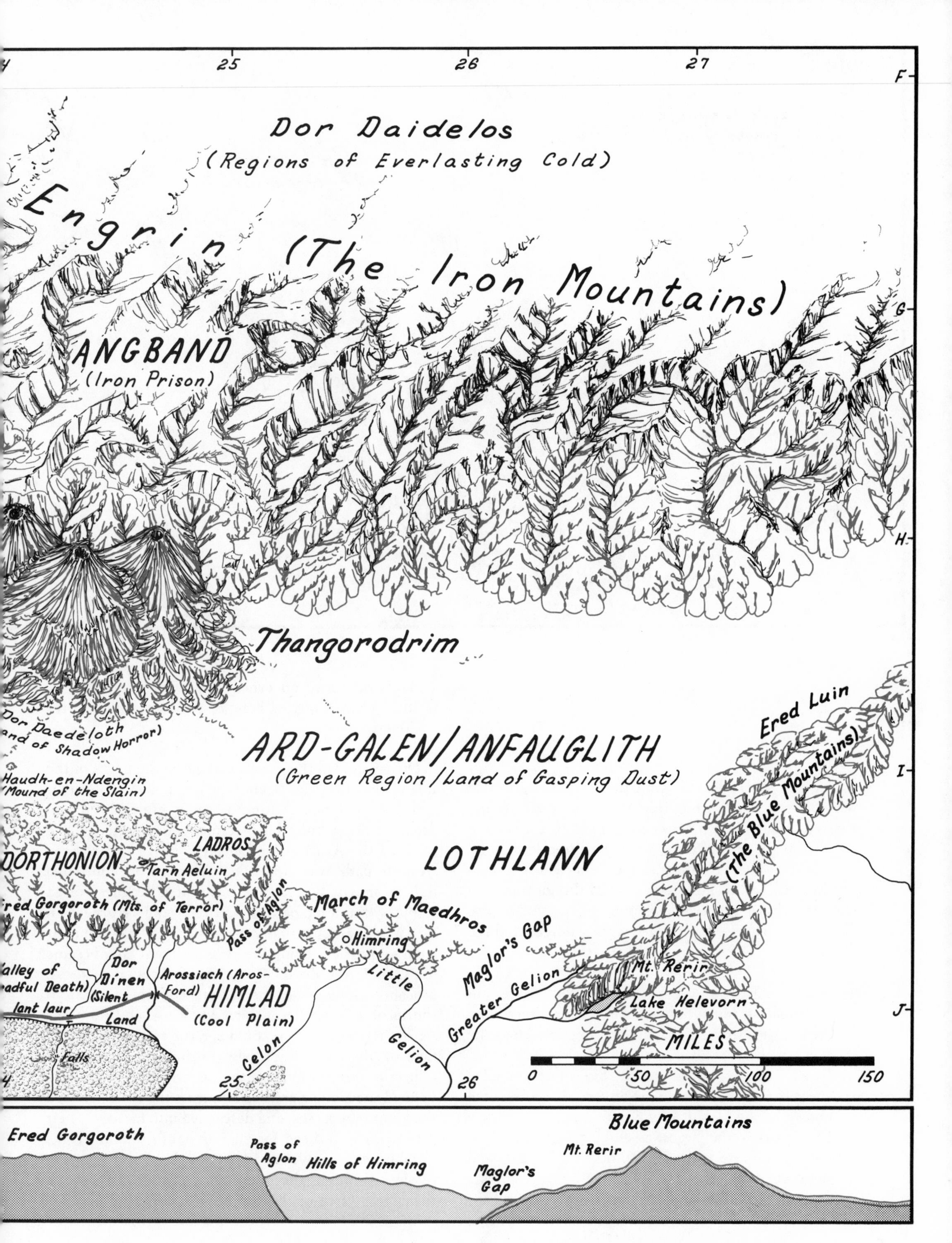
25
26
27
F
G
H
I
J
Dor Daidelos
(Regions of Everlasting Cold)
Engrin (The Iron Mountains)
ANGBAND
(Iron Prison)
Thangorodrim
Dor Daedeloth
Land of Shadow Horror)
ARD-GALEN/ANFAUGLITH
(Green Region/Land of Gasping Dust)
Haudh-en-Ndengin
(Mound of the Slain)
Ered Luin
(The Blue Mountains)
LADROS
DORTHONION
Tarn Aeluin
LOTHLANN
Ered Gorgoroth (Mts. of Terror)
Pass of Aglon
March of Maedhros
Himring
Maglor's Gap
Dor Dínen (Silent Land
Arossiach (Aros-Ford)
Little
Mt. Rerir
Greater Gelion
HIMLAD
(Cool Plain)
Lake Helevorn
Celon
Gelion
MILES
0
50
100
150
Falls
25
26
Ered Gorgoroth
Pass of Aglon
Hills of Himring
Maglor's Gap
Mt. Rerir
Blue Mountains

LANDS TO THE NORTH Cross Section: WEST–EAST

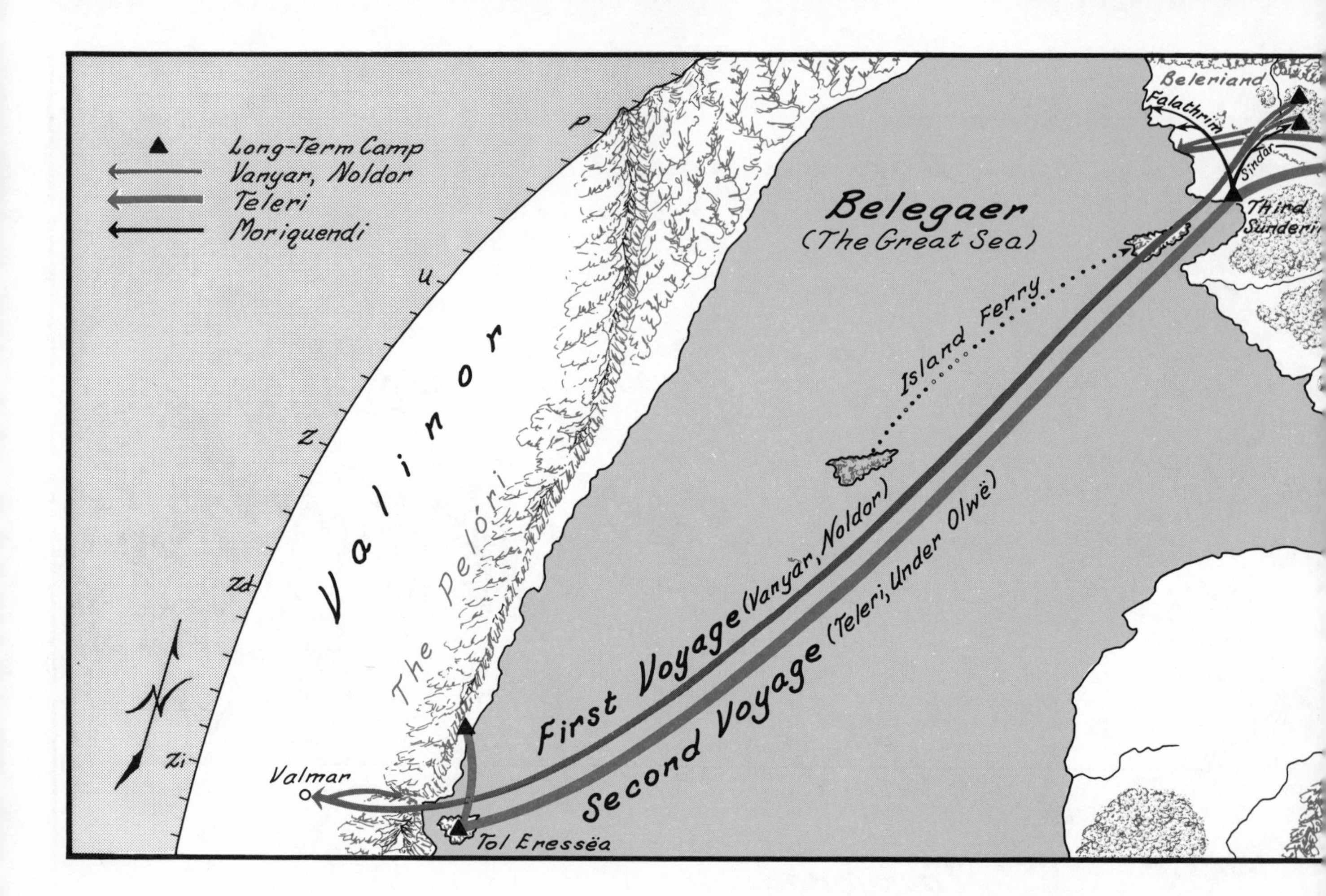

The Great March

AFTER THE VALAR had broken Utumno and imprisoned Melkor, the Elves were free to travel west to the Blessed Realm. When Oromë returned to Cuiviénen, the birthplace of the Elves, with the three leaders he had chosen as heralds, most of the people chose to take the western road. Those who refused the journey and shunned the light became known as the Avari, the Unwilling.[1] Those who accepted were arranged in three hosts:

1) Ingwë's kin — all went west, yet they were still the smallest, but foremost, group. In Valinor they drew closest to the Valar, and became known as the Vanyar, the Fair Elves.
2) Finwë's kin — some stayed, but most travelled always just behind the Vanyar. They became known as the Noldor, the Deep Elves.
3) Elwë's kin — the largest assemblage, and the most reticent on the road. Many never departed, and some turned back very early. Still the numbers were so large that the Host required two leaders, and with Elwë governed Olwë, his brother. Since they always tarried behind, they were dubbed the Teleri.[2]

Oromë guided the great mass along the north of the Inland Sea of Helcar. Seeing the great black clouds that still persisted near Utumno, some grew afraid and departed. They may have returned to Cuiviénen and rejoined the Avari. Whether any or all later trod the western path was not told.[3] Those who continued moved slowly across the uncounted leagues, often stopping for long periods until Oromë returned. In this way they eventually came to those now familiar lands — possibly along the very path that later became the Old Forest Road. They passed through a forest, probably Greenwood the Great; and to the eastern shores of a Great River, later known as the Anduin.[4] Across its waters they could see the towering Mountains of Mist. The Teleri, always the slowest and most reluctant, camped long on the eastern shore. The Vanyar and the Noldor pressed on across the river, climbed the mountain passes, and descended into Eriador. Their path must have been far enough south to allow comfortably warm travel and far enough north to require passing through the mountains instead of around them, to be free of the southern forests, and to allow

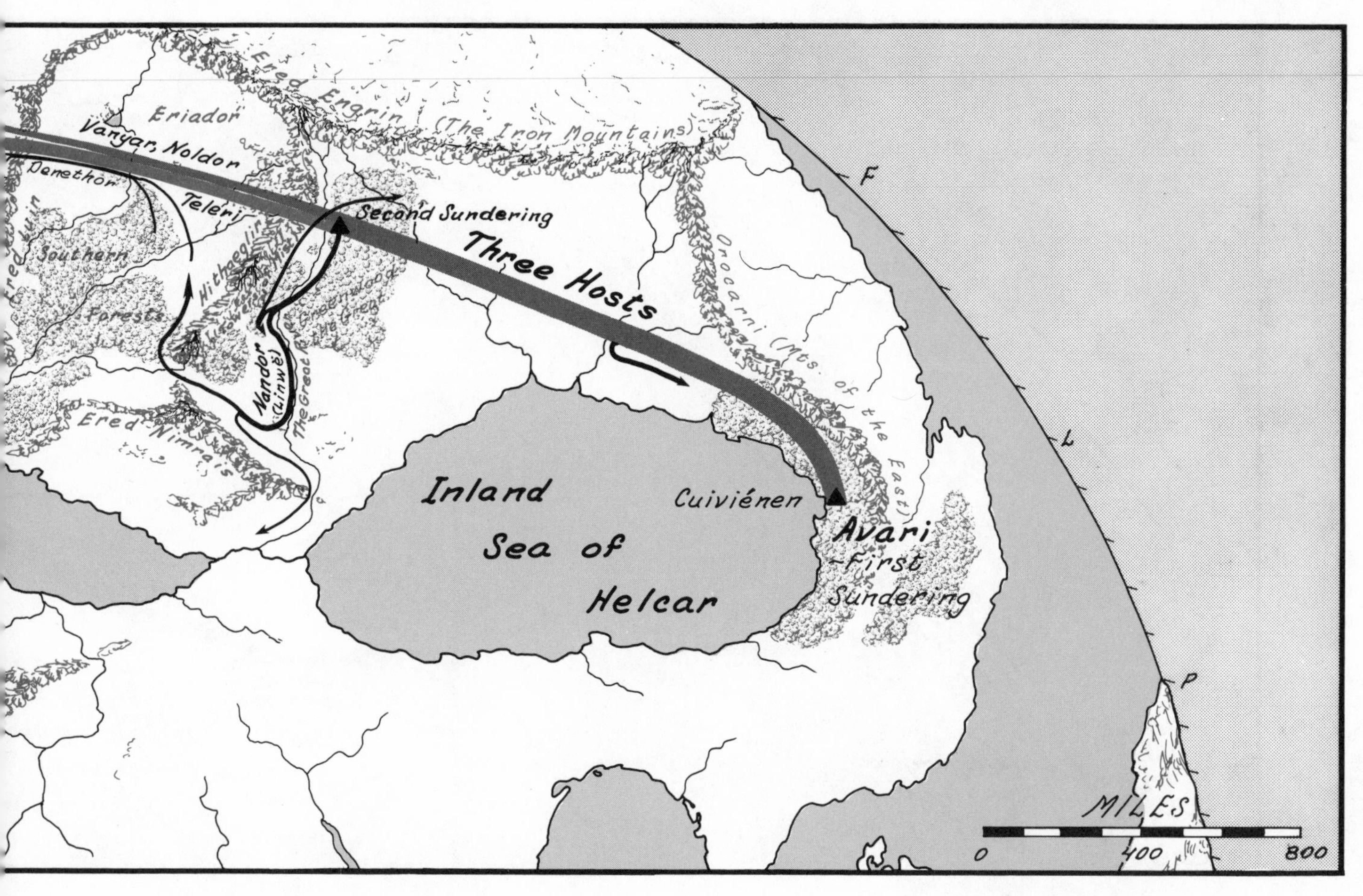

THE GREAT MARCH

fording the major rivers. In short, it was most likely that the Great East Road had its origins in this path of great antiquity.

The Noldor and Vanyar continued west until they reached the Great Sea on the coasts between the Bay of Balar and the Firth of Drengist,[5] after crossing the Sirion.[6] The Elves were awed by the world of water and drew back to the more familiar hills and woods — especially those of Neldoreth and Region where Finwë encamped.[7] There they stayed for long years.

Meanwhile, Lenwë had led some Teleri south down the Anduin; and they afterwards became known as the Nandor: "those who turn back."[8] Some stayed along the Great River, some went to the sea, and some eventually must have passed through the Gap of Rohan into Eriador.[9] Vast forests surrounded them, so they became Wood-elves: possibly the ancestors of the Silvan Elves who inhabited Mirkwood,[10] and Lórien.[11] The people of Denethor, son of Lenwë, at last crossed the western mountains from Eriador into Ossiriand,[12] and eventually were renamed the Laiquendi, Green-elves.[13] The bulk of the Teleri had continued west ages earlier than Denethor, while the Vanyar and Noldor still waited in Beleriand; but once again the Teleri had stopped — this time east of the River Gelion.

At Ulmo's bidding, Ossë grounded an island in the Bay of Balar and drew the Noldor and Vanyar to Valinor (the same isle, according to one tale, that had ferried the Valar to Valinor.)[14] The Teleri were much disconcerted to have been once more left behind, and many of them moved west to the mouths of Sirion. After long years of the sundering, Ulmo returned the island ferry, but many were no longer willing to go. Some had grown to love the Hither Shore, and became the Falathrim, the coast-people — including Círdan the Shipwright, ruler of the Havens of Elgarest and Brithombar.[15] Elwë had vanished in Nan Elmoth,[16] and many of his people returned to the woods, calling themselves the Eglath, the Forsaken People;[17] but upon his reappearance they became the Sindar, the Grey-elves.[18]

The bulk of the Teleri did go forward, but regretted the loss of their familiar land. Upon their wish, Ulmo rooted the island in the Bay, and there it stood through the ages: Tol Eressëa, the Lonely Isle.[19] The Valar opened the Calacirya so that the Teleri could receive the glow from the Pass of Light. Within the pass, the city of Tirion was fashioned and in it dwelt the Noldor and also the Vanyar (until they chose to return to the plain of Valinor).[20] At last the Teleri were drawn to the light. Then Ossë taught them shipbuilding and drew them ashore, where they lived in Alqualondë.

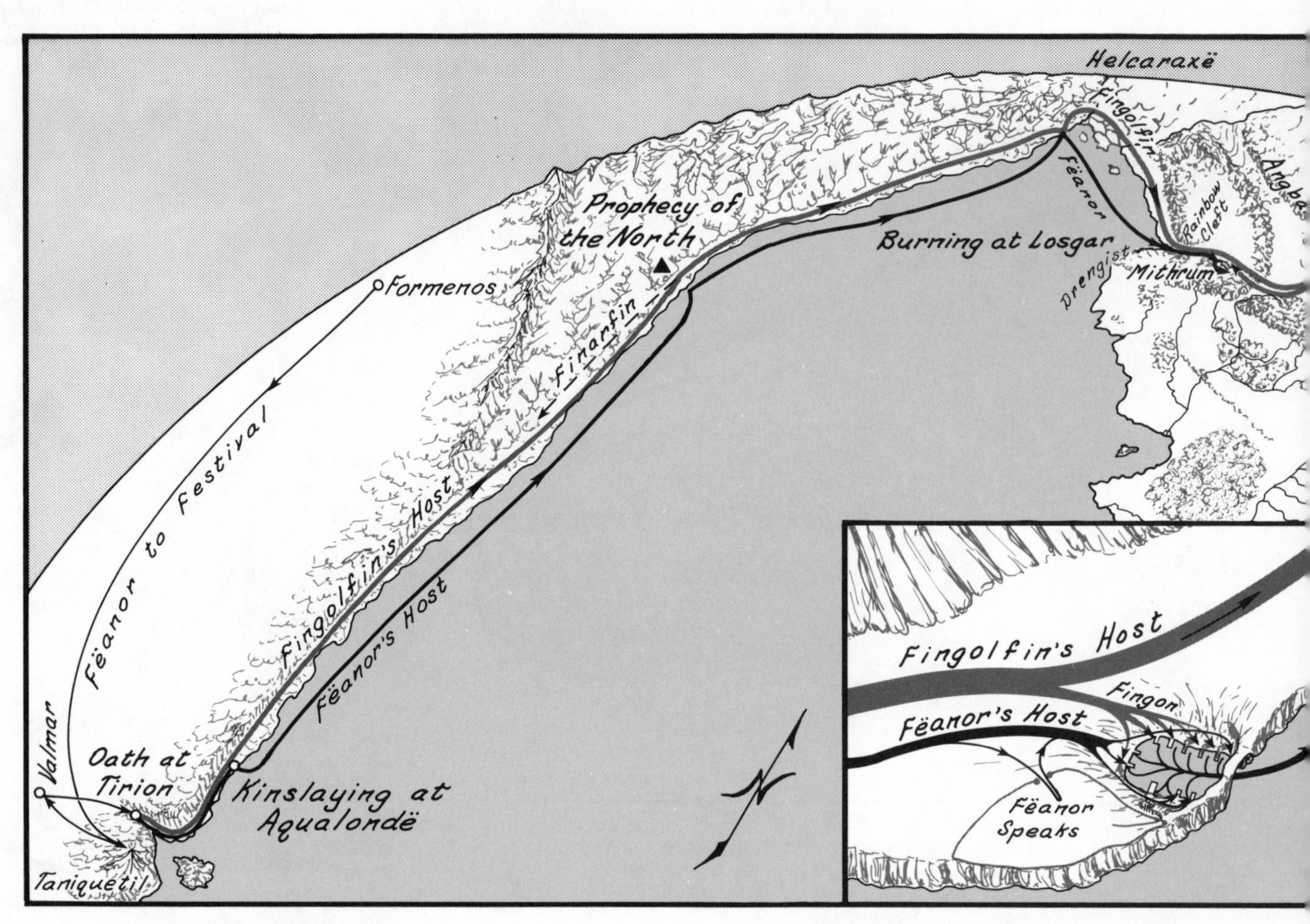

THE FLIGHT Inset: ALQUALONDË

The Flight of the Noldor

ON MANWË'S ORDERS Fëanor was on Taniquetil[1] when Melkor and Ungoliant quenched the light of the Trees and swept through Formenos, taking the Silmarils and slaying Finwë, his father. After the Valar requested the Silmarils Fëanor's anger grew, and he broke his exile and returned to Tirion. In spite of arguments of his half-brothers, his will prevailed over all but a tithe of the Noldor; and with only hasty preparations the Noldor marched forth. Fëanor's host led, followed by the greater host of Fingolfin, with Finarfin in the rear.[2] The way north was long and evil, and the great sea lay beyond; so Fëanor sought to persuade the Teleri to join them, or at least to lend their great ships. Being unsuccessful, he waited until most of his following had arrived, then led them to the harbor and began manning the vessels. The Teleri repulsed them until Fingon arrived, the leading part of Fingolfin's host. His strength was added to the affray, and the Noldor at last won to the ships and departed before most of Fingolfin's host had even arrived. They were left to toil slowly up the rocky coast while the Noldor rowed just offshore in the rough seas.[3]

Long they journeyed, and both the sea and the land were evil enemies. Then, far in the north as they climbed in Araman, they were arrested by a powerful voice that prophesied the Doom of the Noldor. Then Finarfin and his following, least willing from the start, returned to Tirion; but most of the people continued. The hosts neared the Helcaraxë, and while they debated the path to take, Fëanor's folk slipped aboard and abandoned Fingolfin. Sailing east and south, they landed at Losgar, and burned the white ships. Climbing east into Hithlum to the north shore of Lake Mithrim,[4] they were beset by an onslaught from Angband, and Fëanor was slain.[5] Fingolfin's host, angered by the desertion, braved the Grinding Ice floes. Weeks may have passed before they touched the solid ground of Middle-earth with the rising of the moon. After seven days the sun rose just as Fingolfin marched into Mithrim.[6] On he marched to the very gates of Angband, but his challenge went unanswered. He returned to Mithrim, where those who remained of Fëanor's following withdrew to the south shore, avoiding further disturbance.[7]

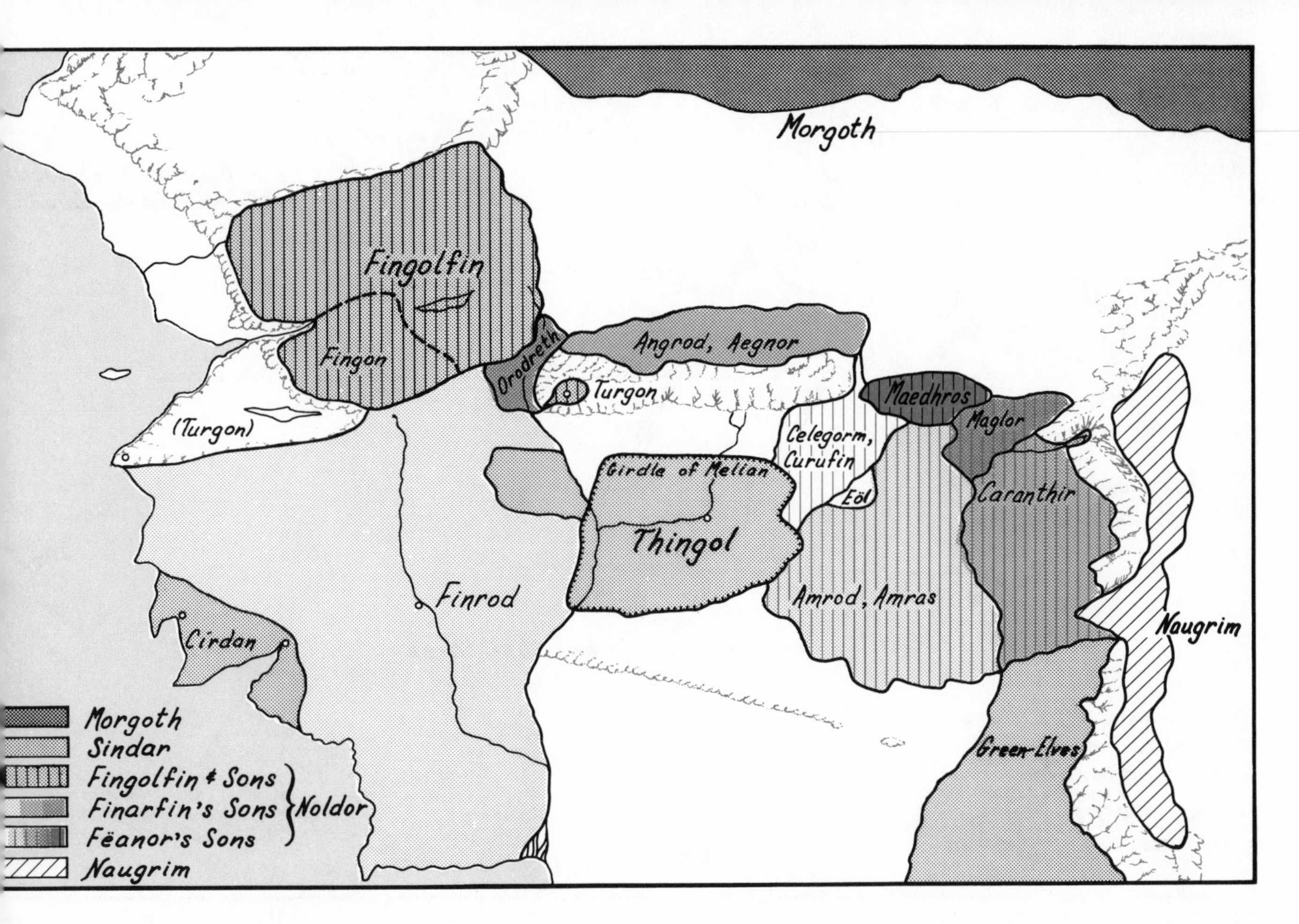

Realms – Before the Great Defeat

As was told, some of the Teleri never left the Hither Shore. They were scattered through Beleriand, but most lived in one of three areas: on the coast, the Falathrim under Círdan; in Ossiriand, the Green-elves; and in the Guarded Realm of Doriath, the Sindar, kin of Elwë/Thingol. The bulk of Thingol's realm lay inside the Girdle of Melian:[1] the Forests of Neldoreth, Region, and part of Nivrim, the west march across Sirion. Outside the Girdle was Brethil, a less populous area. All the Teleri eventually came to acknowledge Thingol as Lord, and so were loosely grouped with the Sindar.

When the Noldor returned from the West Thingol decreed: "In Hithlum the Noldor have leave to dwell, and in the highlands of Dorthonion, and in the lands east of Doriath that are empty and wild . . . for I am the Lord of Beleriand."[2] The Noldor accordingly settled those areas — not only because it was Thingol's wish, but also because it allowed them to beleaguer Morgoth's realm in the north. In the west dwelt: Fingolfin, the high king, in Hithlum; his elder son Fingon, in the subregion of Dor-lómin; and Turgon, in Nevrast.[3] In the center were the sons of Finarfin: Finrod and Orodreth in the Pass of Sirion, and Angrod and Aegnor in northern Dorthonion.[4] The east was guarded by the seven sons of Fëanor: Celegorm and Curufin, at the Pass of Aglon and behind into Himlad; Maedhros, on the Hill of Himring;[5] Maglor, across the gap and into the land between the arms of Gelion;[6] Caranthir, on Mount Rerir and behind into Thargelion.[7] Only Amrod and Amras were set back from the buffer, in the open areas south of the hills.[8]

Fifty years after these lands had been settled, Ulmo spoke to Turgon and Finrod in a dream, suggesting hidden kingdoms.[9] Finrod delved the mansions of Nargothrond, and eventually his lordship was acknowledged by all west of Sirion. Turgon completed building Gondolin in 104.[10] After he moved his people there, Nevrast was left empty.

All these realms survived through the Long Peace until 455, when the Siege of Angband ended. In the short fifty years following, they were overrun one by one until the remaining Elves were pushed to the brink of the Sea.[11]

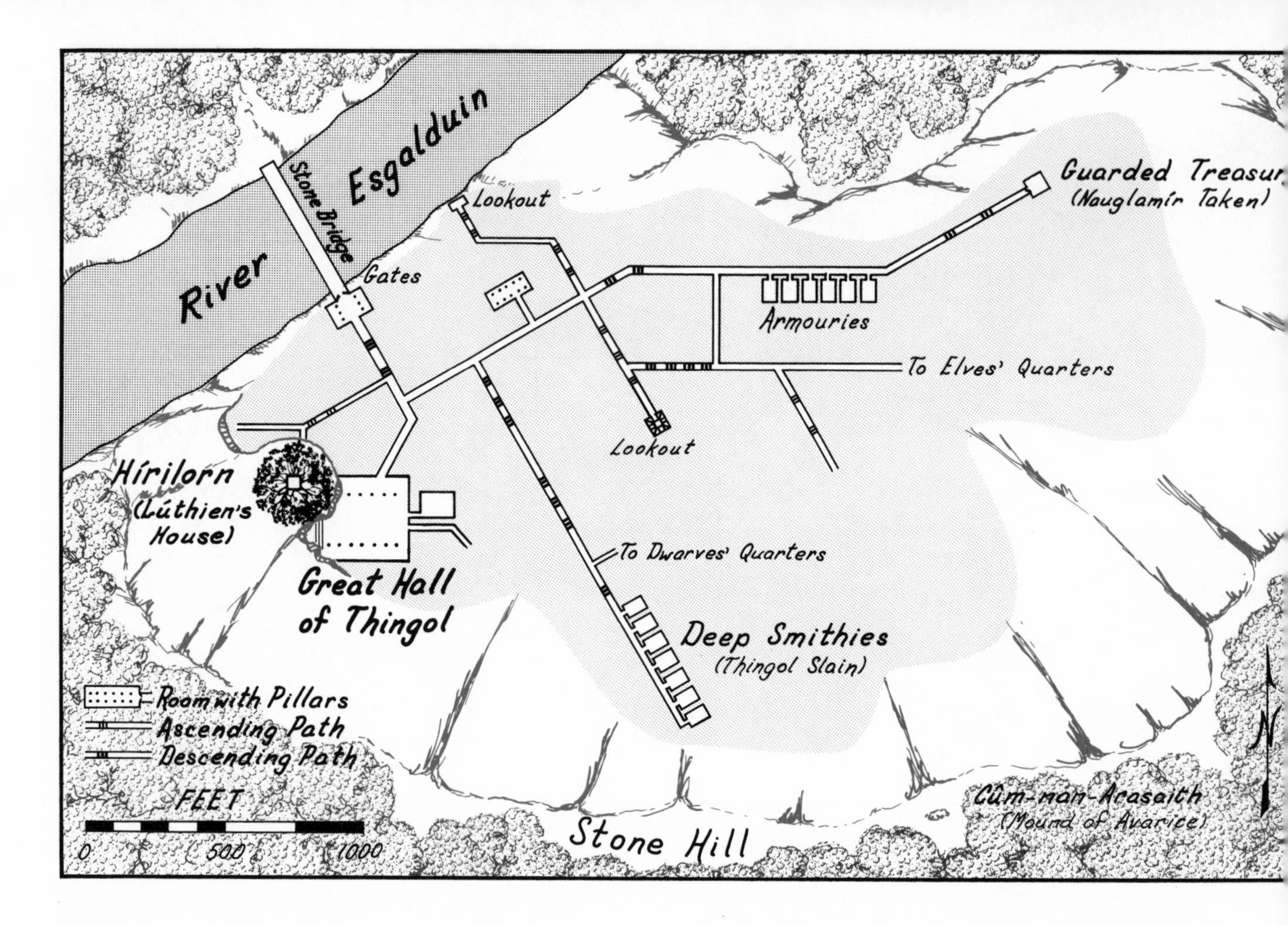

Menegroth, the Thousand Caves

MENEGROTH WAS DELVED for Thingol and Melian by the Dwarves of Belegost.[1] It is uncertain, however, whether the caves were hewn from the solid rock of the hill beside Esgalduin; or whether they were preexisting passages that were simply widened. If the latter were the case, the correct bedrock (such as that found at Nargothrond) would have been necessary for development of a cavern system — but Menegroth was far north of Andram. It has been assumed, therefore, that these were not large natural caverns but were primarily hand-cut. At first thought this might seem unlikely, until one remembers Khazad-dûm, the zenith of the Dwarves' mining achievements. Then anything seems possible!

The hill of stone must have run to the very edge of Esgalduin, for only by crossing the stone bridge could the gates be entered.[2] Near the gates stood a great beech tree whose roots roofed the thronehall: Hírilorn. In it a house was built to prevent Lúthien's escape to rescue Beren.[3] A beech was an excellent choice, for they commonly have no protruding branches for up to half their height.[4] The largest have trunks up to five feet in diameter, and their drip line may be twenty times that.[5]

Countless rooms and paths (many more than have been shown) would have been possible in a square-mile area — especially when delved at several subterranean levels, as these undoubtedly were. Little specific information was given, however. Of the innumerable "high halls and chambers"[6] only three specific locations were mentioned: (1) the Great Hall of Thingol, where Beren came before the throne;[7] (2) the deep smithies, where the Naugrim slay Thingol;[8] and (3) the guarded treasury, where Mablung fell when the Dwarves returned to take the Nauglamír.[9]

Twice Menegroth was the site of battle within the caves. Both were attempts to take the Nauglamír with its Silmaril. About 505[10] the Dwarves returned to avenge the deaths of their kin who fell when Thingol was slain. They succeeded in stealing the necklace, but it was later regained.[11] Four years later, the seven sons of Fëanor, still holding to the accursed oath, initiated the Second Kinslaying, when they fought and killed Dior. They were unsuccessful in their quest, however, for Elwing fled from Menegroth with a remnant of the people, and with them went the Silmaril.[12]

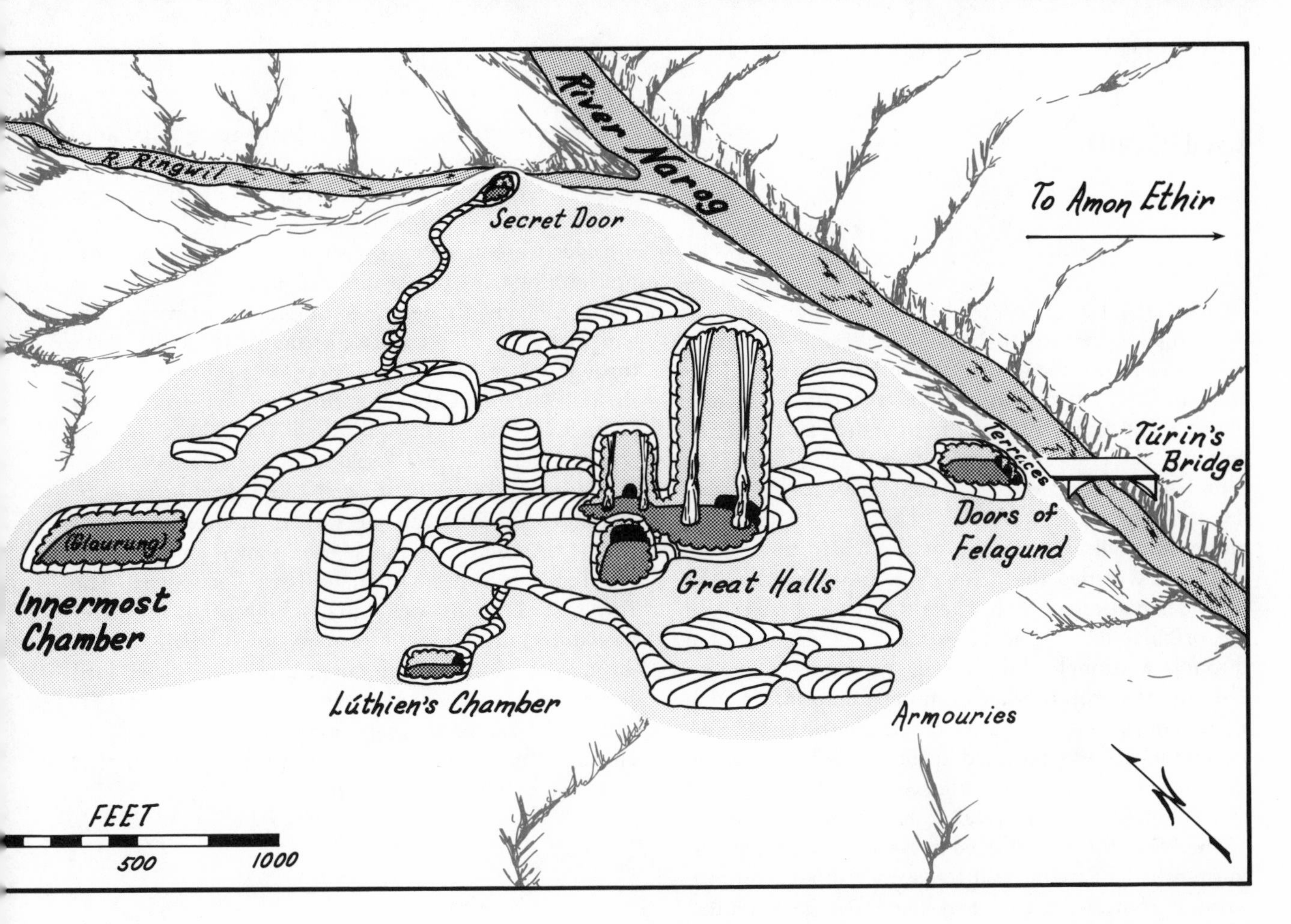

NARGOTHROND

Nargothrond

In a dream Ulmo spoke to Turgon and Finrod, suggesting that each build a hidden fortress. Soon after, Finrod visited Thingol and was inspired to build a stronghold like Menegroth. He learned of the Caverns of Narog and initiated his construction.[1] The area lay south and west of the confluence of the Ringwil and Narog, where those rivers cut through the Andram. The Long Wall was evidently soluble rock, most possibly limestone.[2] That formation, combined with an entrenched river, such as Narog, would have produced ideal conditions for cavern development.[3] Before the return of the Noldor, the caverns were found and widened by the Petty-Dwarves,[4] who called them the Nulukkizdîn.[5] Finrod employed the Dwarves of the Blue Mountains to continue the work. So great was the task that the Dwarves named him "Felagund" — Hewer of Caves.[6]

All that was really necessary to the tale was that the reader envision a complex system of caves, such as those of Carlsbad Caverns, New Mexico, or Mammoth Cave, Kentucky.[7] Such a system would provide a wide variety of sizes and shapes of rooms; would be sufficiently extensive to completely hide a large population; and, after widening, would have had several hallways large enough to allow passage of the dragon. In Nargothrond there were: several rooms used as armouries;[8] a series of great halls in which Finrod, Celegorm, and Curufin addressed the populace;[9] a small, deep chamber in which Lúthien was placed; a secret exit through which she escaped with Huan;[10] and a great inner hall where Glaurung amassed his golden bed.[11]

Tolkien illustrated the entrance to Nargothrond in three separate drawings: Two of those showed three doors; the third, only one.[12] The text always referred in the plural to the Doors of Felagund,[13] so three have been included here. Before the doors was a terrace — broad enough to allow Glaurung to lie upon while the captives were herded away.[14] From there he could see clearly a league east to Amon Ethir, the fateful spot where Nienor fell under his spell.[15] Below the terrace a steep cliff-wall fell to Narog's rapids. Originally, the Elves were forced to go twenty-five miles north to ford the river,[16] but after Túrin came in 487,[17] he persuaded Orodreth to build a mighty bridge. As it could not be lifted to prevent passage, the bridge proved to be their downfall.

Gondolin

GONDOLIN, THE HIDDEN ROCK, was the result of Turgon's long efforts to establish a secret city.[1] Ulmo revealed the location of the Hidden Vale of Tumladen,[2] and after fifty-two years of toil the city was completed.[3] The Echoriath have been shown as a gigantic volcanic caldera, and Amon Gwareth a secondary cone.[4] After extinction, a lake could have formed, similar to Oregon's Crater Lake.[5] Through the towering mountain walls "the hands of the Valar themselves . . . had wrestled the great mountains asunder, and the sides of the rift were sheer as if axe-cloven."[6] In the original tale the river was not yet dry, but ran through a tunnel, and the rift was still to come.[7] Through that rift, the lake eventually emptied, leaving a flat plain, a steep ravine, a tunnel, and the Dry River. When the city was occupied in about 104,[8] these physical properties were well-utilized. The Hidden Way was comprised of the river's abandoned tunnel and ravine. The Way was blocked by a series of seven gates, constantly guarded: built of wood, stone, bronze, wrought iron, silver, gold, and steel.[9] The Dark (Outer) Gate lay within the tunnel; while the ravine contained the remaining gates, and became known as the Orfalch Echor.[10] Once in the Vale, the city could be reached only by climbing the stairs to the main gate,[11] for the hillsides were steep — especially on the north at the precipice of Caragdûr where Eöl died.[12]

The Tale vividly describes Gondolin's many squares and roadways,[13] and adds a second gate in the north through which Maeglin led Morgoth's forces.[14] Scaling the hill was impossible as springs wet the steep, glassy bedrock.[15] The springs inspired Gondolin's original name: Ondolinde, the Rock of the Music of Water.[16]

A drawing by Tolkien[17] was coupled with the original map and analysis of similar landforms in our world.[18] Amon Gwareth has been shown four hundred feet high. It appears to have been flat-topped. The Tower of the King was equally high, with its turret standing eight hundred feet above the Vale. Down through the hill and far north under the plain, Idril directed the excavation of an escape route.[19] In 511, after four hundred years of peace, Gondolin fell. Through the secret way Idril and Tuor led all that remained of the Gondolindrim.[20]

Thangorodrim and Angband

ANGBAND, THE "HELLS OF IRON," was built in the Ered Engrin in the northwest of Middle-earth after the establishment of Valinor as an outpost closer to Aman than Utumno.[1] Its labyrinthine tunnels and dungeons, pits and stairs lay below the fence of the Ered Engrin, with a great tunnel opening beneath the three great smoking peaks: the 'towers' of Thangorodrim.[2]

Thangorodrim, the "oppression mountain group,"[3] was built of slag from the furnaces, and rubble from the redelving of Angband.[4] The hills were solid enough to nail Maedhros to a cliff[5] and imprison Húrin on a terrace.[6] Yet its smoking tops were the highest of the Iron Mountains around Angband — indeed even "the greatest of the hills of the [hither] world."[7] *The Silmarillion* map excluded Thangorodrim and the Ered Engrin, but the "Second 'Silmarillion' Map" illustrates Thangorodrim almost as an 'island' of foothills around the three tall peaks, jutting out one hundred miles from where the curve of the Iron Mountains must lie.[8] Prior to *The History* the only references were the text and a drawing by Tolkien that showed the central peak in the distance.[9] The text stated that these were the "mightiest towers of Middle-earth."[10] The precipice above the gate stood a thousand feet[11] — two-thirds that of our tallest modern building.[12] In the drawing, the central tower, as seen from the Pass of Sirion,[13] appeared immense — far higher than the Ered Engrin. It would have to have been at least five miles in diameter at the base and some 35,000 feet high![14]

The History gives the best close range detail available for the interior of Angband: the Lay of Leithian. The gates were no simple tunnel opening: "they came, as to a sombre court / walled with great towers, fort on fort / of cliffs embattled . . . the gigantic shadow of his gates."[15] Beyond, Beren and Lúthien descended the corridors of the "labyrinthine pyramid" — which rang with the blows of 10,000 smiths, passed vaults filled with Noldor-thralls, marked at every turn by "shapes like carven trolls . . . entombed," and came at last to the "grinning portals" of Morgoth's nethermost hall: "upheld by horror, lit by fire, and filled with weapons of death and torment;" where he held feast beneath "The pillars . . . devil-carven . . . towered like trees . . . boughs like serpents" and across the hall "Beneath a monstrous column loomed . . . the throne of Morgoth" and Fëanor's doom.[16]

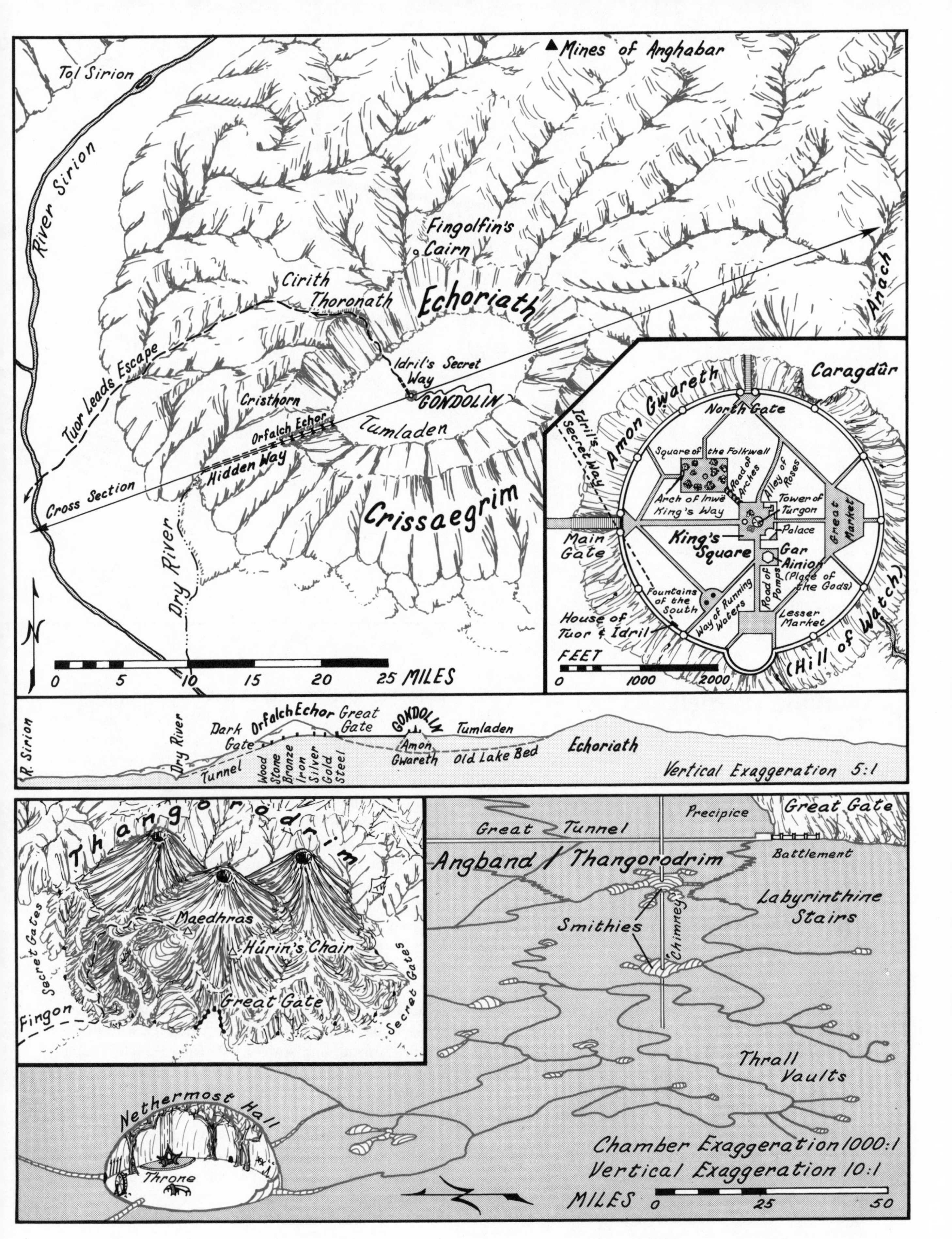

Upper: THE HIDDEN KINGDOM *Cross Section:* WEST–EAST *Inset:* GONDOLIN
Lower: THANGORODRIM *Cross Section:* NORTH–SOUTH

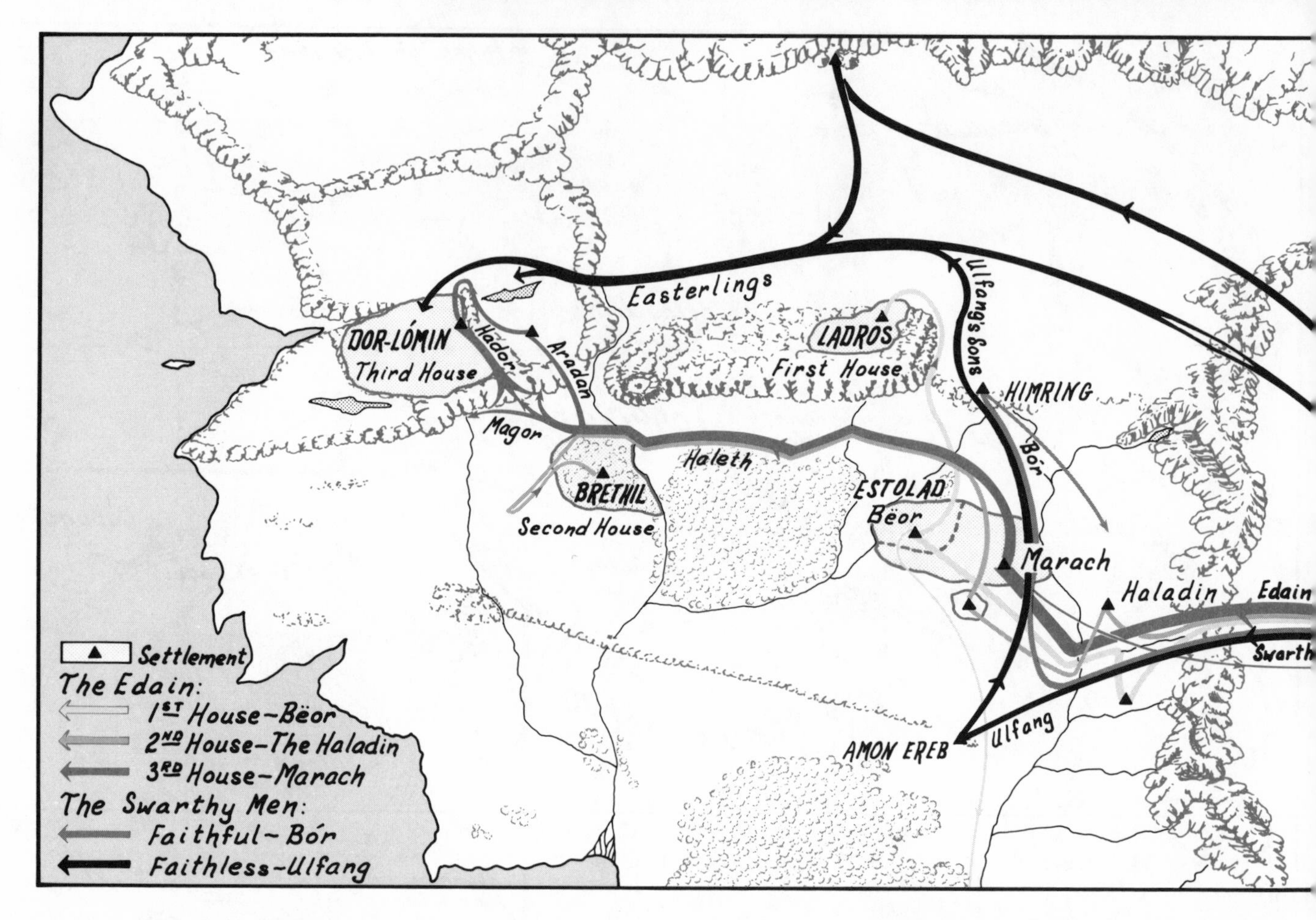

COMING OF MEN INTO THE WEST

Coming of Men

WITH THE RISING OF THE SUN IN THE WEST, mortal Men awoke[1] and over three hundred years later they were discovered by Finrod Felagund near the River Thalos.[2] Three tribes originally crossed into Beleriand in three consecutive years: the Three Houses of the Edain.[3] The first to arrive was Bëor, who moved his people north from Ossiriand into the fields of Amrod and Amras. The land became known as Estolad, the Encampment, and was constantly occupied for about one hundred fifty years.[4] Two years later Bëor's people were joined by the third and largest tribe — that of Marach — who settled to their south and east.[5] Meanwhile the Haladin, the Second House, being sundered in speech and attitude, had colonized southern Thargelion.[6]

During the next fifty years, many of the folk of Bëor and Marach chose to leave Estolad. Some grew disenchanted and were led away south and east out of knowledge.[7] The Noldor, seeking allies, shared their lands, but King Thingol forbade any to settle in the south.[8] Bëor's folk moved to Dorthonion and later were given the land of Ladros in which to dwell.[9] Many of the host of Marach allied with the House of Fingolfin. Some moved to Hithlum, while others remained in the vales south of the Ered Wethrin until they were reunited under Hador, lord of Dor-lómin.[10] The Second House, the Haladin, finally moved to Estolad after having been attacked by Orcs, but passed on through Nan Dungortheb to Talath Dirnen, and then to the Forest of Brethil.[11]

The Edain were not the only mortals to enter Beleriand, however. In about 457, after Dagor Bragollach, the Swarthy Easterlings first appeared.[12] The sons of Fëanor gained their alliance: Those under Bór located in Himring with Maedhros and Maglor, while those under Ulfang lived near Amon Ereb with Caranthir, Amrod, and Amras.[13] During the Fifth Battle, Unnumbered Tears, the folk of Bór remained faithful and were probably forced to relocate with Maedhros to Ossiriand. The sons of Ulfang were traitorous, and with other Easterlings under Morgoth they were later sent to occupy Hithlum, where they preyed upon the families of the valiant Men of Dor-lómin who had fallen around Húrin and Huor.[14]

Travels of Beren and Lúthien

BEREN'S LIFE AFTER DAGOR BRAGOLLACH was a series of journeys. His fame — and Lúthien's — arose from those travels and the related quests. Beren made six important trips, with Lúthien having gone on three: (1) in Taur-nu-Fuin (Dorthonion) from Tarn Aeluin to Rivil's Well, 460; (2) through the Ered Gorgoroth and Nan Dungortheb to Doriath, 464–465; (3) from Doriath to Tol-in-Guarloth via Nargothrond, 466; (4) back to Doriath, then on to Thangorodrim and back, 467; (5) on the Hunting of the Wolf, 467; and (6) to and from the Houses of the Dead, and on to Tol Galen.[1]

After leaving the refuge at Tarn Aeluin, where his father and companions had been slain, Beren tracked the murderous Orcs to their camp at Rivil's Well and retrieved the ring of Finrod Felagund.[2] For the next four years (460–464) he sortied from the highlands, until he was forced to leave during the winter of 464. He looked south to Doriath, and travelled unknown ways to reach it, passing through the enchanted Girdle, even as Melian had foretold.[3] There he wandered for a year, and there he met Lúthien. In summer, 465, she led him before Thingol, her father. Angered by their love, Thingol demanded Beren present a Silmaril as dowry for Lúthien's hand.[4] The 'Tale of Tinúviel' gives an early form of the story, but that in *The Silmarillion* is condensed from the 'Lay of Leithian.'[5]

Beren went out of Doriath, passing above the falls of Sirion to Nargothrond.[6] Then Finrod fulfilled the oath given to Beren's father during Dagor Bragollach.[7] That autumn, he and ten companions travelled north to Ivrin with Beren. They routed a band of Orcs and arrayed themselves in their gear. In the Pass of Sirion, however, Sauron spied them, and they were imprisoned on Tol-in-Guarloth.[8]

Lúthien learned of their predicament; and escaping from her house near Menegroth, she passed west (probably across the bridge of Sirion) into Nivrim. There she was abducted by Celegorm and Curufin, who imprisoned her in Nargothrond.[9] Huan, hound of Celegorm, grew to love Lúthien and helped her escape the deep caverns and reach Sauron's Isle. Between them they defeated Sauron. Then Lúthien bared the pits of the fortress — too late for Finrod[10]

Huan returned to Celegorm and was with him and Curufin later in the winter when they happened upon Beren and Lúthien in the Forest of Brethil. When the brothers assailed the couple, Huan abandoned Celegorm and drove him and Curufin from the wood.[11] Lúthien healed the wound Beren had received in the affray, and they returned to a glade in Doriath. Yet the quest was not achieved, so Beren set out again — only to be followed by Huan and Lúthien. As Beren stood on the skirts of Taur-nu-Fuin, they approached him in the forms they had taken on at Sauron's Isle — a wolf and bat.[12] Beren then was arrayed as the wolf, and Huan returned to the south. Thus disguised, Beren and Lúthien crossed to the Gate of Thangorodrim. There Lúthien enchanted the great wolf Carcaroth, and later, Morgoth. Beren cut a Silmaril from the iron crown and in terror they fled. At the gate Carcaroth had awakened, and engulfed both Beren's hand and the jewel it held. The jewel flamed, and the ravening beast ran wildly away south. The lovers were still not free, for Beren swooned and the hosts of Morgoth had awakened. Then Thorondor and two of his vassals raced north and rescued the valiant pair. The mighty eagles returned them to the glade in Doriath from which they had departed, and there Lúthien ministered to Beren until spring (467). Upon his recovery they returned to Menegroth. Thingol softened, and they were wed.[13]

Meanwhile, Carcaroth had continued his tortuous passage toward Doriath and, at last, was approaching Menegroth. So Beren went forth once more with the Hunting of the Wolf. North along Esgalduin, Carcaroth had stopped by a waterfall. Huan battled the mighty beast, and both fell. So, too, did Beren, whose chest was torn while he defended Thingol. The companions bore him to Menegroth, where he died. At his death, Lúthien withered, and her spirit departed to Valinor. There she was granted the choice of mortality, and Beren was released. They were permitted to return to Menegroth. From thence they went forth to Tol Galen, where they lived the rest of their mortal lives, and that land came to be known as Dor Firn-I-Guinar: the Land of the Dead that Live.[14]

Travels of Túrin and Nienor

WHEN HÚRIN, FATHER OF TÚRIN AND NIENOR, was captured at the Fen of Serech during the Battle of Unnumbered Tears in 473, he defied Morgoth. Then the Dark Lord set a curse upon Húrin and his entire family.[1] So it was that the paths of the children's lives were set, for Morgoth ever sought opportunities to prove his curse.

Túrin's life covered five stages: (1) with Morwen and Húrin in Dor-lómin, 465–473; (2) with Thingol in Doriath, 473–485; (3) with the outlaw band in the woods near Teiglin, and then on Amon Rûdh, 485–487; (4) with Orodreth in Nargothrond, 487–496; and (5) with the Haladin in the Forest of Brethil, 497–501.[2] The pathways shown on the map are those by which he passed from one life stage to the next. Most of the changes resulted directly or indirectly from Morgoth's curse.

The first move was made when Morwen feared that Túrin was endangered by the Easterlings who occupied Dor-lómin after the fall of Hithlum. She sent him to Menegroth, where Thingol fostered him in his youth. On reaching early manhood Túrin helped Beleg guard the northern marches for three years. When he was twenty, however, he fled Doriath after the accidental death of Saeros.[3] In Nivrim he came upon an outlaw band with whom he allied. For a year they bivouacked in the woods near Teiglin, but wishing safer quarters they removed to Amon Rûdh. There Beleg joined them and their land became a haven amongst the Ruin of Beleriand — Dor-Cúarthol, the Land of the Bow and Helm.[4] Unfortunately, the Dragon-helm of Dor-lómin worn by Túrin revealed his whereabouts to Morgoth. Then Túrin was captured, and all his company except Beleg slain. In leisurely fashion, the Orcs travelled up their newly built road through the Pass of Anach and north through Taur-nu-Fuin. On the edge of the northern slopes Gwindor was found, Túrin rescued, and Beleg slain.[5]

Gwindor led Túrin back to Nargothrond, walking through the Pass of Sirion to Ivrin and south along Narog.[6] In Nargothrond Túrin became a great captain and King Orodreth heeded his counsels, even to the building of a mighty bridge and openly pursuing Morgoth's servants. So West Beleriand was freed, allowing Morwen and Nienor to reach Menegroth seeking Túrin.[7] The respite was brief, however. Glaurung led an onslaught against Nargothrond, knowing full well the identity of the great warrior. The dragon taunted Túrin that his family were forsaken.[8] Being deceived, Túrin raced north to Dor-lómin, only to find them gone. Thinking them safe with Thingol, he sought in vain for Finduilas, his love, who had been taken from Nargothrond. Encountering some Men of Brethil, he learned that she had been slain by Orcs and her body lay at Brethil. He stayed with the Haladin, and once more his deeds did not remain secret, though he hid his name.[9]

The evil of the curse had not run its course, for Morwen and Nienor had meanwhile gone west toward Nargothrond. Morwen was lost on the road, and Nienor, standing on Amon Ethir, was bewitched by Glaurung. Her guides led her back to the guarded bridge, but she escaped them during an Orc attack. She ran to the Crossings of Teiglin and was found in Brethil by Túrin. Unaware of her true identity, he named her Níniel. The two eventually wed, and were happy.[10] Then Glaurung came — drawn once more by Túrin's fame. The dragon entered Brethil at Cabed-en-Aras, a narrow gorge of the Teiglin (evidently upstream from the confluence with Dimrost and the ravines shown on *The Silmarillion* map). Túrin reached Dimrost (Nen Girith) at sunset and went on to Cabed-en-Aras in the dark. There he and a companion crossed the treacherous waters and climbed the cliff beyond. At midnight Glaurung made his move — only to be attacked by Túrin. When Túrin recrossed the river to regain his sword, he fainted from the dragon-stench and evil glare.[11]

Meanwhile, Níniel, unable to await news, followed the path to Nen Girith and saw afar the dragon's fire. When Brandir sought to lead her away to the Crossings of Teiglin, she fled. She did not recross Dimrost, but instead dashed south along Teiglin's bank. Soon she reached Glaurung, with Túrin lying beside him — and she thought her love to be dead. Then Glaurung, with his final stroke of malice, released her memory. In despair she cast herself into the water.[12] With the death of the worm Túrin awoke and returned to Dimrost. There Brandir told him of Nienor's death and her true identity. In rage he killed Brandir, then went to the Crossings of Teiglin. There, in a chance meeting with Mablung, Brandir's story was confirmed, and Túrin rushed back to the ravine, where he slew himself.[13] Then the folk of Brethil raised a stone to the hapless: monument of Túrin and Nienor — twice beloved.[14]

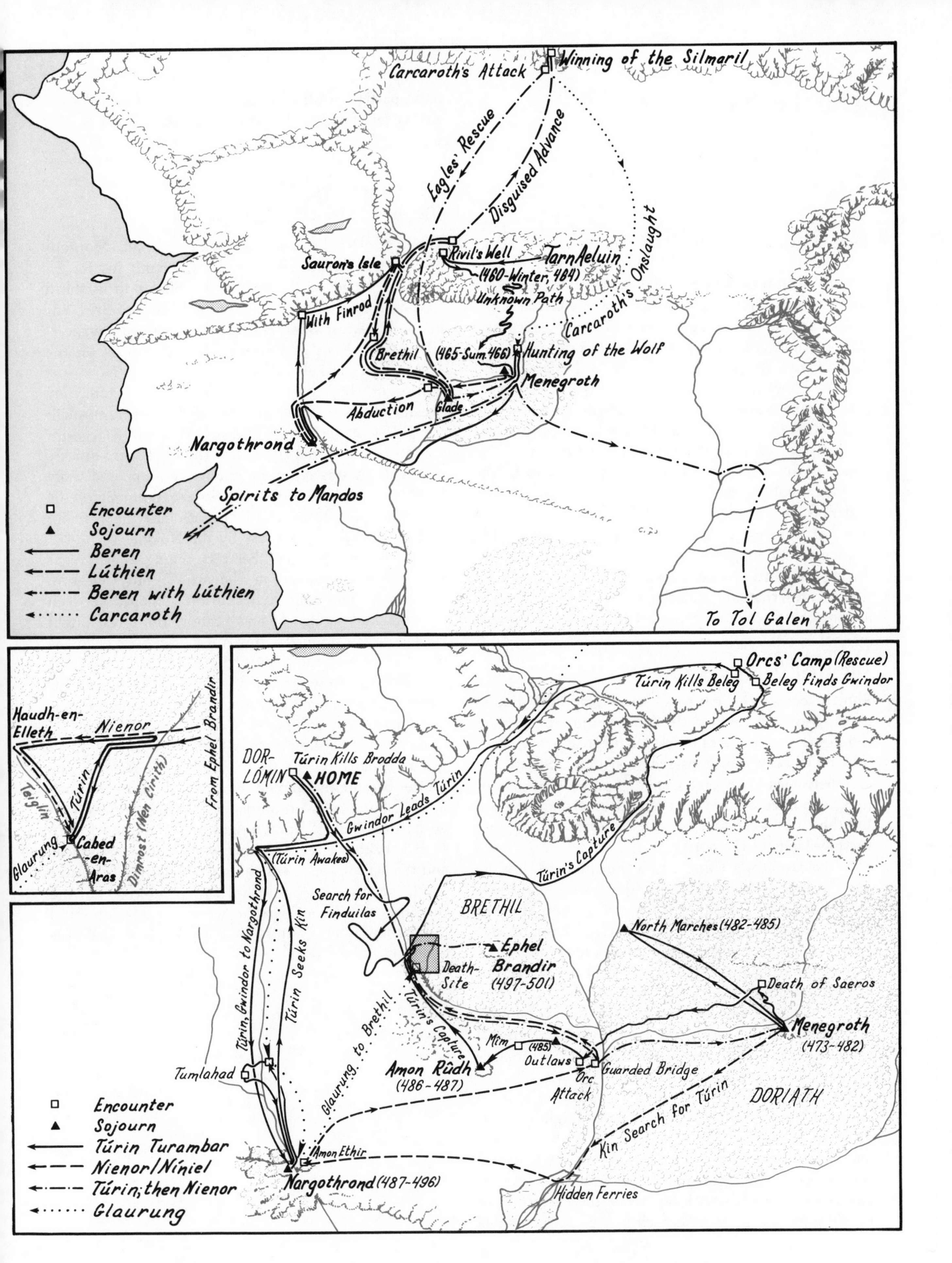

Upper: BEREN AND LÚTHIEN Lower: TÚRIN AND NIENOR Inset: DEATH-SITE

The Battles of Beleriand

THROUGHOUT THE MORE THAN SIX HUNDRED YEARS Morgoth occupied Angband,[1] he strove to master those who lived in northwestern Middle-earth: Elves, Men, and Dwarves. Five major battles and one Great Battle took place in that span of time. Tolkien gave little information about the numbers of troops, and often there were only passing references to the lesser skirmishes. The necessary estimates, therefore, were based upon scattered comments about numbers and location of the populace; and upon knowledge of the topography, existing roads, bridges, and fords. The object is for the reader to gain an impression of the peoples involved, troop sizes and losses, and the ebb and flow of battle. It would be helpful to note that lines of varying width symbolize either increasing numbers marching to the field, or increasing losses during the battle — depending upon the direction of flow. Lines that are superimposed indicate that the action took place later in the battle.

The First Battle

Shortly before the return of the Noldor to Middle-earth, Morgoth assailed the Sindar, thinking to gain the mastery of the area quickly. His great army broke into two hosts, which passed west down Sirion and east betweeen Aros and Gelion. Some of the bands may even have climbed the passes of Anach and Aglon, for the Orcs were said to have "passed silently into the highlands of the north."[2]

In the east, King Thingol took the offensive, leading out the folk of Menegroth and the Forest of Region. He called upon Denethor of Ossiriand, who attacked simultaneously from the east. The Orcs, beset on two fronts, must have turned back-to-back to counter. The east-facing companies of Orcs prevailed over Denethor and encircled him on Amon Ereb, where he fell, before he could be rescued by Thingol's host. When help arrived, the Elves routed the thralls of Morgoth. Of the few Orcs who escaped, most fell later to the axes of the Dwarves of Mount Dolmed.

The bulk of the Western Host camped on the plain between Narog and Sirion, harrying throughout West Beleriand. Led by Círdan, the forces of Brithombar and Eglarest countered but were driven back within their walls and besieged. Thus, the Western Host overran West Beleriand and Falas, while the Eastern Host of Morgoth was destroyed. Each of the opponents had only partial victory. Doriath stood untouched, and thereafter was ringed by the enchanted Girdle of Melian.

The Second Battle
(Dagor-nuin-Giliath, the Battle-under-Stars)

While the Noldor toiled through Araman, Morgoth had already raised Thangorodrim, rebuilt his forces, and fought the battle against the Sindar to establish his dominance. Orcs still beset the havens of Brithombar and Eglarest when Fëanor's host arrived unexpectedly at the Firth of Drengist, and encamped on the north shores of Lake Mithrim.

Morgoth hoped to destroy the Noldor before they became firmly established, so he sent his army through the passes of the Ered Wethrin.[3] Although Morgoth's troops outnumbered the Elves, the Orcs were quickly defeated. (It was often so when slaves opposed those filled with righteous wrath.) So the remnant of the Orcs retreated through the passes into the plain of Ard-galen, followed closely by the Noldor.

The forces that had been besieging the Havens marched north to aid in the affray, but Celegorm ambushed them near Eithel Sirion. Trapped between the forces of Celegorm and Fëanor, the Orcs fought for ten days. Gradually they must have been encircled and forced into the Fens of Serech, where all but a few perished. In wrath the host pressed on across Ard-galen, pursuing even this small troop. Hoping to complete his victory and possibly even come against Morgoth himself, Fëanor raced ahead with only a small group. Soon, at the edge of Dor Daedeloth, the hunter became the hunted. Not only did the Orcs turn in bay, but they were joined by Balrogs from Thangorodrim. There Fëanor fought on alone, and finally — fell. With the arrival of his sons, Fëanor was saved; and the Balrogs and remaining Orcs returned to Angband. Yet they evidently did so by choice, knowing that the wounds of Fëanor were mortal (immortal though he was). Victory was incomplete, and was shorn of glory.

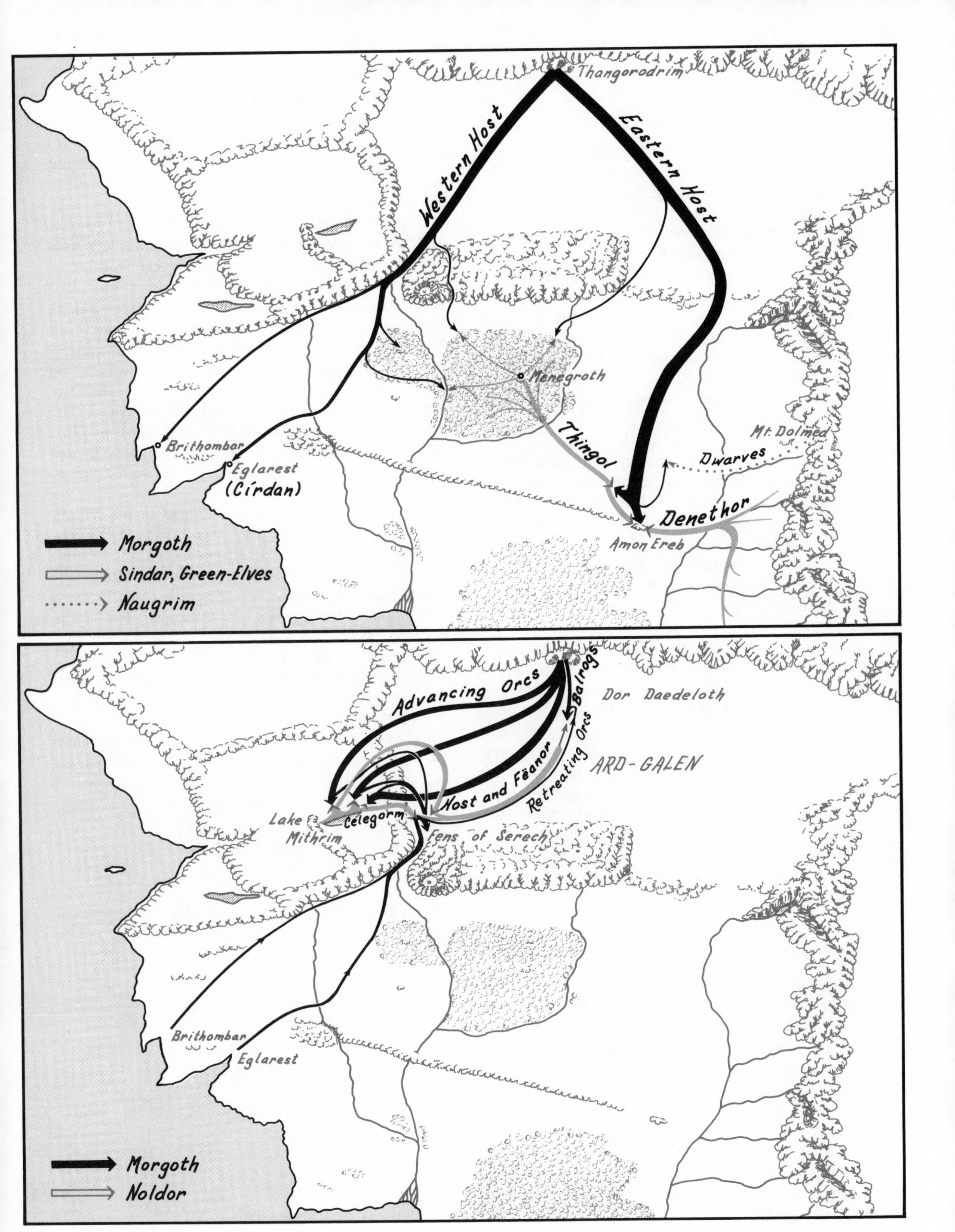

Upper: FIRST BATTLE Lower: SECOND BATTLE

The Third Battle
(Dagor Aglareb, the Glorious Battle)

During the sixty years following Dagor-nuin-Giliath the Noldor established their foothold in Middle-earth.[4] Morgoth's informants thought the Elves were busy with domestic affairs rather than martial vigilance. Again he sent forth a force of Orcs, heralded by eruptions of flame in the Iron Mountains.[5]

Several small bands passed through the Pass of Sirion and Maglor's Gap. In what must have been almost guerrilla warfare, they scattered through East and West Beleriand. In turn, they were countered by the Elves in the area — probably the Noldor, although Círdan may have assisted in the west. Doriath was protected by the Girdle of Melian, and the Green-elves of Ossiriand had refused open encounters after their disastrous losses in the First Battle.[6]

The main host of Orcs meanwhile attacked Dorthonion, where Angrod and Aegnor must have borne the brunt of the assault. When Fingolfin and Maedhros advanced from west and east, the Orcs were trapped in a closing vise and were forced to retreat. They fled to the north, but were closely pursued. The Orc-host was defeated within sight of Angband's gates. For the first time, in a battle against Morgoth, the victory was complete.

The Noldor, having been reminded of their ever-present danger, tightened their leaguer. This was the beginning of the Siege of Angband, which lasted almost four hundred years. Only scattered incidents broke this time of peace. After one hundred years there was a small attack on Fingolfin, which was quickly defeated. A century later Glaurung, then only a half-grown dragon, drove the Elves to the protection of the highlands, but he was forced to retreat from Ard-galen by the archers of Fingon. Morgoth ceased open assaults, and during the Long Peace he employed his powers instead through stealth, treachery, and enchantment of prisoners.[7]

The Fourth Battle
(Dagor Bragollach, the Battle of Sudden Flame)

During the Siege and the Long Peace, the Noldor were able to complete their defenses. Nargothrond was finished, and hidden Gondolin was raised. Numerous fortresses spread all around Ard-galen. Men had appeared from the east, and the Noldorian princes had gained the allegiance of many of these hardy folk. Nor was Morgoth idle. In 455 the peace was broken, and crushing forces were unleashed from Angband.[8]

Once again the battle was heralded by flames, but these were far more deadly than those of the third battle. Rivers of fire rushed along fissures, burning Ard-galen and virtually all the watchful troops encamped there. Swiftly following the fires came a sea of Orcs, led by Balrogs, and Glaurung — who had then grown to his full power.[9] This was no brief battle, fought in a few days. The attacks began in winter and continued in force through spring, and thereafter never completely ceased.

Dorthonion fell soonest to the onslaught. Angrod and Aegnor were slain, and their remaining folk scattered.[10] In the east, all the defenses except those of Maedhros were destroyed and abandoned, for Glaurung came there, leading a mass of Orcs. Maglor's horsemen were burned on the plain of Lothlann,[11] and he retreated to Himring and fought with Maedhros. The Pass of Aglon was breached, and Celegorm and Curufin made their way to Nargothrond.[12] The Orcs took the fortresses on the west side of Mt. Rerir, overran Thargelion, and defiled Lake Helevorn. Then they scattered into East Beleriand. Caranthir fled south, and joining Amrod and Amras, built defenses on Amon Ereb.[13]

In the west, Turgon stayed hidden in his refuge; but Finrod came north from Nargothrond. In the Fens of Serech Finrod became separated from his army. Encircled by Orcs, he would have perished but for the timely rescue by Barahir, who descended from western Dorthonion. Having thus barely escaped, Finrod and his folk retreated to Nargothrond, while Barahir continued his fighting in Dorthonion.[14]

No enemy troops entered Hithlum, although Fingolfin's forces barely managed to defend their fortresses.[15] When news reached Fingolfin, the High King, of the fall of so many of the Noldor, he galloped to Thangorodrim and dueled Morgoth. The Enemy was wounded in body and pride; but Fingolfin fell — valiant, but powerless against such evil.[16]

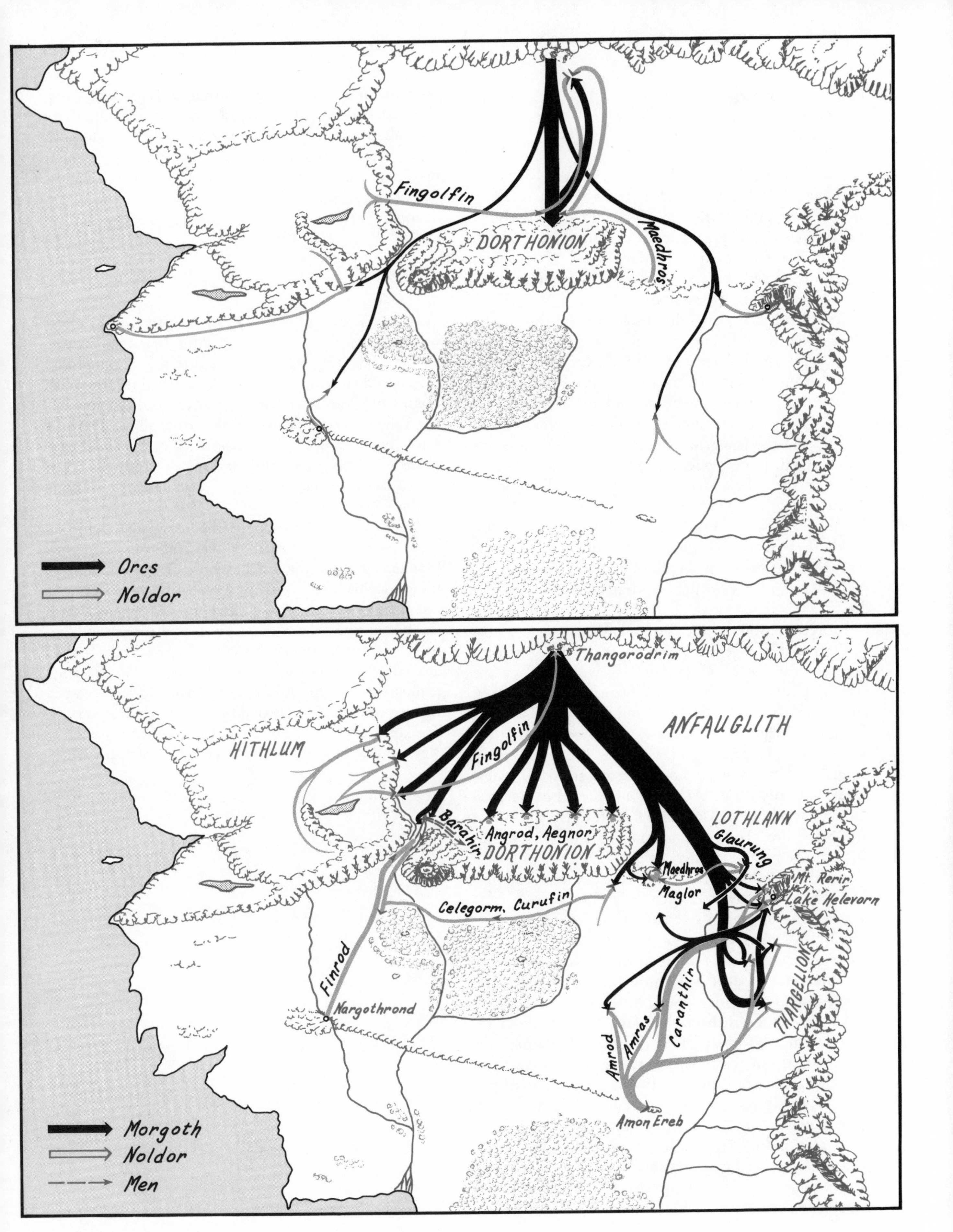

Upper: THIRD BATTLE *Lower:* FOURTH BATTLE

The Fifth Battle
(Nirnaeth Arnoediad, the Battle of Unnumbered Tears)

Inspired by the deeds of Beren and Lúthien, Maedhros decided in 473 that taking the offense against Angband might regain their former possessions. In the eighteen years since Dagor Bragollach, the Noldor had suffered further losses. The Union of Maedhros first ousted the Orcs from Beleriand, and in midsummer they gathered for the assault on Thangorodrim.[17]

In the original plan, Maedhros, leading the eastern host, was to draw out the army of Angband. Then Fingon's host, hidden in the Ered Wethrin, were to attack from the west. In the east were: Elves and Men of Himring, under Maedhros and the sons of Bór; Elves and Men of Amon Ereb, under Caranthir and Uldor; and the Naugrim. In the west were: Elves and Men of Hithlum, under Fingon, Huor, and Húrin; Elves of the Falas; Men of Brethil; a small company from Nargothrond, under Gwindor; and from Menegroth, only two Elves.[18] Unexpectedly, Turgon came forth from Gondolin with a force of 10,000.[19] This probably doubled the strength in the west, and the allies were filled with hope — but victory was not to be . . .

Morgoth, aware of the battle plan, sent forth a host of Orcs to challenge the western host. Most of Fingon's troops — and a few of Turgon's — were fired by the wrath of Gwindor. They broke from the hills without order, defeated the Orc-host, and thrust across Anfauglith. Gwindor's company even passed through the gates into Thangorodrim.[20] Then Morgoth's trap snapped shut. A huge host erupted from all sides. They not only drove back Fingon's host, but pursued and encircled them. Most of the Men of Brethil fell at the rearguard. Turgon, marching up from the south, broke through the leaguer.[21]

At last Maedhros arrived. He had been delayed those five days of battle by treachery.[22] The eastern host never came to Fingon's rescue, however, for still another army was loosed from Angband — led by Glaurung the dragon and Gothmog the Balrog. Glaurung and his forces assailed Maedhros. Simultaneously, the traitorous Uldor broke away, attacking Maedhros in the rear, while on the right Maedhros was beset by more Men who swept from the hills. Embattled on three fronts, the eastern host scattered. The valor of the Dwarves, who held Glaurung at bay, allowed the host to slowly retreat, and escape to Ossiriand.

Meanwhile, Gothmog's forces had thrust aside Turgon, reencircling Fingon. Thus trapped, Fingon fell, and most of his forces perished. With the field lost, Húrin persuaded Turgon to return to Gondolin, protecting the secret of the hidden city. Huor and Húrin with the men of Dor-lómin formed a living wall across the Fens of Serech to guard the withdrawal. There they all died except Húrin, who was taken to Morgoth for torment. Thus, all Hithlum was bereft of its people; and Himring was abandoned. All the highlands, except the realm of Gondolin, lay in the hands of the enemy.

The Great Battle
(The War of Wrath)

Little can be said of the final battle, although its effect was mighty. Over a century after Nirnaeth Arnoediad,[23] the Valar granted the request of Eärendil and prepared their third and last assault on Morgoth. With them from Valinor went the Vanyar and Noldor, but the Teleri only agreed to sail the white ships. The host must have landed in Beleriand, for that land was "ablaze with the glory of their arms."[24] Only the Edain joined the host once it reached Middle-earth — none of the Elves.

The host of Valinor approached Angband. As in all previous encounters between the Valar and Morgoth (the fallen Vala) the earth shook. So powerful were they that his massive army was swiftly destroyed. At last he released the winged dragons, led by Ancalagon the Black. Even the Valar were forced to retreat from these evil creatures. Then Eärendil came, and Thorondor led a swarm of eagles, and they battled the dragons through the night. Just before dawn, Eärendil slayed Ancalagon, who crashed down upon Thangorodrim, breaking its tall towers. The Valar bared the pits of Angband, and obliterated all the realm of Morgoth.[25]

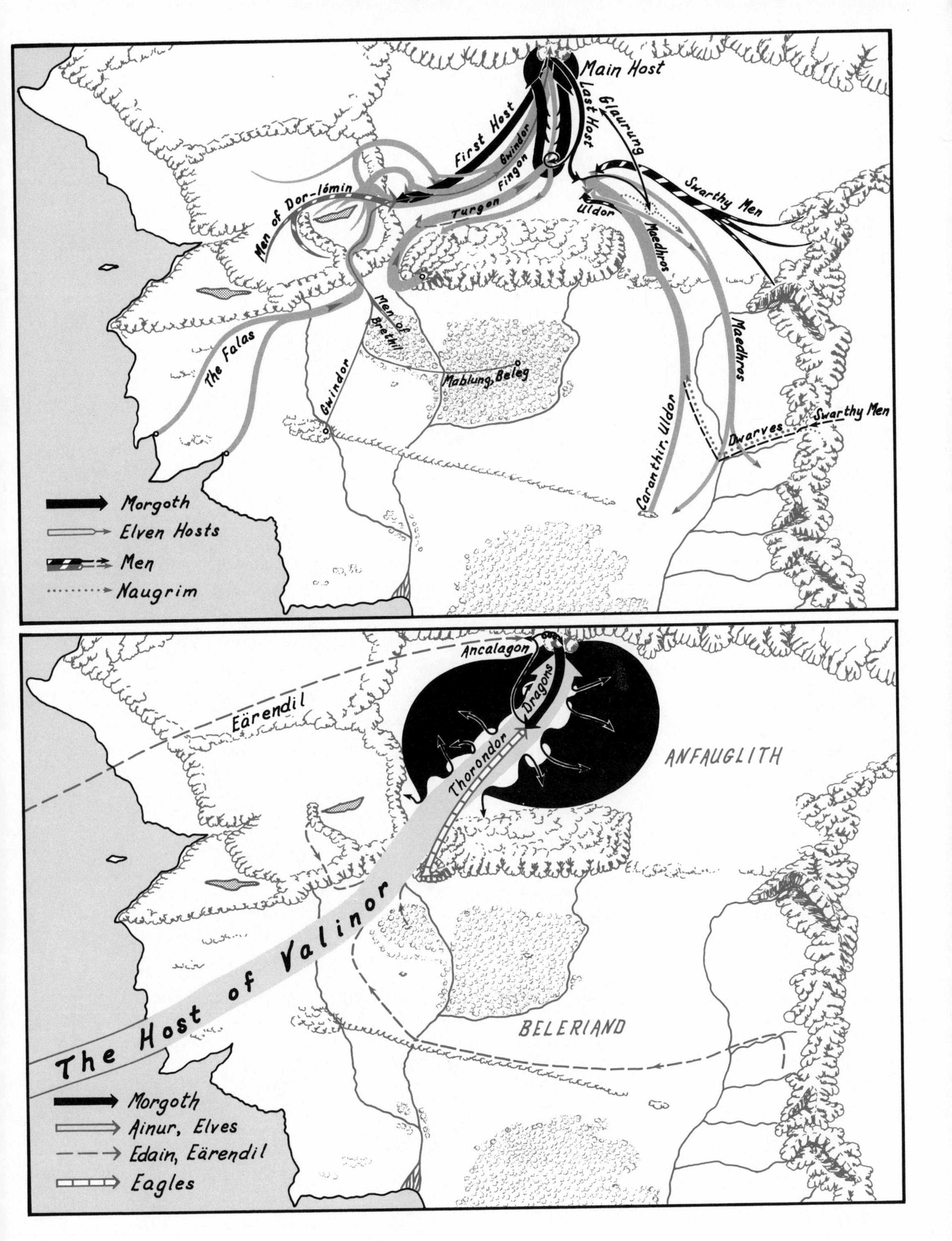

Upper: FIFTH BATTLE Lower: GREAT BATTLE

The Second Age

Introduction

THE DIFFERENCES APPARENT in the land of Aman followed Morgoth's reoccupation of Angband during the First Age. The Valar fortified their land more fully by further lifting the Pelóri, and the Shadowy Seas were darkened with spells as well as the absence of light, and grew far greater in extent, reaching beyond the newly raised Enchanted Isles.[1] The other important physical and cultural changes shown in the map of the Second Age were the result of a single action at the end of the first — the breaking of Thangorodrim in the War of Wrath. During the battle the lands of the northwest were convulsed and most fell beneath the sea.[2] Galadriel foretold that they would some day rise again, but none knew when that would occur.[3]

In Middle-earth the low-lying graves of Túrin and Morwen withstood the turmoils as foreseen.[4] Although Tol Morwen was described as "alone," it was perhaps the 'last' (most western) of the remaining lands. For as Beleriand was destroyed, many retreated to the highlands, and as the waters lapped the hills, they built ships in which to set sail. The last fragments of Dorthonion and the Hill of Himring remained as Tol Fuin and Himling: the Western Isles.[5]

Lindon was the only portion of Beleriand that survived as part of the mainland, although Mount Dolmed and Rerir were both absent. At the River Ascar the Blue Mountains broke apart and the sea roared in, forming the Gulf of Lhûn (Lune). The River Lhûn (which evidently was present in the First Age, but was not mapped by Tolkien), changed course at the time, flowing west into the gulf to which it gave its name.[6] Previously, it was shown as flowing east into Lake Evendim. Nogrod and Belegost were destroyed, and the Dwarves fled to other parts of the mountains. It was possible that the Tower Hills and the west–east ridge of the Ered Luin were newly formed at that time.

The west end of the Ice Bay of Forochel aligned with the former location of the conjunction of the Ered Engrin and the Ered Luin and extended over 300 miles into the lower lands north and east.[7] It has been assumed that the former were utterly destroyed, with only occasional remnants, such as the Grey Mountains. Bays and coastlines were altered elsewhere as well. The submergence of about one million square miles could have raised the level of the sea enough to produce drowned river mouths, embayments (such as near the later sites of Dol Amroth and the fortress of Umbar), and isolation of some higher areas into offshore islands (such as Tolfalas).

One other locale was worthy of note: Mordor. As noted in the discussion of the First Age the map of the world from 'The Ambarkanta' showed the Inland Sea occupying the area which would eventually be the site of Mordor.[8] Although no text supports my conclusions, Mordor might have appeared as part of a worldwide upheaval during the destruction of the Iron Mountains in the area where the Great Gulf partially drained the Inland Sea — the volcanic processes in the formation of that land would allow relatively rapid mountain-building processes.

In Middle-earth, at first the lands were relatively free from evil, but the Men there lived in isolated pockets cut into the forests, or along the coasts and rivers — mostly far from the Elves and Dwarves. The times for them were dark — dark in knowledge, and soon, dark in evil. After only five hundred years Sauron reawoke; and about 1000 S.A. he established himself in Mordor.[9] Many Men, such as the Men of the Mountains near Dunharrow, were drawn under his sway. Eventually his evil influence affected the histories of all the Free Peoples throughout the second and third ages.

The Valar could grant good, as well as destroy evil. So Ossë raised a land in the midst of the sea — Andor, the Land of Gift. It stood slightly nearer to Valinor than to Middle-earth. There, the Edain, the Three Faithful Houses of Men, were as far west toward the Undying Lands as mortal Men could be. So they called their land Númenor — Westernesse.[10] They lived in peace and glory until they destroyed themselves by their own folly.

Fleeing from Beleriand, many Elves chose to leave Middle-earth, but Tirion was closed to them.[11] Thus, they sailed to Tol Eressëa and established the haven of Avallónë on a harbor of the south shore. Avallónë was the first city visible from the east, yet at the time of its founding, it stood closest to Valinor.[12] When, after ages Eriol managed to reach the Cottage of Lost Play,[13] he learned not only many of the 'Lost Tales,' but he also visited other sites on the island. For the Lonely Isle was large enough for many towns and villages, and the Tales told of a greater city eventually built in the midst of the island in the wooded ring of Alalminore, 'the land of Elms': Koromas, the 'Resting Place of the Exiled of Kôr.' There, Ingil, son of Inwë, raised a great tower in memory of lost Tirion on Túna, and so the city came to be called Kortirion.[14] There it would stand until the time of the final Faring Forth, when Ulmo would draw the isle back to mortal lands once more, when the "end was come indeed for the Eldar of story and of song."[15]

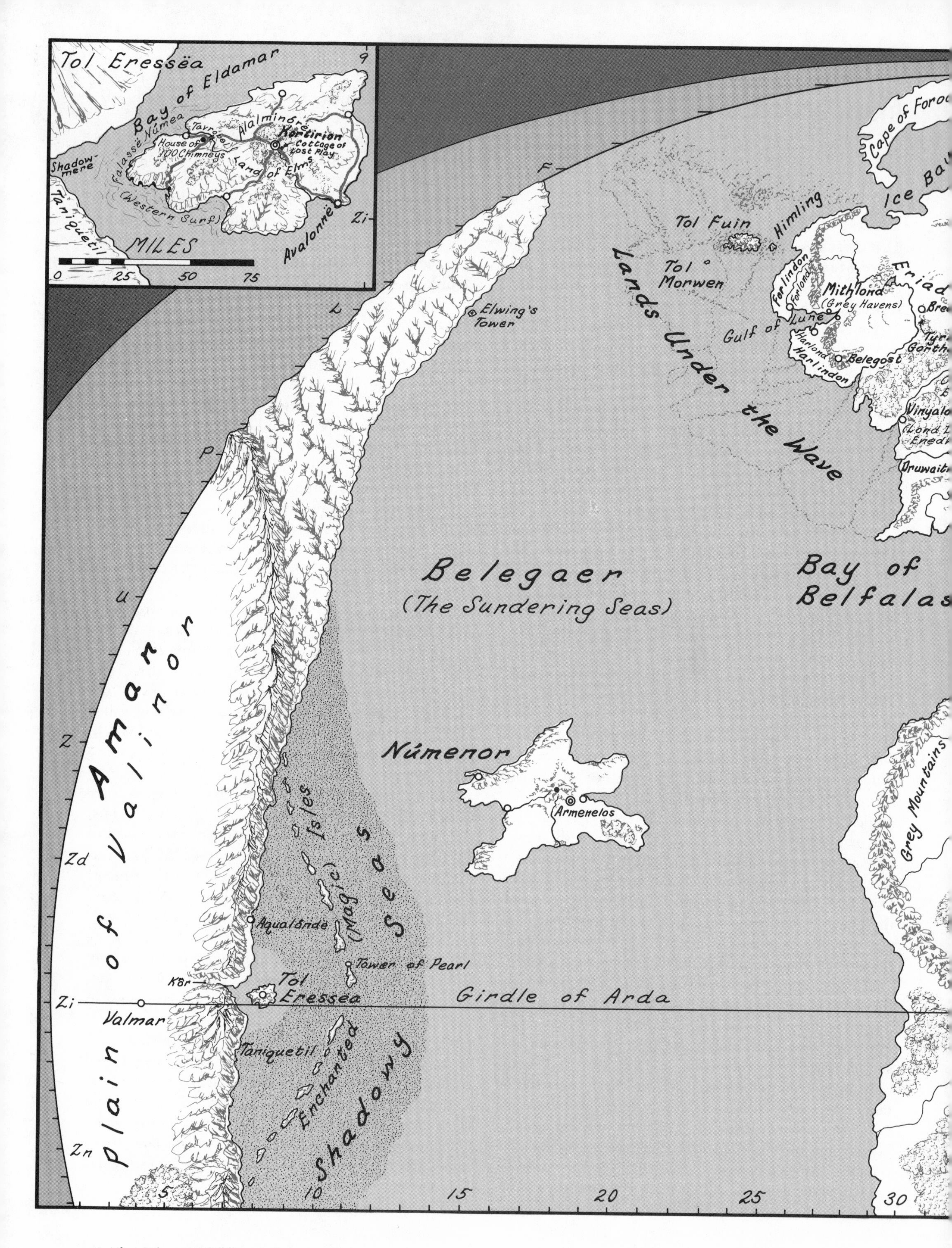
Tol Eressëa
Bay of Eldamar
Bay of Falassë Númea
Tavrobel
Alalminórë
Kortirion
House of 100 Chimneys
Cottage of Lost Play
Land of Elms
Shadowmere
Taniquetil
(Western Surf)
Avalonnë
MILES
0
25
50
75
Cape of Forochel
Ice Bay
Tol Fuin
Himling
Tol Morwen
Lands Under the Wave
Forlindon
Forlond
Mithlond
(Grey Havens)
Eriador
Gulf of Lune
Harlond
Harlindon
Belegost
Elwing's Tower
Vinyalondë
Druwaith
Belegaer
(The Sundering Seas)
Bay of Belfalas
Plain of Aman
Valinor
Númenor
Armenelos
Enchanted (Magic) Isles
Shadowy Seas
Aqualondë
Tower of Pearl
Kôr
Tol Eressëa
Girdle of Arda
Valmar
Taniquetil
Grey Mountains
5
10
15
20
25
30

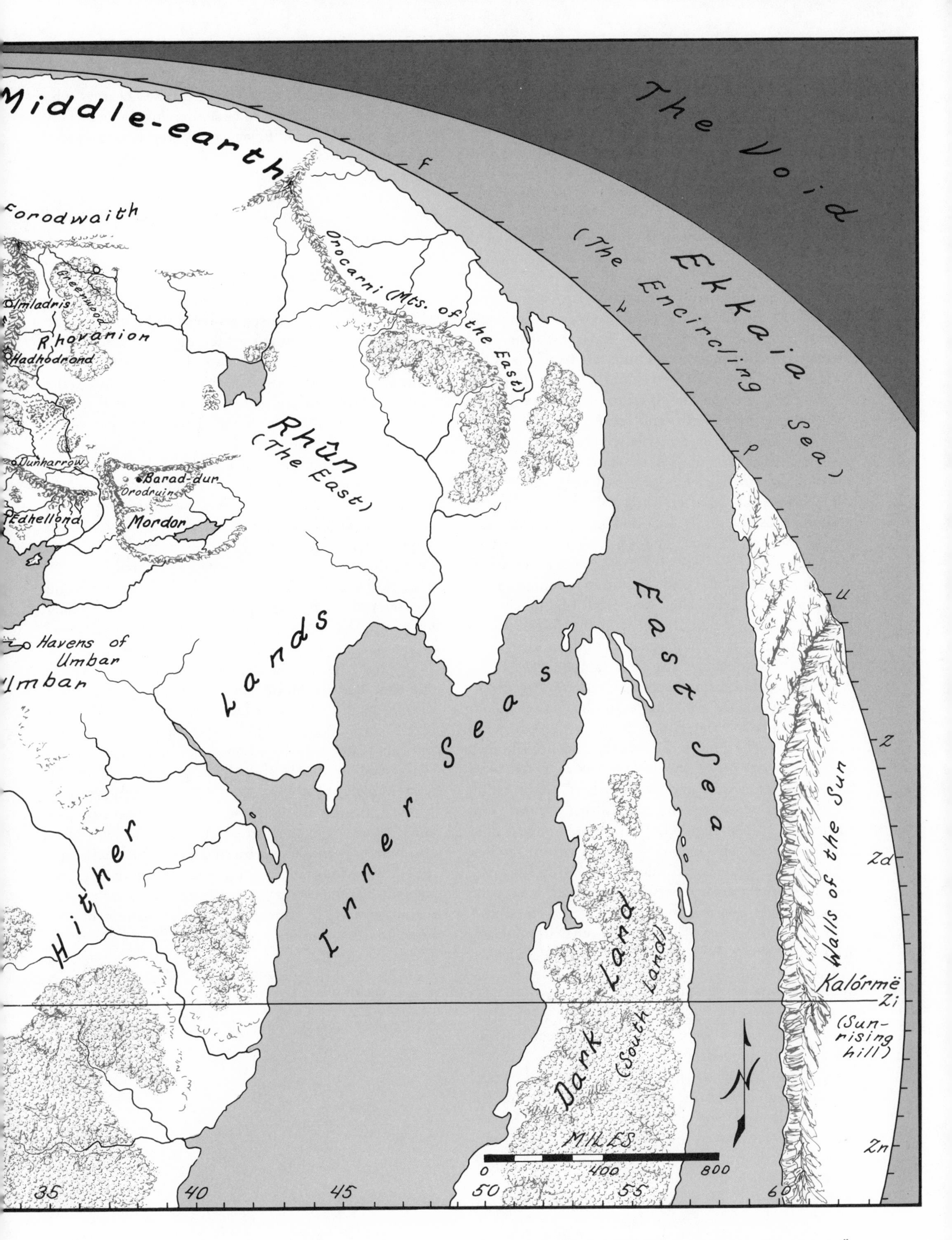

Middle-earth
The Void
Ekkaia
(The Encircling Sea)
Forodwaith
Greenwood
Imladris
Rhovanion
Hadhodrond
Orocarni (Mts. of the East)
Rhûn
(The East)
Dunharrow
Barad-dur
Orodruin
Edhellond
Mordor
Havens of
Umbar
Umbar
Lands
Hither
Inner Seas
East Sea
Dark Land
(South Land)
Walls of the Sun
Kalórmë
(Sun-
rising
hill)
MILES
0
400
800
35
40
45
50
55
60

SECOND AGE OF ARDA Inset: TOL ERESSËA

Refugee Relocation

DURING THE DESTRUCTION OF THE LANDS of the North many survivors escaped — both good and evil. The servants of Angband fled east, while the people of the south either sailed west, or removed to Lindon and beyond. At the end of the Age, two concentrations of Elves remained: On the Isle of Balar, Gil-galad and Círdan governed most of the folk left from the Falas, Nargothrond, Gondolin, and Doriath.[1] Some still dwelt in Ossiriand and on the Western Isles: the Green-elves, Sindar of Doriath, and some Noldor who had followed Fëanor's sons.[2] Some few who heeded Eönwë's summons[3] may have built ships hurriedly[4] and sailed from Balar before it had been submerged, while others did so after being forced to the higher ground. Most of the Noldor and many Sindar chose to take the western path, and left within the first year of the Second Age.[5] On Tol Eressëa they raised the new city of Avallónë, and ever after it remained the haven for those who sailed west from Middle-earth.[6]

Many Sindar, especially those of the Teleri, passed east up until 1600.[7] They joined the Silvan Elves scattered in the woodlands. The most famous was Thranduil,[8] who had probably lived in Doriath, for his dwellings in Greenwood were quite similar.[9] The Noldor who remained on the Hither Shore removed to the land west of the Ered Luin. It once had been known as Lindon,[10] so after the inrushing sea at River Ascar broke the mountains and formed the Gulf of Lhûn, the two portions were renamed. Gil-galad ruled from Forlindon, "North Lindon,"[11] and Círdan resided in Harlindon, "South Lindon."[12] At the eastern end of the Gulf were built the Mithlond, the "Grey Havens," that were the primary ports; but farther west good harborage was also available at Forlond and Harlond.[13] With Gil-galad (son of Fingon) dwelt Elrond Half-elven (son of Eärendil). With Círdan were Celeborn and Galadriel, until they went east to Lórien at some unknown time.[14] Celebrimbor (son of Curufin) also dwelt for a time in Lindon. Later he crossed into Eriador, taking many Noldor. In 750 they reached Eregion (Hollin) and established Ost-in-Edhil.[15]

Few were left of the Edain. It is possible those remaining had hidden in the hills of Dor-lómin, the Forest of Brethil, and perhaps in Ossiriand. At first they may have moved to Lindon, and some even into Eriador and beyond.[16] Most awaited the completion of Númenor, which they finally reached in S.A. 32.[17]

The Dwarf-city of Nogrod probably collapsed when the Blue Mountains broke apart.[18] The Dwarves who escaped the ruin moved to lesser delvings — especially in the south where Belegost apparently survived.[19] Later, many made the long trek east to Moria, where they arrived in S.A. 40.[20]

With the loss of the lands and the forests on them, even the Onodrim, the Ents,[21] withdrew to the lands of the east. Their domain was still great, yet ever-dwindling.[22]

At the time of the fall, Morgoth was taken in his nethermost hall and thrust through the Door of Night.[23] Of his vast hosts, few outlived the battle and destruction.[24] The swarthy Men of the East who had, for the most part, served Morgoth, still lived in Dor-lómin.[25] Those who survived the battle fled back to the east from which they had come, where some became kings; and in after years the hatred they passed on was the cause of many attacks on the Men of Gondor.[26]

The evil servants that had been bred or twisted by Morgoth were mostly destroyed: Balrogs, dragons, Trolls, Orcs, and wolves.[27] They all were creatures of deep, dark places, and those that remained sought such abodes thereafter. If, as has been hypothesized, the Grey Mountains were remnants of the Ered Engrin,[28] it would have been likely for the flight to occur behind the cover of the remaining mountains. Later they may have found unoccupied caves, or they may have joined others of their kind who had never come west.[29]

The only Balrog mentioned in later times was the one that fled to Moria and was found in the early Third Age by the deep-delving Dwarves.[30] There it stayed until it was slain by Gandalf.[31] The dragons (probably mostly winged, such as Smaug)[32] in after years bred in the Withered Heath and lived in the wastes north of the Grey Mountains.[33] Trolls probably spread from the northern valleys of the Misty Mountains.[34] Orcs, and their great allies, the wolves, were also common in the northern Misty Mountains and the Grey Mountains, although their territory expanded with the increase of evil. Mount Gundabad was their chief city.[35] Sauron, Morgoth's lieutenant, refused to seek pardon in Aman, as Eönwë required. Therefore, he hid in Middle-earth until S.A. 500. In 1000 he chose Mordor as his fenced land, and built Barad-dûr, the Dark Tower, which was completed in 1600.[36] Once again the struggles began.

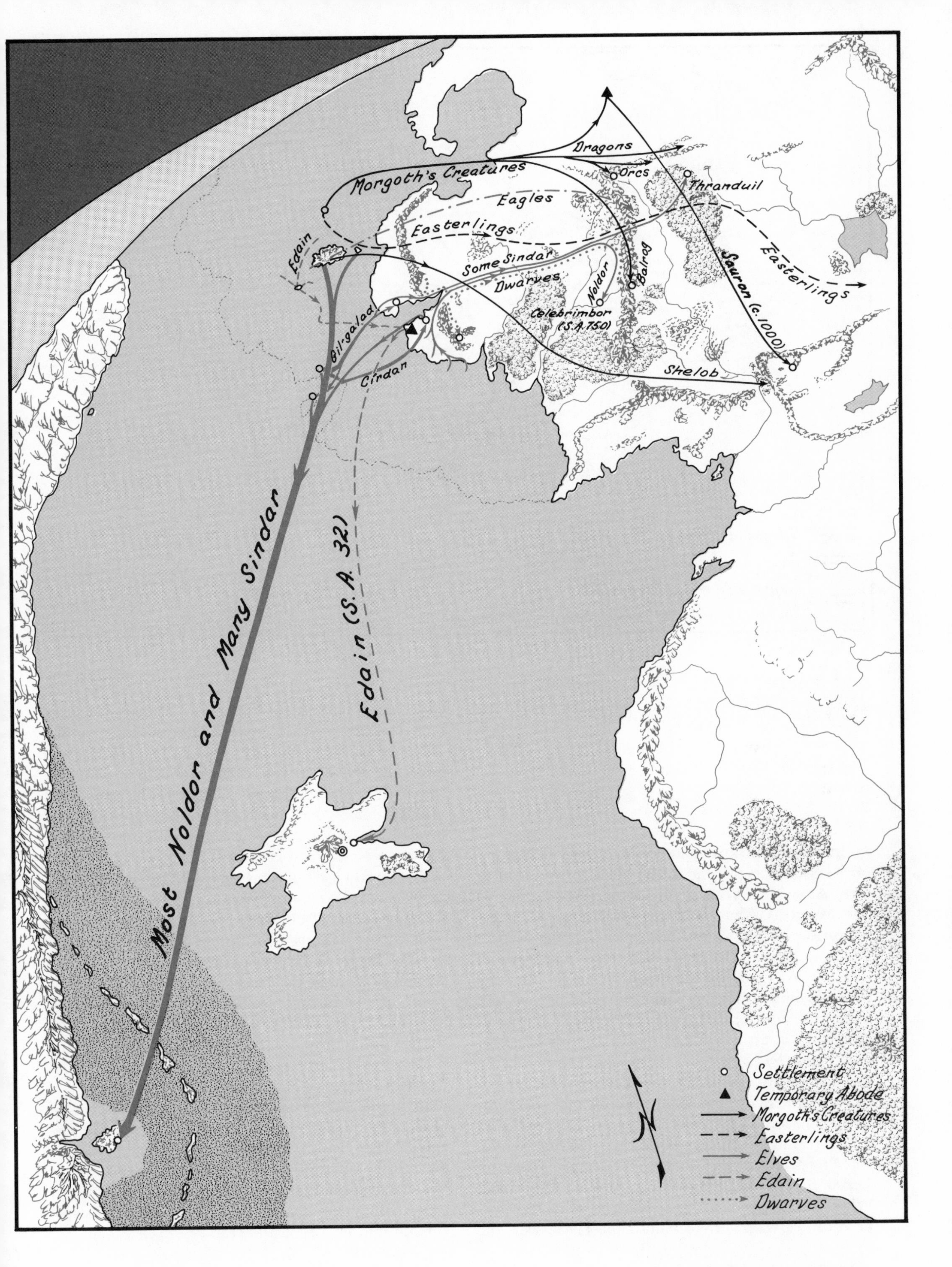

Dragons
Morgoth's Creatures
Orcs
Thranduil
Eagles
Easterlings
Edain
Some Sindar
Dwarves
Noldor
Balrog
Sauron (c. 1000)
Easterlings
Celebrimbor (S.A. 750)
Gil-galad
Cirdan
Shelob
Most Noldor and Many Sindar
Edain (S.A. 32)
Settlement
Temporary Abode
Morgoth's Creatures
Easterlings
Elves
Edain
Dwarves

RELOCATION OF REFUGEES

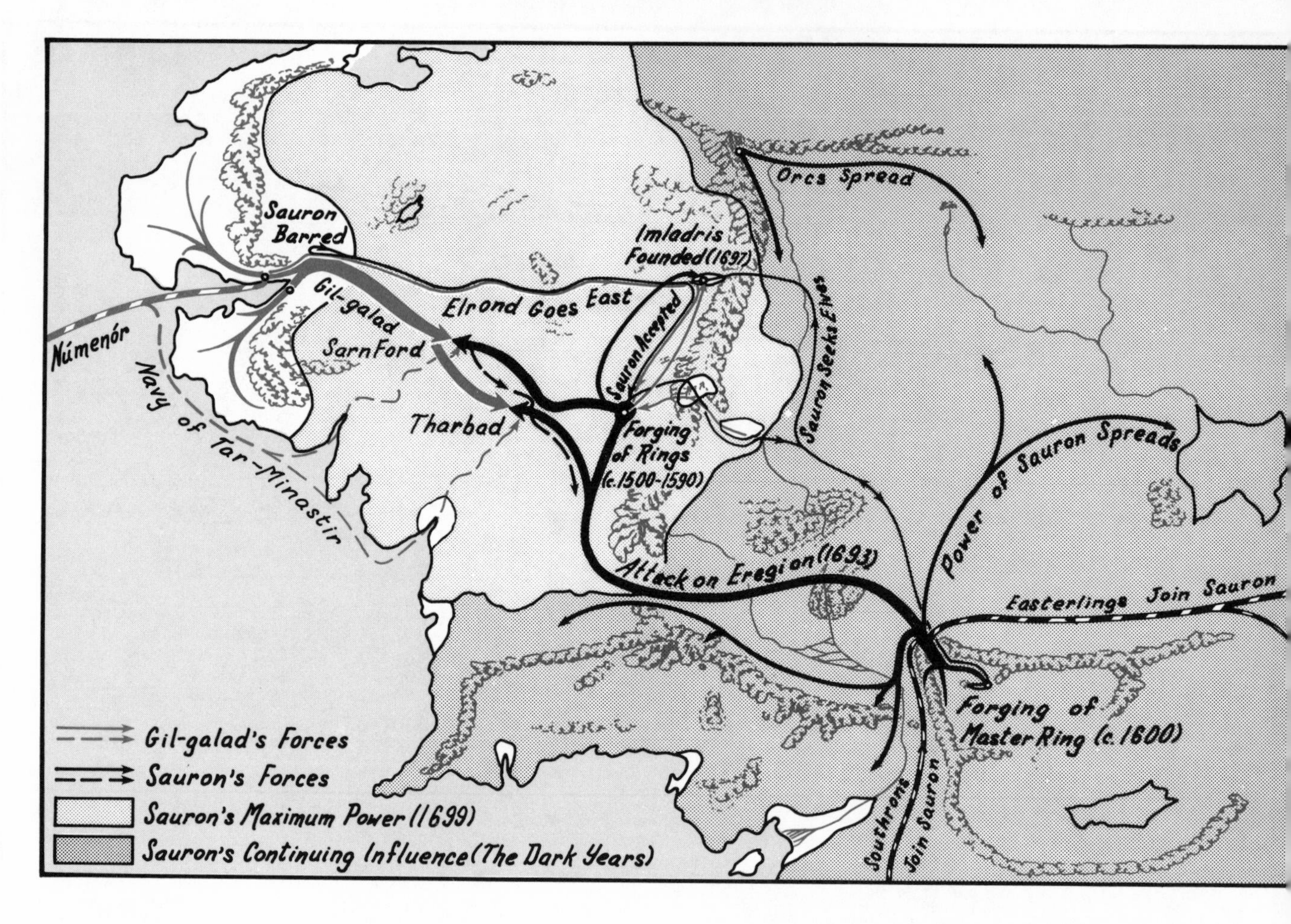

Advent of the Dark Years

As the Númenóreans increasingly visited Middle-earth, Sauron became afraid of their growing influence. After 1000 years of the Second Age he moved into Mordor.[1] There he began gathering his forces: creatures of Morgoth and descendants of the Men of the East. To them he added many new people whom he could sway, mostly Men. Sauron sought after the Eves — going to Lindon, where Gil-galad refused him entrance; and to Eregion, where the jewel-smiths received him heartily.[2] About 1500 the rings of power were begun by Sauron and the smiths. Over probably the next seventy-five years, they devised several lesser rings together. At that point Sauron may have returned to Mordor, for Celebrimbor worked alone until 1590[3] creating the three greatest rings: Narya, Nenya, and Vilya (Fire, Water, and Air). Soon after, Sauron forged the Master Ring in the fires of Orodruin.[4] When he realized that his deceptions were revealed, he chose to wage war to punish the Elves, gain the rings, and establish his dominion. For a century he built his armies. Then in 1695, he assailed Eregion. Gil-galad sent Elrond with aid to Ost-in-Edhil, but before he arrived in 1697 Celebrimbor was slain and the city had fallen.[5] Khazad-dûm and Lórinand assisted Elrond's forces, but they were too few to break the hold of Sauron, and Elrond retreated north with the surviving Noldor and built Imladris.[6]

Sauron still had not achieved his desire, for although he obtained the sixteen lesser rings, the Three Great Rings were out of his reach.[7] Sauron began overrunning Eriador in preparation for an assault on Lindon.[8] By 1699 his forces held sway throughout the land, Rivendell was besieged, and Sauron named himself "Lord of the Earth." People fled to the forests and hills, and Elves sailed west.[9] Within a year help came from a different quarter: Númenor. These were the times when the estrangement had not yet begun, and Tar-Minastir sent a huge fleet to the Grey Havens and more up the Greyflood. Its troops joined with Elves of Lindon, and together they freed Eriador from the Enemy.[10] Then Sauron withdrew slightly, and purposely avoided the places frequented by the Númenóreans.[11] Yet it is evident that away from the coasts Sauron's power continued, for the Men of Dunharrow worshipped him in these Dark Years.[12]

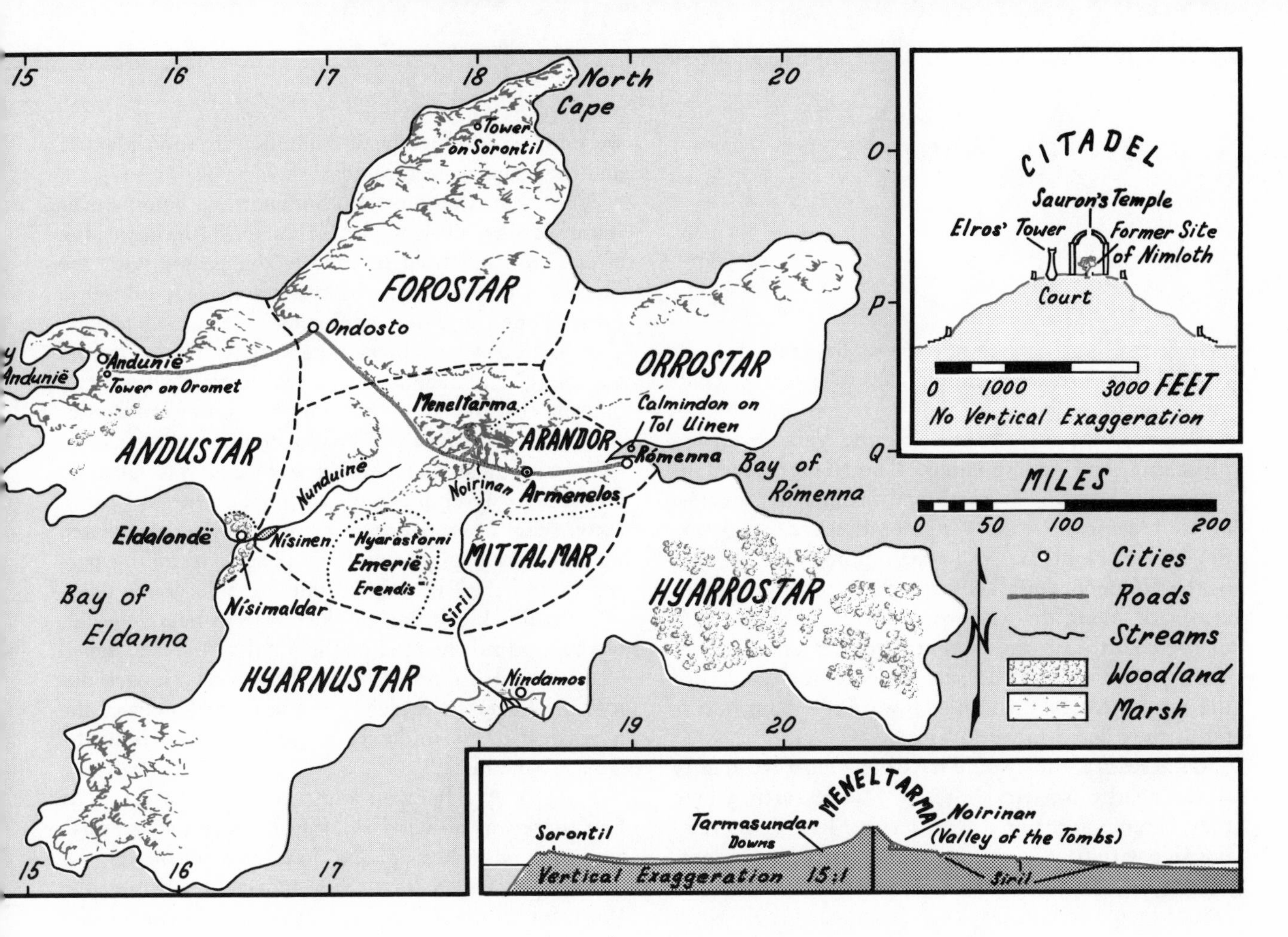

NÚMENOR Cross Section: NORTH–SOUTH Inset: ARMENELOS

Númenor

After the breaking of Thangorodrim, Ossë prepared Andor, the Land of Gift, as a reward for the remnant of the faithful Edain.[1] The Isle was "raised out of the depths" of the sea, and as it was the most western of mortal lands it was called "Westernesse — Númenórë in the High Eldarin tongue."[2] At its center stood the Meneltarma, the Pillar of Heaven, with the "Tarmasundar" (its five roots) extending out into the five peninsulas of the island.[3] Upon two occasions, smoke, and later, fire issued from the mountain,[4] so the land has been interpreted as a volcanic island, with its central peak some 14,000 feet high.[5] Around the Meneltarma, downs eroded back on all sides. Beyond them were fairly flat areas, but due to the northwest–southeast pitch of the island, coastal cliffs were raised on the north shores of all the peninsulas except the one in the southeast.[6] As a free-standing volcanic isle, apart from both Aman and Middle-earth,[7] its size (based upon comparisons with our Primary World) would have been quite limited, yet it measured 167,961 square miles — forty times the size of Hawaii's Big Island![8]

The population was concentrated in Armenelos and Rómenna, with large settlements also at Andúnië and Eldalondë in the west.[9] Originally, the port of Andúnië was the largest city, site of the pleasant seaside estate of Elendil.[10] Eldalondë was also sizable, for the populace gathered there to receive the Eldar, who journeyed from Eressëa. As distrust of the Elves grew, however, the self-centered Númenóreans gradually shifted to Armenelos the Golden. Those folk faithful to the Valar and the Eldar remained in and around Andúnië until Ar-Gimilzor forced them to remove to Rómenna in about 2950.[11] Thereafter the western havens were less important until they became the site of the embarkation of the Great Armament.[12]

In Armenelos Elros had constructed a tower within the citadel.[13] In the Court of the King grew Nimloth, scion of the family of the White Tree of Valinor.[14] Under Sauron's influence a temple to Morgoth was erected — far larger than the Pantheon.[15] From that time on, Númenor's decline was continual, finally precipitating its own destruction. After the island foundered in 3319, it was called "Akallabêth, the Down-fallen, Atalantë in the Eldarin tongue."[16]

Voyages of the Númenóreans

WHEN THE ISLE OF NÚMENOR was first raised, Elves crossed from Eressëa, bringing gifts to enrich it. Their visits continued but could not be reciprocated by the Dúnedain, who were banned by the Valar from approaching the Undying Lands.[1] The Númenóreans instead sailed to Middle-earth and became the greatest of all Mariners — the Kings of the Sea.[2] Crossing Belegaer was only a part of the innumerable voyages of the Númenóreans. They travelled from the Northern Dark, along the western coasts, through the heat of the south, into the Nether Darkness and beyond. They passed into inland seas and eventually reached the eastern coasts, then sailed toward the rising sun as far as they dared to venture.[3]

Of necessity, they would have gone most frequently to the nearby western shores of Middle-earth, where they became acquainted with lesser Men. Their relationship with these people passed through three stages: the Days of Help (600–1700); the Days of Dominion (1800–3200); and the Days of War (3200–3319).[4] Until 1200, the captains made no permanent settlements, although Aldarion built the haven of Vinyalondë (Lond Daer Enedh) in about 750 for lumbering and ship repair.[5] In pity of their fellow men, whom they found living in backward conditions, the Númenóreans taught crafts and supplied unavailable materials and food.[6] The seafarers also made fairly frequent visits to the Grey Havens of Gil-galad and Círdan, for at that time the friendship between the Eldar and the Edain was still firm. In 1700 Tar-Minastir sent a great fleet to the Elves' assistance in the war against Sauron, and helped drive the Enemy from Eriador.[7]

After Tar-Minastir, the Kings of Númenor became enamored of wealth and power. They transformed their havens into armed fortresses, especially in the south, where they went most frequently.[8] The most notable was Umbar, strengthened in 2280.[9] To these walled settlements came increasing numbers of colonists, and being greater in knowledge and weaponry, it was easy for them to change their position from one of teacher/helper to ruler/usurper.[10] Even Sauron came to fear them and retreated from the lands around their havens. Gradually, most of the Edain became estranged from the Eldar. Those who continued secretly to receive the Eressëans and to sail north to Lindon came to be known as the "Faithful."[11] In addition to visiting the Elves, they went south to Pelargir, built in 2350.[12] In the time of Ar-Gimilzôr (possibly about 3150), they were forced to move from Andúnië east to Rómenna; and the Eldar were forbidden.[13]

From that time on, the Númenóreans became ever more warlike. Even while Tar-Palantir (the next king after Gimilzôr) tried to reunite the people with the Elves and the Valar, his brother's son made himself a great captain and warred against the coastal people. The warlord eventually became King Ar-Pharazôn, and was obliged to abandon personal control of the fleet. Sauron threatened to reclaim the shoreward settlements, but in 3261 Ar-Pharazôn led forth such an impressive host that he submitted and was taken to Númenor.[14] From this came the final downfall. Within sixty years after Sauron's arrival, he had completed the corruption of most of the people, including persecution of the Faithful. In time, he induced Ar-Pharazôn to break the Ban of the Valar. Amandil, leader of the Faithful, learned of this final vanity and sailed west toward Valinor to plead for mercy. It was not told if he ever succeeded. His son Elendil went to the northwest to try to descry his sails, but saw only the Great Armament.[15]

In 3319, Ar-Pharazôn launched his vast navy.[16] At first there was no wind and the slaves rowed. At dusk an east wind picked up, and they were out of sight by morning. Nevertheless, "they moved slowly into the West, for all the winds were stilled . . . in fear of that time."[17] For thirty-nine days they journeyed, and on the final day they surrounded Eressëa at sunset and camped that night at Túna. The next day at midmorning the world was broken. The only Númenóreans who escaped were the settlers already on Middle-earth and some of the Faithful.[18] On advice of Amandil, Elendil and his sons had prepared ships: four for Elendil, three for Isildur, and two for Anárion.[19] The ships were blown wildly east when the cataclysm occurred. Elendil was cast upon Lindon, and the brothers made their way to Pelargir. With them they bore the fruit of Nimloth, the palantíri, and the stone that was set at Erech — all valuable in the establishment of the Realms in Exile.[20]

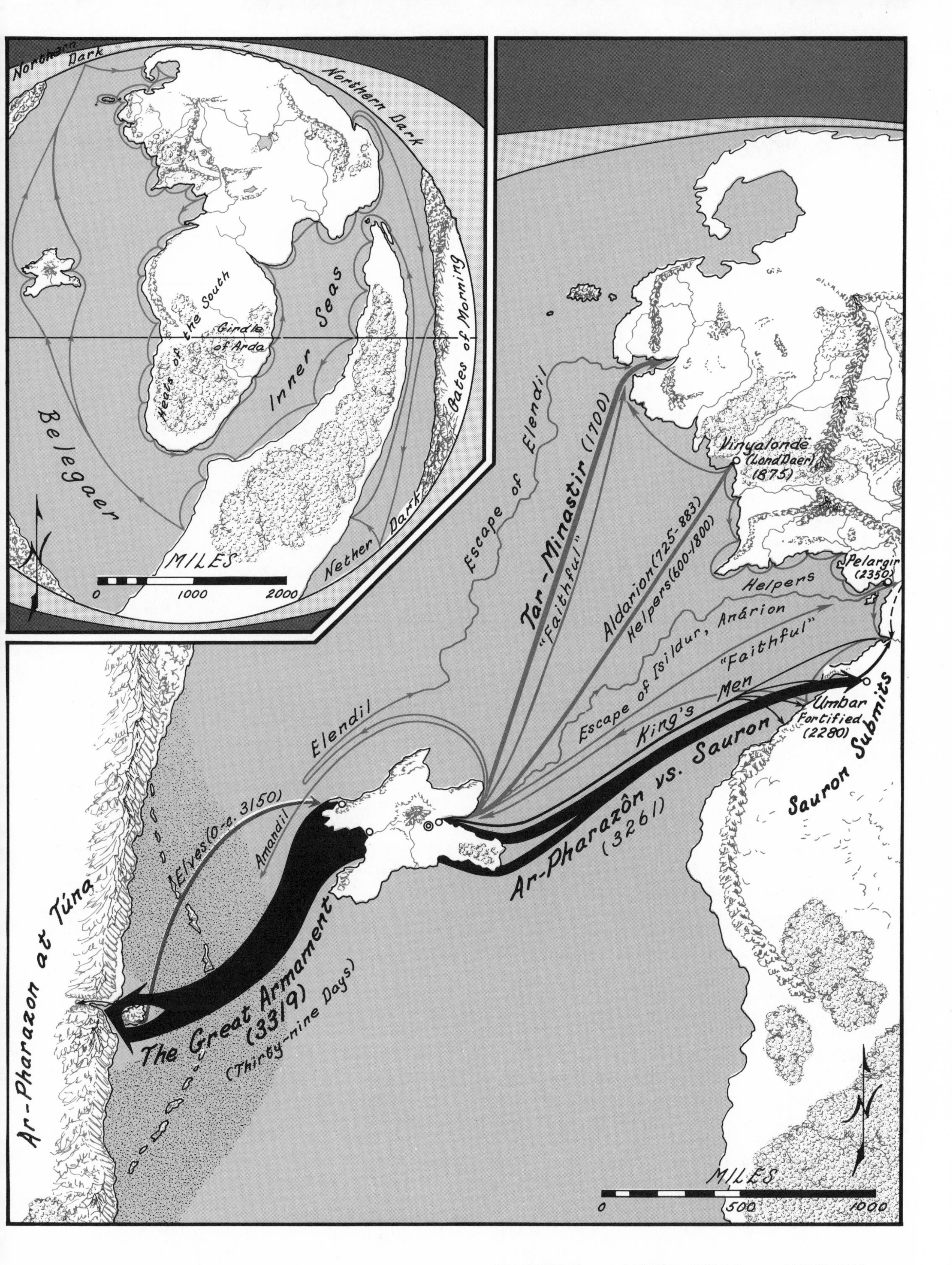
Northern Dark
Northern Dark
Gates of Morning
Inner Seas
Heads of the South
Girdle of Arda
Belegaer
Nether Dark
MILES
0
1000
2000
Escape of Elendil
Tar-Minastir (1700)
"Faithful"
Vinyalondë
(Lond Daer)
(875)
Aldarion (725-883)
Helpers (600-1800)
Pelargir
(2350)
Helpers
Escape of Isildur, Anárion
"Faithful"
Men
King's
Umbar
Fortified
(2280)
Elendil
Amandil
Elves (0-c. 3150)
Ar-Pharazôn vs. Sauron
(3261)
Sauron Submits
Sauron
Ar-Pharazon at Túna
The Great Armament
(3319)
(Thirty-nine Days)
MILES
0
500
1000

VOYAGES Upper: WORLD-WIDE Lower: BELEGAER

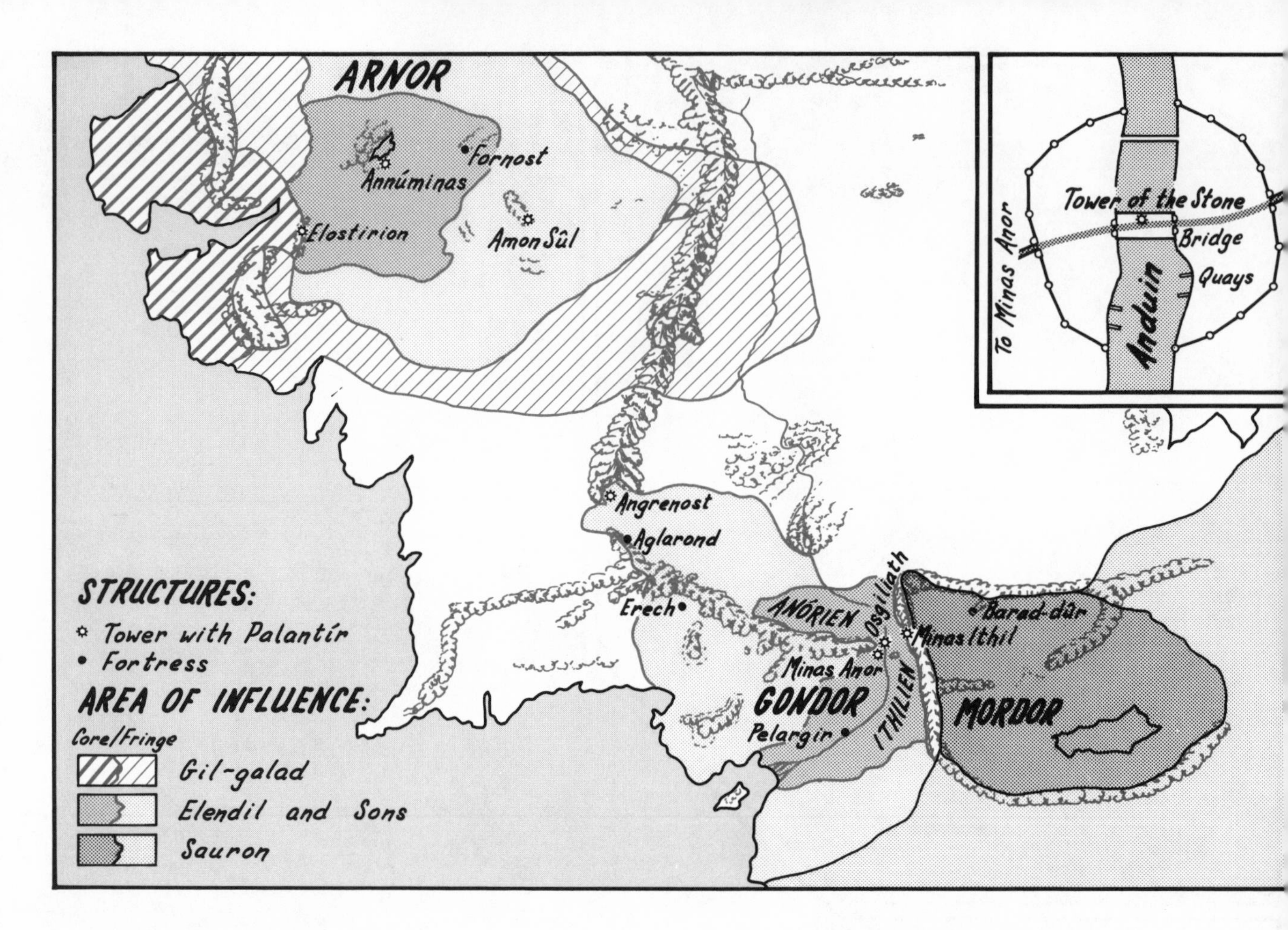

REALMS IN EXILE Inset: OSGILIATH

The Realms in Exile

WITHIN A YEAR AFTER THE FALL OF NÚMENOR, Elendil and his sons in 3320 had established the Realms in Exile: Arnor and Gondor.[1] Arnor lay in Eriador, where most of the people had paid allegiance to Gil-galad — but few of the Eldar lived outside of Lindon, except in Imladris.[2] Elendil reigned from Annúminas, beside Lake Nenuial.[3] The most notable other structures were: the city of Fornost on the North Downs; the dwellings on Tyrn Gorthad (the Barrow-downs);[4] and forts on the hills north of the Great Road east of the Last Bridge.[5]

The palantíri were divided between the two realms.[6] The Seeing Stones of Elendil were placed at Annúminas, in the Tower of the West;[7] on Weathertop, in the Tower of Amon Sûl; and on the Tower Hills, in Elostirion, the highest and most westward of the three white towers.[8] Gondor spread from the Anduin valley until it had fortifications as far west as Erech, Aglarond, and the unbreakable tower of Orthanc, which housed a palantír. The other three palantíri were placed in towers raised in Minas Ithil, dwelling of Isildur; Minas Anor, home of Anárion; and in Osgiliath, the Citadel of the Stars, which was the chief city of the realm.[9] The most central feature of Osgiliath was the River Anduin, whose waters were so wide and deep at that point that even large vessels could anchor at the city's quays. From Minas Anor and Minas Ithil roads approached the city along walled causeways.[10] To permit easy passage, a great bridge was constructed. It was even possible that the bridge was the citadel, for towers and stone houses stood upon it.[11] One of those may have been the Tower of the Stone, with its Great Hall and Dome of Stars, for when Osgiliath was burned in T.A. 1437, the Tower fell and the palantír it held was lost in the river.[12]

Against Arnor, and especially Gondor, was set Mordor. Although Sauron's body fell with Númenor, his spirit escaped, and soon returned to the dark tower of Barad-dûr.[13] He, too, speedily ordered his realm, reorganizing not only his evil creatures, but the Men of Harad, Rhûn, and Umbar as well. Among these were scattered the Black Númenóreans, renegades of the King's Men, who hated the Faithful as much as did Sauron.[14] Thus, the stage was set for the next confrontation.

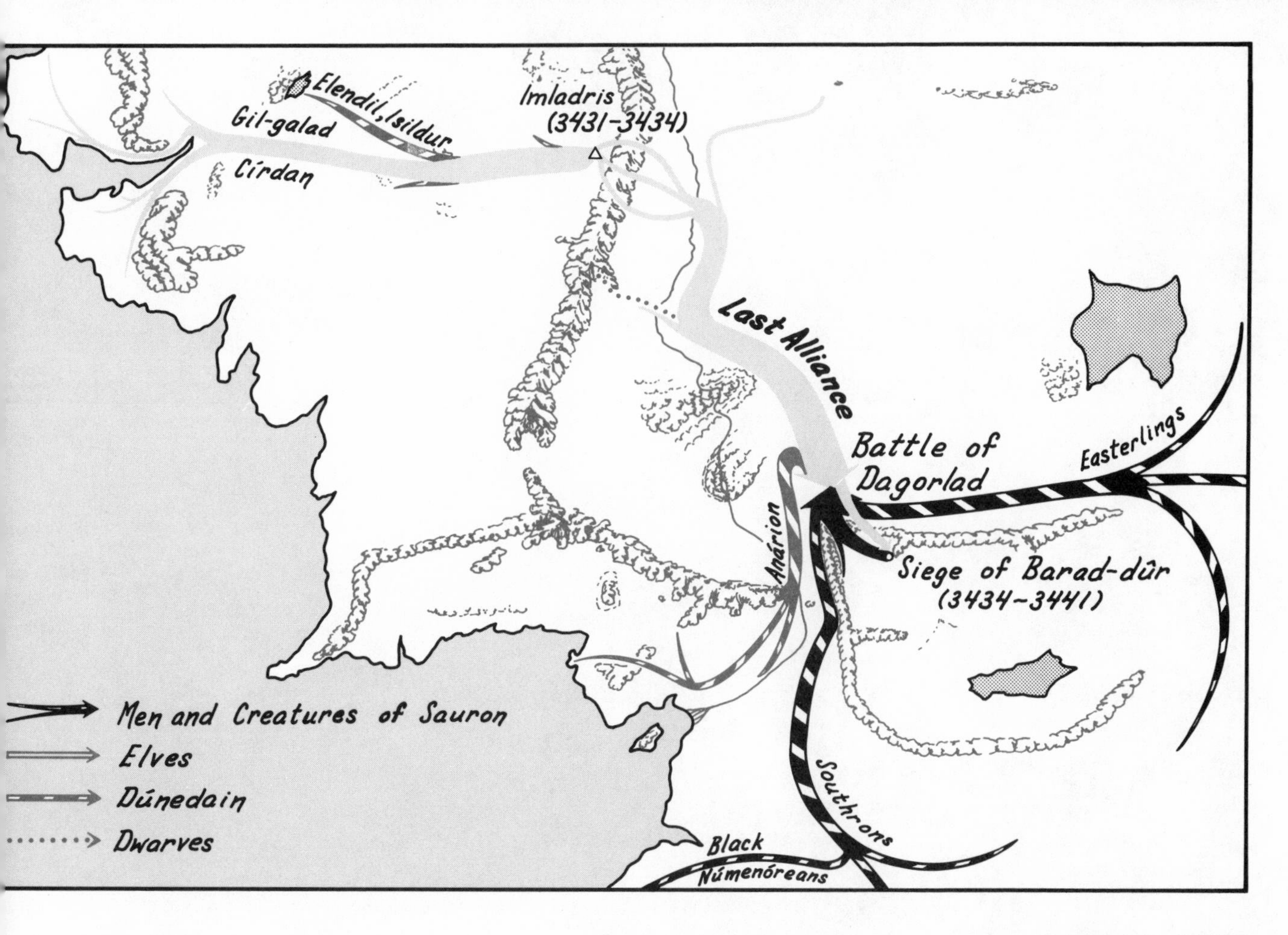

THE LAST ALLIANCE

The Last Alliance

IN 3429, Sauron attacked Gondor, hoping to crush the fledgling realm before it was fully defended.[1] Isildur and his family were forced to flee from Minas Ithil to Annúminas, and Sauron's forces moved on toward Osgiliath. Anárion successfully defended the city and even drove the Enemy from Ithilien, but it was only a temporary reprieve.[2] In hopes that the Enemy, too, was not fully prepared, Gil-galad and Elendil proposed a unified attack on Sauron's land: the Last Alliance.[3] All beings except Elves were said to have been divided between the League and the Enemy, even beasts and birds, although few Dwarves fought,[4] and probably no Ents.[5] As they were on the offensive, the League gathered their forces for two years, and in 3431 the northern troops marched.[6] On Amon Sûl, Elendil awaited the arrival of Gil-galad and Círdan,[7] and together they continued to Imladris, where they spent three years — undoubtedly making plans, forging weapons, training. In 3434 they climbed the Misty Mountains and passed down the Anduin.[8] They still gathered troops as they went along: Elves from Greenwood and Lórien, Dwarves from Moria, and Anárion with the forces from Gondor.[9] The final host was second only to that which had fought in the War of Wrath.[10]

The battle was waged on the stony plain of Dagorlad, north of the Black Gate of Mordor, "for days and months," and the bodies were buried in what became the Dead Marshes.[11] In the end, the Alliance prevailed, and Sauron's forces retreated to Barad-dûr. For seven years they besieged the fortress and many skirmishes were fought, until in 3446 Sauron was so pressed that he at last came forth.[12] He faced his challengers on the flanks of Mount Doom, where his ring was at its fullest power. With Gil-galad stood Círdan and Elrond; and with Elendil was Isildur.[13] Gil-galad and Elendil both were slain; yet Sauron stumbled and fell. When Isildur sliced the Ring and finger from Sauron's hand, his spirit fled. Then the forces of the Alliance routed his thralls, and leveled his fortress; but the victory was incomplete, for the Ring was not destroyed.[14]

The Third Age

Introduction

By the beginning of the Age of Men, Arda had been reduced from its former size.[1] Beleriand had submerged, Númenor foundered, and Valinor was removed from the circles of the world. "New lands" were found to the west, and some said that the peak of Meneltarma again rose above the waters over fallen Númenor.[2] Only the areas originally mapped in *The Lord of the Rings* remained of any importance to the telling of the tale.

When Númenor was toppled and Valinor taken away, great changes were reported — new isles, new hills, drowned coasts.[3] No specific information was given, however, about where the alterations occurred. Logic would suggest that far more upheaval would have been associated with the catastrophic change of the world's being made round after the Downfall of Númenor than with the destruction of Thangorodrim. Tolkien, too, must have struggled with this, for he attempted some rewritings in this vein — especially regarding the final inundation of Beleriand.[4] Nevertheless, extensive writings were already in existence, in which most of the major features had already been mentioned before the cataclysm, and so were obviously not newly made. Even the coastlines may not have been re-formed sufficiently to be evident on a world map, for the havens of Middle-earth that the Númenóreans had settled were still present in later times — notably Umbar.

It has been necessary, therefore, to map few, if any, of the physical variations that might have been likely. There were two notable exceptions, both vegetative: forests and marshes. The cutting over of forests had begun slowly in the First Age and was greatly amplified during the Second by the lumbering activities of Númenor.[5] By the beginning of the Third Age only the Old Forest, Fangorn, and a few scattered woods continued as remnants of the once-vast primeval stand.[6] Additionally, the "Secondary World" powers blasted the green areas and created wastelands: the Desolation of the Dragon[7] and the Desolation of the Morannon.[8] The denudation resulted in spreading of nearby marshes. The fens in eastern Mirkwood spread after the coming of Smaug.[9] The Dead Marshes grew larger during the Third Age, swallowing up the graves from the Battle of Dagorlad.[10]

Although Sauron was hidden through much of this Age, the evil forces he had unleashed continued to create havoc. For the Elves it was a period of waiting, with occasional involvement in the concern of the other Free Peoples.[11] They fenced themselves in Lindon, Imladris, Lórien, and northern Greenwood. In times of turmoil many Elves departed from the Grey Havens or the havens of Edhellond near Dol Amroth.[12] For the other peoples it was a time of fairly frequent upheavals: conquest, retreat, escape, and migration. Orcs, dragons, Men, Dwarves, and the previously unmentioned Hobbits all migrated through the lands with the ebb and flow of the times — evacuating when necessary, then moving on to better lands as they became available.[13]

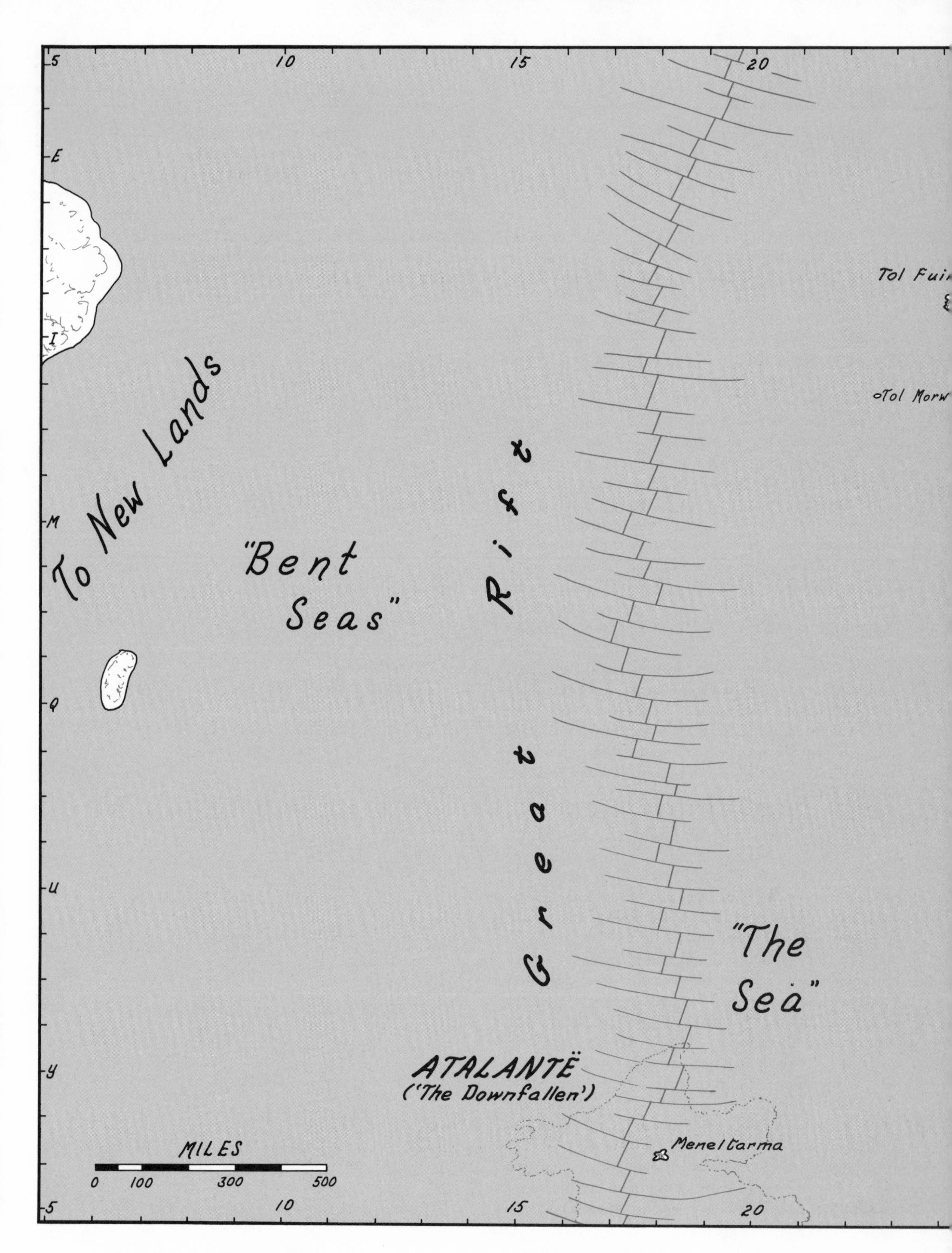
To New Lands
"Bent Seas"
Great Rift
"The Sea"
ATALANTË
('The Downfallen')
Meneltarma
MILES
0
100
300
500
10
15
20
5
E
I
M
Q
U
Y

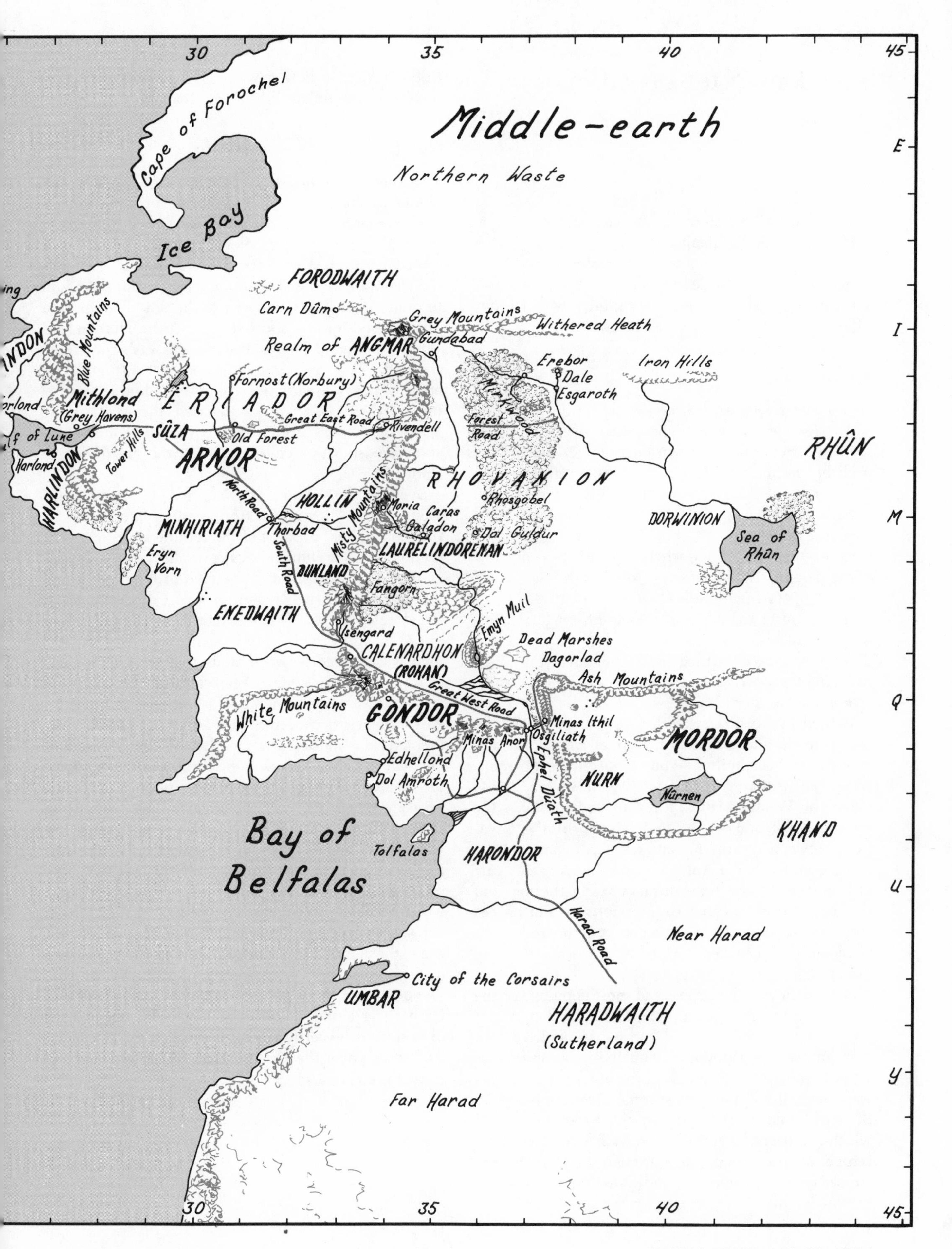

(EARLY) THIRD AGE OF ARDA

Kingdoms of the Dúnedain

T.A. 1050

Arnor and Gondor originally had been only separate fiefs under the final authority of Elendil.[1] After his death and those of his sons, the realms increasingly functioned as two divided kingdoms, until they ceased even to act as allies — each being busy with its own affairs.[2]

Arnor

Arnor never recovered after the slaughter of its folk at the first of the Age.[3] The sphere of its influence seemed never to have grown much larger than it had probably been under Elendil.[4] At its greatest extent, the borders ran south down the River Lune and the coast to the mouth of the Greyflood; up the Greyflood, then the Loudwater to the Misty Mountains; then west to the Bay of Forochel,[5] though possibly not encompassing the Snowmen of the North.[6] It totalled about 248,540 square miles.

In 861, after the death of the eighth king, quarrelling among his sons was so great that the realm was divided into three: Arthedain, in the northwest; Rhudaur, in the northeast; and Cardolan, in the south. Arnor was no more.[7]

Arthedain's boundary with Cardolan ran from the coast, up the Baranduin to the Great East Road, and along it to Weathertop. From there to the northern fringe Arthedain bordered with Rhudaur in a line along the Weather Hills. Rhudaur and Cardolan lay on the north and south, respectively, of the Great Road between Weathertop and the upper waters of the Greyflood, while the Angle beyond the river was part of Rhudaur. All the kingdoms met at Weathertop, and the desire to obtain that frontier fortress and its palantír caused further enmity between the realms of Cardolan and Rhudaur, who had no other "Seeing Stone."[8]

Arthedain was the largest and most populous of the three, having been the core of the original kingdom;[9] but even its population had become so depleted that Annúminas was abandoned, and the new capital was set at Fornost.[10] The capitals of the other two divisions were never listed, but at least some guess can be made. Bombadil told of the ruins in the Barrow-downs,[11] which had been the burial grounds, and later, the final refuge of the people of Cardolan.[12] The Hobbits crossed their northern dike and wall after escaping the barrow-wights.[13] Farther east, in the area of Rhudaur, Bilbo and Frodo both saw stone walls and crumbling towers on the hills north of the Road.[14]

Gondor

The southern Dúnedain had not suffered as many casualties in the War as the northern, and their indigenous population seems to have been more numerous. From the original core along the Anduin, Gondor spread to its greatest extent, including all the lands west to the Greyflood/Sirannon; north along Anduin to the Field of Celebrant; east to the Sea of Rhûn; and (excluding Mordor) south to the River Harnen and along the coast to Umbar. Haradwaith was a conquered tributary. The area under direct rule was probably about 716,425 square miles, with Harad possibly adding another 486,775. Additionally, the Men of the Vales of Anduin acknowledged Gondor's authority, and friendship was cultivated with the Northmen in Rhovanion.[15]

West of the Anduin, the increase of Gondor's size seems to have resulted from natural accretion, although the hold in some of the remote lands was very tenuous — the Dunlendings certainly never were assimilated.[16] They lived in the land of Enedwaith, and "In the days of the Kings it was part of the realm of Gondor, but it was of little concern to them."[17] East of the Anduin, the history was entirely different. Ithilien was penned between lands that were either uninhabited or unfriendly. Against these the Dúnedain retaliated in self-defense and/or conquered for gain. After the victory of the Last Alliance, Mordor was desolate and its passes embattled — the Morannon, Durthang, Cirith Ungol — but still war never ceased on Gondor's borders.[18] The first mention of a specific invasion was in T.A. 490, when Easterlings from Rhûn crossed through Dagorlad. They were not finally defeated until about 550.[19] In these battles Gondor was assisted by a prince of Rhovanion (which at that time seems only to have referred to an area east of Greenwood).[20] In 830, Gondor's emphasis changed from defense on land to offense at sea. The first action was the extension of the realm south along the coasts east of Ethir Anduin[21] — apparently resulting in the possession of South Gondor. In 933, the great haven of Umbar was besieged and won; but it rose above a sea of enemies who battled the walled haven for 117 years. At last, in 1050, the king led great forces overland and routed the Haradrim.[22]

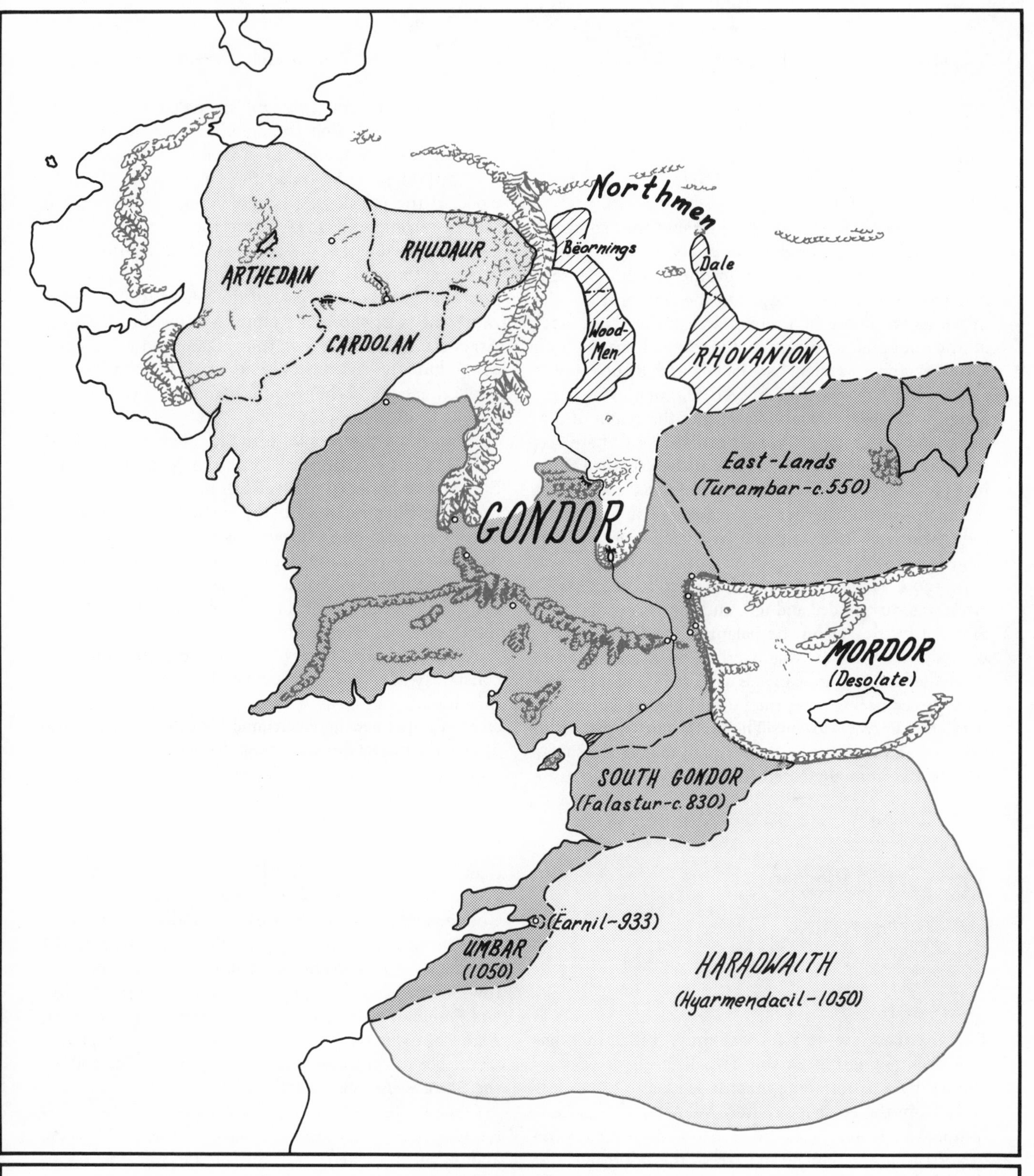

LEGEND

- Known City or Fortress
- Fortified Wall
- New Lands Gained in Battle
- Sub-Kingdoms
- North Kingdom-Realms of Arnor
- South Kingdom-Realm of Gondor
- Tributaries to Gondor
- Allies of Gondor

KINGDOMS OF THE DÚNEDAIN

Battles

T.A. 1200–1634

IN 1050, SAURON REAPPEARED, establishing an abode at Dol Guldur. As Gondor was at its greatest power, Sauron chose to strike first in the north. He sent Angmar, chief of the Nazgûl, to the land north of the Ettenmoors, where he ordered a realm on both sides of the mountains. By 1350 the royal lines in both Rhudaur and Cardolan had failed, and Rhudaur was ripe for seizure of power by evil Hillmen. When the King of Arthedain sought to reunite the realm of Arnor under his crown, Rhudaur resisted, and there was battle along their common border at the Weather Hills. In 1356, Arthedain fortified the highlands, and later set guard on the frontier of Cardolan. For fifty years they held back the evil, and Rivendell was also besieged.

In 1409, Angmar mustered a great force. Weathertop was surrounded and fell, and the Tower of Amon Sûl destroyed. Taking the palantír, the Dúnedain retreated, and Rhudaur was overrun by Angmar. From there the land of Cardolan was assaulted, and its people were forced back among the burial fields of Tyrn Gorthad, the Barrow-downs. The Arthedain returned to Fornost, and with the help of Círdan, managed to drive the enemy from the North Downs. When help came in the rear from Lórien and Rivendell, attacks lessened.[1]

While the North Kingdom struggled for survival, Gondor was becoming entangled in both internal and external strife. Sometime after Gondor had reached its widest borders, they ceded the lands south of Mirkwood to the people of Rhovanion as a buffer against the Easterlings. In 1248, after the Easterlings once more initiated skirmishes, a great force from Gondor destroyed not only the enemy armies, but even all the camps and settlements east of the Sea of Rhûn. Afterward, the west shore of Anduin was fortified, and the Argonath sculpted, as a warning against entering Gondor;[2] but the friendship with the Northmen was strengthened, and the twentieth king even wed a princess of Rhovanion.

As some of the people were unwilling to accept the half-Dúnedain Eldacar as lord, the Kinstrife began. Eldacar was besieged in Osgiliath in 1437, and escaped from the burning city to the north. After only ten years Castamir, the usurper was hated and the Dúnedain rallied around the rightful king. Eldamir marched south and won the battle at Erui. Castamir fell, but his men retreated to Pelargir and escaped, becoming the Corsairs of Umbar.[3]

Allied with the men of Harad, the Corsairs were constantly at war on both land and sea: In 1551, Hyarmendacil II significantly defeated the men of Harad; in 1634, the Corsairs devastated Pelargir and killed the king; in 1810, Gondor retook Umbar and destroyed Castamir's descendants.[4]

The Great Plague

T.A. 1636–37

THE READER VIEWING THIS MAP must realize that disease does not lessen or stop at a finite line, such as implied by a pattern on a map. It gradually grows less away from the epidemic center, following the concentrations of people. Tolkien gave no specific date, no list of casualties, but he did stress the importance of the resulting depopulation.

In 1636, only a year after the king had been killed in the Corsairs' raid on Pelargir, an evil east wind carried the seeds of further disaster into Gondor. The new king and all his children succumbed to a ravaging disease.[5] They were certainly not alone. The disease had affected the Easterlings and the land of Rhovanion first, and "When the Plague passed it is said that more than half of the folk of Rhovanion had perished."[6] From Osgiliath the plague rapidly spread through Gondor and much of the western lands.[7] Minhiriath, the southern portion of Cardolan, was hard hit. All the remnant of the Dúnedain hidden among the Barrow-downs also died, and evil spirits from Angmar and Rhudaur were free to enter there. Farther north Arthedain was only marginally affected, so its people were able to continue defending Fornost.[8] The folk of the Shire were heavily afflicted.[9]

Outside Rhovanion, Osgiliath had the highest casualties. Many fled from the city to the countryside and never returned, and the capital was moved to Minas Anor. So many died that the troops stationed at remote camps must have been recalled and the forts overlooking Mordor were unmanned. Such weakness could have left Gondor wide open to attack, but her enemies (possibly both the Easterlings and the Southrons) had also suffered.[10] For almost two centuries Gondor did little but try slowly to regain its strength.

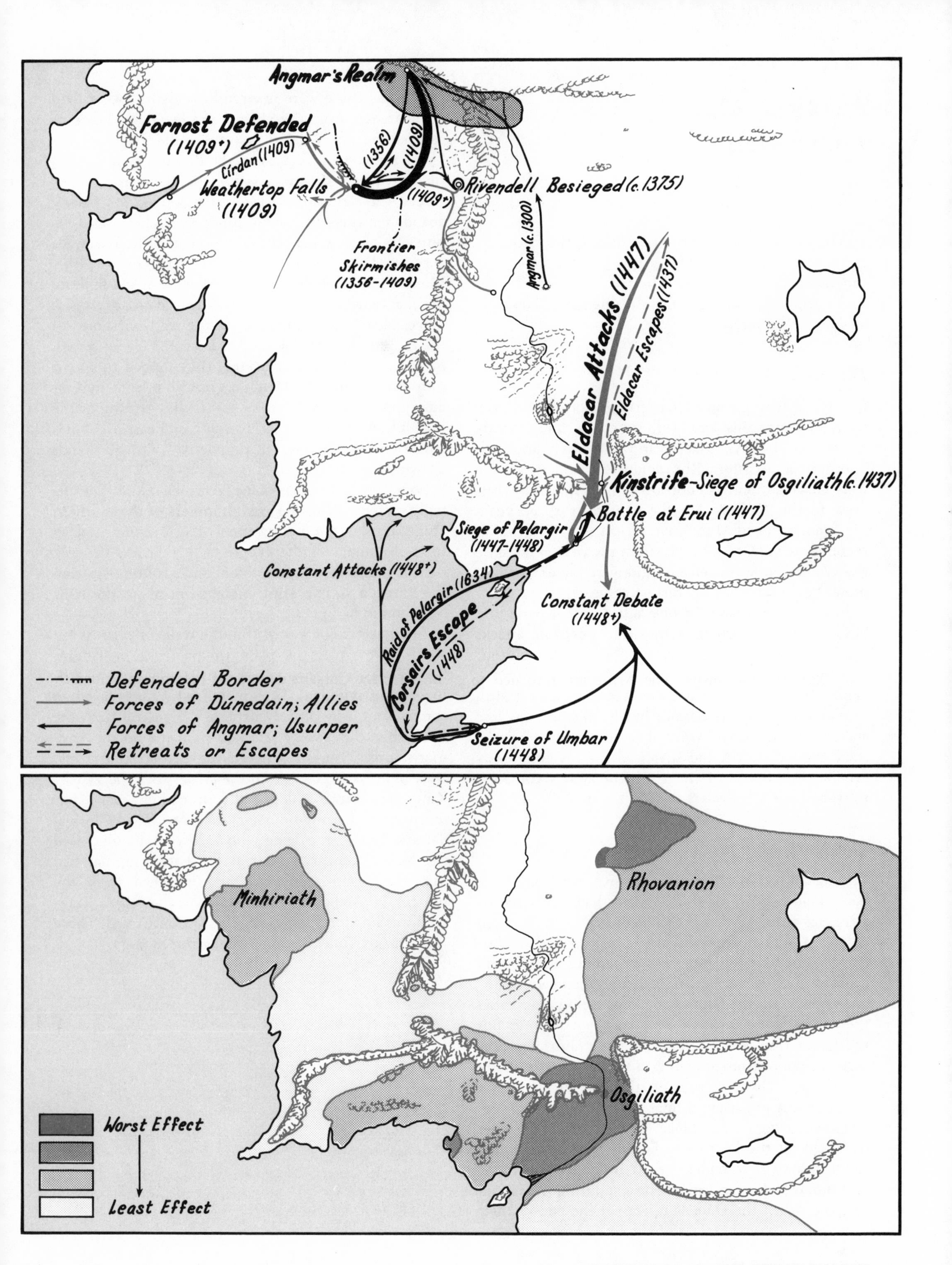

Angmar's Realm
Fornost Defended
(1409+)
Círdan (1409)
(1356)
(1409)
Weathertop Falls
(1409)
(1409+)
Rivendell Besieged (c.1375)
Frontier Skirmishes
(1356-1409)
Angmar (c.1300)
Eldacar Attacks (1447)
Eldacar Escapes (1437)
Kinstrife-Siege of Osgiliath (c.1437)
Battle at Erui (1447)
Siege of Pelargir
(1447-1448)
Constant Attacks (1448+)
Raid of Pelargir (1634)
Corsairs Escape
(1448)
Constant Debate
(1448+)
Seizure of Umbar
(1448)
Defended Border
Forces of Dúnedain; Allies
Forces of Angmar; Usurper
Retreats or Escapes
Minhiriath
Rhovanion
Osgiliath
Worst Effect
Least Effect

Upper: BATTLES Lower: THE GREAT PLAGUE

Wainriders and Angmar

T.A. 1851–1975

LITTLE HISTORY WAS REPORTED during the two centuries following the Plague. While Gondor slowly recuperated, Arthedain (less affected by the epidemic) continued in its struggle against Angmar. Then new onslaughts began.

The South Kingdom

In 1851 a new group of Easterlings appeared in the west — numerous and well-armed — and became known as the Wainriders. In 1856 they attacked. Southern and eastern Rhovanion fell, and its people were enslaved; and Gondor lost at Dagorlad and withdrew to the Anduin. For the next forty-three years the Wainriders ruled the east, but in 1899 Rhovanion revolted, while Gondor attacked in the west. This time the Wainriders were defeated and were forced to withdraw. Peace returned for forty-five years.[1]

In 1944, the eastern people allied with Khand and Near Harad, launching a massive two-front attack. The northern battle was fought before the Morannon, and the easterners won the day. As the enemy advanced into North Ithilien, the Dúnedain were in full retreat. The southern assault by the alliance was less successful. The South Army of Gondor was victorious, then marched north and surprised the revelling easterners. The Battle of the Camp became a complete rout, and the Wainriders fled.[2]

The North Kingdom

Through all of the time the massive invasions were being held back in the south, Arnor had continued its struggles against Angmar. Rhudaur had fallen through default. Cardolan from disease.[3] Only Arthedain continued, but its population was dwindling and its will probably was wavering. In 1940 they had sworn alliance anew with the South Kingdom, seeing at last that they were being accosted by a common enemy, but the losses from the battles with the Wainriders prevented Gondor from providing any assistance for many years after. Then, in 1973, Arthedain perceived that Angmar was preparing a final great stroke. Messages were sent begging assistance. Gondor readied a great fleet, led by the king's son Eärnur, but by the time the fleet arrived in mid-1975, Arthedain was lost.[4]

Angmar had come against Fornost during the winter of 1974, when the Dúnedain were at the end of their resources. There were few reinforcements, other than some archers from the Shire;[5] and few defenders ever escaped the city. Most of those who did, including the king's sons, went west across the River Lûne and eventually reached Círdan. Arvedui, the "Last-king," continued the fight from the North Downs, but finally abandoned the struggle.[6] On horseback he evaded his pursuers and raced north and west until he reached a deserted Dwarf-mine in the far north of the Blue Mountains. With little food and inadequate clothing for that northern clime, he was forced to seek assistance. Near the mountains, on the western shores of the Ice Bay, he found a camp of Lossoth, the Snowmen of Forochel. At first reluctant, they agreed to succor him until spring. In March a great ship, sent by Círdan, appeared in the Bay. Against the warning of the Lossoth, Arvedui boarded the ship and cast off; but a storm arose, the vessel foundered, and all hands drowned.[7]

Sometime later that same year, Gondor's fleet finally arrived. With the great numbers of the southern Dúnedain came mounted men of Rhovanion. Added to the remnant of the people of Arthedain, the folk Círdan summoned from Lindon, and a contingent from the Shire, a sizable army marched north to the Hills of Evendim.[8]

Angmar did not wait within the walls of Fornost but went west across the plain to meet the onslaught. Seeing this, the cavalry was sent north into the hills to wait in ambush. The main host had engaged in combat and were already driving the enemy from the field when the cavalry attacked from the north. Angmar's forces, caught between the two striking arms, were obliterated. Out from the affray rode the Witch-King, and Eärnur galloped after him; but when Angmar turned, Eärnur's horse shied away. Then Glorfindel attacked — the same who with the Hobbits faced the Nazgûl centuries later at the Ford. Angmar fled into the shadows of dusk and vanished from the north.[9] So Arthedain was freed; yet the North Kingdom was no more, for its people were destroyed. Those few who remained became wandering rangers.[10]

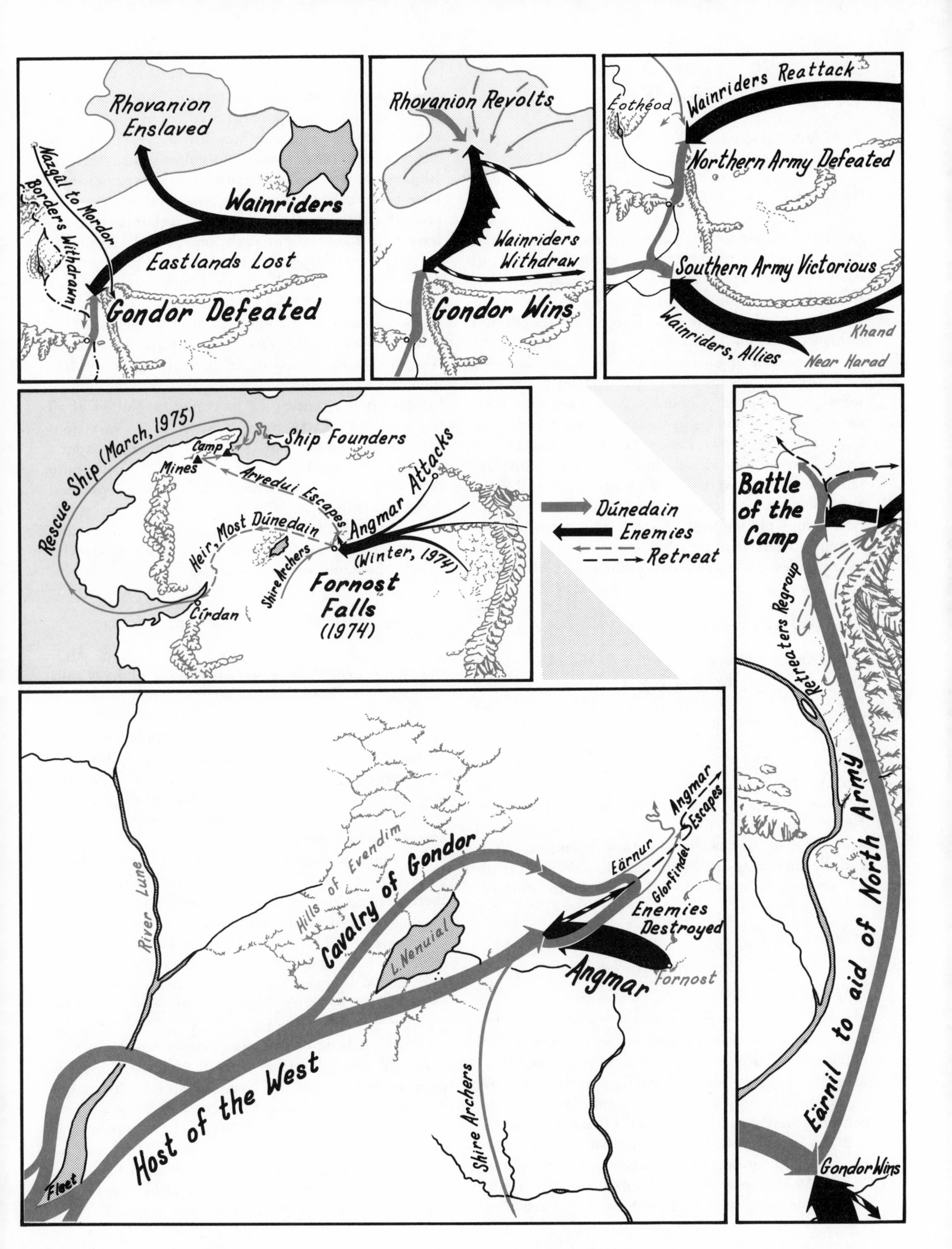

GONDOR VERSUS WAINRIDERS Top, 1856, 1899, 1944 Right: BATTLE OF THE CAMP (1944) ARTHEDAIN VERSUS ANGMAR
Center Left: FALL OF FORNOST (1974) Lower: DEFEAT OF ANGMAR (1975)

Deepening Difficulties

T.A. 2000–2940

In the millennium following the end of the North Kingdom, troubles increased until virtually all the known lands were affected in some way. Much of the evil was due directly or indirectly to Sauron. In spite of the loss of the One Ring, his strength and influence grew until even the weather was affected. At times the forces of good were able to counter Sauron's advances, but always those that had been defeated were soon replaced. Gondor was attacked and reattacked: in 2060 and again in 2475, from Mordor; in 2510, from the Brown Lands; in 2758, from Umbar; and in 2885, from Harad. Interspersed with the assaults on Gondor were Orc-raids into Eriador, Rohan, and Wilderland; plunderings by dragons; and two horribly long, cold winters.[1] All the lands seem to have become a chessboard on which the black was supplied with limitless pawns and an infinite variety of moves.

The Last of Gondor's Kings (2000–2050)

After Angmar escaped the battle in the plain of Evendim, he made his way back to Mordor and once again readied a force. In 2000, twenty-five years after the fall of Arnor, he marched through the Pass of Cirith Ungol and besieged Minas Ithil, which fell two years later.[2] The city was occupied by the Nazgûl and renamed Minas Morgul, Tower of Sorcery.[3] From his new abode Angmar began his campaign in the south. He sent forth no warlike hosts. Instead, in 2043 and again in 2050, he challenged Eärnur to single combat; and the king went east to fight the duel. When Eärnur did not return, there was no heir and the stewards ruled.[4]

The Watchful Peace and Its End (2060–2480)

Gandalf, whom the Elves called Mithrandir, was the first to perceive that the growing evil power in Dol Guldur was Sauron himself.[5] In 2063 Mithrandir went to the Dark Lord's fortress, and Sauron retreated east — but it may only have been a feint. The next four centuries were called The Watchful Peace, because the evil was less; but evil had certainly not vanished. Orcs continued to spread. The Dwarves were driven from Moria. Most important, Sauron used the opportunity to gain additional support from Men in the east.[6]

In 2460 Sauron returned to Dol Guldur with his new allies, and once more his thralls were under direct control. His first assault was fifteen years later, in 2475. Uruks from Minas Morgul marched through Ithilien and attacked Osgiliath. Reinforcements must have been rushed from Minas Anor and other nearby areas, for the partially deserted city certainly could not have withstood the onslaught on its own. Boromir I defeated the enemy and drove them back to the mountains; yet Osgiliath fell into final ruin. In the fighting the great bridge was broken and the last citizens fled — as did many of the inhabitants of Ithilien. Yet the defeat had once more restrained the forces sent by the Nazgûl. The Uruks continued guerrilla warfare in Ithilien, but there were no more major battles at Osgiliath for over half a century.[7] The cumulative drain of all the harrying attacks from many sides — east from Mordor and south from Umbar — reduced Gondor's striking arm until the country could do little more than defend its own borders. At times it even had difficulty with that.[8] To further disrupt assistance, Orcs spread through most of the Misty Mountains, blocking passage and harrying those few peoples who dared to remain near the mountains.

The Balchoth and the Rohirrim (2510)

The next major onslaught came in the north. After the defeat of the Wainriders, when many of the Northmen had left Rhovanion and settled among the folk of Gondor, a new group of Easterlings had taken the lands east of Mirkwood. They were called the Balchoth, and their allegiance was given to Sauron. At first they passed through Mirkwood and raided the Vale of Anduin, until the lands south of the Gladden were deserted. Then they prepared for an assault against Gondor itself.[9]

On numerous rafts the Balchoth crossed Anduin, passing from the Brown Lands to the Wold. At first there must have been little resistance in the sparsely populated plains of Calenardhon, until the bulk of the troops arrived. The North Army probably counterattacked earliest, and in their fervor had already driven into the Wold and were cut off from the later companies. The Balchoth forced further separation by pushing them north across the Limlight. By chance or command, a band of Orcs descended from the mountains and blocked further retreat, and the Dúnedain were backed against the river. In such an hour the Éothéod arrived. Although a summons had been sent to Gondor's allies before the attack, it had taken long to reach the horsemen in the far north. In haste the host of Eorl had galloped down the east side of Anduin, crossed the river at the Undeeps, and broken on the rear of the attacking Balchoth — unexpected by friend

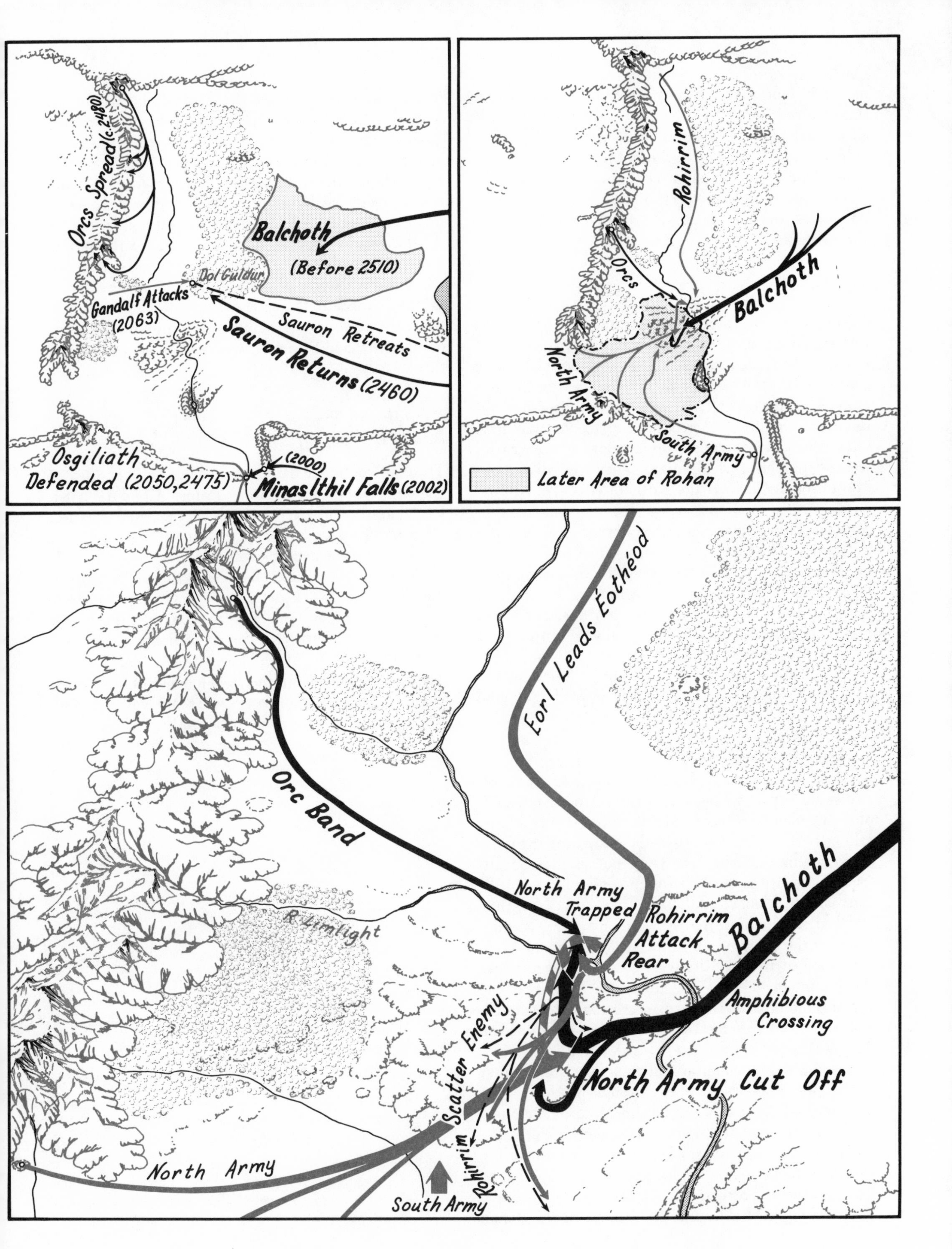

Upper Left: BEFORE AND AFTER THE WATCHFUL PEACE Upper Right: FORCES TO FIELD OF CELEBRANT
Lower: BATTLE OF CELEBRANT

or foe.[10] Not only did they rout the attackers, but they crossed back into northern Gondor and scattered all the Balchoth in Calenardhon as well.

In reward Gondor gave the Éothéod all the depopulated land of Calenardhon between the Isen and the Anduin. They held the territory as a separate realm, under their own kings. Gondor's lands once again were shrunken.[11]

The Days of Dearth (2758–2760)

During the 250 years following the coming of the Rohirrim, once more there was a respite. In 2545 more Easterlings invaded the Wold, but were driven back by the Horse-lords.[12] Except for the increase of dragons plundering northern Dwarf-mines, no other difficulties were specifically listed until 2740. At that time Orcs began new invasions of Eriador — even as far west as the Shire, where in 2747 they were driven out by Bullroarer Took, at the Battle of Greenfields.[13]

The nearly fatal year was 2758. War and weather combined almost finished the westerners from Eriador to Gondor. The Corsairs of Umbar allied with the men of Harad and sent three great fleets to assault the coast of Gondor all the way from the Isen to the Anduin. Many of the invaders established beachheads and cut their way inland. All Gondor was alive with war.

Rohan could not come to Gondor's assistance, because of difficulties of its own. From its founding Rohan had been opposed by the Dunlendings, who viewed the Northmen as trespassers. Almost immediately, skirmishes began along the Isen — the boundary between Rohan and Dunland. In 2710 some Dunlendings had managed to capture and hold Isengard. A dispute between King Helm and a large landholder of the Dunlendings increased grievances.[14] When Easterlings crossed into Anduin at the same time the fleets were assailing Gondor, the Dunlendings took advantage of the situation. Allied with some of the Southrons who had landed at the Isen and the Lefnui, they attacked Rohan from the west. Helm's army was defeated at the Crossings of Isen. The Riders of the Mark who escaped the conflicts were forced to retreat into the mountain valleys. The fortress at Aglarond and the ancient hold of Dunharrow were probably filled, while the leader of the Dunlendings sat enthroned in Edoras.[15]

In addition to the military losses, a long, hard winter settled in. From November through March, snow blanketed all the lands from Forochel to the Ered Nimrais. Food and fuel ran short, making famine a problem by midwinter. Loss of stock and late spring planting worsened the situation, and many thousands perished throughout the northwest.

The refugees hidden in the mountains of Rohan made desperate raids on the encamped enemy, and from such deeds came the fame of Helm Hammerhand.[16] The weather was cruel to the enemy as well, and in the spring, turned to the favor of the Rohirrim, for rushing meltwaters flooded the plains. When a frantic band led by Helm's nephew drove the Dunlendings from Edoras, the usurpers had no place to go. As the weather had been kinder south of the mountains, Gondor had been able to battle its attackers, and by spring were free to assist Rohan. With the arrival of the Dúnedain the last enemies were driven out. Even Isengard was regained and Saruman allowed to occupy Orthanc in hopes he could prevent its recapture.[17]

Remaining Events Prior to the Battle of Five Armies (2770–2940)

Troubles continued after the Days of Dearth: Orcs in Rohan, 2800–2864; Harad against Gondor, 2885; Uruks in Ithilien, 2901; the Fell Winter, 2911.[18] These were scattered and of limited importance. Far more notable were the activities of the Dwarves — not only as the prelude to *The Hobbit* but also as a part of the greater history. The defeat of the Orcs at Moria in 2799 and later at Lonely Mountain in 2941 helped reduce the northern Orc troops available in the War of the Rings. The slaying of Smaug eliminated a creature that could have been used by Sauron with devastating effect.[19] As these events are covered elsewhere, they have not been repeated here.[20]

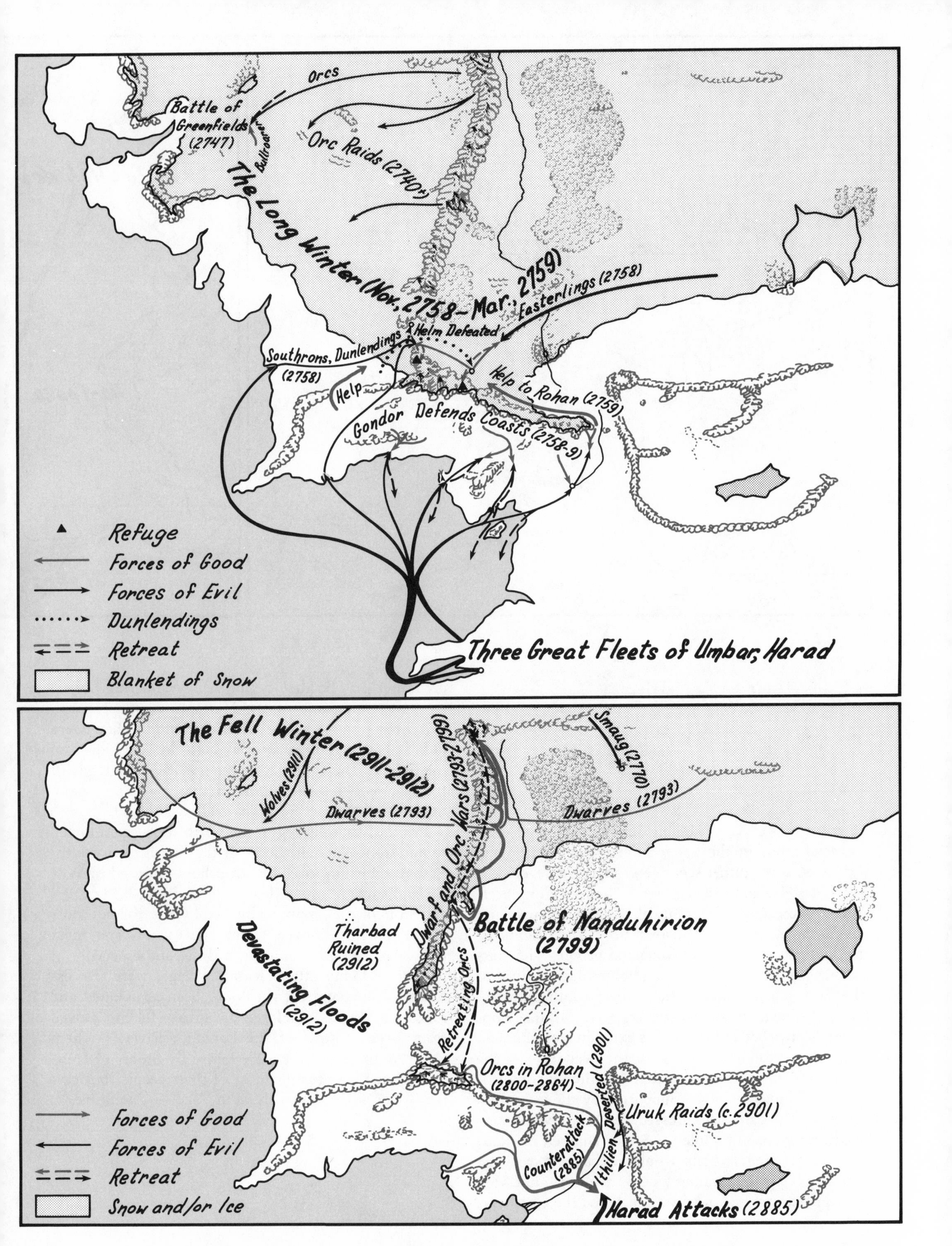
Orcs
Battle of Greenfields (2747)
Bullroarer
Orc Raids (2740's)
The Long Winter (Nov., 2758 – Mar., 2759)
Easterlings (2758)
Helm Defeated
Southrons, Dunlendings (2758)
Help
Help to Rohan (2759)
Gondor Defends Coasts (2758-9)
Refuge
Forces of Good
Forces of Evil
Dunlendings
Retreat
Blanket of Snow
Three Great Fleets of Umbar, Harad
The Fell Winter (2911-2912)
Wolves (2911)
Dwarves (2793)
Dwarf and Orc Wars (2793-2799)
Smaug (2770)
Dwarves (2793)
Battle of Nanduhirion (2799)
Tharbad Ruined (2912)
Devastating Floods (2912)
Retreating Orcs
Orcs in Rohan (2800-2864)
Ithilien Deserted (2901)
Uruk Raids (c. 2901)
Counterattack (2885)
Forces of Good
Forces of Evil
Retreat
Snow and/or Ice
Harad Attacks (2885)

Upper: DAYS OF DEARTH Lower: REMAINING EVENTS PRIOR TO THE HOBBIT

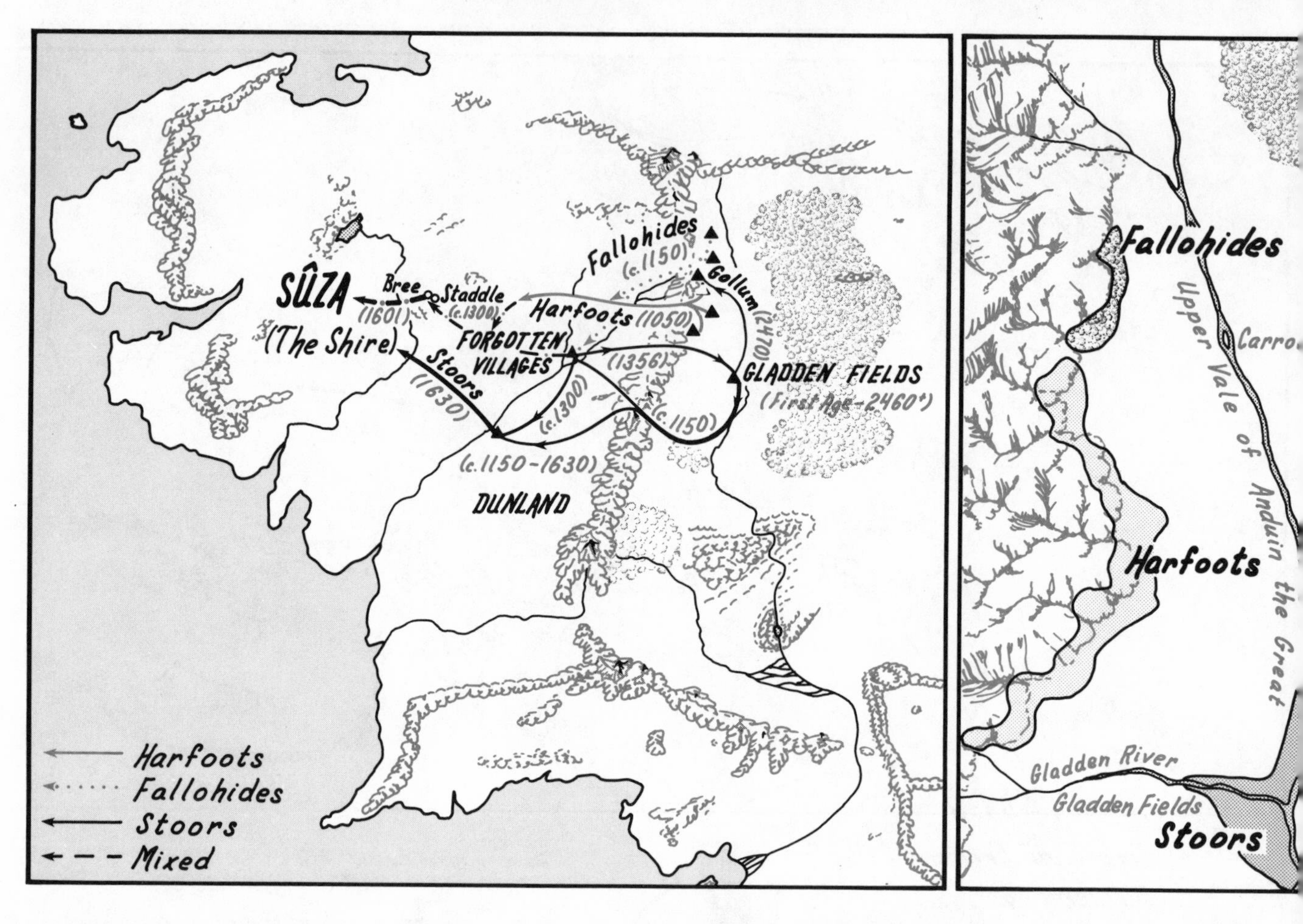

Left: MIGRATIONS Right: ANCESTRAL LANDS

Migrations of Hobbits

THROUGH THE AGES Hobbits lived quietly in their ancestral lands in the upper vales of Anduin.[1] Over the years, three rather separate groups had developed: Fallohides, Harfoots, and Stoors. Their dwelling preferences were quite different, although they may not have been as separated as shown here. The Fallohides, the most northerly, were woodland people. The Harfoots chose the uplands, delving homes in the hillsides. The Stoors apparently lived farthest south and preferred the lowlands and riverbanks.[2] The original Hobbit lands have been illustrated as extending on the west along the Great River, between the Gladden and the Carrock — the area inhabited at one time by the Rohirrim.[3] The location was supported by the migration patterns: The Fallohides crossed the Misty Mountains north of Rivendell,[4] while the Stoors climbed the Redhorn Pass.[5] The Hobbits would probably have been perfectly happy continuing where they were, but Men were increasing, and nearby Greenwood the Great was becoming evil. So they began their Wandering Days.[6] In T.A. 1050, some of the Harfoots went west into Eriador — some as far as Weathertop. They were joined about a century later by both the Fallohides and the Stoors. The Fallohides were few and mingled with the Harfoots and the Stoors of the Angle, but many Stoors settled apart near Tharbad in Dunland.[7]

In 1300, those living in the north were again forced to flee from Angmar. Some of the Stoors went south, joining their kin in Dunland; others returned to Wilderland, where they dwelt along the Gladden[8] — ancestors of the infamous Sméagol/Gollum;[9] but most of the Hobbits moved west. The earliest and most important settlements were in Bree, and especially in Staddle.[10] Many other pleasant villages were also established but later seem to have been abandoned and forgotten. In 1601 a large group of Hobbits moved from Bree to west of the Baraduin River,[11] where thirty years later they were joined by Stoors of Dunland;[12] and eventually, most of their people (but certainly not all)[13] settled there in Sûza — The Shire.[14]

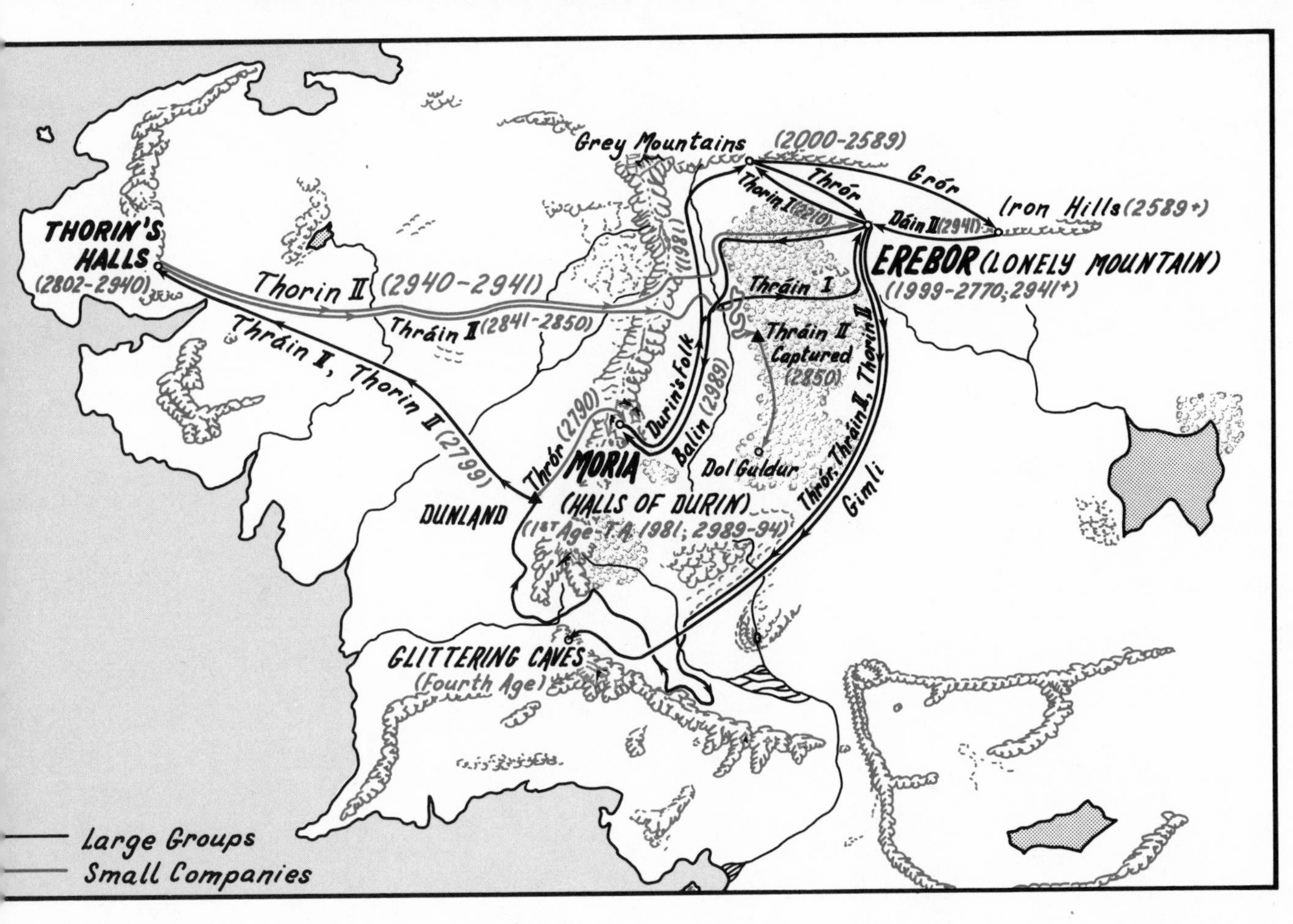

MIGRATIONS OF DURIN'S FOLK

Migrations of Dwarves

Durin was the first of the Seven Dwarf Fathers to awake,[1] and the other families were rarely mentioned.[2] Some of Durin's people went west in the First Age to the Ered Luin,[3] but most remained in Khazad-dûm until T.A. 1980, when they delved too deep and released the Balrog, which had hidden there almost 5500 years before. Most went north to the Grey Mountains; but Thráin I, heir to the throne, wandered to the Lonely Mountain, where he established the Kingdom under the Mountain in 1999.[4] In 2210, under his son Thorin I, many of the people joined their kindred in the rich Grey Mountains, where they prospered until 2570.[5] When the king was killed by a cold-drake, the Dwarves again forsook their home. Some returned to Erebor with Thrór, the king's eldest son, while others went east to the Iron Hills with a younger brother, Grór. Both communities prospered, and there was much commerce between them. To Thrór, Sauron gave the first-made of the Dwarf Rings, and with it a great hoard was built.[6] Thus, their success was also their downfall, for in 2770 Smaug descended on the gate and routed the halls. Many escaped and scattered. Some accompanied Thrór, Thráin, and Thorin, who wandered south, stopping wherever work could be found.[7]

Twenty years later, when they were eking out a living in Dunland, Thrór returned to Moria and was beheaded by Orcs. The Dwarves gathered from all corners — not only Durin's folk, but also "Houses of other Fathers" — to destroy the Orcs, ending with a great battle in 2799.[8] Afterward Thráin led his folk west to the Blue Mountains, and their people began to reassemble. Yet once again, the evil power of the Ring was at work. Thráin led a small company east toward Erebor. They were pursued, and Thráin was captured and imprisoned in Dol Guldur, where the Ring was taken.[9] Before his death he was found there by Gandalf,[10] and that led to all that happened afterward — Thorin and Company, the Battle of Five Armies, and the resettlement of Erebor. Only two more large migrations remained: Balin's disastrous attempt in 2989 to reoccupy Moria[11] and Gimli's colonization of the Glittering Caves.[12]

Regional Maps

Introduction

THE FOLLOWING REGIONAL MAPS include all of the place names of northwestern Middle-earth at the time of Bilbo's and Frodo's quests as mentioned in *The Lord of the Rings* and *The Hobbit.* Some of the names were locational, such as *Far Harad,* "far south"; some were descriptive, for example, *Lithlad,* "ash plain"; and some were inspired by nearby cultural features, as *Ithilien,* "moon land," was named for *Minas Ithil,* "Tower of the Rising Moon."[1] The Shire and Rohan were the only political units with boundaries set by decree,[2] so only their borders have been drawn.

Except for the Shire, no history has been given here. Instead, the accompanying texts explain the necessary decisions reached in drawing the physical base maps.[3] Tolkien's maps and text were compared with each other and with the Primary World, and the resulting landscape explained as if its formations were on Earth, rather than Middle-earth. The index marks shown here are 100 miles apart, as are Tolkien's originals, but they are off 50 miles east–west and are 25 miles north on the north–south grid.[4]

The Shire

THE HOBBITS OF BREE obtained permission from the high king at Fornost in 1601 to settle the lands between the Brandywine River and the Far Downs. The boundaries shown were based on the stated distances: from the Far Downs to the Brandywine Bridge, forty leagues (120 miles); and from the *western* moors to the marshes in the south, fifty leagues (150 miles).[5] The latter was measured from northwest to southeast, for had the line run due north–south it would have ended in hills, not marshes. The total area was about 21,400 square miles and was divided into four farthings. These have no official function but fit the subregions of the Shire: cooler, drier fields of the north; downlands of the west; sheltered croplands of the south; and the mixed lands of the east — woods, marshes, croplands, and quarries. Two adjacent areas were added to the Shire later: the Eastmarch (Buckland) and the Westmarch. Buckland was occupied in T.A. 2340, almost 700 years before the War of the Rings; while the Westmarch was granted by Aragorn in F.O. 32.[6]

Assorted references mentioned other settlements not shown on Tolkien's map, so it has been assumed that they lay beyond its edges.[7] The map even indicated the direction to several towns. Some topographic clues also were given: Michel *Delving* was on the White Downs (so presumably Little *Delving* was also); Greenholm was in the Far Downs; Undertowers was at the east edge of the Tower Hills,[7] the Emyn Beraid, where Gil-galad built the White Towers for Elendil upon his arrival from fallen Númenor.[8] Each of these was placed along the Great East Road. The names themselves also have topographic references. Long *Cleeve* (a village occupied by the *North* Tooks)[9] suggests a narrow valley cut through uplands; while Long*bottom* probably lay in a river bottom (though none was shown in that area other than the Brandywine). History, too, added insight. Longbottom was close enough to ship tobacco conveniently to Saruman via Sarn Ford; and Bullroarer Took defeated the Orcs at the Battle of Greenfields in Northfarthing — probably not far from the north bounds.[10]

Lobelia Sackville-Baggins was originally a Bracegirdle from Hardbottle. The name means "hard dwelling"[11] so the town was probably in some rocky area such as the downs; but was it north or south, White or Far Downs? The Bracegirdles were shown in the area west of Girdley Island,[12] yet there was no indication of Hardbottle even in the nearby hills of Scary. The family owned many tobacco plantations, and the Sackville-Bagginses had land in South Farthing, so Hardbottle was placed on the White Downs at their south end.[13] Another village associated with the Sackville-Bagginses was never mentioned by Tolkien: Sack*ville.* The author used the name only as a surname, yet it seems reasonable to have been a village occupied by some members of the Sackville-Baggins family. The location was suggested by the Sackville-Bagginses' tobacco land in South Farthing and the connection between the Bagginses and the Bracegirdles.

The Gamgees may have originally come from West Farthing. Their hometown of Gamwich was probably close to Tighfield, for there was much migration between the two. Two things suggested placement of Tighfield in West Farthing: From Tighfield one cousin moved *to* Northfarthing, and Sam said his uncle ran a "ropewalk *over by* Tighfield."[14]

Once the villages had been placed, the cut-off roads were extended to them. The final product, although not authenticated, helps show the Shire as it was — well-settled, yet uncrowded, with lots of Hobbits but plenty of elbow room.

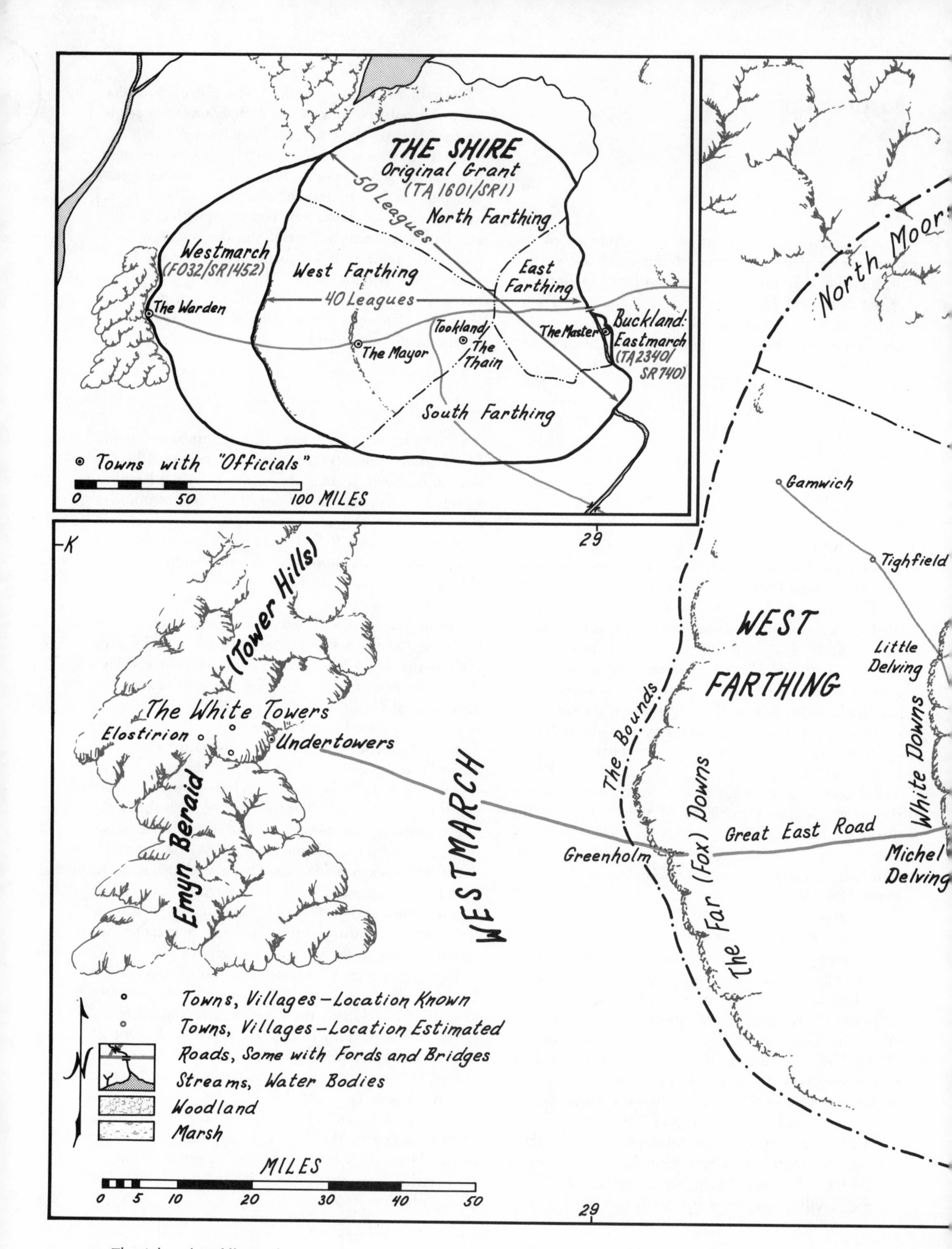
THE SHIRE
Original Grant
(TA 1601/SR1)
50 Leagues
North Farthing
Westmarch
(FO32/SR1452)
West Farthing
East
Farthing
40 Leagues
The Warden
Tookland
The Thain
The Mayor
The Master
Buckland:
Eastmarch
(TA2340/
SR740)
South Farthing
Towns with "Officials"
0
50
100 MILES
29
K
North Moors
Gamwich
Tighfield
(Tower Hills)
WEST
FARTHING
Little
Delving
The White Towers
Elostirion
Undertowers
The Bounds
White Downs
Emyn Beraid
WESTMARCH
The Far (Fox) Downs
Great East Road
Greenholm
Michel
Delving
Towns, Villages–Location Known
Towns, Villages–Location Estimated
Roads, Some with Fords and Bridges
Streams, Water Bodies
Woodland
Marsh
N
MILES
0
5
10
20
30
40
50
29

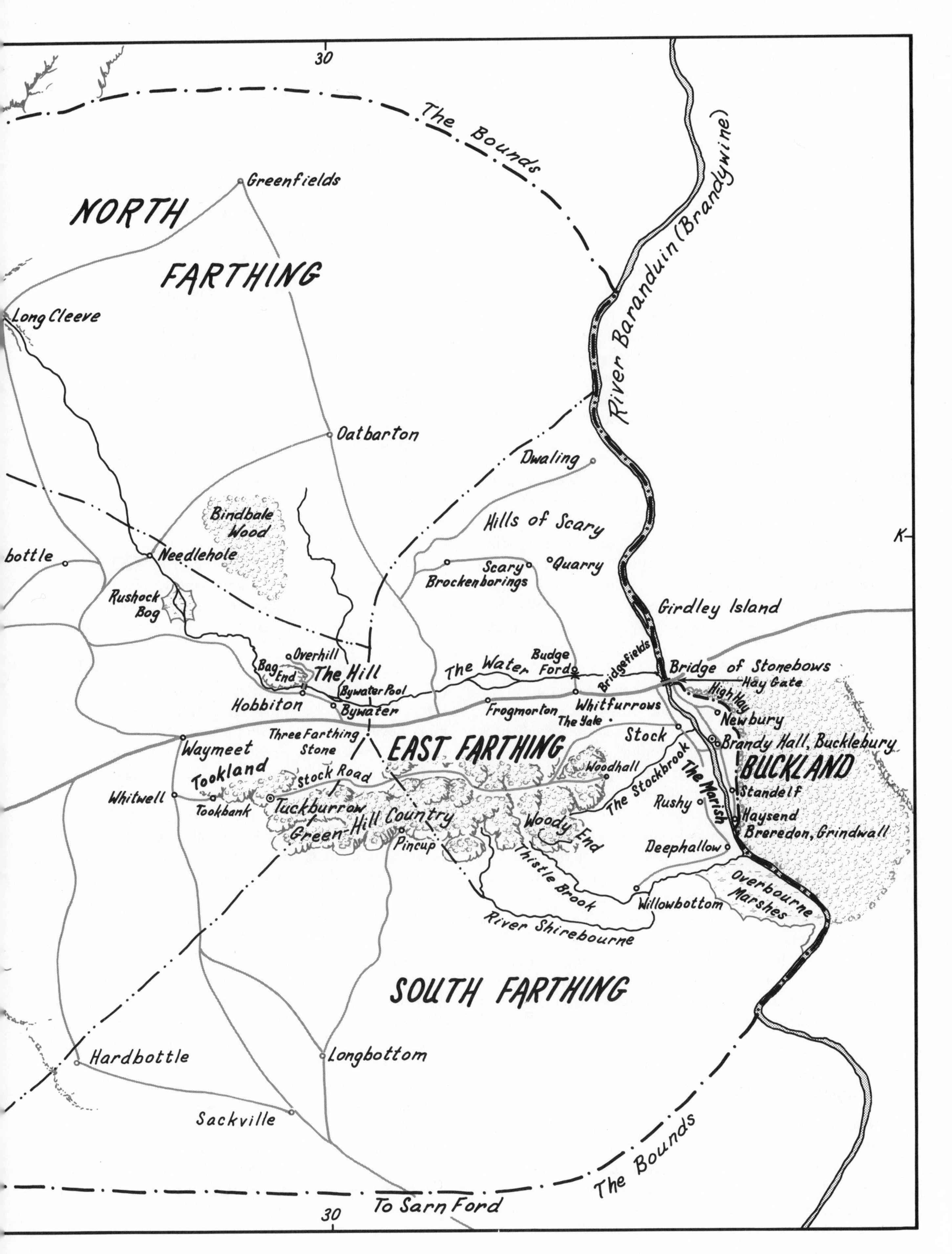

THE SHIRE Inset: POLITICAL DIVISIONS

Eriador

ERIADOR WAS THE NAME of all the lands between the Misty Mountains and the Blue.[1] On Tolkien's map the entire region appeared as one integrated whole, with a series of uplands whose longitudinal axes formed concentric rings.[2] Many of those uplands were *downs* — the Far (Fox) Downs, the White Downs, the North Downs, the South Downs, and the Barrow-downs. Interspersed with the downlands were the Hills of Evendim and the Tower Hills, which also fit the ring-like pattern; and the Green-Hill Country and the hills of Scary, which did not fit, but instead appeared to run perpendicular to the downlands.[3]

Some readers may have heard of downs, without understanding what they are (other than hills of some sort). Downs occur when layers of sedimentary rock dip away from hills or mountains and begin eroding back, peeling off layer after layer of rock. The more resistant rock layers stand up as long ridges, sometimes extending hundreds of miles,[4] while weaker sediments are eroded more quickly, forming lowlands. The ridges have a steep erosional face called the *scarp* and a long, gently dipping *backslope*.

Circular down ridges most often develop around a *dome*, such as the Wold and Downs near Fangorn. Less commonly, the concentric ridges could erode back from hills enclosing a broad round basin. Eriador centered on the Weather Hills, but also was almost encircled by the Blue Mountains on the west and northwest and the Misty Mountains on the east, northeast, and north; so its assorted downs could have been eroding back from either the central hills, or the outlying mountains, or both. The only clues given were about the Barrow-downs and Bree-hill and have been discussed in detail under that section. Evaluation of those two features has resulted in the illustration of Eriador as one gigantic round basin. This roughly circular shape was retained as a series of sedimentary layers eroded back over the eons of time — circular ridges and complementary lowlands.

The Weather Hills and the Midgewater Marshes

The sedimentary rock layer, which originally lay on the surface, was exposed to the erosional processes for the longest period of time. Gradually the outer edges of the layer were washed away, until at last the only portion left intact was the remnant towering almost a thousand feet above the surrounding landscape — the Weather Hills.[5] The ridges were barren and rocky, indicating that the bedrock was possibly a flinty limestone, such as in the Flint Hills of eastern Kansas. This permeable stone would have allowed such rapid downward percolation of water that tree growth could not have been supported because of excessive soil aridity. Some of the water, collecting in a crack, could have formed the spring found by Sam and Pippin at the foot of Weathertop.[6]

The underlying layer was less resistant, and its erosion resulted in a lowland. The low gradients there, coupled with continental glaciation that would have disrupted stream courses, left numerous bogs and marshes — the best-known being the Midgewater Marshes.

The Barrow-downs and Bree-hill

The third group of sediments was relatively resistant. From them were formed the North Downs, Barrow-downs, and the South Downs. Their scarps have been illustrated facing northwest, southwest, and south, respectively — away from the center of the bowl formation. No downlands were shown east of the Weather Hills. Their absence could have been due to any of several variables, including changes in gradient, dip, or rock type.

Only the Barrow-downs were described in any detail by Tolkien. They had no surface drainage and were rather barren, supporting only grasses. Therefore they must have been composed of a highly permeable rock, such as chalk.[7] To visualize the paths trod by the Hobbits, the orientation of the down ridges was of prime importance. Tolkien gave several clues, which had to be integrated: (1) As the Hobbits led their ponies north away from Bombadil's house, the "hill-brow" was so steep they had to dismount to climb it; yet they were able to ride easily down the gentle slope behind. (2) Continuing *north* toward the road, they climbed the steep face and descended the long backslope of ridge after ridge of hills. (3) When standing atop a hill looking *east*, the Hobbits could see "ridge behind ridge." (4) After leaving the hilltop on which they had been fogbound, the Hobbits rode *north* through a valley. (5) When Frodo heard cries for help he turned *east* and went steeply uphill.[8] Almost all of these references indicate that the down scarps faced south and the ridges themselves ran east–west. The long north–south valley was a series of *gaps* through the ridges.[9] This orientation, however, conflicts with the circular pattern of downs shown on the map, as well as with processes found in the real world — both of which require the downs to face more to the west. As a compromise, the long axis has been illustrated as trending from northwest to southeast — a reasonable explanation in view of the distinct southwesterly flow of the Withywindle.

Both the barren knob in the Old Forest and Bree-hill may have been associated geologically with the Barrow-downs. The knob was not far from the east edge of the forest; and when Bombadil guided the four Hobbits to the northwest edge of the downs, he told them they had to go only four miles to reach the Prancing Pony.[10]

The Shire

West of the inner ring of downs, the Brandywine lowland lay in an area of weak rock strata. The river course bulged westward from the North Downs to just north of Sarn Ford. Within the lowland two hilly areas cropped out: the Green-Hill Country and the hills of Scary. These probably were not downlands, for they ran perpendicular to the down ridges, and notably Tolkien did not call them downs. They may have been old hill remnants of highly resistant rock, covered by a veneer of weak sediments that later eroded away. In Northfarthing was still another formation — the North *Moors*.[11] Moors are poorly drained uplands that can occur on granite.[12] If that were the case in the Shire, the gray stones of the Green-Hill Country,[13] the rock quarried near Scary,[14] and the moorlands may all have been granite.

West of the Green-Hill Country lay the White Downs and the Far Downs. Nothing was told of the Far Downs, but the White Downs were certainly chalk. Not only was the name, based on the color of the bedrock, indicative, but poor Mayor Whitfoot was buried in chalk when the roof of the Town Hole collapsed.[15]

The Tower Hills and the Hills of Evendim

Tolkien noticeably chose to call these *hills,* rather than *downs,* even though at first glance at the pictorial *Lord of the Rings* map they appear to fall into the same pattern of concentric rings. Even so, it is evident that the Hills of Evendim were much more extensive than any of the downlands. The 'hatchured' maps in *The History* are more revealing, and clearly show the more complex topography.[16] As these hills lay near the Blue Mountains, they may have been folded rather than merely the product of erosion of sedimentary rock layers. The Tower Hills, although not more widespread, must also have been rather steep. In his dream, Frodo had to struggle to reach the White Towers on the ridge top.[17]

The Blue Mountains

The Ered Luin were little described, for they lay on the fringes of all Tolkien's tales. Their elevation must have been lower than that of the Misty Mountains, for the Blue Mountains did not form as significant a barrier to the early westward migrations. The range appeared to run in twin ridges in places — especially as shown on the map from *The Silmarillion.* These have been illustrated in the atlas as upfolded with their peaks eroded down by streams — a *breached anticline,* an erosional pattern most commonly occurring in sedimentary rock. The outer layers seem to have been underlaid by metamorphic rocks formed in contact with numerous igneous intrusions. This environment is often necessary to produce veins of ore such as those mined by Dwarves from the earliest days.[18]

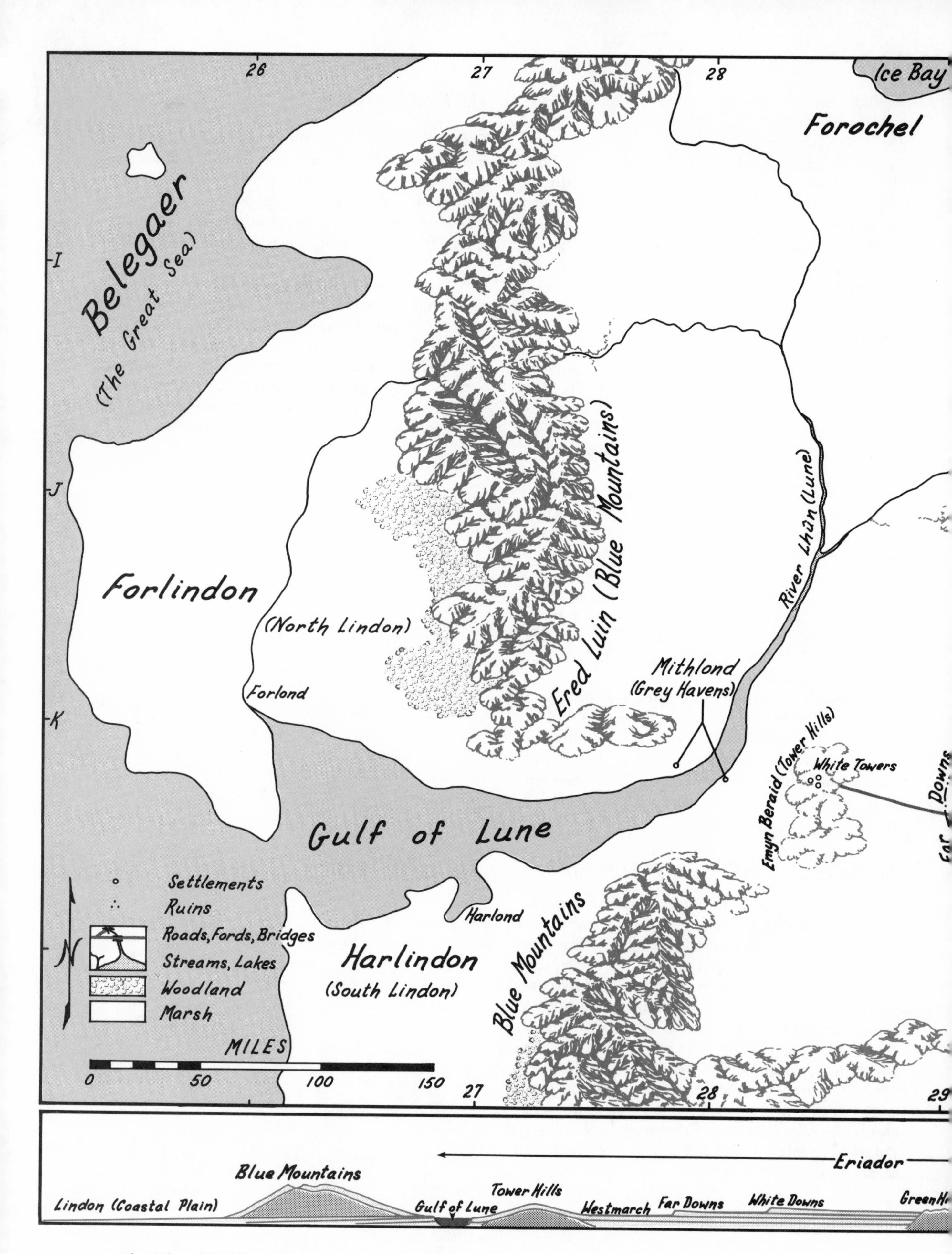
Ice Bay
Forochel
Belegaer
(The Great Sea)
Forlindon
(North Lindon)
Forlond
Ered Luin (Blue Mountains)
River Lhûn (Lune)
Mithlond
(Grey Havens)
Emyn Beraid (Tower Hills)
White Towers
Downs
Gulf of Lune
Harlond
Harlindon
(South Lindon)
Blue Mountains
Settlements
Ruins
Roads, Fords, Bridges
Streams, Lakes
Woodland
Marsh
MILES
0
50
100
150
26
27
28
29
I
J
K
Eriador
Blue Mountains
Tower Hills
Lindon (Coastal Plain)
Gulf of Lune
Westmarch
Far Downs
White Downs

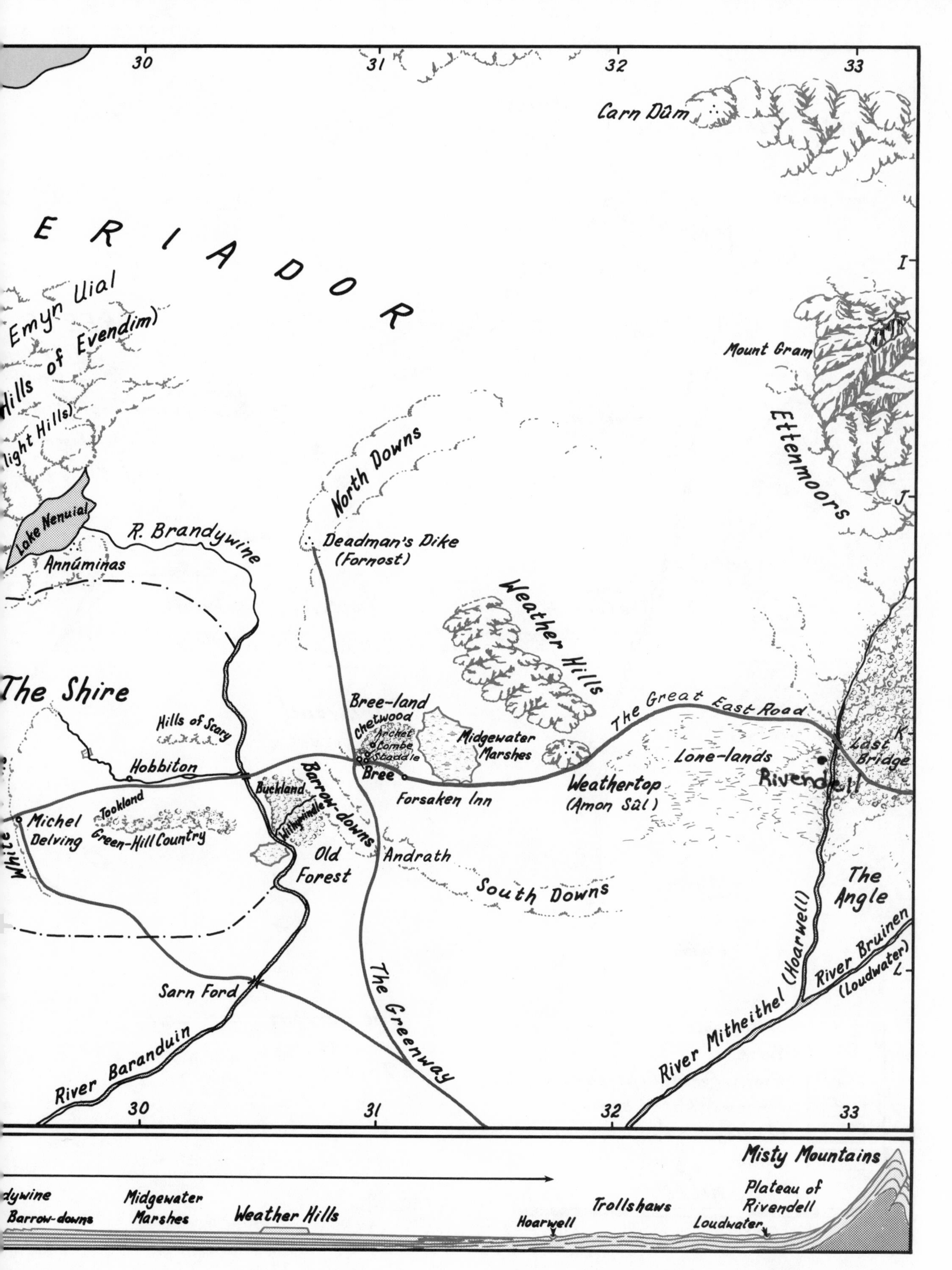

ERIADOR Cross Section: WEST–EAST (OFFSET WEST)

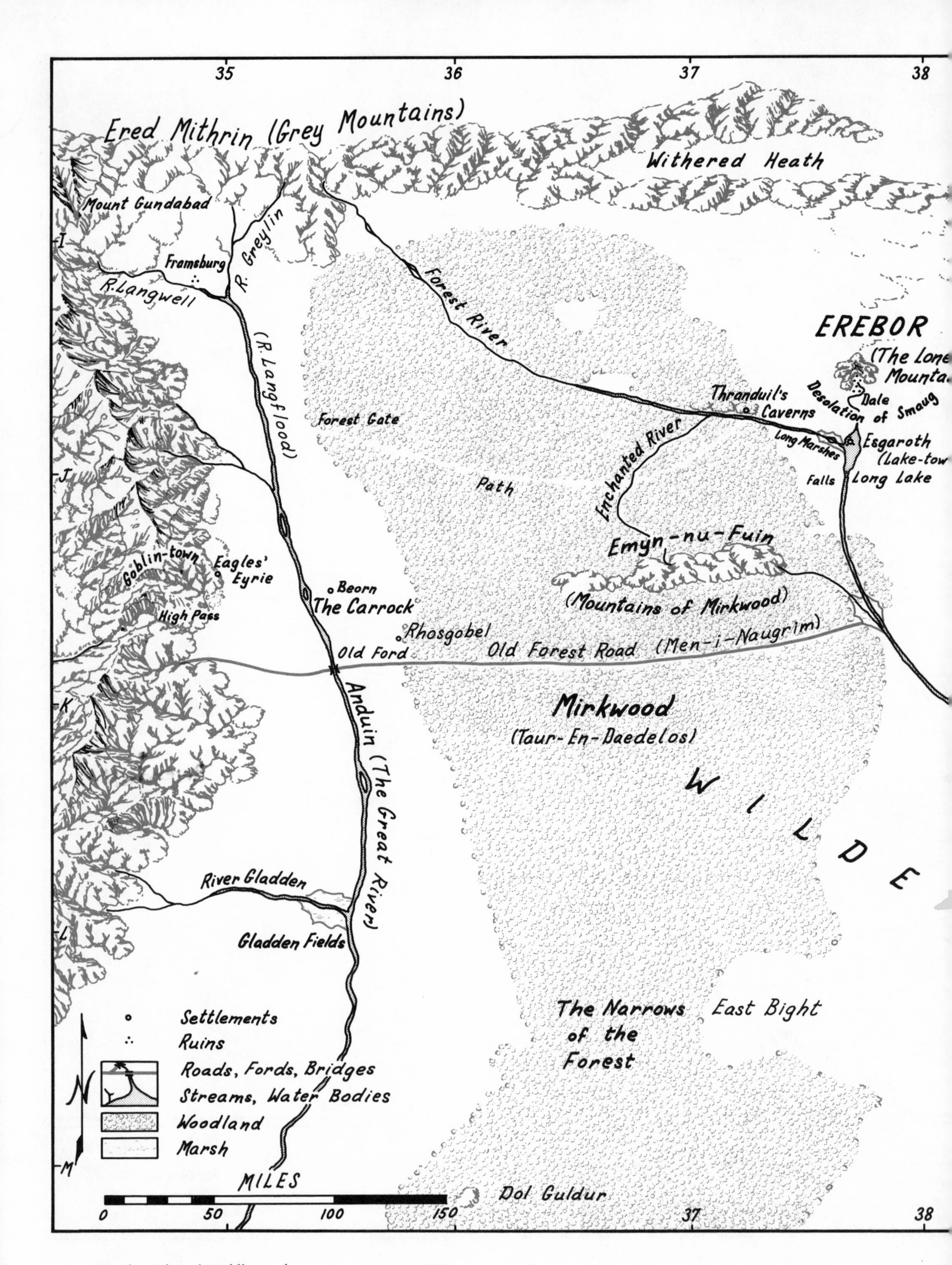

35
36
37
38
Ered Mithrin (Grey Mountains)
Withered Heath
Mount Gundabad
R. Greylin
Framsburg
R. Langwell
Forest River
EREBOR
(The Lone
Mounta
Thranduil's
Caverns
Desolation of Smaug
Dale
(R. Langflood)
Forest Gate
Enchanted River
Long Marshes
Esgaroth
(Lake-tow
Falls
Long Lake
Path
Emyn-nu-Fuin
(Mountains of Mirkwood)
Goblin-town
Eagles'
Eyrie
Beorn
The Carrock
High Pass
Rhosgobel
Old Ford
Old Forest Road (Men-i-Naugrim)
Anduin (The Great River)
Mirkwood
(Taur-En-Daedelos)
W I L D E
River Gladden
Gladden Fields
The Narrows
of the
Forest
East Bight
Settlements
Ruins
Roads, Fords, Bridges
Streams, Water Bodies
Woodland
Marsh
MILES
0
50
100
150
Dol Guldur
I
J
K
L
M
N

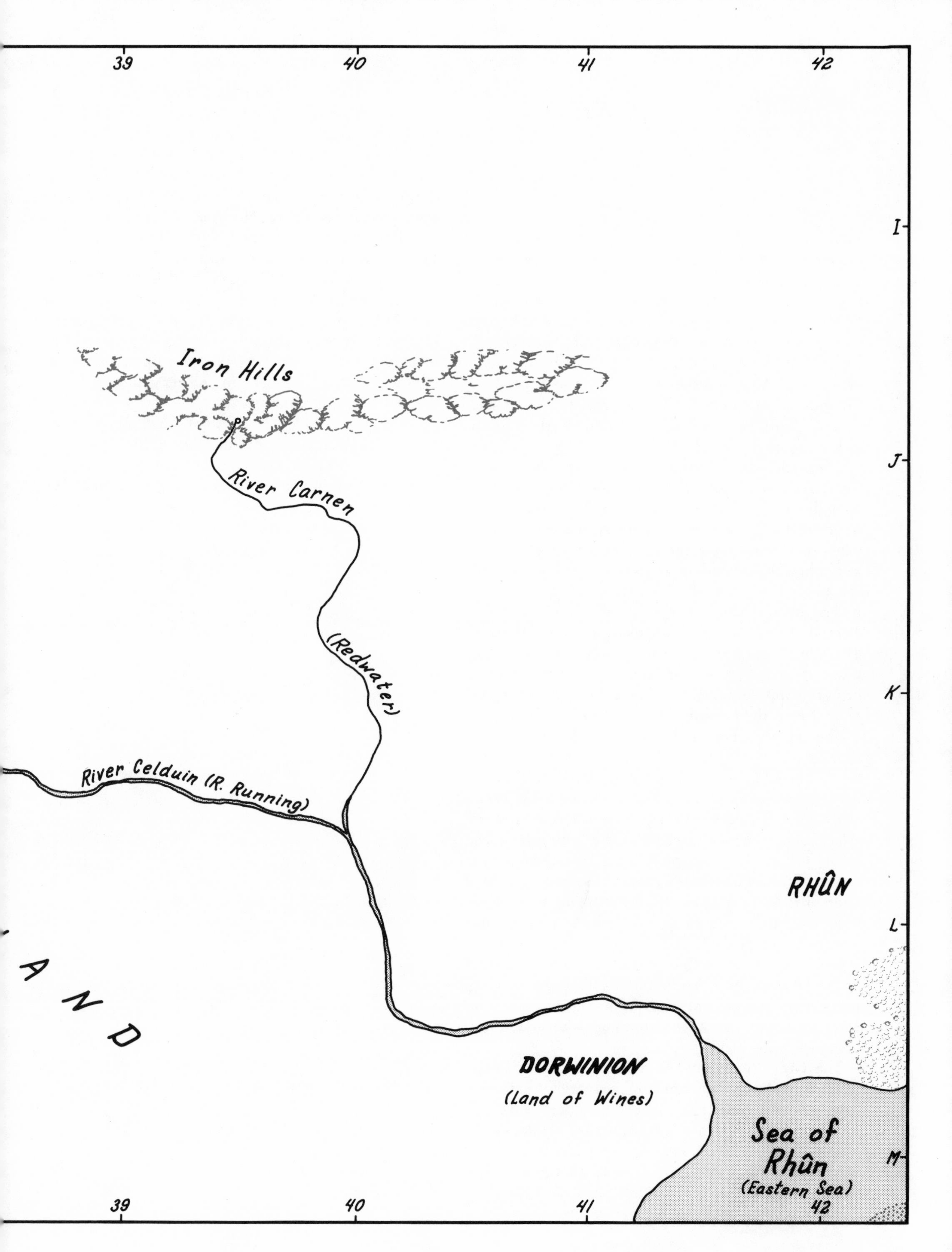
39
40
41
42
I
J
K
L
M
Iron Hills
River Carnen
(Redwater)
River Celduin (R. Running)
RHÛN
AND
DORWINION
(Land of Wines)
Sea of
Rhûn
(Eastern Sea)

Wilderland

WILDERLAND WAS SHOWN ON TOLKIEN'S MAP as synonymous with Rhovanion;[1] yet a broader definition would include all of the lands east of the Ford of Bruinen and north of Lorien — the area known as "The Wild."[2] Less has been said about this region because, perhaps, there was less to be said, and because fewer clues were given. Only three things were evident: (1) Soluble limestone probably was present at Thranduil's dwellings; (2) continental glaciation had occurred; and (3) crystalline rock formed the core of at least some of the hills.

The path across Mirkwood taken by Thorin and Company was apparently fairly level but had just enough ups and downs to prevent Bilbo from even noticing that he was at the bottom of a wide valley when he climbed the great oak.[3] This bowl-like valley might have been a hollow — that is, a valley in which the water seeps into the limestone and flows out in underground rivers. It was close enough to King Thranduil's to be in a soluble limestone bedrock. Thranduil's underground palace, complete with columns of "living stone" and "underground river,[4] were probably limestone solution caverns, reportedly enhanced with the assistance of Dwarves.[5]

The extensive bogs and marshes at the end of both forest roads, the Long Marshes along the Forest River, the "tumbled land" between Lonely Mountain and its nearest neighbors to the northeast,[6] and most especially the description of Long Lake, all point toward effects of continental glaciation. The "shingles" piled at the feet of the promontory near Lake-town[7] could easily have resulted from glacial till — a conglomeration of rocks ranging from gravels to boulders, which the glacier had captured and carried along. Most importantly, Long Lake "filled what must once have been a great deep rocky valley."[8] It is reminiscent of the finger lakes of New York. South of Long Lake the ruggedness was absent, for, between the eaves of Mirkwood and the River Running, Rhovanion had occupied "wide plains."[9]

The Grey Mountains, Iron Hills, and the Lonely Mountain all were richly mineralized. Erebor harbored both gold and jewels, the most fabulous being the Arkenstone.[10] The major yield of the Iron Hills is self-evident. No specific references were made to the products of the Grey Mountains, only that they were rich.[11]

The Grey Mountains may originally have been part of the extensive Iron Mountains. This assumption was based on three clues: (1) Once the location of Thangorodrim was set, the approximate position of the Iron Mountains aligned perfectly with this later range.[12] The great parent chain might have been only partially destroyed by the Valar, leaving remnants scattered across Middle-earth. (2) North of the Ered Engrin lay the "Regions of Everlasting Cold."[13] North of the Ered Mithrin was the "Northern Waste."[14] These may have been synonymous. (3) Dragons bred in the Withered Heaths even before the coming of Thorin I in the Third Age.[15] Orcs long held the area around Mt. Gundabad.[16] Both of these were creatures of Morgoth, and with the breaking of Thangorodrim, the most likely relocation for them would have been in any remaining portions of the Iron Mountains.

All things considered, Wilderland had much potential but was historically plagued by evil Men and creatures — Easterlings, Orcs, Trolls, dragons, wolves. In spite of long years of settlement it still remained "The Wild."

The Misty Mountains

The towering Mountains of Mist were undoubtedly one of the most important features in Middle-earth. It is quite likely that they, as well as the White Mountains, were inspired by the European Alps, in which Tolkien had hiked in 1911.[1] The Hithaeglir, raised by Melkor early in the First Age as a hindrance to the riding of Oromë, were a barrier to early westward migrations[2] and to the quests of both Bilbo and Frodo. The north–south orientation of some 900 miles would also have blocked the predominating moist winds from the west. The orographic lifting, possibly to as high as 12,000 feet,[3] would have produced the cloudy conditions that not only gave the range its name, but that were more locally important in naming Fanuidhol (Cloudyhead), and especially in producing the tremendous thunder-battle from which Thorin and Company sought shelter.[4]

Landscape Morphology

Few clues were given by Tolkien to allow any analysis of the forces involved in producing the Misty Mountains. If they were comparable to the Alps, they would have been formed by a complex mixture of faulting, folding, doming, and volcanic activity.[5] This ruggedness extended into the area west of the mountains, producing tortuous lands all the way from the Ettenmoors in the North,[6] through the extremely dissected plateau around Rivendell with its many gullies, ravines, and deep valleys,[7] the tumbled hill lands traversed by the Nine Walkers in Eregion,[8] and down to the hilly wastelands of Dunland.[9] East of the range the Anduin followed a relatively straight course amidst a broad green valley until it reached the wolds south of Lórien.

The one process clearly in action at some time was alpine glaciation. Two of Tolkien's key terms were features left behind by abrading ice: *horn,* the sharp-pointed peak cut by ice on three or more sides; and *trough,* a valley eroded by a glacier until it is U-shaped — broad, with steep walls. Some other landforms described by Tolkien also appeared glacial in origin. For example, an advancing glacier may form *rock steps,* while a retreating one may leave *recessional moraines.* Either process could dam lakes or *tarns* that might empty over the dam in falls or rapids.[10] Many of these features were found in the region of Moria: Caradhras meant the Red*horn;*[11] after defeating the Balrog, Gandalf lay atop Silvertine on the "hard horn";[12] just past the point where the Nine Walkers turned back from the Redhorn Pass, the path ran "in a wide shallow *trough*";[13] and the Silverlode went "leaping down to the *trough* of the valley."[14] Rapids bubbled down the Dimrill *Stair* into the Mirrormere. The Mirrormere itself was a classic example of a moraine-dammed lake — "long and oval thrusting into the upper dell." The Silverlode did not, however, empty directly from the lake but filtered through the loose till of the moraine and appeared from an icy spring about a mile below. Together with a tributary it plunged over a fall downstream at what may have been still another moraine.[15] The valley at the west gate of Moria was possibly also glacially carved, for it was relatively flat, with towering walls, and the lake dammed by the otherworldly agent was typically long and narrow.[16]

Because alpine glaciation appeared in the central part of the mountains, it had probably occurred in the higher elevations throughout the range — especially in the colder north. Tolkien's drawing of the Goblins' gate as viewed from the eagles' eyrie[17] and his description of the peaks as "spikes of rocks"[18] reinforced the impression of jagged mountaintops. Even in the south, tall Methedras was snowcapped.[19]

Rock Type

Mountain ranges usually have as complex a mixture of rock types as they have mountain-forming processes. In the Misty Mountains only three types of clues could aid in discerning the bedrock: color, minerals, and landforms.

Most of the colors mentioned were not pertinent to the main range but to the hill lands to its west. Red stone was mentioned near both Rivendell and Moria. In the Trollshaws the East Road cut through "moist walls of red stone"[20] on its last leg, descending to the Ford of Bruinen, where the Black Riders attacked. In the western part of the Trollshaws Thorin and Company crossed a "rushing red" river, indicative that it was carrying sediment from the red soil (although if this were the Mitheithel ["*grey*-spring"], red may not have been its usual color).[21] Near Moria the Fellowship scrambled through a barren country of "red stones" north of the Sirannon, which also had "brown and red-stained stones [on] its bed."[22] The rock west of Moria may have been the same as that west of Rivendell. It could have been either sandstone or quartzite, for both of those can be red.

In the mountain range itself, only Caradhras was noted as the "*Red*horn," while the other mountain rock was described as gray.[23] It seems unlikely that Caradhras, the tallest of the Mountains of Moria, would have been composed of the same red rock found

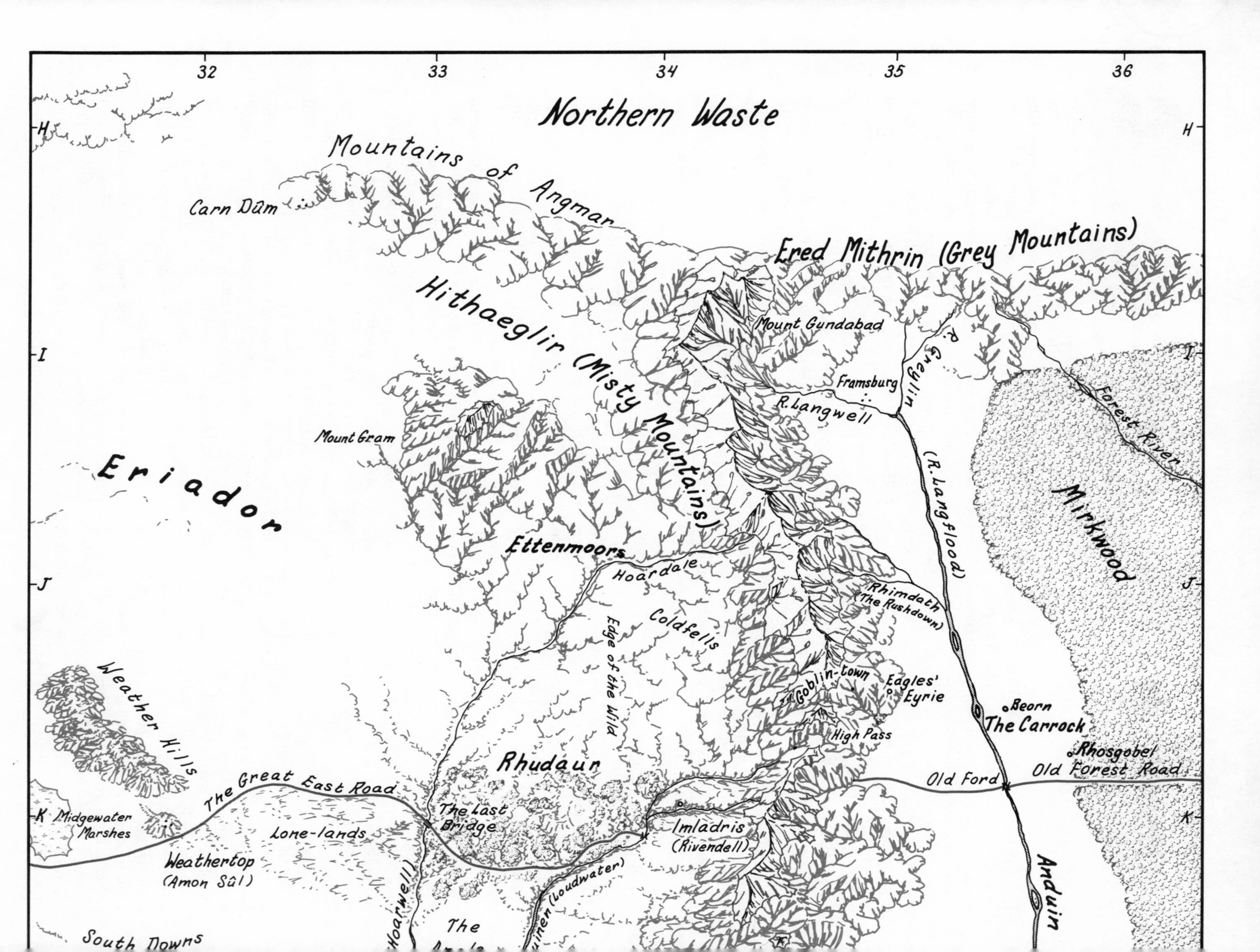

32
33
34
35
36
H
I
J
K
Northern Waste
Mountains of Angmar
Carn Dûm
Ered Mithrin (Grey Mountains)
Hithaeglir (Misty Mountains)
Mount Gundabad
R. Greylin
Framsburg
R. Langwell
(R. Langflood)
Forest River
Mirkwood
Mount Gram
Eriador
Ettenmoors
Hoardale
Rhimdath (The Rushdown)
Coldfells
Edge of the Wild
Goblin-town
Eagles' Eyrie
Beorn
The Carrock
High Pass
Rhosgobel
Old Forest Road
Old Ford
Rhudaur
Weather Hills
The Great East Road
The Last Bridge
Midgewater Marshes
Lone-lands
Imladris (Rivendell)
Weathertop (Amon Sûl)
(Loudwater)
Hoarwell
The
Anduin
South Downs

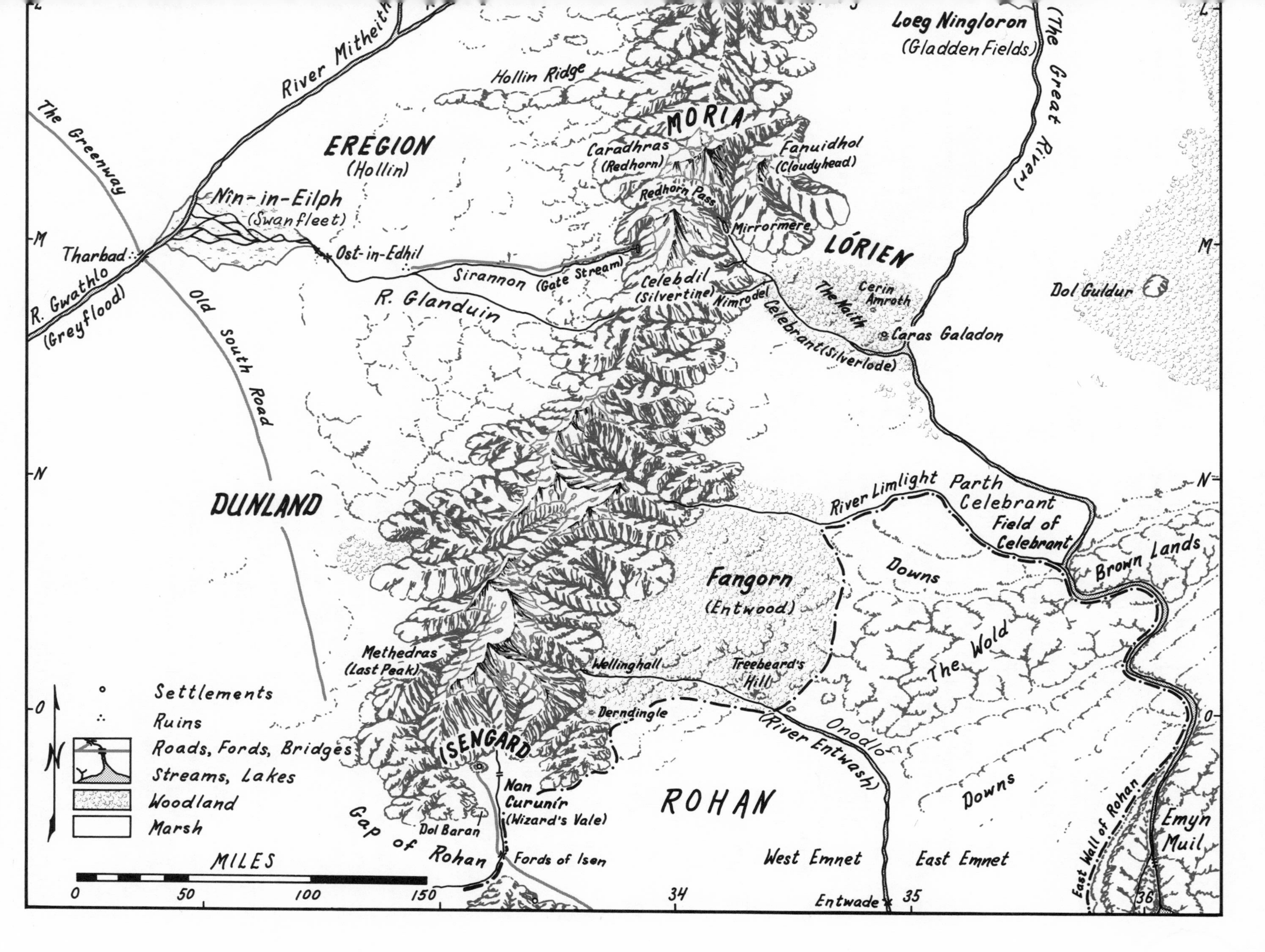

River Mitheithel
Hollin Ridge
Loeg Ningloron
(Gladden Fields)
(The Great River)
The Greenway
EREGION
(Hollin)
MORIA
Caradhras
(Redhorn)
Fanuidhol
(Cloudyhead)
Nîn-in-Eilph
(Swanfleet)
Redhorn Pass
Mirrormere
Tharbad
Ost-in-Edhil
LÓRIEN
R. Gwathlo
(Greyflood)
Sirannon (Gate Stream)
Celebdil
(Silvertine)
Nimrodel
The Naith
Cerin Amroth
Dol Guldur
R. Glanduin
Old South Road
Celebrant (Silverlode)
Caras Galadon
River Limlight
Parth Celebrant
Field of Celebrant
DUNLAND
Brown Lands
Downs
Fangorn
(Entwood)
The Wold
Methedras
(Last Peak)
Wellinghall
Treebeard's Hill
Derndingle
Onodlo
(River Entwash)
ISENGARD
Nan Curunír
(Wizard's Vale)
Dol Baran
Gap of Rohan
Fords of Isen
ROHAN
Downs
East Wall of Rohan
Emyn Muil
West Emnet
East Emnet
Entwade
Settlements
Ruins
Roads, Fords, Bridges
Streams, Lakes
Woodland
Marsh
MILES
0
50
100
150
34
35
36
L
M
N
O

in the foothills — especially as the other peaks were obviously of different material. One of two things may have accounted for its color: Its bedrock was a third rock type not present in either the foothills or the surrounding mountains, or its bedrock was not red at all but merely reflected rays of the rising sun.[24]

One additional factor may shed light on the subject — mineralization. The lodes of mithril, an ore found nowhere else, were "north towards Caradhras, and down to darkness."[25] Veins of precious ores normally result from repeated igneous intrusions into faults.[26] If intrusions had occurred, extrusions might have also been present; and the Redhorn might have been an isolated peak of igneous rock, such as andesite porphyry, which is dull pink or red.[27]

The other mountains in the area were, as mentioned, gray at the surface. So many rock types are gray that it would be futile to attempt any discussion without further information. The rock at the core, however, was probably crystalline. Moria was a highly mineralized area, with lode veins of silver, gold, and iron. The jewels of Moria, "beryl, pearl, and opal pale,"[28] were such an unlikely mixture that some may not have been mined there at all. Instead, they were perhaps received in trade — especially the pearls, which are usually "mined" from fresh- or saltwater animals, not rock, unless of course they referred to cave pearls, which sometimes can form in gypsum cavern systems.[29] Perhaps a better explanation is that Tolkien originally listed rubies instead — a gem that would have been far more likely to occur with the others.[30]

It is difficult to determine if any of the formations elsewhere in the mountains were the same as those at Moria. Similar processes may have been involved in the south, for not only was Isengard volcanic,[31] but the ore for the copper and iron pillars was probably mined in that vicinity.[32]

In the northern part of the range where Thorin and Company "toured" the Goblin-tunnels, a very different process was present — cavern formation. Gollum's cave, complete with its slimy island and subterranean lake that emptied into a dark stream,[33] would probably have been in soluble limestone. Blocks of a more resistant limestone may have constituted the "wide steep slope of fallen stones" that the Dwarves disturbed in their flight from the Goblins.[34] The same rock may have formed the "wide shelf" on the outlying mountain where the eagles made their eyries.[35] As illustrated by Tolkien, the peak appeared to be capped by layers of limestone.[36]

Rivers and Roads

In one respect this revised map differs from both the prior *Atlas* and *The Lord of the Rings* map: the course of the River Bruinen and the route of the Great East Road between Weathertop and the Ford of Bruinen. As more material became available in print, Tolkien eventually decided, "'. . . where this is possible and does not damage the story, to take the *maps* as "correct" and adjust the narrative.'"[37] This was apparently part of the decision-making process in the Second Edition of *The Lord of the Rings*. The First Edition "shows the Road running along the Loudwater 'for many leagues to the Ford'" while in the Second Edition, this was changed to read "'along the edge of the hills.'"[38] The river course shown here is a compromise based on the more detailed analysis in *The History*.

Tolkien's original maps showed much wider curves of the Great East Road, but when redrafted for publication by Christopher Tolkien, the latter in retrospect realized that he had flattened the curves of the road:

> In 1943 I made an elaborate map . . . the course of the Road from Weathertop to the Ford is shown exactly as on my father's maps, with the great northward and southward swings. On the map that I made in 1954 . . . however, the Road has only a feeble northward curve between Weathertop and the Hoarwell Bridge, and then runs in a straight line to the Ford.[39]

Here, as with the River Bruinen, the map has been revised to reflect Tolkien's original intent, as clarified on two sketch maps from *The History*.[40]

The Brown Lands, the Wold, The Downs, and the Emyn Muil

TOLKIEN MAPPED AND REMAPPED this area repeatedly, changing far more than just names. Four distinct designs showed the evolution of the hill lands through which the Anduin flowed. In the first map Nen Hithoel was 120 miles north, lying just south of the Green Hills, which ran east–west in much the same location as shown for the Wold and the Brown Lands. The Border Hills further south lay roughly in the location of the Eastern Emyn Muil.[1] As Nen Hithoel shifted south, three additional maps displayed the development of the Emyn Muil (then called the Sarn Gebir, although that term eventually applied only to the rapids.)[2] The hills were first shown as a simple east–west ridge, then gradually became a complexly curved series of ridges centering on the lake.[3] While the maps did not show as clearly the formations of the Wold area, the illustrations here are carefully designed to fit both story and Primary World features and processes.

All of these areas were related in rock type and morphology. They have been interpreted as layers of sediment gently folded along a southwest–northeast axis. The result was a broad upfold or *anticline* that narrowed to the northeast. This was complemented by a downfold or *syncline* that narrowed to the southwest. The Brown Lands, the Wold, and the Downs were all upfolded; the Emyn Muil, downfolded. At the eastern edge of the fold the strata not only bent but broke, forming the cliffwall which Sam and Frodo had such difficulty descending.

The Brown Lands, the Wold, and the Downs

Wold is a Middle English term comparable to the west Saxon *weald,* a forested area.[4] In southeastern England there is a domed region of hills called "The Weald." Tolkien's Wold structurally was very similar, although unforested. It, too, was an upfolded ridge or *anticline,* from which sedimentary layers, with varying degrees of resistance, eroded back to form concentric rings of hills — the Downs.

Downlands occurred both north and south of the Wold. The company floated past the north downs after passing the Limlight. Several days later the great race toward Isengard took much of the company along the western edge of the south downs. Ten miles west lay the Entwash.[5] The hills were drier than the valley bottoms, so the Orcs held close to them for more solid footing.

These hills were low because the strata were relatively thin. They sloped away gently from the center of the Wold but had a much steeper drop facing inward — "green slopes rising to bare ridges."[6] The sediments may have been chalk, a type of limestone. The Downs of England are chalk and are so permeable that they "are notoriously short of water and are used as grazing lands for sheep."[7] The downs north of the Wold were "rolling downs of withered grass,"[8] and those to the south were "long treeless slopes"[9] at whose feet "the ground was dry and turf short. . . ."[10]

The Wold was described as bleak and treeless, and higher than the Downs. The Wold and the Brown Lands were actually parts of the same feature, merely bisected by the Anduin. The resistant rock was highly dissected. The Wold might have been suited to some cultivation just as the Brown Lands had once flourished under the care of the Entwives before the Enemy "blasted all that region."[11]

As in the Weald of England, a valley probably lay between the Wold and the in-facing escarpments of the Downs — both north and south. The intersections of these valleys with the west bends of the Anduin created the North and South Undeeps that were utilized by both the Balchoth and the Éothéod for easier river-crossing at the Battle of Celebrant.[12]

The Emyn Muil

Just as the varying thickness and degree of resistance played a role in the formation of the Wold and the Downs, they continued to do so in the Emyn Muil. These strata were much thicker than those of the Downs. Three main layers of downfolded sediment composed the rocky land. These were most clearly apparent in the western Emyn Muil, where "the Highlands . . . ran from North to South in two long tumbled ridges."[13] The three layers appeared as: (1) the inner eastern ridge, which was the highest, and therefore thickest, layer; (2) the outer western ridge, which was about 120 feet thick, for it stood "twenty fathoms"[14] above the third layer; (3) the "wide and rugged shelf which ended suddenly in the brink of a sheer cliff: the East Wall of Rohan."[15]

The inner layer of strata had been eroded back from all directions, leaving only a bowl-shaped remnant, known as a *synclinal valley.* It had relatively long inward slopes and steep outfacing cliffs. The rapids of Sarn Gebir churned through the northern cliffwall of this layer. The rock closest to the river at this location was highly eroded, leaving "chimneys." The limestone must have been chemically dissolved in some parts, for there were some features of *karst topography,* such

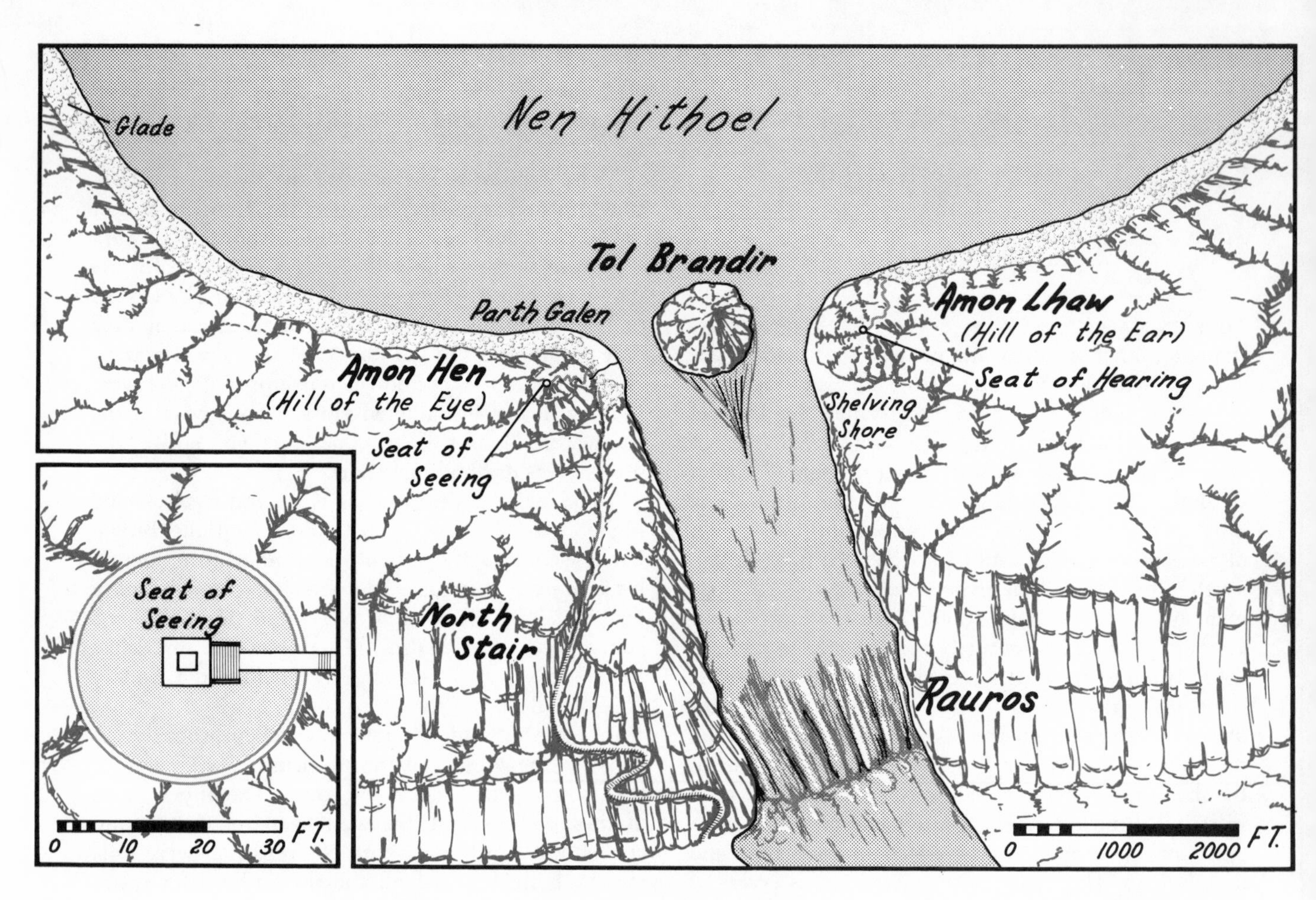

RAUROS Inset: AMON HEN

as that found in the Mammoth Cave (Kentucky) area of the United States and the Dalmatian region of Yugoslavia. Where rock below the surface had been dissolved and the overlying strata collapsed, varying sizes of *sinkholes* occurred. So as the Fellowship toiled in the mile between the river and the portage-way, they came upon many "hidden holes" and "sheer dales."[16]

Between Sarn Gebir and the Argonath the river had eroded down sharply, so that cliffs rose "to unguessed heights on either side."[17] Nen Hithoel, the lake behind the natural dam of the southern ridge, also lay at the base of high cliffs. These cliffs had been eroded somewhat, and alluvial terraces were left at their feet, such as the lawn of Parth Galen and the "shelving shore" where Sam and Frodo hid their boat.[18] South of the lake the river must have downcut through the ridge, leaving behind three hills. On the west and east were Amon Hen and Amon Lhaw, the Hills of the Eye and the Ear, with their battlemented summits and high stone seats of Seeing and Hearing. In the center, surrounded by rushing waters, stood Tol Brandir.[19] Beyond that isle the three layers converged, forming the cliff over which Rauros pounded. So sheer was the drop that portaging was possible only by descending the ancient North Stair.[20]

As Aragorn, Gimli, and Legolas pursued the Orcs, they climbed westward up the more gradual eastern slope, then down a deep valley on the west. At the base of the cliff a "dale ran like a stony trough between the ridge hills."[21] This valley marked the separation of the two major rock strata. The outer ridge conformed to the pattern of the inner. It had a gentle slope rising away from the creekbed and a steep escarpment facing the plains of Rohan.

East of Nen Hithoel, Sam and Frodo must have crossed the same layers, but differences in slope, some faulting, and other factors replaced the two distinct ridges and shelf of the western Emyn Muil with a "strange twisted knot of hills."[22] There was evidently a fault line at the eastern edge, highest in the south. Northward "the cliff-top was sinking towards the level of the plains."[23]

Erosion and mass wasting probably made the tumbled land where the cliff had "slipped and cracked . . . leaving great fissures and long slanting ledges that in places were almost as wide as stairs."[24] Still, the end of the gully towered about 108 feet (eighteen fathoms),[25] and most of Sam's rope of "thirty ells, more or less"[26] was required to help them escape the Emyn Muil at last.

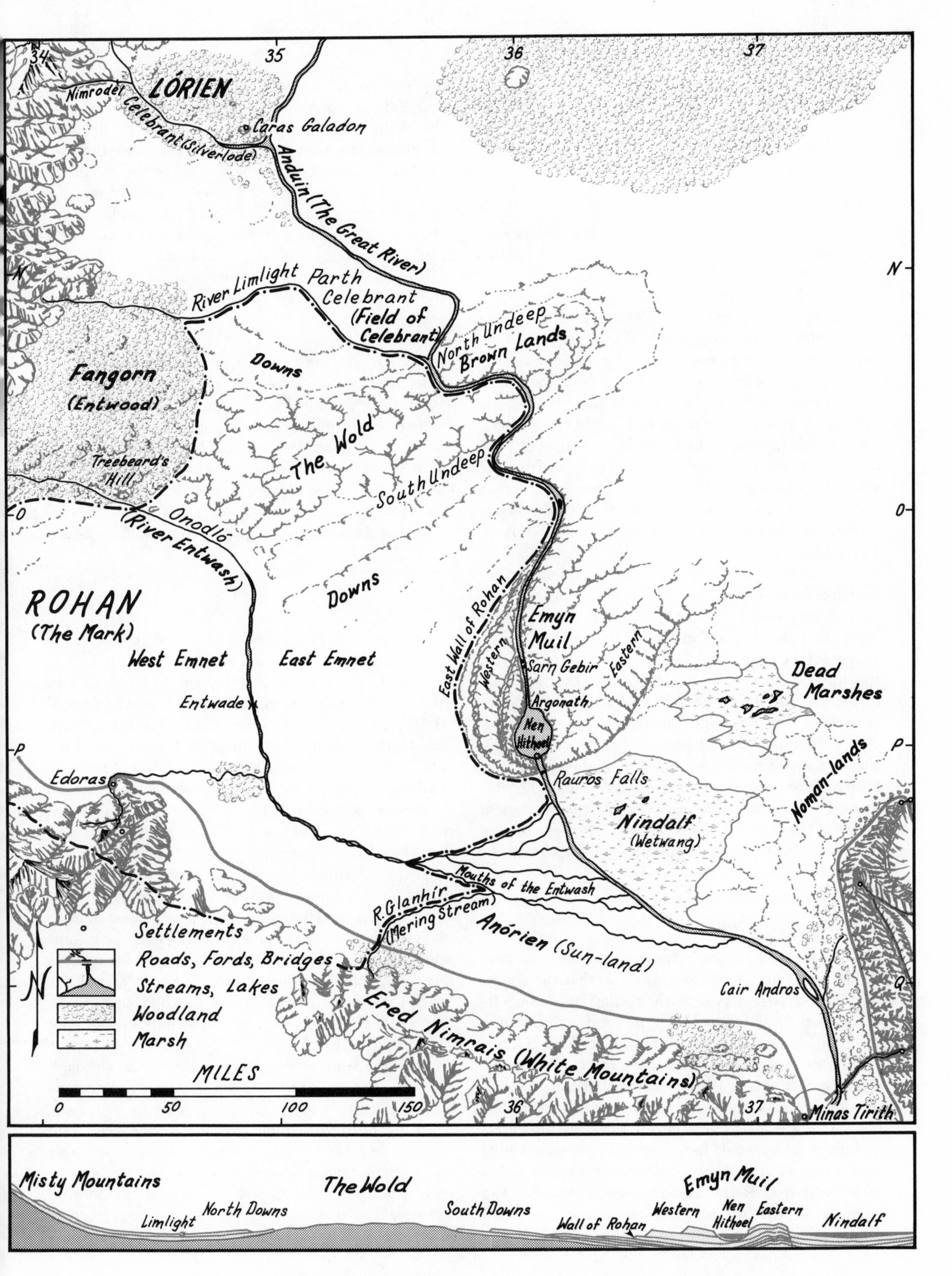
34
35
36
37
LÓRIEN
Nimrodel
Celebrant (Silverlode)
Caras Galadon
Anduin (The Great River)
N
River Limlight
Parth Celebrant (Field of Celebrant)
North Undeep
Brown Lands
Fangorn (Entwood)
Downs
The Wold
Treebeard's Hill
South Undeep
O
Onodló (River Entwash)
Downs
ROHAN (The Mark)
East Wall of Rohan
Emyn Muil
Western
Eastern
Sarn Gebir
Argonath
Nen Hithoel
West Emnet
East Emnet
Entwade
Dead Marshes
P
Noman-lands
Edoras
Rauros Falls
Nindalf (Wetwang)
Mouths of the Entwash
R. Glanhír (Mering Stream)
Anórien (Sun-land)
Settlements
Roads, Fords, Bridges
Streams, Lakes
Woodland
Marsh
Cair Andros
Q
Ered Nimrais (White Mountains)
MILES
0
50
100
150
Minas Tirith
Misty Mountains
The Wold
Emyn Muil
Limlight
North Downs
South Downs
Wall of Rohan
Western
Nen Hithoel
Eastern
Nindalf

THE HILL-LANDS Cross Section: NORTH-NORTHWEST TO SOUTH-SOUTHEAST

The White Mountains

THE SECOND MAJOR RANGE of mountains spanned some 600 miles, west to east. The White Mountains were present in the First Age[1] and were quite likely raised at the same time as the Towers of Mist. Their northern arm even appeared to be an extension of that north-south range, merely eroded away at the Gap of Rohan. West of Dunharrow and south of Helm's Deep, where the forces forming the east–west and the north–south ranges met, the land was heaved upward and tortuously twisted into a *knot.* There were probably some of the highest peaks in the known lands of Middle-earth (after the destruction of Thangorodrim and the Iron Mountains) — possibly even higher than those of the Alps. Many other portions of the White Mountains must also have been as high as most of the Misty Mountains, or higher, in order to remain snowcapped at the more southerly latitude. Tolkien's contour-like lines on the map in *The Return of the King* gave the impression that Mt. Mindolluin and the Starkhorn were hardly higher than the heights of the Emyn Muil or the Ephel Dúath; yet those peaks were snowcapped, while the other highlands were not. Originally, Tolkien stated the White (then 'Black') Mountains were "not very high, but very steep on the north side."[2] At least the first part of this view must have changed, for to have been snowcapped they must have been at least 9500 feet in elevation.[3] Also, either due to elevation or rugged topography or a combination of the two, there were apparently no passes, or Aragorn would not have been desperate enough to hazard the Paths of the Dead.

Landscape Morphology

Once again Tolkien gave clues that alpine glaciation had occurred in at least the area of Dunharrow. Stark*horn* had a jagged peak with everlasting snow.[4] Irensaga was "saw-toothed"[5] — an apt description of a series of jagged peaks formed by the heads of glaciers, or *cirques,* cutting back until they meet, forming *arêtes.* Even at this southerly latitude, glaciers had apparently extended into the main vale of the Snowbourn. It was deep, with steep sides, as any great mountain valley would have been. The clues indicating glaciation were the width of a "little more than half a mile" where Théoden's riders crossed[6] and the two tributary valleys that hung high above the floor of the main vale. The stream in the western valley ran in a "narrow gorge" and emptied over the cliff in "waterfalls,"[7] so it was probably not glaciated, even though the main vale was. East across the river the road of Púkel-men slowly wound up the towering cliff "hundreds of feet above the valley" to the "wide upland . . . the Firienfeld."[8] The glen ran deep into the mountains until it ended at the "sheer wall" of the Haunted Mountain.[9] This high dell was typical of a glaciated *hanging valley* — broad and long, with the glacier having scoured steep walls along the sides and shattered the rock at its head, forming a crowning amphitheater.[10]

Glacial landforms were not mentioned elsewhere in the range, although they may have been present — especially in the "knot." Atypically, the Stonewain Valley was described as a "trough," but its low elevation would indicate it was not glacial, so the term may have been applied loosely. The valley could have been stream-cut, although there was no stream there in the Third Age. It could have been a fault or a downfold, or it might not have been a natural feature at all but a colossal stone quarry, as implied by Ghân-buri-Ghân.[11]

Rock Type

Only two rock types can be identified in the White Mountains with any assurance: limestone (metamorphosed into marble in certain areas) and intrusive igneous. Soluble limestone was evident in the area of Helm's Deep and can be inferred near Mt. Mindolluin, due to the proximity of limestone formations in the Emyn Muil, the Downs, and North Ithilien. The white walls of Minas Tirith were probably locally quarried limestone of resistant type. The Tower of Ecthelion that "glimmered like a spike of pearl and silver"[12] may have been white marble.

The Glittering Caves of Aglarond were basically found in a soluble limestone layer. The formations were typical of extensive cavern systems — columns, wings, ropes, curtains, underground pools. Less common were the "gems, crystals and veins of precious ore,"[13] which could have been the result of igneous intrusions. Some of the finest rubies and sapphires in our world are found as secondary deposits in solution cavities in northern Burma.[14] No mention was made of any ore deposits elsewhere in the range, although the exclusion certainly does not mean they were nonexistent.

In contrast to Aglarond, the Paths of the Dead were as "dry as dust."[15] Dry caverns can occur as upper galleries, but no cavern-type formations were mentioned, so they probably were not solution cavities. Instead, they may have resulted from water, frost, or even lava enlarging existing cracks and joints, then evacuating the channel. The Paths may have resulted from any of these causes, or may even have been mined in whole or in part. The color clues in the area support the possibility of igneous rock, which is often black. The sunrise view revealed peaks that were "white-tipped and streaked with black,"[16] and the Haunted Mountain was called "black Dwimorberg."[17]

In spite of the predominance of white rock used in the construction of Minas Tirith, the hill itself may have been volcanic. The outer wall was the same invincible black rock as that forming Orthanc, and the "vast pier of rock" could easily have been a weather resistant 'dike' such as those sometimes found in extinct, eroding volcanic cones.[18]

The Lowlands

Arms of the White Mountains extended far to the south, some almost to the Bay of Belfalas. Between the ridges lay deep-cloven river valleys, such as that of the Morthond, where the Grey Company descended from the Paths of the Dead — "a great bay that beat up against the sheer southern faces of the mountains."[19] These alluvial valleys coalesced as they neared the bay, producing the fair green coastlands of Anfalas and Belfalas.

The broad plain north of the White Mountains and southeast of the Misty was entirely drained by one huge river system, that of the Entwash. Although it had its source in the springs leaping down Mount Methedras above Treebeard's abode,[20] most of its tributaries ran from the White Mountains. It would also have drained part of the south downs and the Wold through groundwater discharge. The Entwash had one unusual feature, the large inland delta. Such a formation might give the impression that the river was quite muddy, yet an *inland* delta is not indicative that a river carries large amounts of sediment. Instead, this pattern develops where there is a sudden decrease in slope from the extremely high mountains down to the flat valley bottom. The abrupt change sharply reduces the river's ability to carry particles in suspension, and the accumulation of sediment that results disrupts the main river channel. This action is apparent in the Entwash from the braided stream shown above the delta.[21] The breakdown of current further reduces the carrying capacity, causing more deposition. The rivulets wander farther, and the cycle continues until the adjustment has been made and the river reconsolidates itself or, as in the case of the Entwash, enters another river.

Prairie grasses normally occur in relatively dry areas; yet the plain must have been easily flooded. After the Long Winter it became "a vast fen,"[22] and even in drier years Shadowfax led the way around "hidden pools, and . . . wide and treacherous bogs" between Fangorn and Edoras.[23] Apparently there was just enough water to produce the marvelously lush grasslands of Rohan.

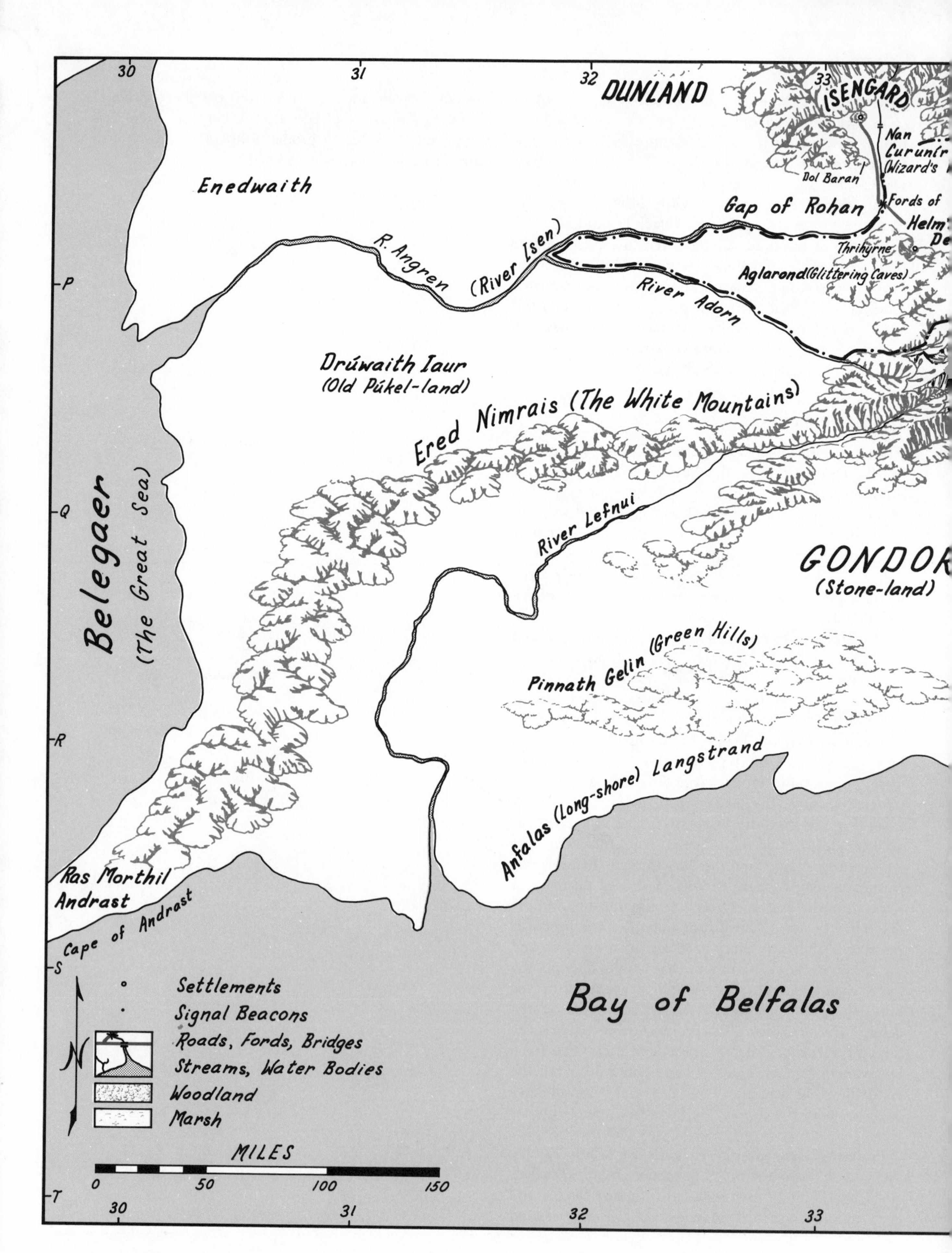
DUNLAND
ISENGARD
Nan Curunír (Wizard's
Dol Baran
Fords of
Helm's De
Enedwaith
Gap of Rohan
Thrihyrne
R. Angren (River Isen)
Aglarond (Glittering Caves)
River Adorn
Drúwaith Iaur (Old Púkel-land)
Ered Nimrais (The White Mountains)
River Lefnui
GONDOR (Stone-land)
Belegaer (The Great Sea)
Pinnath Gelin (Green Hills)
Anfalas (Long-shore) Langstrand
Ras Morthil Andrast
Cape of Andrast
Bay of Belfalas
Settlements
Signal Beacons
Roads, Fords, Bridges
Streams, Water Bodies
Woodland
Marsh
MILES
0
50
100
150
30
31
32
33
P
Q
R
S
T

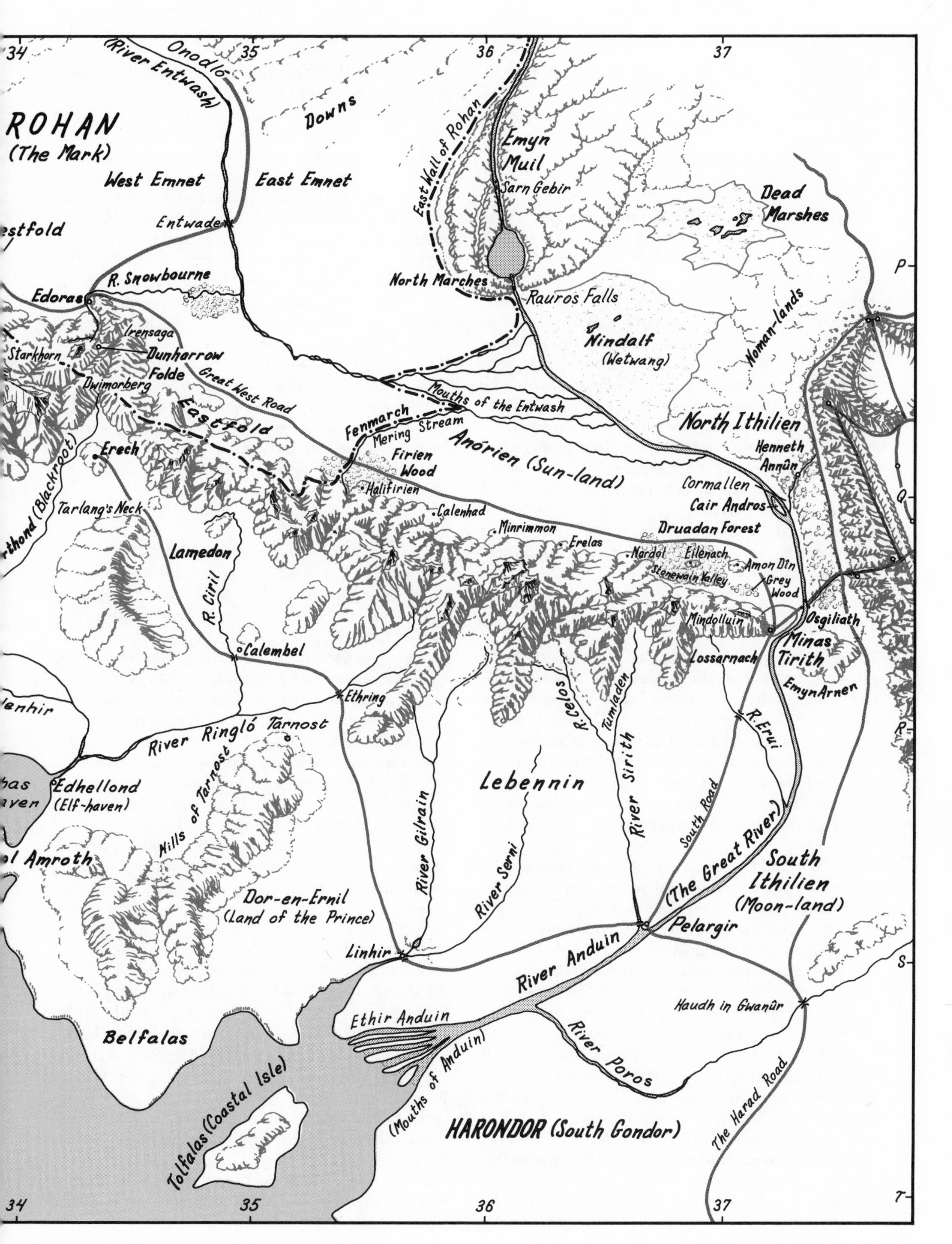
ROHAN
(The Mark)
Onodló
(River Entwash)
Downs
West Emnet
East Emnet
Entwade
Edoras
R. Snowbourne
Irensaga
Dunharrow
Starkhorn
Folde
Dwimorberg
Great West Road
Eastfold
Erech
Tarlang's Neck
Lamedon
R. Ciril
Calembel
Ethring
River Ringló
Tarnost
Hills of Tarnost
Edhellond
(Elf-haven)
Dor-en-Ernil
(Land of the Prince)
Belfalas
Tolfalas (Coastal Isle)
Emyn Muil
East Wall of Rohan
Sarn Gebir
North Marches
Rauros Falls
Nindalf
(Wetwang)
Mouths of the Entwash
Fenmarch
Mering Stream
Firien Wood
Halifirien
Anórien (Sun-land)
Calenhad
Minrimmon
Erelas
Nardol
Eilenach
Druadan Forest
Stonewain Valley
Amon Dîn
Grey Wood
Mindolluin
Minas Tirith
Osgiliath
Dead Marshes
Noman-lands
North Ithilien
Henneth Annûn
Cormallen
Cair Andros
Lossarnach
Emyn Arnen
R. Erui
R. Celos
Tumladen
River Sirith
South Road
Lebennin
River Gilrain
River Serni
(The Great River)
South Ithilien
(Moon-land)
Pelargir
Linhir
River Anduin
Ethir Anduin
(Mouths of Anduin)
River Poros
Haudh in Gwanûr
The Harad Road
HARONDOR (South Gondor)
34
35
36
37
P
Q
R
S
T

THE WHITE MOUNTAINS

Mordor (and Adjacent Lands)

TOLKIEN ONCE COMMENTED that Mordor corresponded more or less with the Mediterranean volcanic basin; and Mt. Doom, Stromboli.[1] At every turn the volcanism was suggested: Mordor, the Black Land; Ephel Dúath, mountains of black rock; Ered Lithui, ash mountains; Lithlad, ash plain; Gorgoroth, a volcanic plateau; and of course, Mt. Doom, an active volcano. The landscape was sinister, in keeping with its master. The lands outside the Ephel Dúath (the "outer fence") were noticeably nonvolcanic: North Ithilien, a quick-falling land filled with streams and grottoes; marshlands; moors of the Noman-lands; and even Dagorlad, the hard battle plain. They, too, added to the mystique. The lands in the northwest, near the Morannon where Sauron's power was strongest, fell under his power and were ruined; but Ithilien had only recently come under the evil influence and "kept still a dishevelled dryad loveliness."[2]

The Adjacent Lands

The northern lands were swept by bitter eastern winds carrying fumes from the slag mounds and from the increasingly active Mt. Doom.[3] The climate became arid, and the landscape was slowly denuded of its growing things. As the lands became more barren, the little rain that fell ran off the surface of the nearby highlands and fed more and more water into the bracken swamps. The Dead Marshes grew until they had swallowed up the graves dug after the battle of the Last Alliance.[4]

As Frodo and Company left the Dead Marshes they climbed "long shallow slopes" of the "arid moors of the Noman-lands."[5] These were probably the receding end of a sedimentary layer that continued south through Ithilien, dipping away from the Ephel Dúath. The edge of the sediments had eroded back from the range, leaving the "long trenchlike valley between it and the outer buttresses of the mountains" over which the Hobbits peered toward the Morannon.[6]

As the mountain chain turned east, the crest fell away, and the valley widened into a plain — Dagorlad, scene of many battles — over which the Hobbits watched the Southrons enter the Black Gate. The plain was "stony," probably a *pediment* — the rubble of innumerable rocks washed out from the mountains, but never weathered due to the arid climate.[7]

The Hobbits turned south, following the path of the road that was built between the crests of the western slopes and the eastern mountains. They passed into an increasingly pleasant land, with ample rainfall blown in on the moist southwest winds from the Bay of Belfalas.[8] There the water collected into numerous streams, which fell quickly down to Anduin, cutting steep gorges. Sometimes the streams found their way into a crevice and followed the weak fissures under the surface, reappearing far below in springs. One such "grot" was sealed to form Henneth Annûn.[9] Farther south the sediments must have continued to dip steeply, for after leaving Faramir's refuge the Hobbits stayed west of the road until they reached the gorge of the Morgulduin. Turning east, they climbed continually, and "if ever they went a little downward, always the further slope was longer and steeper." At last they struggled "onto a great *hog-back* of land"[10] — a sharp-crested ridge of resistant sediments with a backslope exceeding 45° and an even steeper scarp.[11] Beyond the Cross-roads lay the first "tumbled lands" of Mordor.[12]

Mordor

The land of Sauron was composed of three major features: the mountains, which were "parts of one great wall"; the plateau of Gorgoroth; and the plains of Lithlad.[13] All the lands were arid and all were volcanic. Climbing the mountains, the Hobbits were surrounded by constant examples of the volcanic rock, which made the range predominantly black. Gabbros may have been thrust up; basalts extruded at lower levels or exposed in necks and dikes. All could have given the black appearance. Along the Winding Stair the Hobbits passed "tall piers and jagged pinnacles . . . great crevices and fissures . . ."[14] These could have resulted from the columnar weathering of basalt.

Around them the peaks rose high above, but were apparently lower than those of the White and Misty Mountains. No mention was made of snow, although "forgotten winters had gnawed and carved the sunless stone."[15] Still, the peaks were probably quite high, for the top of the pass of Cirith Ungol was more than 3000 feet above the Cross-roads.[16] Possibly the ranges could have been folded and faulted as well. Faulting probably produced the trough between the Ephel Dúath and the Morgai through which the Hobbits crept north from Cirith Ungol. "The eastern faces of the Ephel Dúath were sheer," and the slopes of the Morgai were jumbled, notched, and jagged.[17] Transverse faults were apparent too, for Sam and Frodo drank from a gully that appeared to have been "cloven by some huge axe."[18]

At the north end of the Ephel Dúath, at its junction with the Ered Lithui, lay a deep circular valley ringed by sheer black barren cliffs — Udûn. Tolkien described the vale as being encircled by arms sent out by the two ranges.[19] The symmetry of the valley suggests either a *caldera* or a *ring-dike*. A caldera is the remnant of a volcano that has exploded and/or collapsed. A ring-dike is a circular ridge of cooled igneous rock surrounding a deep valley. It occurs when a round block subsides into an underlying magma chamber and the fluid magma is forced up around the edges. Often the upwelling is intermittent, leaving passes such as the Isenmouthe and Cirith Gorgor.[20] Either process could have resulted in the feature shown by Tolkien, although compared with our world either would have been gigantic. Imagine the original height of a volcano with a forty-five-mile base. This colossus would have towered almost 29,000 feet! In contrast Mt. Doom was only seven miles across and stood 4500 feet.[21]

As the Hobbits turned east and south from Udûn, they faced the final path across Gorgoroth, a *lava plateau*.[22] Its level would have been higher than that of Udûn (a "deep dale") and the plain of Lithlad.[23] Tremendously thick layers of *flood basalts* were deposited through the years by slow upwelling from the many fissures that pocked the landscape. These were supplemented by flows from volcanoes, most of which had previously been active but had left only the skeletons — necks and dikes, low mounds, and in the southeast where erosion was more advanced, mesas and buttes. At the time of the quest, fissures were numerous, and the remnants of activity gave the plateau its rugged and evil appearance;[24] yet none was more imposing than the smoking peak at the very heart — Mt. Doom.

The plateau was barren, and had all Mordor been of that formation Sauron would have had little to feed his countless troops; but conditions were somewhat better in Lithlad — the ash plain. There the flows of more solid material were apparently less, or were mostly eroded. If the rock were highly weathered, the resulting soil would have been quite fertile. In the semi-arid climate, water was in short supply, for the bitter Sea of Nurnen (with its interior drainage) was salty.[25] Still, a recent deposition of ash would have helped with conservation (for ash is a highly effective mulch, reducing evaporation),[26] allowing dry-land farming in the "great slave-worked fields."[27]

Originally, the geography of Mordor was rather different, notably in the northwest. Gorgoroth was present from the beginning, but extended almost to the Sea of Nurnen, and only the eastern ridge with Barad-dûr at the end was shown.[28] The Gap of Gorgoroth, which eventually was blocked by the fortress of the Morannon, was once the site of Cirith Ungol.[29] The Vale of Udûn and the Isenmouthe, the ridge of the Morgai, and the eastern and western ranges separating Gorgoroth from Lithlad were all absent until late in the story.[30] The near-encirclement of Gorgoroth and addition of Nurn to its south on *The Lord of the Rings* map left Lithlad in its original placement — *east* of Gorgoroth, south of the Ash Mountains.[31] Even the southern Ephel Duath were changed, originally bulging in two arcs nearly 150 miles wide toward Harad, and narrow only at the Nargil Pass, at the source of the southern river feeding into the Sea of Nurnen.[32]

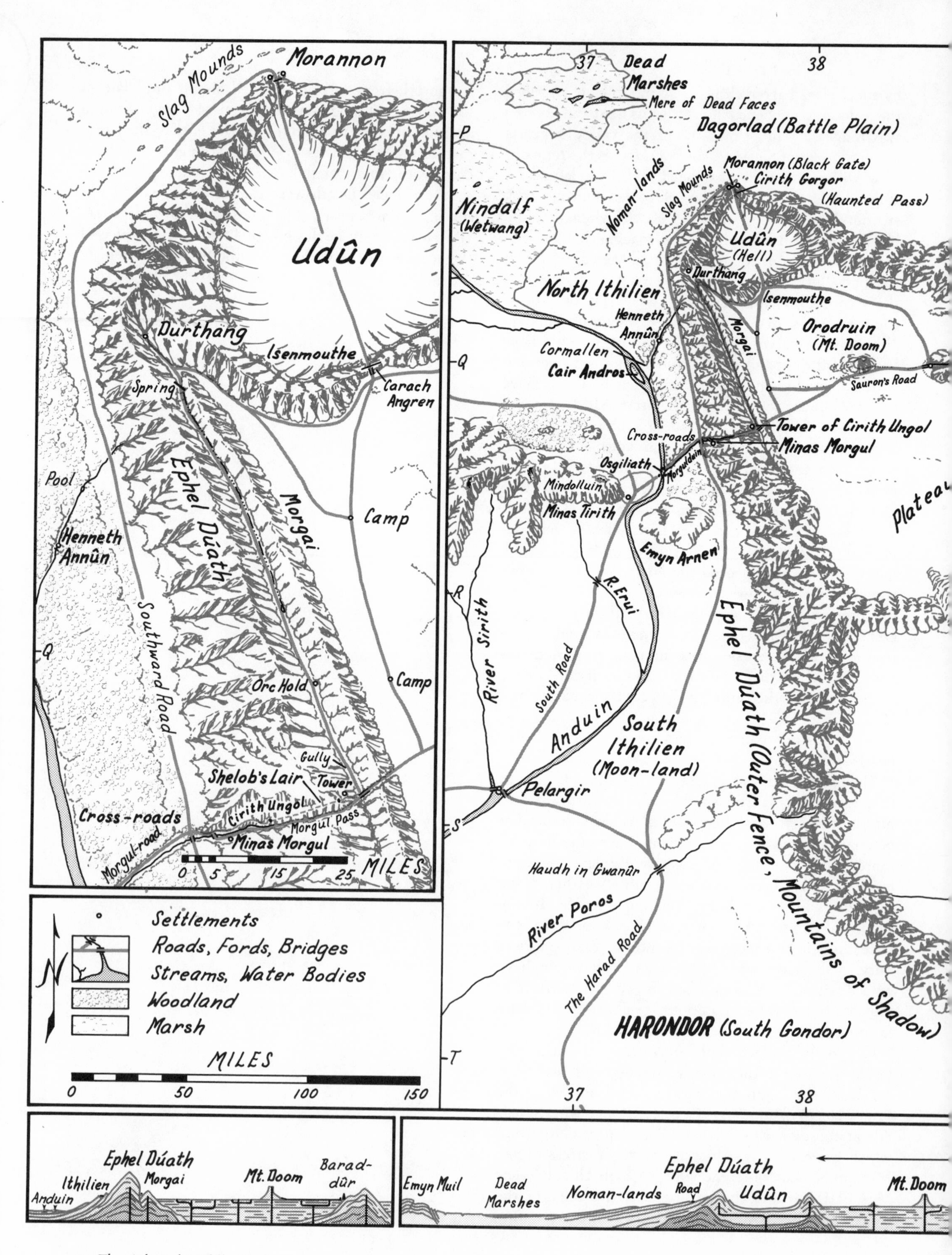
Morannon
Slag Mounds
Udûn
Durthang
Isenmouthe
Carach Angren
Spring
Ephel Dúath
Morgai
Pool
Henneth Annûn
Camp
Camp
Southward Road
Orc Hold
Gully
Shelob's Lair
Tower
Cross-roads
Cirith Ungol
Morgul Pass
Morgul-road
Minas Morgul
0 5 15 25 MILES
Settlements
Roads, Fords, Bridges
Streams, Water Bodies
Woodland
Marsh
MILES
0 50 100 150
Dead Marshes
Mere of Dead Faces
Dagorlad (Battle Plain)
Morannon (Black Gate)
Cirith Gorgor
(Haunted Pass)
Noman-lands
Nindalf
(Wetwang)
Udûn
(Hell)
Durthang
Isenmouthe
North Ithilien
Henneth Annûn
Orodruin
(Mt. Doom)
Cormallen
Cair Andros
Sauron's Road
Tower of Cirith Ungol
Minas Morgul
Cross-roads
Osgiliath
Morgulduin
Mindolluin
Minas Tirith
Plateau
Emyn Arnen
R. Erui
River Sirith
South Road
Anduin
South Ithilien
(Moon-land)
Pelargir
Ephel Dúath (Outer Fence, Mountains of Shadow)
Haudh in Gwanûr
River Poros
The Harad Road
HARONDOR (South Gondor)
37
38
P
Q
R
S
T
Ephel Dúath
Ithilien
Anduin
Morgai
Mt. Doom
Barad-dûr
Emyn Muil
Dead Marshes
Noman-lands
Road
Udûn
Mt. Doom

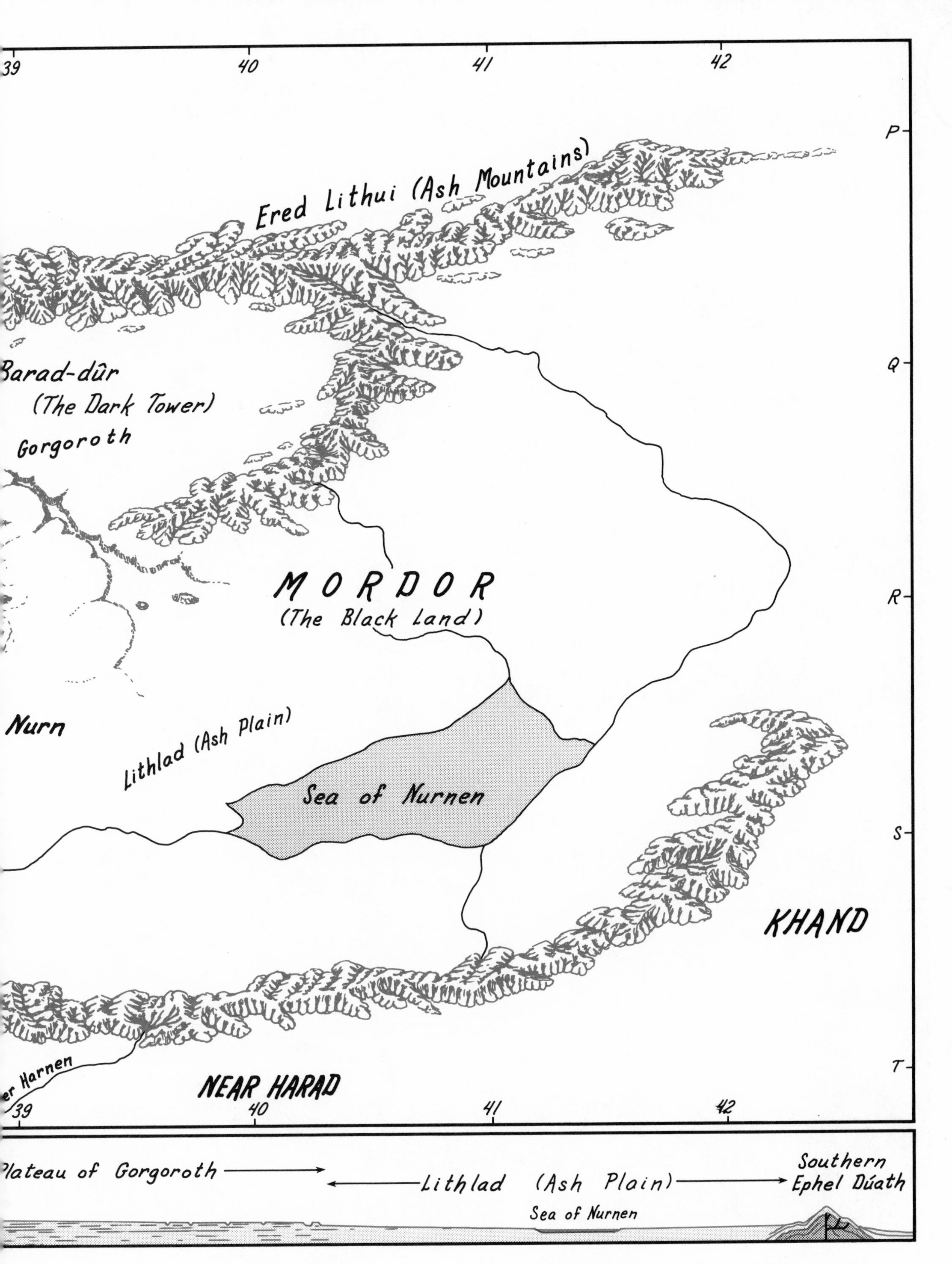

MORDOR Cross Section Left: WEST–EAST Cross Section Right: NORTHWEST–SOUTHEAST

The Hobbit

Introduction

In "The Hobbit" Tolkien provided some vivid descriptions, but stated few dates and no distances, and showed no scale on the original map of Wilderland. Therefore, the pathway maps could be drawn only by using the map scale and other information from *The Lord of the Rings.* The Shire Calendar explained the day/date system, which allowed analysis of the few dates given in *The Hobbit.*[1] Once the number of travelling dates had been established, it was possible to calculate the miles covered daily by mere measurement, combined with occasional clues such as rising early, riding late, and factors that might have altered the company's speed.

All the dates given for the War of the Rings were said to have utilized the Shire Calendar,[2] so that was used here as a basis for *The Hobbit* dates as well. It is possible Tolkien had not yet contrived the Shire Calendar when *The Hobbit* was written, but even our own calendar would have resulted in just a few days' variance. Only three dates could be pinpointed in the journey east: April 27 — departure from Hobbiton on Thursday "just before May";[3] Midyear's Day — departure from Rivendell on midsummer morning (intrepreted as synonymous with Midyear's Day, the summer solstice);[4] and September 22 — arrival in Lake-town.[5] The encounter with the Trolls was when it would "soon be June."[6]

Bag End to Rivendell

The number of days spent on the road between Bag End and Rivendell could only be estimated by calculating backward. The company left Bag End on April 27 and Rivendell on Midyear's Day (where they had spent "fourteen days at least"),[7] so they could have been on the road for as much as fifty-one days. The distance from Bag End to Rivendell was slightly more than 400 miles, so the company might have averaged as little as eight miles per day. Perhaps they did not hurry on their way. The weather until late May had been fine and the inns plentiful; whereas camping in the rain and going hungry would have encouraged them to speed up a bit later in the journey. Perhaps they spent more than two weeks in Rivendell — mortals seemed to have great difficulty keeping track of time in the Elvish cities. As a compromise the final estimate was that they travelled for thirty-eight days and spent twenty-seven in Rivendell — still only an average of ten miles per day!

As Frodo and friends later travelled between the same two points, the map west of Rivendell lists for comparison the distances covered in both *The Hobbit* and *The Lord of the Rings.* Even on ponies the dwarves appeared to be travelling at snail's pace, while Frodo was in a continual forced march. Only once did the Dwarves seem more speedy than the Hobbits: in the Trollshaws. The inconsistency arose from the distance between the rushing river and the clearing where Bilbo met the Trolls. The river was not named in *The Hobbit,* although the revised version of the story specifically mentioned that it had a stone bridge.[8] As the *Last* Bridge crosses the Hoarwell, then the distances disagree. The Trolls' fire was so close to the river that it could be seen "some way off,"[9] and it probably took the Dwarves no more than an hour to reach; whereas Strider led the Hobbits north of the road, where they lost their way and spent almost six days reaching the clearing where they found the Stone-trolls. Lost or not, it seems almost impossible that the time-pressed ranger would have spent six days reaching a point the Dwarves found in an hour. *The History* series helps explain the discrepancy: the addition of the stone bridge was made as part of an elaborate rewriting done in 1960, which was never published. The proposed revision was that Thorin and Company cross the Last Bridge early in the morning and only reach the campsite near the Trolls in the evening after travelling several miles.[10]

Unfortunately, even this revision does not significantly improve the situation of Frodo and Company while drastically altering the story line of *The Hobbit.* Perhaps the most effective solution is that shown by Strachey: interpreting the events to have occurred by a lesser stream (unmapped by Tolkien) closer to the Bruinen, and ignoring both the presence of the bridge and the statement that the river's source was in the mountains.[11] The alternate route shown is based on a sketch map in *The History,* with the stream added. This is the clearest indication of Tolkien's true intent, but even it is not ideal, as the distance to the Ford is short given the time and mileage covered after Frodo and friends met Glorfindel.[12] Consistently the Dwarves went slower in all their travels than the Hobbits did in the later story. We can only surmise reasons for such variance. It is possible Tolkien had longer distances in mind for *The Hobbit* travels, and either did not check the effect of the scale placed on the map in the later book or chose to ignore it. Had the scale of the Wilderland map been about twice that of the rest of Middle-earth, the Dwarves' pace would have been nearer normal. Tolkien "was greatly concerned to harmonise Bilbo's journey with . . . *The Lord of the Rings*

. . . but he never brought this work to a definitive solution."[13] Rather than analyze too closely, it is preferable we merely gain a general impression of the seemingly endless toil necessary to reach Lonely Mountain.

Rivendell to the Lonely Mountain

Eighty-four days passed between the departure from Rivendell on Midyear's Day and the arrival in Lake-town on September 22. All of that time was spent en route except the one day of rest at Beorn's and the days of captivity in the Elvenking's caverns. The time can be broken into four stages: in the Misty Mountains, the Anduin valley, Mirkwood, and Thranduil's caverns. The first leg of the journey was spent in climbing the mountains. Rivendell lay west of the range, so the company had to reach and cross the foothills and the lower skirts of the mountains before they even began the long weary ascent to the High Pass. The Dwarves were going so slowly that Bilbo thought, "They will be harvesting and blackberrying, before we even begin to go down the other side at this rate."[14] During their two-day short cut through the Goblin's tunnels on a Tuesday and Wednesday he found "the blackberries were still only in flower . . . and he ate three wild strawberries."[15] At that latitude, strawberries would probably fruit and blackberries blossom between mid-June and mid-July,[16] and later comments about there being an "autumn-like mist" in spite of its being "high summer"[17] suggested the latest possible date: mid-July. This would result in a twenty-five day ascent between Rivendell and the Goblins' Front Porch — certainly longer than the "two marches" Gandalf estimated the Fellowship of the Ring would require to reach the top of the Redhorn Pass.[18]

After escaping from the Goblins' back-door the company made a speedy descent to the eastern skirts of the mountains, and with the eagles' assistance reached Beorn's the next day. On his ponies they made good time, galloping along Anduin's grassy valley — a respectable twenty miles per day. Although they left Beorn's just after noon they covered "many miles" before evening, then continued north for three more days. They travelled especially late on the second day and started at dawn on the last so they could reach the Forest Gate in the early afternoon.

On foot in Mirkwood, progress was slow and "days followed days" — even before Bombur fell into the Enchanted Stream and had to be carried, slowing them more.[19] The length of the forest path was 188 miles, of which they had already covered 143 when they reached the stream. Their marches east of there required about a week, so they might have spent up to four weeks crossing the forest, covering little more than six and a half miles each day.

The time spent in captivity in Thranduil's caverns was "a weary long time."[20] It took Bilbo "a week or two" to find Thorin, and he still had to make and implement his escape plans — possibly requiring another two weeks.[21] When at last he put his plan into action, it was the afternoon of September 21. That afternoon and all the next day were spent barrel-riding to Lake-town in time for arrival on Bilbo's birthday.

The company made preparations for the last leg of the journey and after only "a fortnight" asked the Master of Lake-town for assistance.[22] Assuming at least two days were required to assemble provisions, they would have departed about October 9. They rowed for three days up the Long Lake and the River Running, then rode to the Mountain. They camped for a short time west of Ravenhill, then moved camp to the valley between the western spurs and again to the hidden bay on the mountainside. There they stayed until Durin's Day allowed them to open the secret door and enter. Calculating backwards, with time allowed for the armies' march, the siege, the battle, and Bilbo's return to Beorn's before Yule,[23] Durin's Day would not have been later than October 30. That was the estimate shown, but if precise calculation of Durin's Day was beyond the skill of the Dwarves, it certainly was beyond mine.

The Third Age, Year 2941–42

The important dates of *The Hobbit* appear in the following chronology. It should be remembered that only April 27, Midyear's Day, September 22, 2941, and May 1, 2942,[24] were stated or were clearly traceable to Tolkien. All the other dates were calculated and are highly speculative.

April 25.	Gandalf visits Bilbo at Bag End.
April 26.	Wednesday. The unexpected party.
April 27.	Thorin and Company ride out of Hobbiton at 11:00 a.m.
May 29.	The company crosses a river and are captured by the Trolls.
June 4.	They ford the Bruinen and reach Rivendell at dusk.
1 Lithe.	Midsummer's Eve. Elrond discovers the moon-letters on Thror's map.
Midyear's Day.	The company leaves Rivendell.
July 16.	Monday. They are captured by the Goblins during the night.
July 19.	Thursday. Gandalf and the Dwarves escape, Bilbo finds the Ring, meets Gollum, escapes. The company is

trapped by wolves and rescued by eagles.

JULY 20. They fly to the Carrock and reach Beorn's in midafternoon.

JULY 22. They ride out from Beorn's in early afternoon.

JULY 25. Gandalf departs with ponies at the west edge of Mirkwood.

AUGUST 16. The company crosses the Enchanted Stream. Bombur falls into a trance.

AUGUST 22. They leave the path at night.

AUGUST 23. Before dawn Thorin is captured by the Wood-elves, and the other Dwarves by giant spiders. Bilbo rescues the Dwarves.

AUGUST 24. At dusk the Dwarves are captured by Wood-elves and taken to the Elvenking's Halls.

SEPTEMBER 21. The company escapes the Elvenking in the afternoon and reaches the huts of the Raft-men at dusk.

SEPTEMBER 22. They reach Lake-town just after sunset.

OCTOBER 9. The company departs from Lake-town by boat.

OCTOBER 12. They leave the river and ride to the Lonely Mountain.

OCTOBER 14. The camp is moved to the western valley.

OCTOBER 19. Bilbo discovers the hidden path. The camp is moved to the hidden bay.

OCTOBER 30. Durin's Day. The Secret Door is opened at dusk. Bilbo visits Smaug and returns to the Dwarves at midnight.

NOVEMBER 1. Bilbo returns to Smaug's chamber in the afternoon. In the evening Smaug smashes the door, attacks Lake-town, and is killed.

NOVEMBER 2. Goblins, Beorn, and Gandalf hear of Smaug's death.

NOVEMBER 3. Elvenking's host leaves Mirkwood. Thorin learns news.

NOVEMBER 4. Elves turn toward Lake-town.

NOVEMBER 6. Elves reach Lake-town. Dáin receives summons.

NOVEMBER 12. Elves reach Lake-men pass the north end of the Long Lake.

NOVEMBER 15. The joint forces reach Dale at dusk.

NOVEMBER 16. Lonely Mountain is besieged.

NOVEMBER 22. Bilbo gives the Arkenstone to the Elvenking and Bard.

NOVEMBER 23. Dáin arrives in early morning. The Battle of Five Armies. Thorin and Bolg slain.

NOVEMBER 27. Gandalf, Bilbo, and Beorn leave Lonely Mountain.

DECEMBER 30. They arrive at Beorn's and stay until spring.

MAY 1. Gandalf and Bilbo reach Rivendell.

MAY 8. They leave for Hobbiton, which they reach in June.

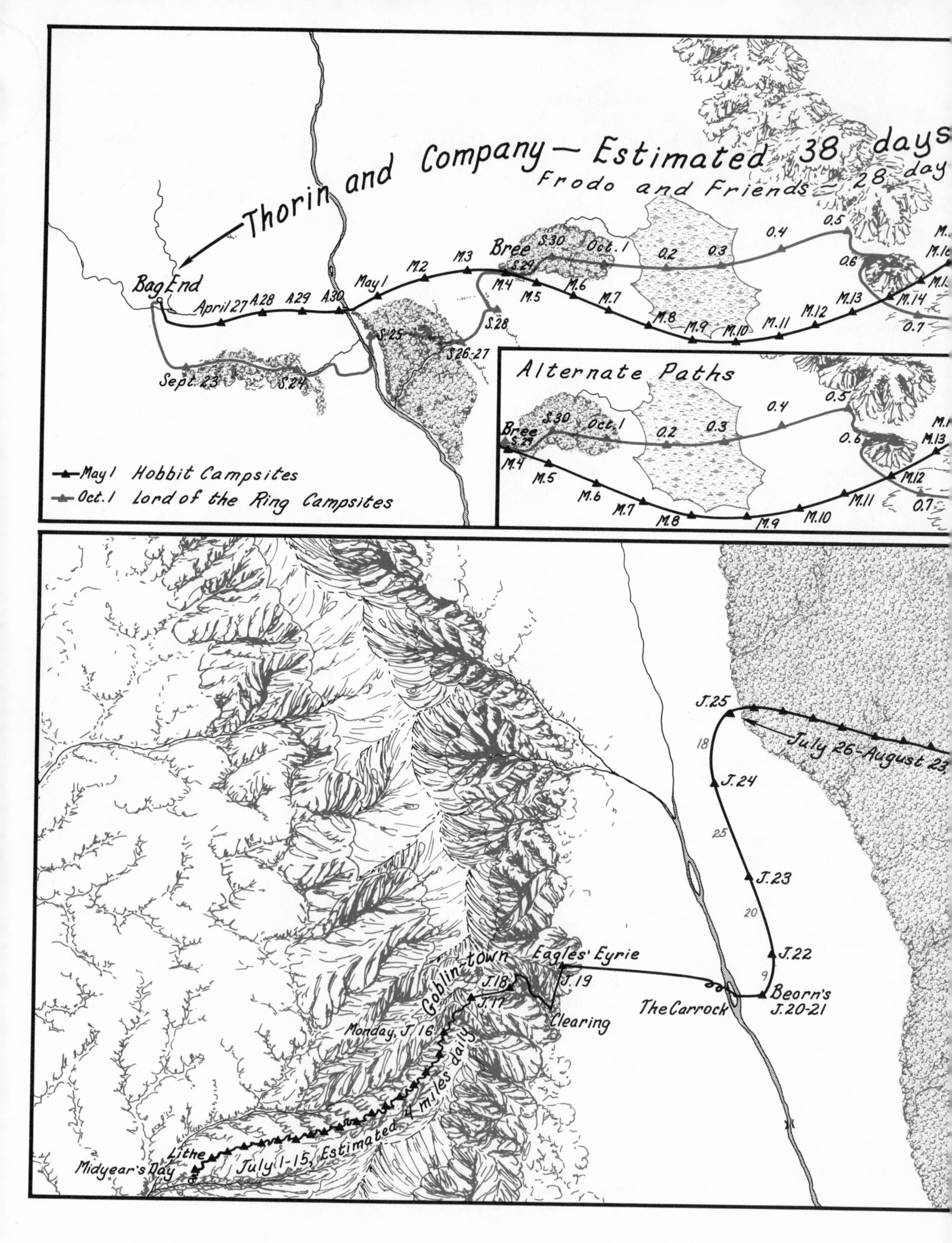
Thorin and Company — Estimated 38 days
Frodo and Friends — 28 days
Bag End
April 27
A.28
A.29
A.30
May 1
M.2
M.3
Bree
S.29
S.30
Oct. 1
0.2
0.3
0.4
0.5
0.6
0.7
M.4
M.5
M.6
M.7
M.8
M.9
M.10
M.11
M.12
M.13
M.14
Sept. 23
S.24
S.25
S.26-27
S.28
May 1 Hobbit Campsites
Oct. 1 Lord of the Ring Campsites
Alternate Paths
J.25
July 26-August 23
18
J.24
25
J.23
20
J.22
9
Beorn's
J.20-21
The Carrock
Eagles' Eyrie
J.19
Clearing
Goblin-town
J.18
J.17
Monday, J.16
4 miles daily
July 1-15, Estimated
Lithe
Midyear's Day

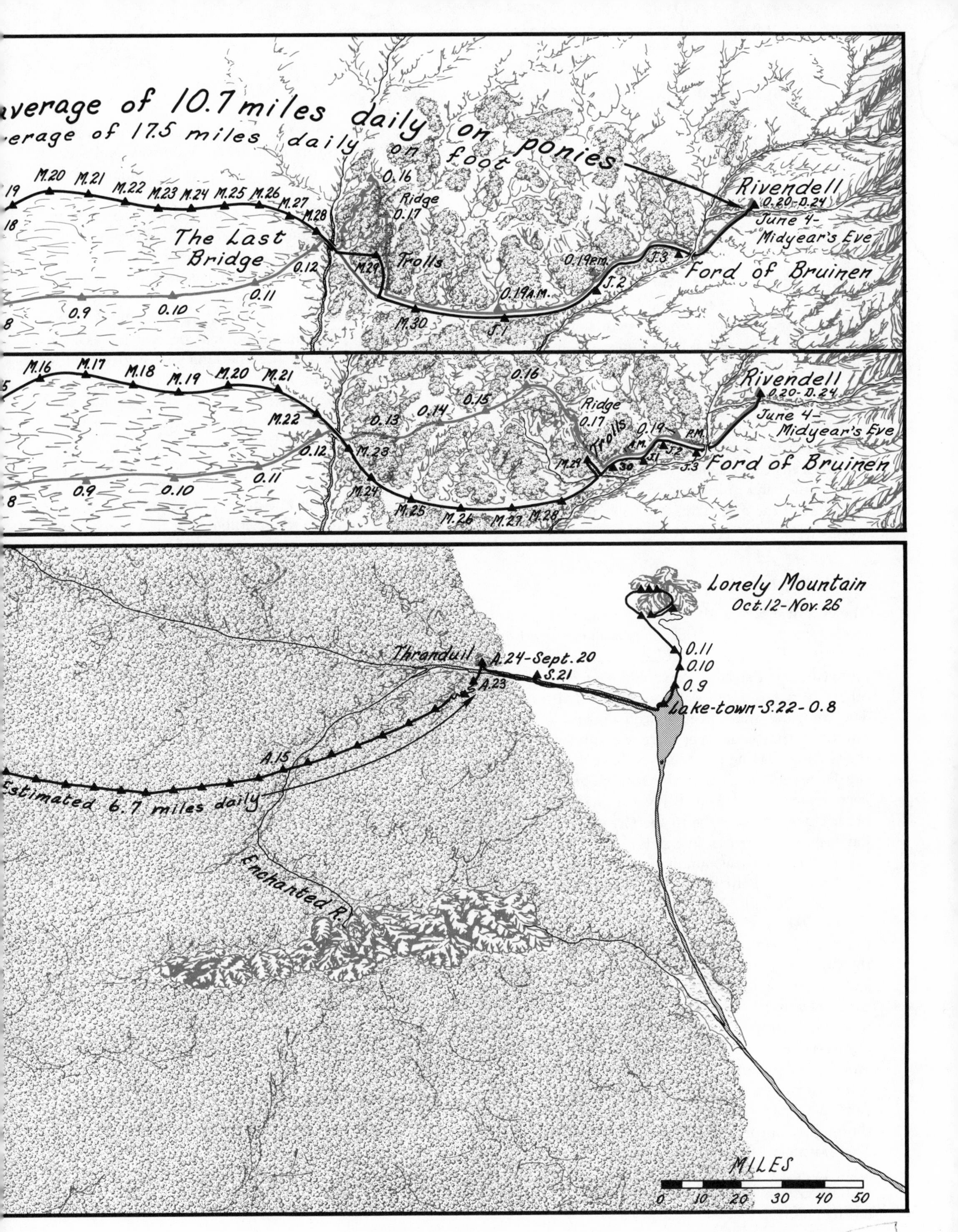

HOBBIT PATHWAYS Upper: BAG END TO RIVENDELL (VERSUS LOTR)
Inset: ALTERNATE PATHS Lower: RIVENDELL TO LONELY MOUNTAIN

Over Hill and Under Hill: Goblin-town

SEEKING SHELTER from a mountain storm, the company found a cave near the top of the High Pass, which turned out to be the newest opening to a vast and intricate network of passages and caves inhabited by Goblins.[1] The main entrance had in the past opened on "a different pass, one more easy to travel by . . . ,"[2] possibly farther south and nearer the East Road. The tunnels have been estimated as thirty-five miles from the Front Porch to the back-door, because the Dwarves spent about two and a half days and had gone "miles and miles, and come right down through the heart of the mountains . . ." to a point west of the Carrock.[3]

The Capture

The entrance cave itself was "quite a fair size, but not too large . . ."[4] In the back wall was a cleverly hidden door: the "black crack."[5] It led to a wide passage that plunged almost steadily down and soon was joined by others that were "crossed and tangled in all directions."[6] The company was forced to run down the paths as quickly as they could; yet there was sufficient time for the Goblins leading the ponies to have drawn ahead of the Dwarves so far that the saddlebags had already been removed and were being rummaged.[7] With no other clues, the distance to the Great Goblin's cavern has been estimated as five miles. The cavern appears not to have been astoundingly large, so it has been illustrated as about three hundred feet long by one hundred feet high.

After escaping from the cavern the Dwarves' lead must have been significant. At first they could hear the Goblins' shouts "growing fainter"; then they ran, and "not for a long while did they stop, and by that time they must have been right down in the very mountain's heart."[8] When the Goblins caught up, the Dwarves were at a point where the passage had gone around a slight curve, then ran straight for a while before turning a sharp corner. Around that bend Gandalf and Thorin turned to parry, and succeeded in thoroughly surprising and scattering their pursuers. The skirmish bought more time, and the Dwarves "had gone on a long, long way" before they were reattacked.[9] In the confusion Bilbo was dropped and left behind.

Bilbo's Escape

Bilbo probably took the same path as that followed by Gandalf, because he held to the main way and seems merely to have missed turning at the smaller side-passage that led to the outside. Instead, he followed the route to Gollum's cave, where the passage stopped.[10] The distance he covered alone was probably not far, for Bilbo noticed side tunnels almost immediately that, upon his return, seemed only about a mile from the cave.[11]

Gollum's cave was natural: Water seeping through the overlying rock had dissolved some of it, washing the residue down to the lake and out into the little stream that Gollum had first followed underground.[12] In the center of the lake stood the "slimy island" that was Gollum's home. The lake was "wide and deep and deadly cold"; yet it has only been shown as four hundred feet in diameter, because from the island Gollum could see Bilbo, could easily carry on a conversation, and could paddle quickly to shore.[13]

On the return, when Bilbo was fleeing, Gollum counted the side-passages: "'One left, yes. One right, yes. Two right, yes, yes. Two left, yes, yes. . . . Seven right, yes. Six left, yes!'"[14] The last was the way to the back-door, and it was not far, because Gollum could smell the Goblins in the guard room. The passage at first went down, then up, then climbed steeply, turned a corner, went down a bit, then finally around another corner — just where it entered the guard room.[15] The room centered on the great stone door and must have been relatively small, for the Goblins were "falling over one another" trying to find Bilbo. Once through the outer door Bilbo leaped down the few steps and into the valley.[16]

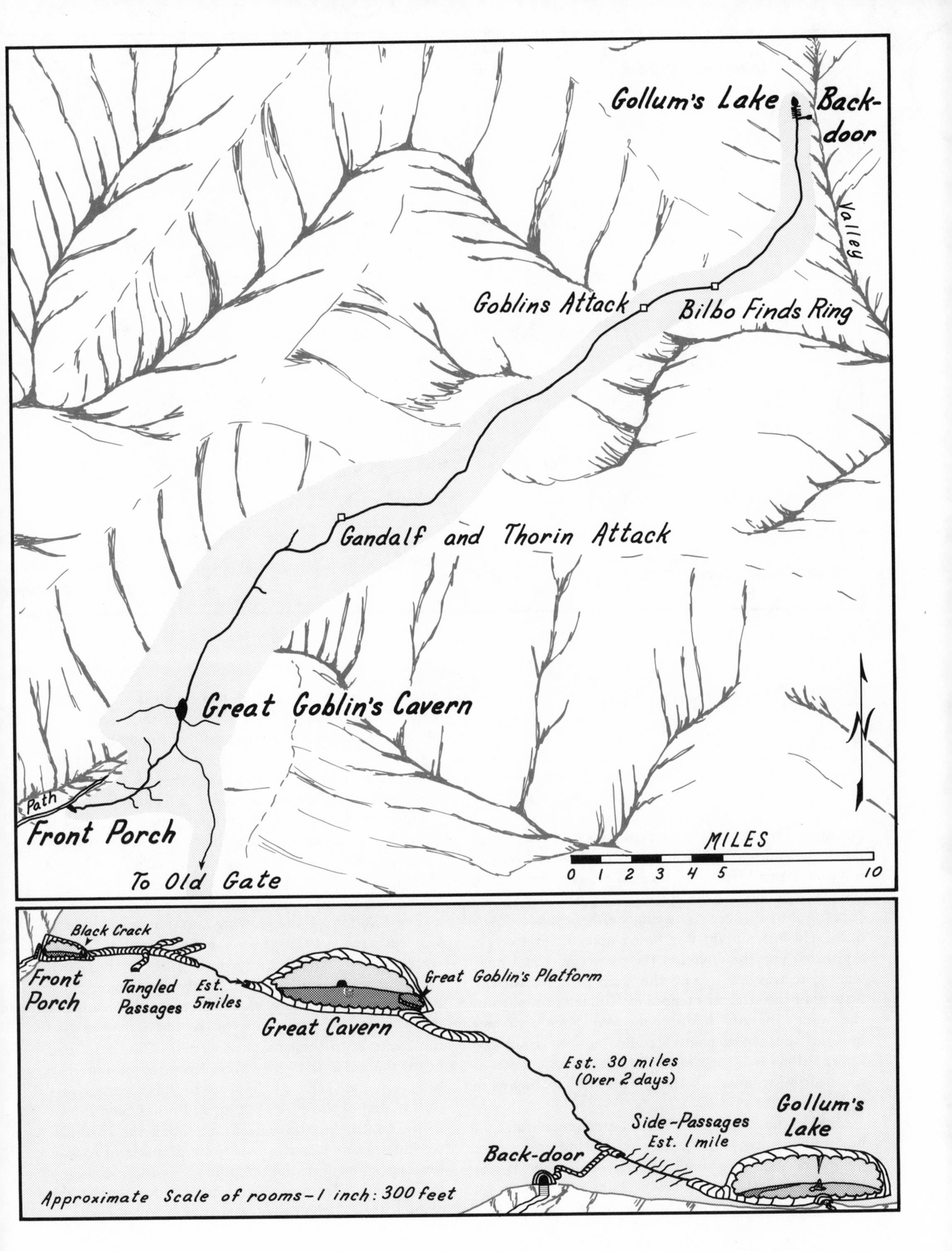

GOBLIN-TOWN *Cross Section:* SOUTHWEST–NORTHEAST

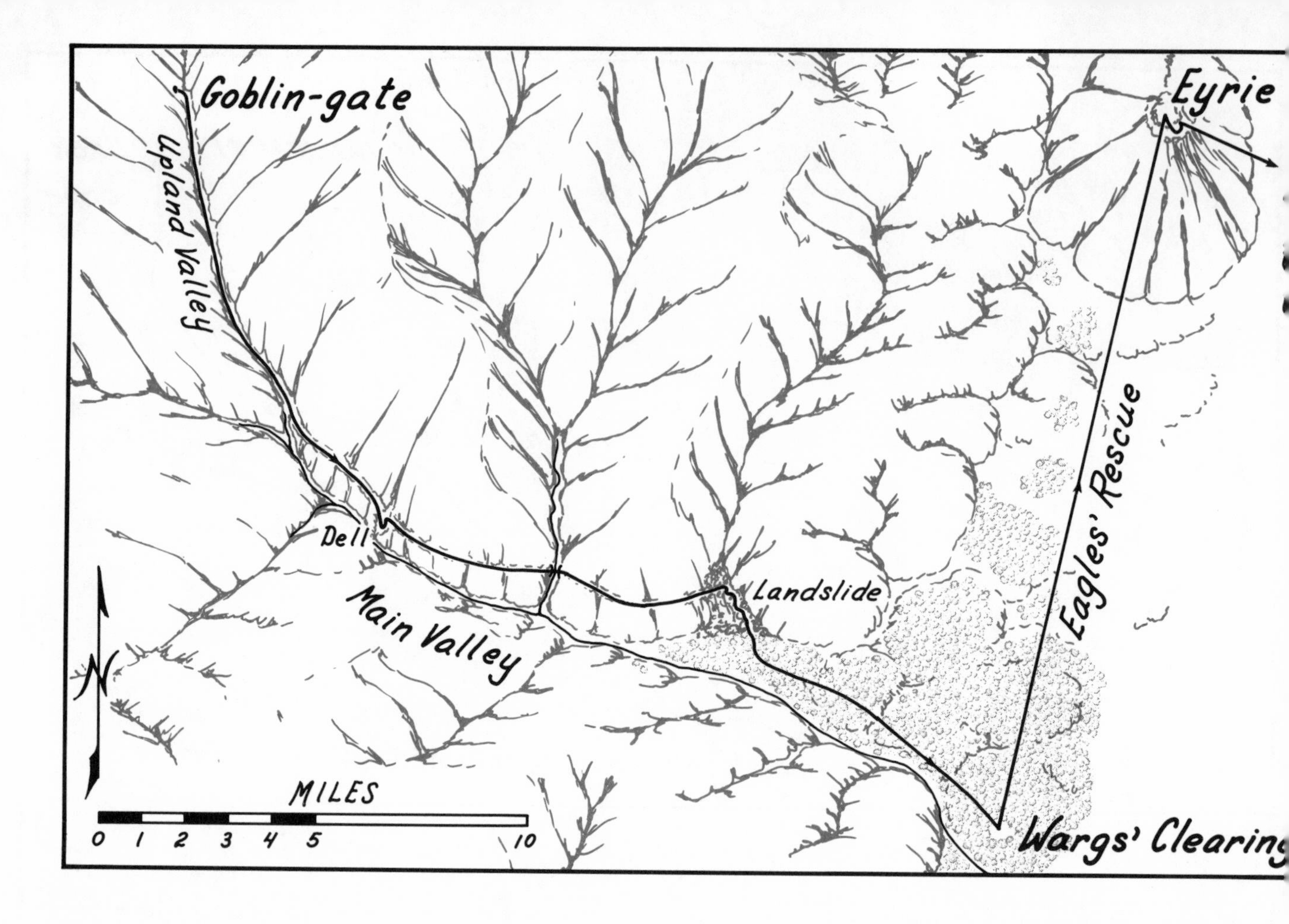

Out of the Frying Pan

After Bilbo left the Goblin tunnels he leaped down the stairs to a path in "a narrow valley between tall mountains" from which could be seen glimpses of the plains beyond.[1] This upland valley has been shown running into a larger vale going southeast toward Anduin. The orientation was based upon several clues: Southeast was the direction the company would have wanted to travel to regain the main road; it was the way all of the streams mapped by Tolkien flowed from the mountains into Anduin; the Woodmen's villages in "the southward plains" could be seen from the lower valley and must have been reasonably close to the clearing from which the wolves and Goblins were to have made a raid.[2]

Once in the larger vale, Bilbo crept along a trail that hugged the north slope, with a wall rising on his left. Below the path in a small dell he found Gandalf and the Dwarves. It was probably about five o'clock on Thursday afternoon, for the sun had already started sinking shortly after Bilbo had escaped the Goblin-gate. The dell was still "pretty high up," so after a short conversation the company continued along the rough path as quickly as possible, crossed a small stream, and just before night fell (about 8:30 as it was midsummer), they encountered a landslide.[3] After skidding to the base of the rock fall, they turned aside into the pine woods that filled the lower valley. Through the trees the Dwarves travelled along "a slanting path leading steadily southwards," and after "what seemed like ages" they came to a clearing.[4]

The location of the clearing was not given, but it was apparently still within the foothills, for wolves were heard howling "away down hill."[5] Those evil Wargs soon surrounded the Dwarves and were joined by Goblins, who were about to roast the company when eagles suddenly came to the rescue and carried the Dwarves to their mountain eyrie. The eagles had heard the noise and "flew away from the mountains" to investigate.[6] This might seem to indicate the clearing lay east of the eyrie, but instead it has been shown to the south; for the woods lay among the foothills, while the eyrie was atop "a lonely pinnacle of rock at the eastern edge of the mountains," which according to Tolkien's illustrations and maps stood amidst the plain at the far end of an east-running ridge.[7]

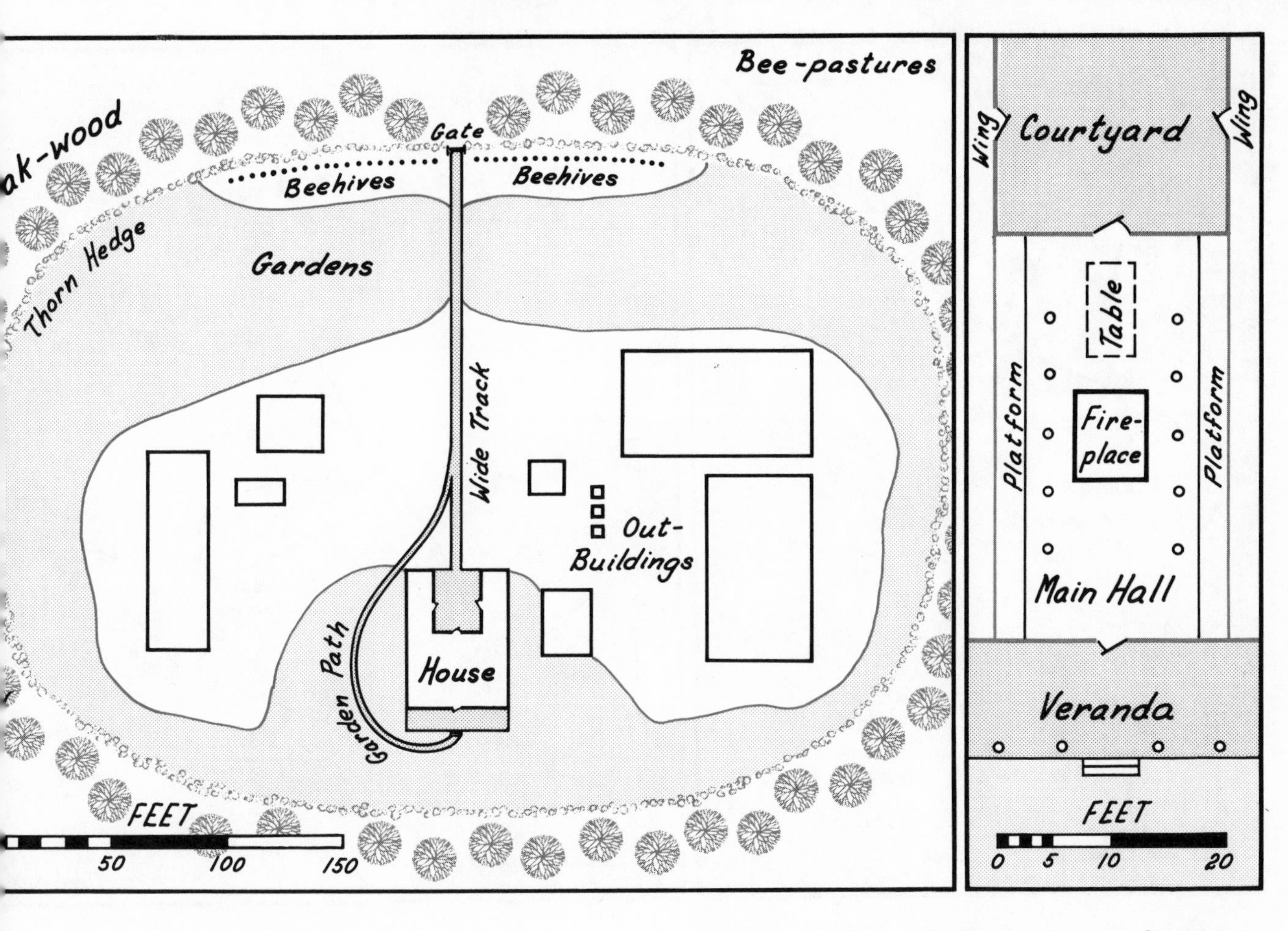

Left: FARMSTEAD Right: HOUSE

Beorn's Wide Wooden Halls

BEORN'S FARMSTEAD lay due east of the Carrock, and the company walked much of the day to reach it. They knew they were close when they reached "great patches of flowers . . . his bee-pastures."[1] A belt of oaks and a thorn-hedge surrounded the farmstead itself, and the hedge allowed entry only where it was broken by a high, broad, wooden gate. Inside the gate and past the beehives on the southward side were more gardens and a wide grassy track that led to the "long low wooden house" and its collection of outbuildings: "barns, stables, sheds."[2]

The house was apparently U-shaped, for the track came to the open side of a courtyard that was enclosed in the rear by the house and on the sides by the two long wings.[3] The central portion was most likely the hall into which Beorn led the two visitors — the same hall where the company later ate and slept. An illustration by Tolkien gave much information about the room:[4] It appeared longer than it was wide, and if the temporary trestle table were about four by eight feet, the room would have been about twenty by thirty-five feet, and the central fireplace about six by eight feet. Running along both side walls were the raised platforms in which the boards and trestles for the table were stored, and on which the travellers' beds were laid.[5] The side walls probably abutted the wings, so they had no windows, making the hall dimly lit.[6] The door shown in Tolkien's drawing was probably that which exited to the veranda. The pleasant roofed porch faced south and had steps leading down to a path that passed through the gardens and back around the house to the main track. It was along that path the Dwarves appeared as Gandalf told his tale.[7]

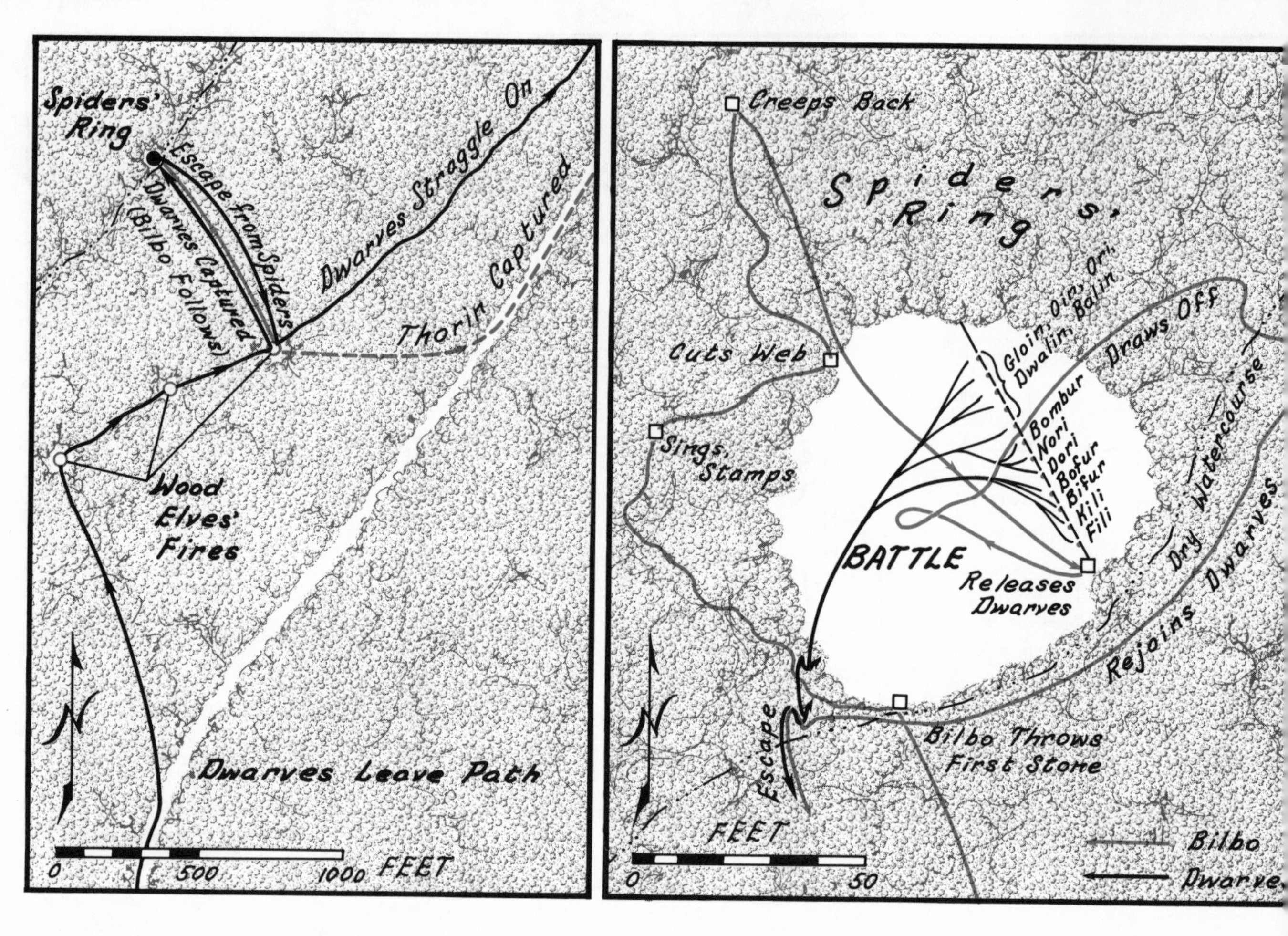

Left: OFF THE PATH *Right:* THE SPIDER BATTLE

Attercop, Attercop

STRUGGLING ALONG THROUGH MIRKWOOD, the Dwarves saw Elf-fires off the path. Against all advice they left the trail. The distance shown was based on the fire's being "a longish way off."[1] The company's efforts were in vain, for the Elves around the fire immediately vanished. Two more times this scene was repeated with each fire being "not far way."[2] The third attempt resulted in Thorin's capture by the Wood-elves, the other Dwarves' wandering away and being caught by spiders, and Bilbo's being left alone only to find himself partially enmeshed in a web.[3]

After Bilbo killed the spider he correctly guessed the direction the Dwarves had been taken and reached their ring after going "stealthily for some distance."[4] It has been assumed the spiders' glade lay even farther from the path than the fire-rings, for both of those were kept clear of spiders.[5] Upon reaching the clearing, Bilbo spotted the Dwarves hanging from a line on the far side. He stoned a creature about to poison Bombur, then attempted to lead the spiders away from the glade. Many followed, but others closed the openings around the clearing, so Bilbo was forced to return briefly and cut an entrance. Then he continued his diversion, before creeping back, leaving the hunting spiders in the woods. He had managed to release seven of the twelve Dwarves before their captors returned, then fought while the remaining Dwarves were freed. To get out of the losing battle Bilbo once more chose to draw off the spiders, going alone to the right; while he instructed the Dwarves, under Balin's command, to break through "to the left . . . towards the place where we saw the last elf-fires."[6] The spiders split and followed both Bilbo and the Dwarves, so the weary company was still having to stop frequently to fight when Bilbo returned to help. At last the spiders quit, just as the company reached an Elf-clearing.

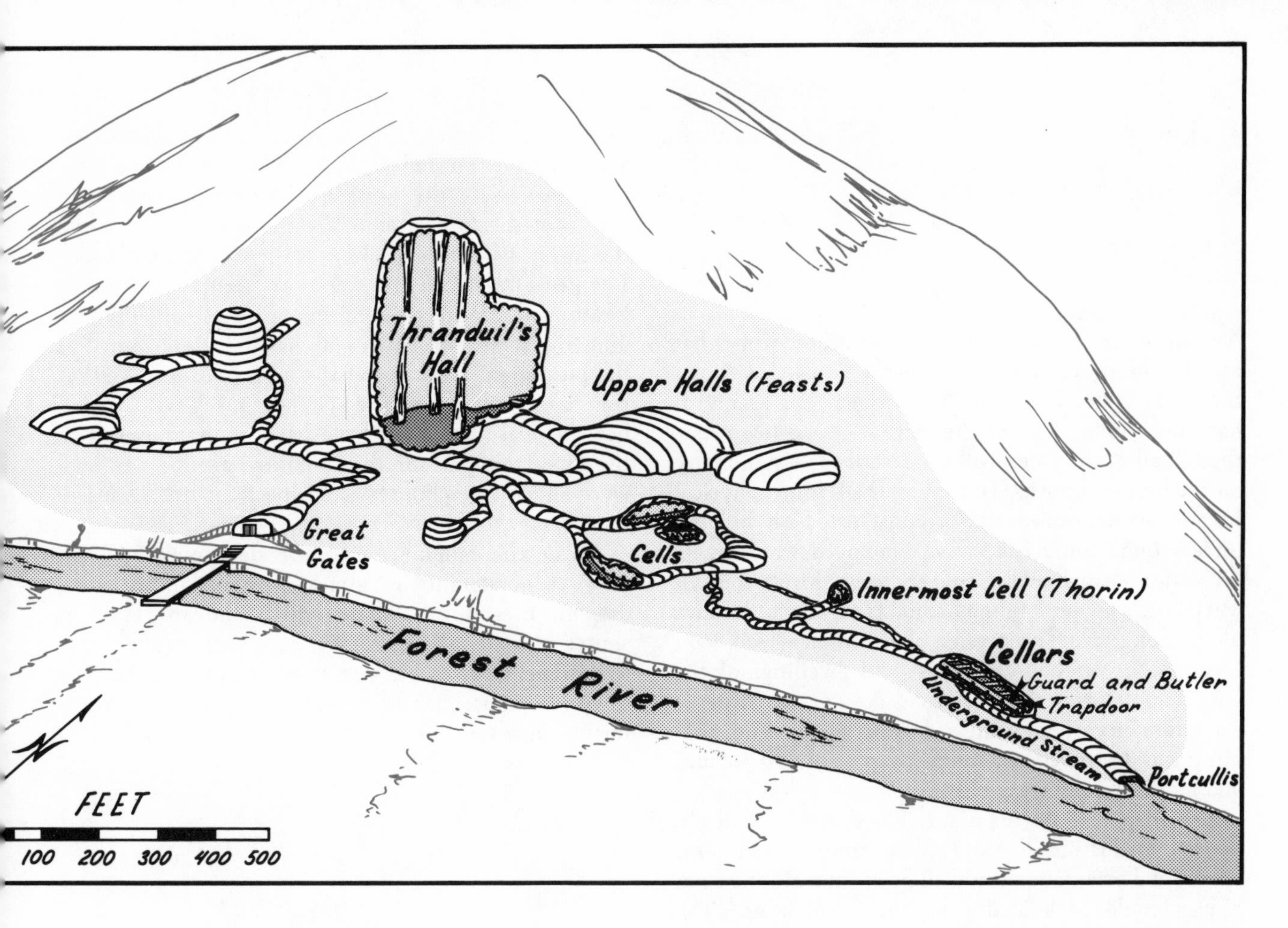

THRANDUIL'S CAVERNS

Thranduil's Caverns

THE ELVENKING WAS THRANDUIL, who once had lived with Thingol and Melian, so his dwellings were understandably reminiscent of both Menegroth and Nargothrond:[1] All lay under a wooded hill beside a river, with a stone bridge leading to the great gates; all had a great pillared hall used as a throneroom, and many twisting passages leading to other rooms of varying sizes at different levels; all had been enhanced by the mining efforts of Dwarves.[2] Thranduil's dwelling was different in two ways: Although extensive, it seems to have been somewhat smaller than the great ancient underground kingdoms; and it had an underground stream. The Forest River apparently dropped rather steeply between the gate and the stream, for the main passage led to the upper galleries, while the stream originated in the heart of the hill and "flowed under part of the lowest regions of the palace, and joined the Forest River some way further to the east, beyond the steep slope out of which the main mouth opened."[3]

When the Wood-elves captured them, the Dwarves were led over the bridge, up a stair cutting through the steep bank, across a grassy terrace, through the great gates that "closed by magic," and down twisting passages to Thranduil's great hall.[4] As they refused to tell the Elvenking their purpose, they were imprisoned in "twelve cells in different parts of the palace." Thorin's was in "one of the inmost caves with strong wooden doors."[5] One of these same dungeons may have been used years later to imprison Gollum.[6] Little was told of the remainder of the rooms except that there were upper halls large enough to allow feasting, and that "the lowest cellars" overlay the tunnel of the underground stream.[7] It was to those cellars Bilbo led the Dwarves to escape: first Balin and last Thorin, whose cell was "fortunately not far from the cellars."[8] The guard and butler were in the small room adjacent to the one with the trap-door, and Balin watched them while Bilbo packed the Dwarves in barrels. Once the Elves had cast the barrels into the stream, the distance seemed fairly short to where they floated under the arched portcullis into the main river.[9]

Lake-town

As the barrels floated past the promontory that formed the rocky gates between the Forest River and the Long Lake, Bilbo saw the village that seems to have been unique in Middle-earth — Lake-town. Although all of the cities Tolkien described — and many of the smaller towns as well — had some physical barrier, being walled and/or constructed on hills or underground, only Lake-town employed water as its protection against evil. Using the great forest trees of Mirkwood, gigantic pilings sunk far into the bottom of the Long Lake supported a platform on which were erected the warehouses, shops, and dwellings of the Lake-men. During the prestigious days of the Dwarves the larger city of Esgaroth had stood on the same site, but it was destroyed at some point (possibly by Smaug) and its rotting pilings could still be seen at low water.[1]

The map of Lake-town was based almost entirely upon an illustration by Tolkien from which size, shape, and orientation could all be estimated; and even houses could be located from their roof-lines.[2] The platform paralleled the west shore of the lake north of the Forest River. In the lee of the promontory lay a protected bay with a shelving shore on which stood "a few huts and buildings," probably used for storage of the barrels collected there.[3] One was a guardhouse at the end of the great wooden bridge that ran out to the town.[4]

At the far end of the bridge were gates, and beyond was a very small compact village, only about two city blocks in size but with numerous two-storied buildings constructed with only narrow openings between, utilizing every square foot of space. Depending on the size of families and apartments, the tiny area could have housed a population of four hundred or more. A wide quay was left on all sides of the platform, from which steps led down to the water. Passing between the buildings near the bridge the company was led beside "a wide circle of quiet water" that functioned as the central market place.[5] By descending one of the pool's numerous stairs and ladders one could reach the lake by rowing through a canal that passed under an arched tunnel that pierced the walkways and even one building.

Only four specific structures were mentioned within the village: the "great hall" where the Dwarves found the Master at feast, the large house where the company lived during their stay, the Town Hall from which they departed, and the "Great House" that was smashed by Smaug.[6] One or more of these terms may actually have referred to the same location. It is tempting to correlate the great feast hall with the Town Hall, but the former stood by the market-pool while the latter had steps leading down to the lake itself. The great feast hall has therefore been shown in the location of a large building in the center of Tolkien's drawing, while the Town Hall has been interpreted as the prominent structure at the bridge corner. Neither the "large house" nor the "Great House" was located, but the feast hall may have been synonymous with the Great House, for the buildings around the pool were all "greater houses" and the feast hall seems to have been the largest.[7]

All of the buildings were wooden, making them very vulnerable to an attack by the fire-breathing dragon. In spite of valiant efforts and an abundant source of water the buildings were well on their way to destruction even before Smaug fell to his ruin. The town was subsequently rebuilt "more fair and large" farther north up the shore.[8]

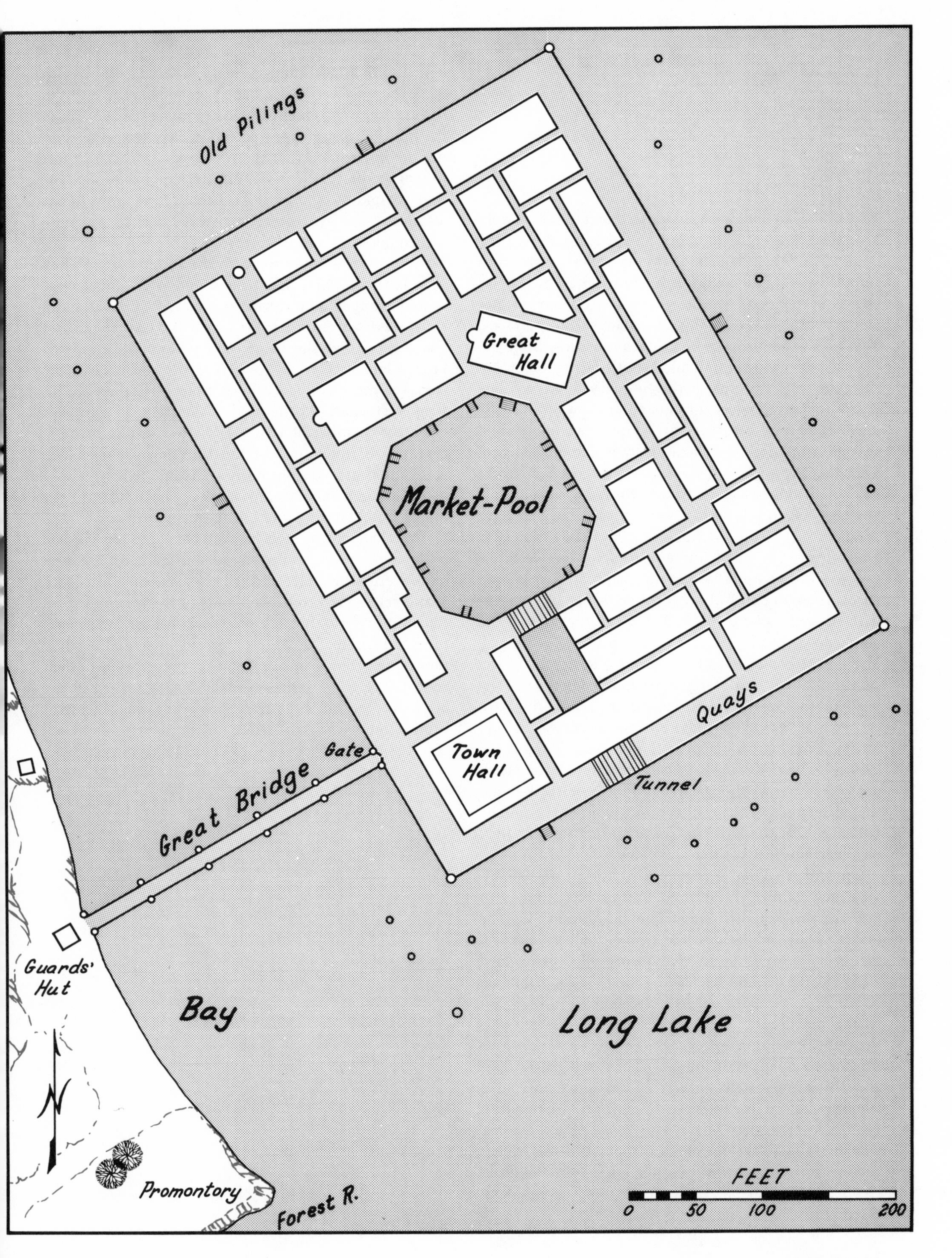
Old Pilings
Great Hall
Market-Pool
Quays
Gate
Great Bridge
Town Hall
Tunnel
Guards' Hut
Bay
Long Lake
N
FEET
0
50
100
200
Promontory
Forest R.

LAKE-TOWN

Lonely Mountain

THROR'S MAP indicated that the diameter of Lonely Mountain was equal to about half the distance to the Long Lake, which lay about twenty miles south.[1] The summit was high enough to be snowcapped at least as late as spring, and so was possibly 3500 feet in elevation.[2] The shape of the mountain's spurs showed clearly on Thror's map: six ridges radiating from the central peak. Within the broad south-facing valley lay the ruins of Dale, once a thriving city of Men.[3] The Running River, which originated from a spring just inside the Front Gate,[4] descended over two falls,[5] then swirled around Dale in a wide loop that passed first near the eastern spur, then west beyond Ravenhill, before turning east and south to Long Lake.[6] Just north of Ravenhill, on the western side, the company made its first camp. Within a few days they moved to a narrower vale, about three miles long, between the two western spurs. There at the east end, just behind an overhanging cliff of 150 feet, was the hidden bay with its secret door.[7] Bilbo discovered the foot of the path "down the valley . . . at its southern corner."[8] There were rough steps that ascended to the top of the southern ridge and along a narrow ledge across the head of the vale. Directly above the camp the path turned east behind a boulder into the steep-walled bay. Sitting with his back against the far wall, Bilbo could look west toward the Misty Mountains; yet the opening was so narrow it appeared only as a crack. Beyond the grassy terrace the trail continued along the mountain-face, but the Dwarves went no further, for they were certain this was the "doorstep."[9]

On Durin's Day Thorin opened the magical Side-door and gained entrance to the ancient tunnels of Erebor, the kingdom under the Mountain. Of the many "halls, and lanes, and tunnels, alleys, cellars, mansions and passages,"[10] the only ones mentioned were the secret tunnel leading to the "bottommost cellar" and the stairs and halls ascending to the "great chamber of Thror" near the Front Gate, which was the only remaining entrance.[11] The secret tunnel was considered small, even though "five feet high the door and three may walk abreast."[12] It descended in a smooth straight line to Smaug's chamber. As the dungeon-hall lay at the "Mountain's root,"[13] and the bay was at the eastern end of the valley, the tunnel has been estimated as being two miles long. In the dark, creeping along to prevent echoes, Bilbo spent about three hours traversing that distance.[14]

In the hall lay Smaug's hoard, attesting the wealth of gold and jewels that had been mined there.[15] An illustration by Tolkien allowed estimates of the size of the hall.[16] Smaug appeared about sixty feet long, giving the impression that the room was at least 180 feet in length. Its vast size was further emphasized by the ever-shrinking light of Bilbo's torch "far away in the distance."[17] Two great stairways exited through arched doors on the eastern wall. Thorin led the company up one of these to reach the Front Gate. "They climbed long stairs and turned and went down wide echoing ways, and turned again and climbed more stairs and yet more stairs again."[18] As the lower chamber was in the heart of the Mountain, and the Front Gate was in the center of the south face, the passages must generally have gone east, then south, then west again. At the head of the steps they entered the great chamber of Thror, and after passing through came upon the source of the Running River, which was routed in a straight narrow channel to a fall at the gate. Beside it ran a wide road that passed beneath the tall arching gateway and onto a rocky terrace.[19]

The old pathway and bridge below the terrace had crumbled, but across the stream the stairs on the west bank were still intact and led the company to a path that ascended the southwest spur to the watch-post on Ravenhill: the only such post described of the several present.[20] It had a large outer chamber and a small inner one. The company stayed there briefly, then returned to the Front Gate, where they walled in the arch and flooded the terrace (including the old path), leaving only a narrow ledge on the west to approach the gate. There they awaited the coming armies.[21]

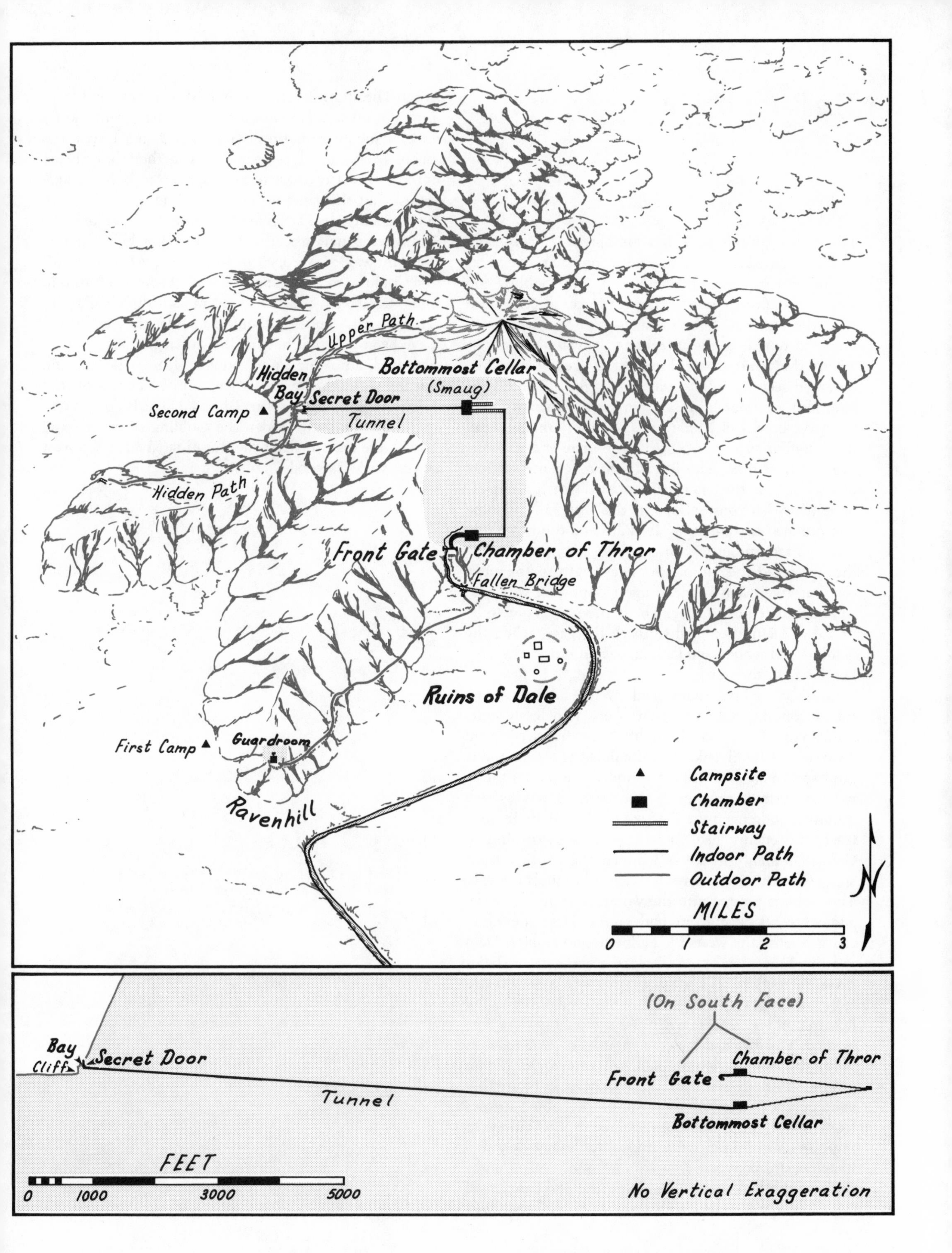

Upper Path
Hidden Bay
Secret Door
Bottommost Cellar
(Smaug)
Second Camp
Tunnel
Hidden Path
Front Gate
Chamber of Thror
Fallen Bridge
Ruins of Dale
First Camp
Guardroom
Ravenhill
Campsite
Chamber
Stairway
Indoor Path
Outdoor Path
MILES
0
1
2
3
(On South Face)
Bay
Cliff
Secret Door
Chamber of Thror
Front Gate
Tunnel
Bottommost Cellar
FEET
0
1000
3000
5000
No Vertical Exaggeration

LONELY MOUNTAIN Cross Section: WEST–EAST

The Battle of Five Armies

THE NEWS OF SMAUG'S DEMISE spread quickly, and within days much of the north was on the move seeking to gain the unguarded treasure. The Goblins and wolves had already mustered great forces at Gundabad after the slaying of the Great Goblin and were well prepared to utilize the unexpected advantage. Immediately they started east through the Grey Mountains, observed secretly by the watchful eagles.[1] The Elvenking also was marching east but turned toward Laketown on Bard's plea. Eleven days after Smaug's fall their combined forces passed the north end of Long Lake.[2] Meanwhile, Thorin had sent raven messengers to his "kin in the mountains of the North" and especially to his cousin Dáin in the Iron Hills,[3] some two hundred fifty miles away. Bard and the Elvenking arrived first, and in response to Thorin's grim refusals they besieged the Mountain. The length of the siege was not given, but it ended upon Dáin's arrival: possibly about ten days later. The battle was about to be joined as Dáin attempted to reach the gate, when the Goblins and wolves suddenly appeared out of the broken lands to the north.[4]

Quickly the Elves, Men, and Dwarves allied against the oncoming enemies. They were hopelessly outnumbered: Dáin had brought "five hundred grim dwarves";[5] the Elvenking commanded at least a thousand spearmen, plus archers;[6] and while Bard's forces were uncertain, they may have been as few as two hundred, judging from the size of the town. In contrast, the enemy had "a vast host."[7] According to Gandalf's plan, the Elves manned the southwestern spur, and the Dwarves and Men, the southeastern. The Goblins poured into the valley, seeking the gate, and were attacked from both sides. First the Elves charged from the west, then allowing no respite, Dáin and the Lake-men plunged in from the east, and the Elves reattacked. The strategy was working successfully, with the Goblins pinned in the head of the valley fighting on two fronts; when the ambushers were ambushed. Goblins had scaled a mountain path that divided just above the gate and had gained the higher ground on both spurs of the mountains. From that vantage they attacked the rear of the allied armies from above, allowing the Goblins in the valley to regroup and bring in fresh troops, including Bolg and his powerful bodyguard.[8]

The Elves had been pushed back near Ravenhill, and Dáin and Bard were losing ground east of the river when Thorin broke the newly built gate wall and leapt into the affray. He thundered "To me! O my kinsfolk!" and to him they went: all Dáin's forces and many Men and Elves as well.[9] Together they thrust into the heart of the enemy, right up to Bolg's bodyguard; but they had no rearguard and gradually they were encircled. The defenders who had not left the spurs faced new assaults and could not help. Just in time the eagles swooped in from the west, casting off the Goblins from the upper ridges. With the Mountain thus freed, all the forces went into the valley to Thorin's assistance. Still outnumbered, they might yet have been defeated but for Beorn. In the last hour he appeared, "no one knew how or from where," and cutting through the ring of enemies he carried off the fallen Thorin, then returned and killed Bolg.[10] With the death of their leader the Goblins scattered, and most were lost in either the Running River, the Forest River, or Mirkwood.

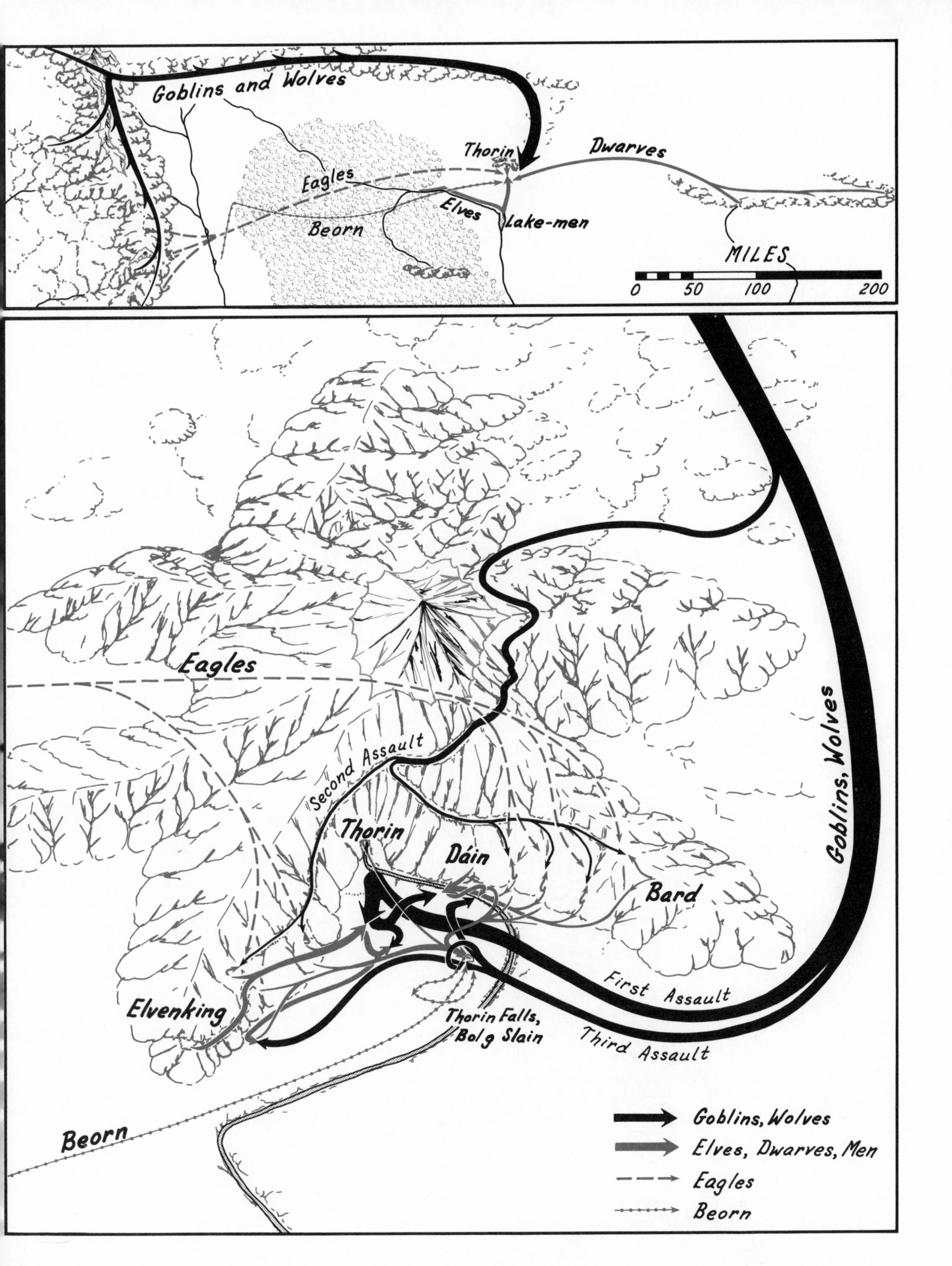

Upper: TO THE BATTLE Lower: THE BATTLE

The Lord of the Rings

Introduction

During the seventy-seven years between Bilbo's finding the Ring and Frodo's quest to destroy it, Sauron reestablished his power in Mordor; Balin attempted to recolonize Moria; Saruman turned wholly to evil; Aragorn undertook great journeys; Bilbo moved to Rivendell; and Gollum went in search of *Thief* Baggins.[1] Gollum left his mountain cave in 2944, and his wanderings took him through Mirkwood to Esgaroth and Dale. In 2951 he was heading west toward the Shire when he was drawn toward Mordor. He lurked on the borders until he was captured in 3017, and later that year he was allowed to leave, only to be caught again — this time by Aragorn.[2] He was held in Mirkwood by Thranduil, but was rescued by Orcs and reached Moria.[3]

Gollum's imprisonment in Mordor had allowed Sauron to learn of Bilbo's finding the Ring but not the location of the Shire. After the Battle for Osgiliath,[4] the Nazgûl crossed the river and passed up the Vale of Anduin, searching unsuccessfully for Halflings. It was mid-September before they returned and were sent by Sauron to Isengard for information. From there they rode west toward the Shire.[5] Meanwhile, Saruman's treachery had delayed Gandalf. In late June, Gandalf had gone to the borders of the Shire, and while journeying up the Greenway met Radagast and learned of the Nazgûls' ride and Saruman's offer of help.[6] He spent the night at Bree, then rode to Isengard, where he was imprisoned atop Orthanc until September 18.[7] After Gwaihir the eagle carried him to Edoras, he tamed Shadowfax. On that swiftest of steeds he galloped toward Hobbiton like the wind, only to arrive too late: Frodo had gone, with the Black Riders in close pursuit.[8]

THE STAGE IS SET

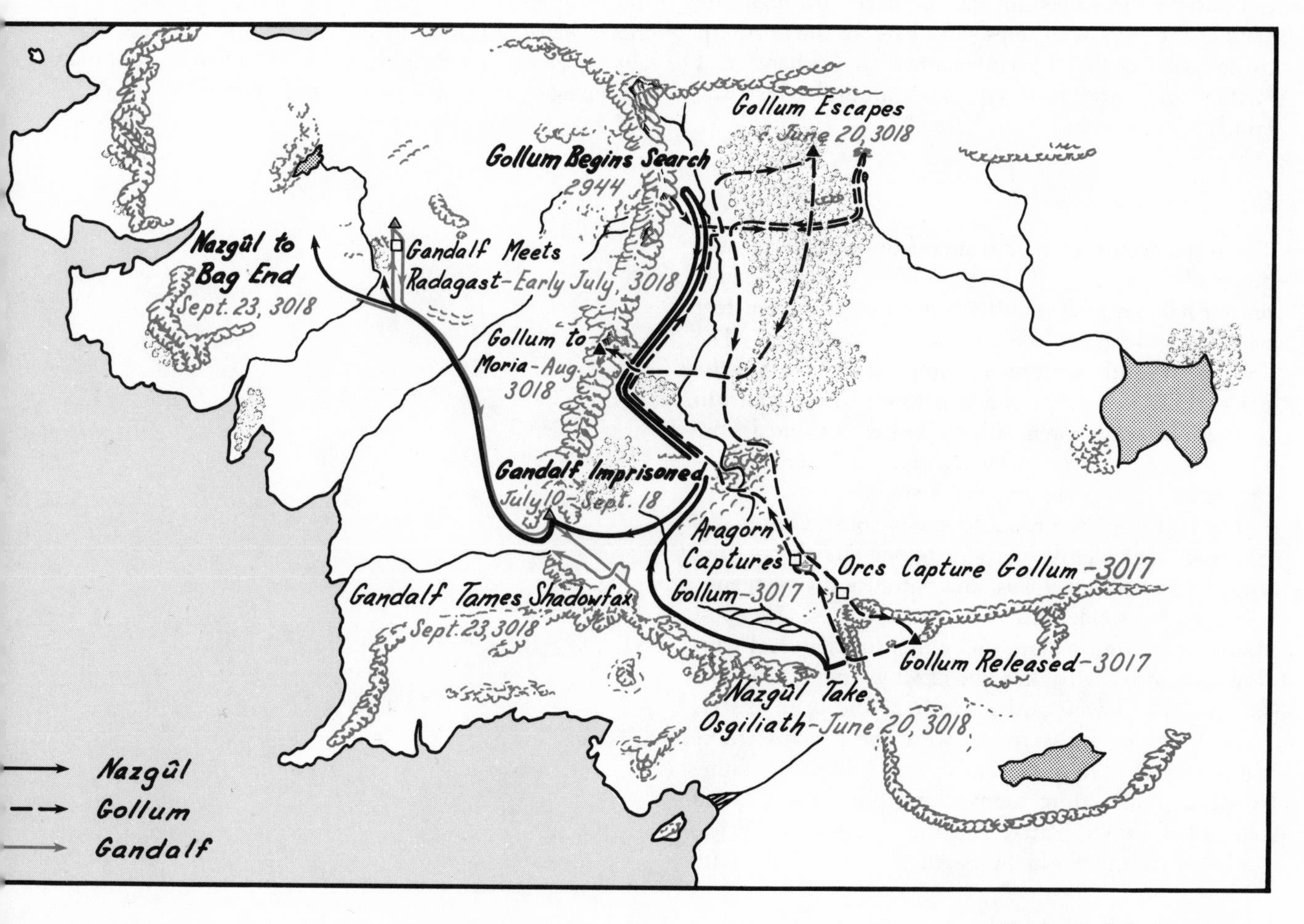

Hobbiton and Bag End

Hobbiton was both mapped and illustrated by Tolkien, providing firm knowledge of the village and the surrounding countryside.[1] The village was so small that it had no inn or public house, and its residents were forced to walk "a mile or more" to Bywater to visit *The Ivy Bush* and *The Green Dragon*.[2] Its principal buildings were Sandyman's Mill on the Water and the Grange on the west side of the road to The Hill.[3] South across the bridge on both sides of the Bywater Road were most of the residences,[4] but the most luxurious home of the village (indeed of the area) was to the north — Bag End Underhill.[5]

Bag End was not a building, of course, but a Hobbit-hole excavated into the side of the only suitable hill around.[6] Below it on the south flanks were other, smaller holes, including Number Three Bagshot Row, occupied by the Gaffer Gamgee and his son Sam.[7] Between the Row and the door of Bag End was a large open field, the site of Bilbo's great birthday party. For the party a new opening had been cut through the bank to the road, with steps and a gate. In the northern corner was set the "enormous open air kitchen," and farther south was the Party Tree around which the family's pavilion had been raised.[8]

Bag End

The residence of Bag End wound from the great green door west into the side of the hill. The door opened onto a hallway that may have been up to fifteen feet wide, judging from one of Tolkien's drawings.[9] The door faced south, with the opening cut steeply into the bank where the path ran east before turning south to the gate. On the porch Bilbo talked with Gandalf, the Dwarves left their instruments, and Frodo set the hiking packs while preparing to depart.[10]

The hall itself served as an entry closet, with hooks for coats and plenty of room to set out the parting gifts Bilbo had left.[11] Past the entrance doors opened "first on one side and then the other."[12] The best rooms were "on the left, going in," for they had windows cut into the bank, some of which overlooked the kitchen and flower gardens west of the open 'Party' field.[13] Among those rooms were the parlour where the Dwarves met with Gandalf and Bilbo, the dining room, a small sitting room where Bilbo and Gandalf talked before The Party, and the study where Frodo spoke with the Sackville-Bagginses, and later with Gandalf.[14] At least the study and the parlour had hearths.[15] Additionally there was a drawing room where Bilbo was "revived," two or more bedrooms, wardrooms, a kitchen, and "cellars, pantries (lots of those)."[16] All in all it was a most comfortable residence.

Hobbiton: Before and After

Before the War of the Rings, Hobbiton lay amid the picturesque countryside of well-managed fields separated by neat hedgerows, where tree-lined lanes led to cozy cottages and holes edged by bright gardens. After the war the Hobbits returned to find a very different view. Along the Bywater Road all the trees were cut, as were all the chestnuts on the lane to The Hill. The hedgerows were broken and the fields, brown. A gigantic chimney, presumably a smelter, choked the air; shabby new houses stood thickly along the road; and Sandyman's Mill was replaced by a larger building, which straddled The Water, befouling the stream. The old farm past the mill had been turned into a workshop with many windows added.[17] The Grange was gone, and tarpaper shacks stood in its place. Bagshot Row was "a yawning sand and gravel quarry," Bag End could hardly be seen for the large huts built right up to its windows, the 'Party' field "was all hillocks, as if moles had gone mad in it," and the Party Tree was gone![18] It was a sad sight, but a year of work restored the village, and "All's well as ends Better!"[19]

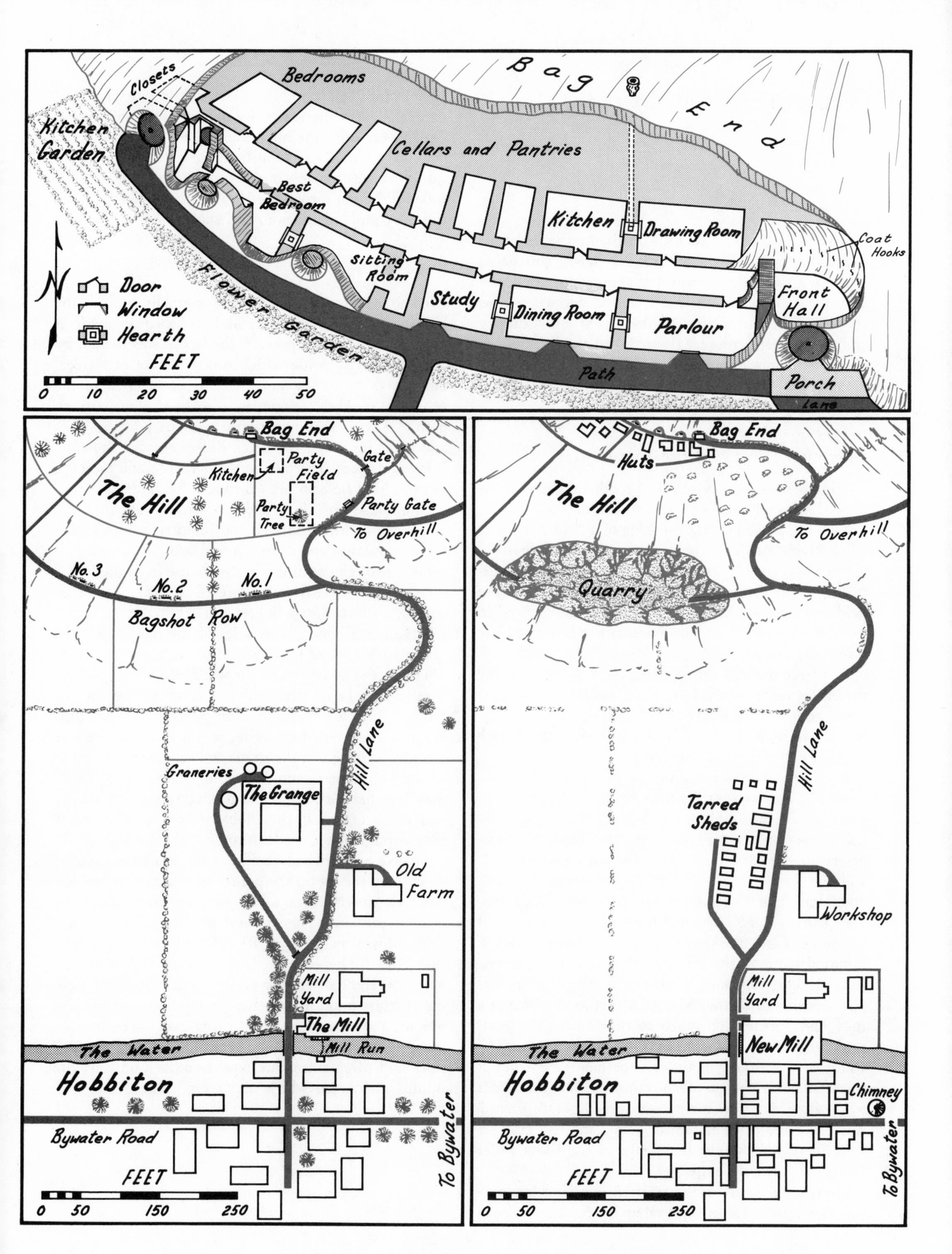

Upper: BAG END *Lower Left:* HOBBITON: BEFORE THE WAR *Lower Right:* HOBBITON: AFTER THE WAR

Along the Brandywine

WHEN FRODO LEFT BAG END on the first stage of his quest, he headed east toward his newly purchased house at Crickhollow. Instead of going along the Great East Road and crossing the Bridge of Stonebows, he chose to hike south through the Green-Hill Country and the Marish, crossing the river on the Bucklebury Ferry. The appearance of the Black Riders forced the Hobbits off the road, so they reached the Ferry in a rather unorthodox way.

Maggot's Farm and the Ferry

Cutting across country east of Woodhall, the Hobbits headed through the well-kept fields of the Marish. They were passing along the edge of a field of turnips when Pippin suddenly realized where they were — old Farmer Maggot's.[1] They were actually trespassing until they went through the stout gate at the edge of the field and into the hedge-lined lane beyond. Ahead in the distance was a clump of trees that concealed the farmstead. Within the trees stood a high brick wall with a large wooden gate opening onto the lane. Inside the enclosure stood the farm buildings (including, possibly, houses for the three ferocious dogs), and a large house where the company had a bite of supper before Maggot drove them to the Ferry.[2]

Maggot's farm was a mile or two from the main road. The land west of the Brandywine was apparently quite wet, as the word *Marish* hints. Tolkien originally had shown only a road, but soon decided it was necessary to raise the road above the surrounding fields and meadows on a high-banked *causeway*.[3] A deep dike along the west side of the road also helped alleviate the drainage problem.[4] About five miles north of Maggot's Lane the ferry lane ran straight east a hundred yards to the landing. This, too, was changed from the early versions in which the ferry landing was placed south of Farmer Maggot's, yet in the final tale they had "turned too much to the south . . . [and] could glimpse . . . Bucklebury . . . to their left.[5] The width of the Brandywine was not mentioned, but it was a major river, possibly comparable to the upper Mississippi. It "flowed slow and broad before them," was too wide for a horse to swim, and the Hobbits could barely make out the figure of the Black Rider "under the distant lamps."[6]

On the east shore of the river was another landing-stage from which a path wound up the bank to the road past Brandy Hall and Bucklebury. Brandy Hall was excavated into the west face of Buck Hill and on the flanks were built the holes and houses of Bucklebury.[7] The ferry lane passed south of the hill to an intersection with the north–south road of Buckland. Half a mile up the main road the Hobbits took a lane that led them a couple of miles to Crickhollow.[8]

Crickhollow

Crickhollow was a small house, originally built as the hideaway of Brandy Hall, and its isolation made it ideal for Frodo's purposes.[9] The house was hidden by a thick hedge, inside which was a belt of low trees. Passing through the narrow gate in the hedge, the travellers crossed "a wide circle of lawn" along a green path.[10] There were apparently gardens both in front and back, for when the Black Riders entered the gate, Fatty saw them "creep from the garden"; and escaping out the back he also ran "through the garden."[11]

The house was "long and low, with no upper story; and it had a low, rounded roof of turf, round [shuttered] windows, and a large round door."[12] A wide hall passed through the middle of the house from the front-door where the friends entered to the back-door through which Fatty Bolger ran from the Nazgûl.[13] Doors opened along both sides of the hall. One door at the back opened onto a firelit bath large enough to hold three steaming tubs, so while the hikers bathed, Merry and Fatty prepared a second supper in the kitchen "on the other side of the passage."[14] The number and character of the other rooms in the house was not given, but given the shape and relatively small size of the house there could have not been many. There may not have even been a dining room, for supper was eaten at the kitchen table.[15] It was, after all, a cozy cottage and did not need an elaborate layout.

Frodo spent only one night at his new home, and at dawn they picked up the ponies from a nearby stable[16] and rode to where the Old Forest was bounded by the Hedge: the High Hay.[17] West of the Hedge the path sloped down, edged by brick retaining walls on either side. Directly beneath the Hedge was an arched tunnel, barred at the east end by an iron gate. Once through, the Hobbits found themselves on the floor of a treeless hollow, and about a hundred yards away on its far side the path climbed into the edge of the Old Forest — thick and threatening, an expanse broken only by the Bonfire Glade, for which they were headed.[18]

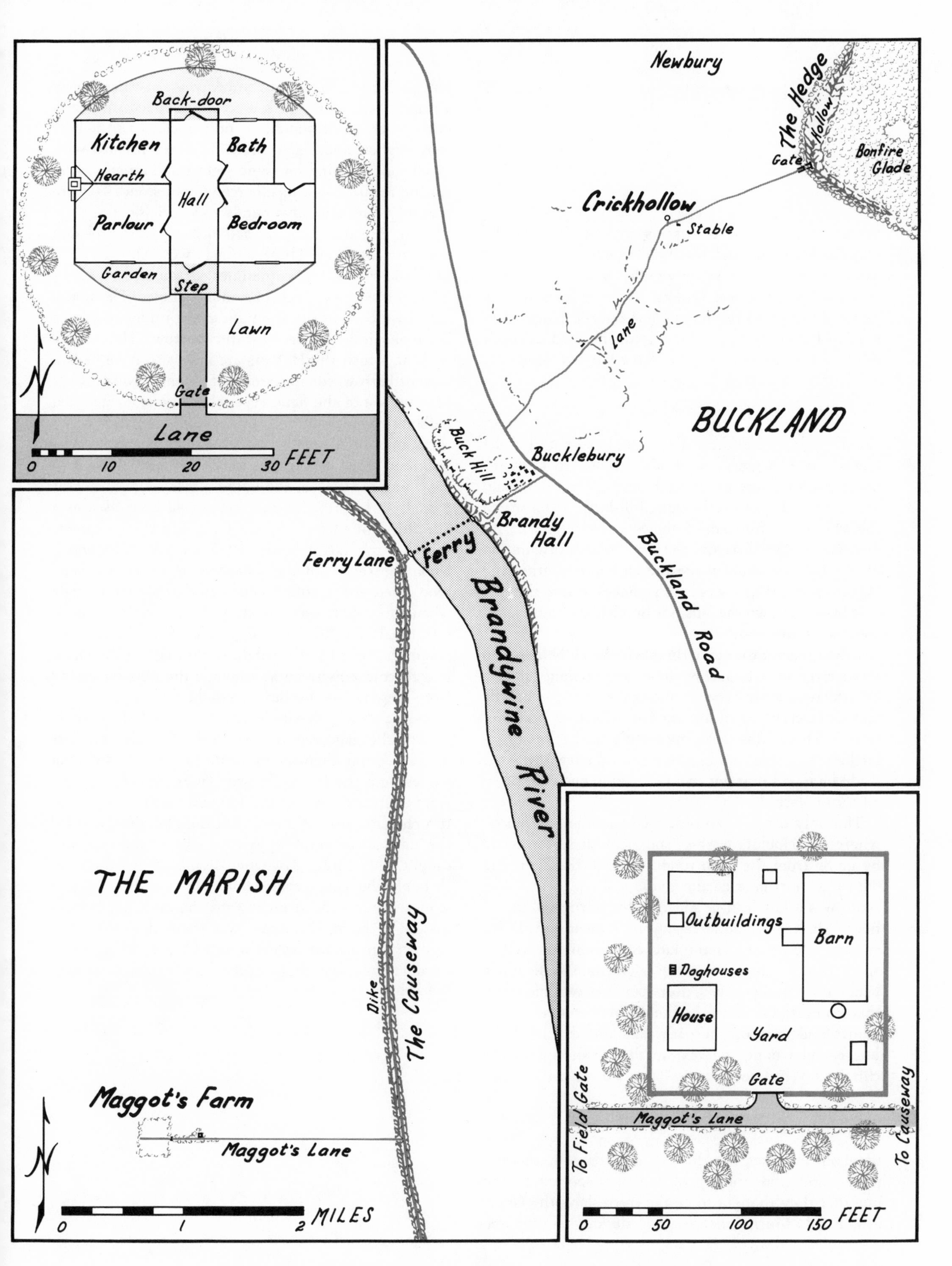

ALONG THE BRANDYWINE Upper Inset: CRICKHOLLOW Lower Inset: MAGGOT'S FARM

On the Barrow-downs

WHILE ATTEMPTING TO CROSS NORTH through the Old Forest, Frodo and his three friends were instead forced south to the Withywindle, where they were entrapped by the Great Willow.[1] By good fortune Tom Bombadil came to the rescue, and led the Hobbits up the Withywindle to his home, which stood between the forest eaves and the first of the Barrow-downs.

The Home of Tom Bombadil

Coming out of the forest, the stone-lined path led the Hobbits over a grassy knoll and beyond that up another rise to where the stone house of Tom Bombadil sheltered under an overhanging hill-brow, from which the young Withywindle bubbled down in falls.[2] As discussed under "Eriador" the predominant orientation of the Downs would make the cliff face southwest.[3] However, the Withywindle must have cut into the cliff as it bubbled down the falls, for Bombadil's house faced *west* not *southwest*.[4]

Crossing over the stone threshold the Hobbits found themselves in a long low room with a long table, a hearth, rush-seated chairs, and opposite the door, the fair Goldberry seated among her reflecting bowls of lilies.[5] There was also apparently a back-door, a kitchen, and stairs leading to a second story, for Tom could be heard (but not seen) clattering and singing in all those places.[6]

The only other room described was the *penthouse*, where the Hobbits washed and slept. It was reached by going from the main room, through the door, and "down a short passage and round a sharp turn."[7] The room was a low lean-to added to the north end of the house. It had windows facing west (over the flower garden) and east (over the kitchen garden), as well as space for the four mattresses along one wall and a bench on the opposite.[8] After spending two nights in that comfortable lodging, the Hobbits fetched their ponies and rode up the path that passed behind the house and wound its way up the north end of the cliff.[9] They had entered the Barrow-downs.

The Barrow-downs

By about mid-day, the Hobbits had crossed numerous ridges, and from the top of one they spotted a dark line that they thought to be the trees along the Great East Road. Much relieved, they decided to stop for lunch. The hill they had climbed was flat-topped with a ring "like a saucer with a green mounded rim," and in its center was a standing stone. To the east the hills were higher, and "all those hills were crowned with green mounds, and on some were standing stones."[10] All the features — rings, barrows, and stones — were probably remnants of funerals and burials.

As in England the great *bell barrows* were probably the least common. These mounds were built of carefully laid turves, and sometimes surrounded by a *peristalith*, a close-set circle of standing stones. The stones may have been of ritual significance, or may only have been physical supports for the barrow. The hollow circle in which the Hobbits ate may also have been a type of barrow, for in Exmoor, England, "Most of the barrows are of the *bowl* type, shaped like an inverted pudding basin [and] . . . [in] case of cremations . . . there may be a narrow circle of piled stones."[11] The different types of barrows may have been related to varying practices at the same time, or at different periods in history, for the downs had been used as a burying ground even in the First Age by the forefathers of the Edain before they entered Beleriand.[12] Upon the return of the Dúnedain the area had been reoccupied and fortified, and new burials were made when the region was known as Tyrn Gorthad, and it was the last refuge of the people of Cardolan from Angmar. After the Dúnedain succumbed to the Great Plague, the downs became evil, inhabited by spirits from Angmar — the Barrow-wights.[13]

Riding slowly in single file from the hollow circle toward the gap seen to the north, the four Hobbits instead found themselves facing a pair of standing stones, and the horses bolted. Frodo headed east toward his friends' voices and found himself going steeply uphill toward the south. On the flat summit stood the dark shadow of a barrow where he, too, was caught.[14] The next day when Bombadil led them on through the gap, Frodo could not see the standing stones. They headed on toward the dark line which, instead of being the Road, was the hedge, dike, and wall that had once been the northern fortification of Cardolan. At last they reached the road and trotted toward Bree.[15]

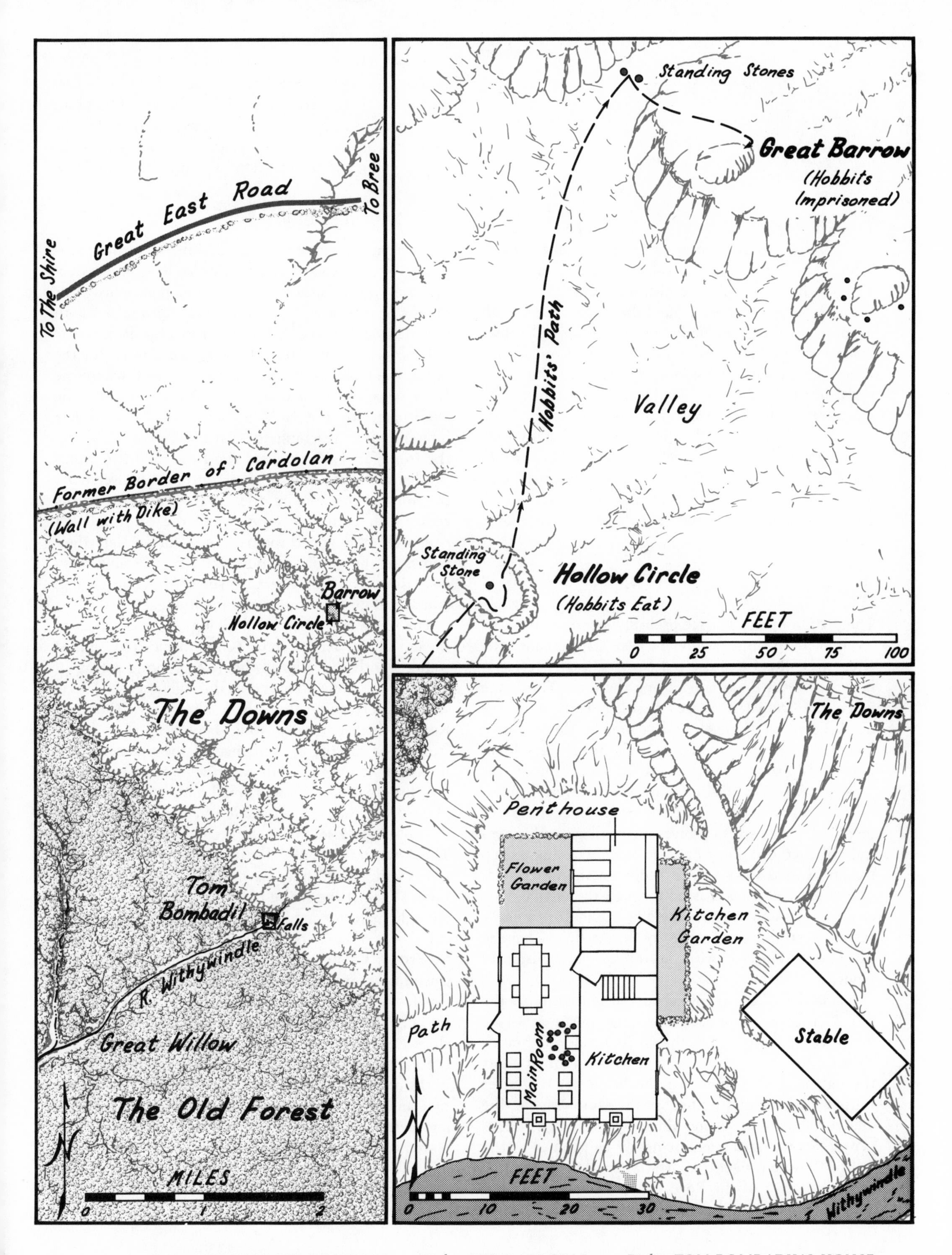

Left: THE BARROW-DOWNS Upper Right: THE BARROW Lower Right: TOM BOMBADIL'S HOUSE

At the Prancing Pony

East of the Barrow-downs the Hobbits came to Bree-land, "a small country of fields and tamed woodlands only a few miles broad."[1] Bree-land had four villages: Bree, Staddle, Combe, and Archet. The settlements were clustered around the slopes of Bree-hill — Bree on the west, under the frowning hill-brow; Staddle on gentler southeastern slopes; Combe in a valley on the eastern flanks; and Archet in the Chetwood north of Combe.[2] Of the four, the largest and most important was Bree. Tiny as it was, the little country had bent with the ebb and flow of many centuries, for it had been settled by Men of Dunland in the Elder Days.[3] About 1300 the Big Folk had been joined by Hobbits fleeing Angmar,[4] and the Little Folk settled especially in Staddle, but there were also some in Bree.[5]

Bree

The predominance of Bree probably stemmed from its location at the intersection of two major roads: the Great East Road and the old North Road. The latter had been most important during the early Third Age when the Dúnedain passed between Fornost in the north down to Tharbad, and beyond to the realm of Gondor. After the fall of Arnor the road was seldom used and became known as the Greenway for it was grass-grown.[6] The road-crossing was just west of Bree-hill, and as with many ancient settlements the Bree-men had attempted to protect their village with physical obstructions. They built no walls, but dug a deep trench or *dike* with a thick hedge on the inner side. The Great East Road passed through the village, so a causeway was built across the dike at the Road's entry in the west and exit in the south. At the hedge the Road was blocked with sturdy gates, constantly tended.[7]

Inside the village the Road curved south around the hill, then turned east again.[8] A drawing shows a lane which curves north from the Great Road, one branch climbing to the crest of the hill, while another leads through a small opening in the hedge for a shorter route to Combe and Archet. In the same drawing the dike is shown as being almost semicircular.[9] This gently sloping area was not nearly as popular as the hill of Bree, however, for most of the houses of Bree were built east of the Road, with few between there and the dike. The village held about a hundred stone houses, mostly on the lower slopes of the hill. East and above them were delved Hobbit-holes.[10] Only four structures were specifically mentioned: lodges for the two gatekeepers, Bill Ferny's house (the last before the South-gate), and the excellent inn, the Prancing Pony.

The Prancing Pony

Tolkien stated that *bree* meant "hill," a term appropriate for the locale;[11] but it may also have been a dual play on words (although it was not mentioned), for bree is also Scottish for "liquor" or "broth" — both of which were served by Butterbur in large measures.[12]

Looking for some refreshments and a room for the night, the Hobbits rode to the inn. It stood where the Road began to turn east, yet was not far from the West-gate, for the Hobbits had passed only a few houses before reaching the yard.[13] The windows on the front faced west toward the Road, and two wings ran back into the hill, with a courtyard between. As the inn had three floors, there was an archway in the center that permitted entrance to the courtyard yet supported the upper rooms. The Hobbits left their ponies in the yard, and Bob was sent to stable them — possibly on the ground level of the south wing, which had no doors nor steps mentioned.[14]

The inn was entered by climbing the broad steps on the left side under the arch.[15] Once inside Frodo almost collided with Butterbur, who was carrying a tray of mugs "out of one door and in through another."[16] He was probably going from the kitchen to the Common Room, which normally would have been close to the front-door for the convenience of the villagers. The innkeeper led the Hobbits down a short passage to "a nice little parlour." It was small and cozy, had a fireplace, some chairs, and a table.[17]

They were also shown to their rooms to wash up. These were apparently farther along the hall of the north wing,[18] and may have been at the far end; for tucked against the rising hill there may not have been enough space for a full-sized room, but only for the small beds of Hobbits. The location was also supported by Strider's statement that the rooms' windows were close to the ground;[19] and while steps were needed at the front of the inn, in back the lower story was actually shorter than the upper ones due to the rising slope.[20] Those low-set windows were so unsafe that the ranger wisely insisted the Hobbits spend the night in the parlour. The kitchen, a private dining room used by Gandalf (in an early version), Butterbur's chamber, and a side door would also have been conveniently placed on the ground floor.[21]

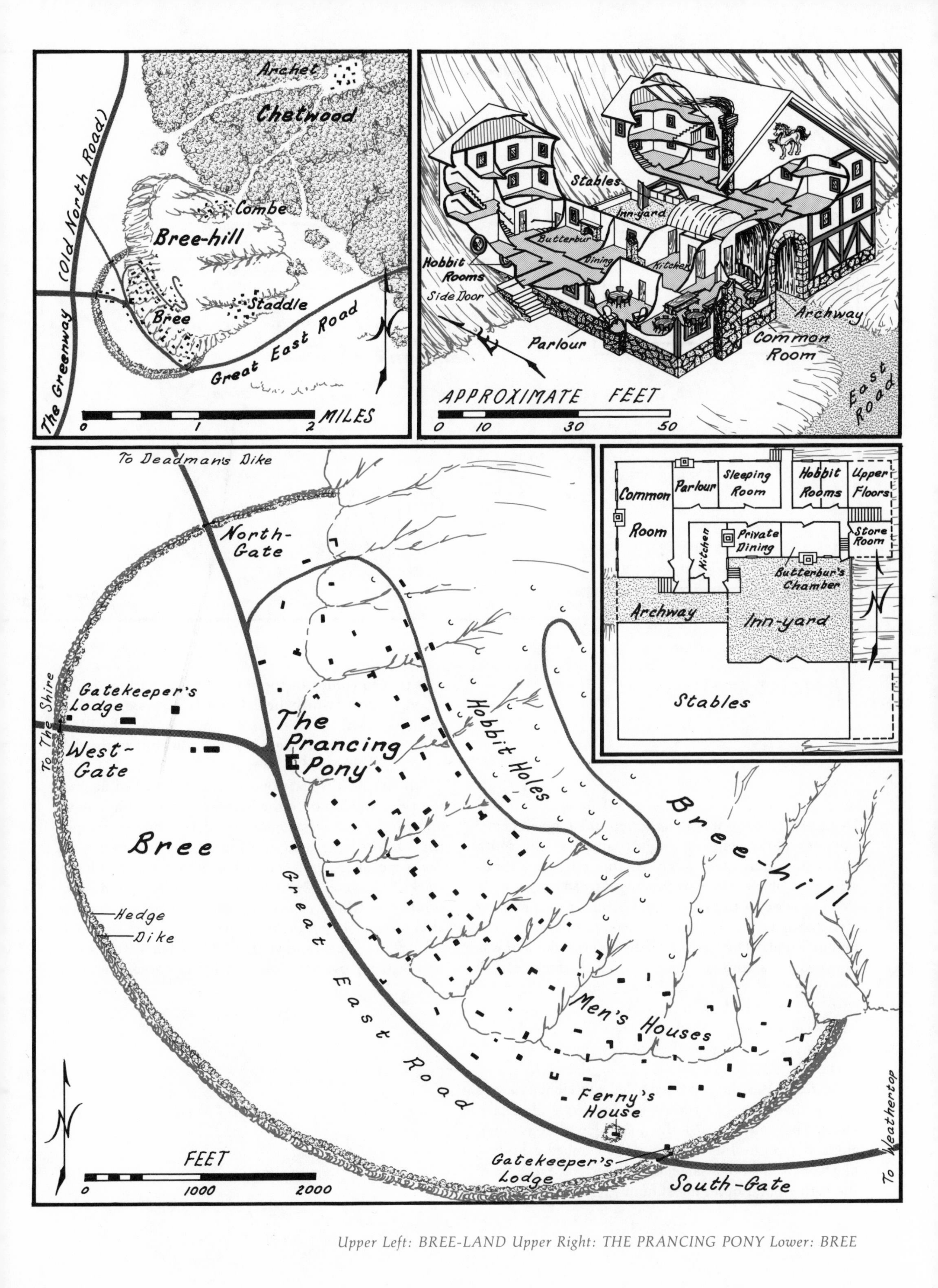

Archet
Chetwood
The Greenway (Old North Road)
Combe
Bree-hill
Staddle
Bree
Great East Road
0
1
2
MILES
Stables
Inn-yard
Butterbur
Hobbit Rooms
Dining
Kitchen
Side Door
Archway
Parlour
Common Room
East Road
APPROXIMATE FEET
0
10
30
50
To Deadman's Dike
North-Gate
Common Room
Parlour
Sleeping Room
Hobbit Rooms
Upper Floors
Kitchen
Private Dining
Store Room
Butterbur's Chamber
Archway
Inn-yard
Stables
Gatekeeper's Lodge
To The Shire
West-Gate
The Prancing Pony
Hobbit Holes
Bree
Bree-hill
Great East Road
Hedge
Dike
Men's Houses
Ferny's House
Gatekeeper's Lodge
South-Gate
To Weathertop
FEET
0
1000
2000

Upper Left: BREE-LAND Upper Right: THE PRANCING PONY Lower: BREE

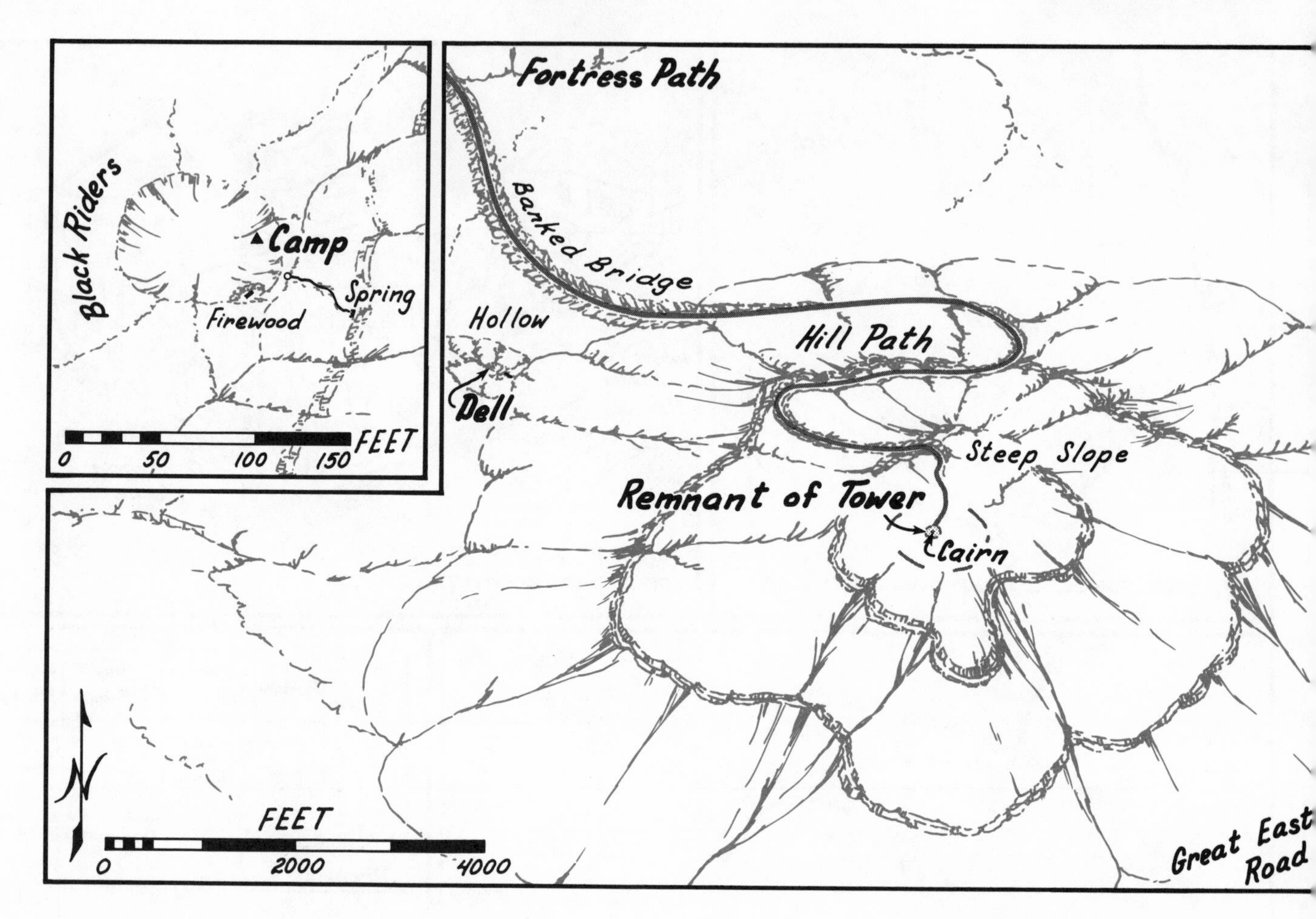

WEATHERTOP Inset: THE DELL

Weathertop

FAR EAST OF BREE was Weathertop, the highest of the Weather Hills, standing slightly apart, at the south end of the undulating ridge. Its summit rose a thousand feet above the surrounding lowlands, giving a clear view of all the terrain and lifting it to the upper airs that gave the hill another name: Amon Sûl, the Hill of Wind.[1] The top of Weathertop was flat and was crowned by a tumbled ring of stones, which was all that remained of the watchtower built in the early days of Arnor.[2] The tower and the hills to the north had been further fortified after the fall of Rhudaur to Angmar, but in 1409 all was lost, and the tower burned.[3]

To reach Weathertop Strider led the Hobbits along a path that once had served the fortresses along the Hills. The path hugged the west slopes, continuing along the connecting ridge until it climbed a bridge-like bank to the north edge of Weathertop.[4] From there the path wound up to the summit, reaching the top in a last steep climb. In the midst of the blackened ring stood a cairn, which held Gandalf's message stone. Looking down the East Road, Frodo spotted the Black Riders, and the travellers hurried downhill to the dell where they planned to camp.[5]

On the northwest slope of the hill tucked against the ridge which ran to the Weather Hills was a hollow, and within that was a bowl-like dell.[6] Sam and Pippin had explored the area and found a spring nearby in the slope of the hill, and a fall of rocks concealing a stack of firewood.[7] Near the spring Strider found boot-prints and feared to stay the night; yet they had no alternative. They built their fire in the most sheltered corner of the dell and waited.[8] Their fears were well-founded, for over the western lip appeared five black shapes.[9]

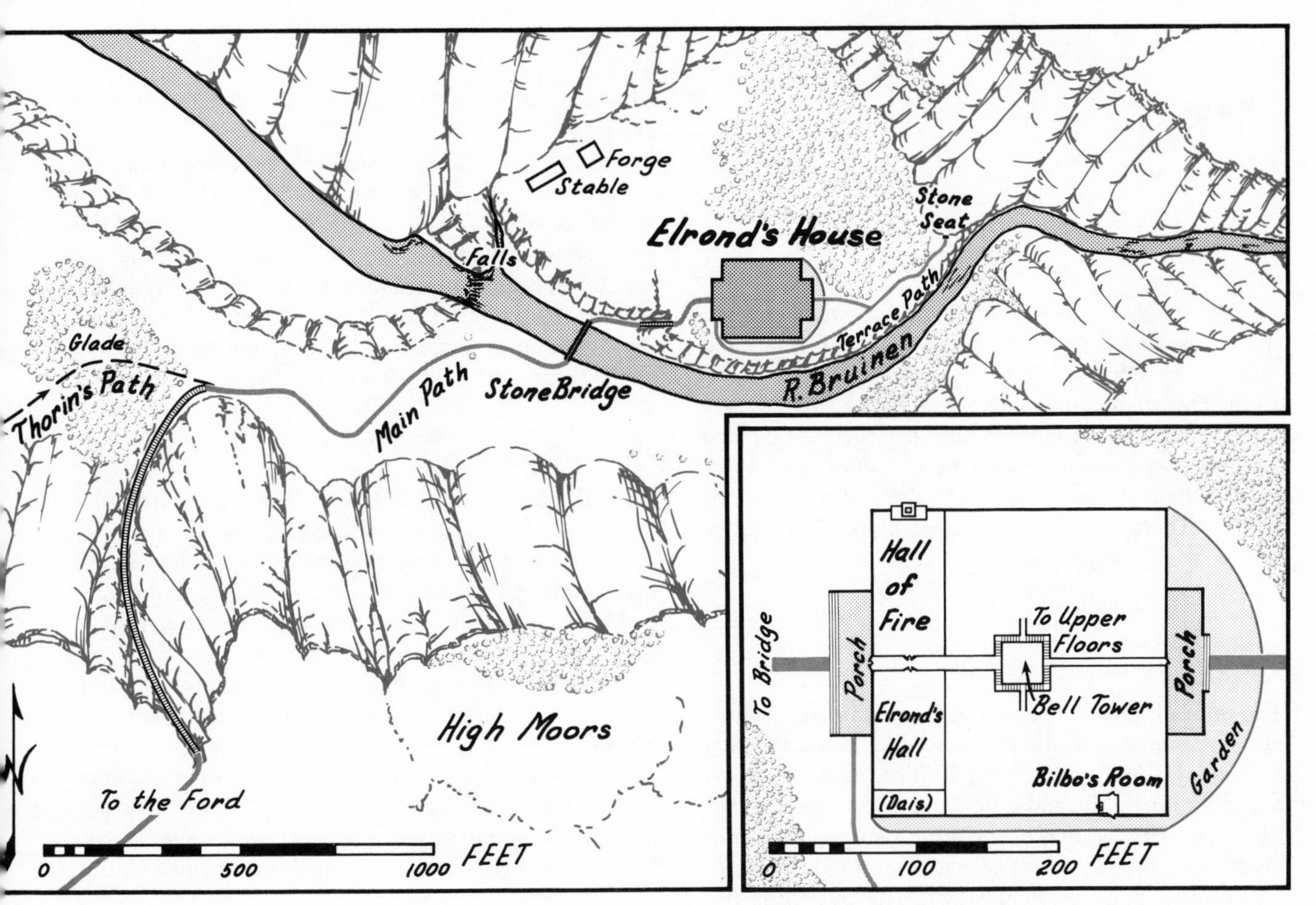

RIVENDELL Inset: THE LAST HOMELY HOUSE

Rivendell

AFTER THE FALL OF OST-IN-EDHIL in S.A. 1697, Elrond led the Elves of Eregion north and founded the refuge of Imladris — Rivendell.[1] The settlement subsequently headquartered many of those in the Last Alliance, assisted in the battles against Angmar, and housed Isildur's heirs through many generations.[2] There Aragorn met Arwen, Thorin and Company rested, Bilbo retired, and Frodo was brought for recovery from his knife-wound.[3]

The deep valley was one of many cutting through the moors sloping up to the Misty Mountains.[4] Its sides were so steep that Gandalf's horse almost slid over the edge when he led the Dwarves east, and the company "slithered and slipped . . . down the steep zig-zag path."[5] There was apparently at least one other path on the south slope, for when the Dwarves met Elves in a glade, the hosts led them to a "good path," possibly the one in Tolkien's illustration, shown descending from a long flight of stairs.[6] The path led across a narrow bridge that crossed the River Bruinen above the falls, and went on to the house of Elrond.[7]

The Last Homely House was "'a big house . . . [always] a bit more to discover.'"[8] There were at least two large halls: Elrond's Hall, where the feast was held, and the pillared Hall of Fire, which was just across the passage.[9] These were evidently next to the front door, for Frodo could see the glow of the firelight from the outside before the Fellowship's departure.[10] Only three other features were mentioned in the house: Frodo's room, which was upstairs;[11] Bilbo's room, which was on the ground floor facing south and had a fireplace and a window and door next to the garden;[12] and the east-facing porch, where Frodo rejoined his friends and where the Council of Elrond was held.[13] Tolkien's drawing also showed a front porch and a small central tower, which may have held the bells used to signal for meals and for the Council.[14] Outside the house there were gardens on the east and south and a path that led along the terrace to a stone seat where Gandalf, Bilbo, Frodo, and Sam met.[15] There may also have been stables, where "Bill" was kept; and a forge, where Anduril was prepared for Aragorn.[16]

Moria

IN THE DEEPS OF THE FIRST AGE, Durin discovered the caves above Azanulbizar, the Dimrill Dale, and there he founded what was to become the greatest of all the Dwarf kingdoms — Khazad-dûm.[1] The Dwarves remained there, carving mines that were "vast and intricate beyond the imagination,"[2] until T.A. 1980, when a Balrog was released and the realm was abandoned.[3] Thereafter the mines were more often named Moria, the *black pit*.[4]

The Mountains of Moria

The mines lay in the bowels of three towering mountains: Caradhras, Redhorn; Celebdil, Silvertine; and Fanuidhol, Cloudyhead.[5] The Redhorn was the tallest and most northerly, and it held the lode veins of mithril silver.[6] The location of the other two peaks was not given, but Tolkien's map showed one to the west of Mirrormere and one to the east. The Silvertine has been placed in the west because it held the Endless Stair leading to Durin's Tower, where Gandalf fought the Battle of the Peak;[7] and as all of the tunnels mentioned were west of the Dimrill Dale, that great spiraling passage seemed likely to be there as well.

South of Caradhras was a steep winding path over which one could cross the Misty Mountains: the Redhorn Gate.[8] The western road was "twisting and climbing . . . in many places had almost disappeared."[9] At the east end it descended into a deep dale, beside "an endless stair of short falls."[10] Gandalf had reckoned it would take "more than two marches" to reach the top of the pass; but the Fellowship was forced down by snow, and instead moved southwest to the Hollin Gate.[11]

The West-door

During the early part of the Second Age Noldorian Elves had built their city of Ost-in-Edhil in the land of Eregion west of Khazad-dûm. A road ran between the two cities along the River Sirannon, ending at the West-door of the Dwarrowdelf.[12] The gate opened onto a shelf that stood "five fathoms" (thirty feet) above the riverbed, over which the Sirannon had originally tumbled in falls. Beside the Stair Falls were steep steps, but "the main road wound away left and climbed up with several loops," as clearly showed in Tolkien's drawing.[13]

The shallow valley was about three eighths of a mile between the falls and the gate, and possibly two miles from end to end.[14] The road had originally crossed the shelf between hedges,[15] but the Fellowship found the valley had been dammed and was flooded, leaving only a narrow rim around the edge. They skirted the water, crossing a creek at the north end (possibly the source of the Sirannon), and reached the Doors of Durin.[16]

The Mines

Gandalf calculated it was at least "forty miles from the West-door to East-gate in a direct line."[17] Past the steps at the entrance there were twists in the tunnel, many passages going off in all directions, and cracks and holes across the floor.[18] At last Gandalf arrived at a point where an arch opened into three eastward passages — one ascending, one descending, and one level. The travellers camped beside the archway in a guardroom with a well.[19] The guardroom has been shown about 3900 feet deep, but there were hammer sounds heard through the well shaft from a lower level.[20] The mines could have been as deep as 12,500 feet and still have been within limits reached in our Primary World.[21]

The ascending passage climbed in great mounting curves with no intersecting tunnels until it came at last to a lofty pillared hall with entrances on each side: the Twenty-first Hall of the North-end.[22] They camped in a corner, far from the west door,[23] and the next morning they went through the north door toward light, and found the sunshine came from a small chamber on the right of the corridor — the Chamber of Records, which held Balin's tomb.[24] There they were attacked, but they fled through the east door down a steep stair (which apparently ran due east, for Gandalf was thrown backward down the steps).[25] To reach the Great Gates Gandalf had said to look for "'paths leading right and downwards,'" yet he made no turns for the passage they were following "seemed to be going in the direction that he desired."[26]

After having descended many flights of steps and having gone a mile or more, they reached the Second Hall in the First Deep; but the passage must have veered south during that distance, for they entered the hall on the north with the Gates "away beyond the eastern end, on the left."[27] The hall was much larger than the other they had seen. The Fellowship was on the east end, between a chasm in which fire burned and the abyss spanned by Durin's Bridge.[28] After Gandalf and the Balrog fell into the pit, the others fled "'not more than a quarter mile . . . up a broad stair, along a wide road, through the First Hall, and out!'"[29]

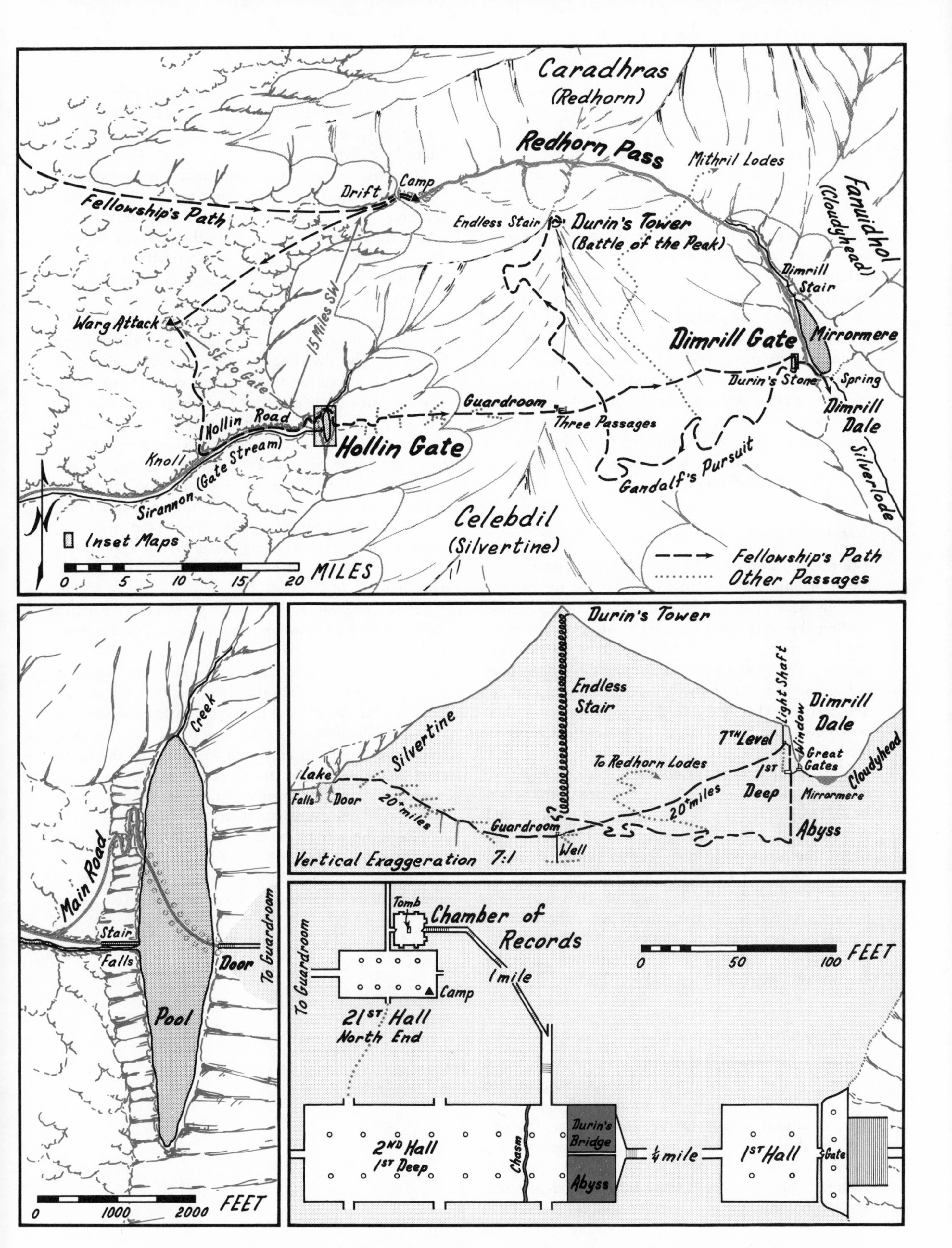

Upper: MORIA Oblique Cross Section: WEST–EAST Lower Left: WEST END Lower Right: EAST END

Lothlórien

CARAS GALADON WAS "the city of trees."[1] The name was Silvan, adapted to Sindarin, and most of its inhabitants were of Silvan origin;[2] although they were governed by Celeborn, a Sindar, and Galadriel, noblest of the Noldor still in Middle-earth.[3] Lórien was settled by the Silvan Elves in the First Age, when it was called Lórinand, but there were differing versions of when they were joined by Celeborn and Galadriel.[4] Galadriel reportedly planted the mallorns, and under the power of her ring the forest realm became *Laurelindórinan*, Land of the Valley of the Singing Gold; but through the wearing of centuries it faded and so became *Lothlórien*, the Dreamflower.[5]

Nimrodel and Cerin Amroth

The travellers entered the Golden Wood about a mile north of Nimrodel — the stream named for the Elf-maiden who once had lived beside the falls.[6] After fording the water they decided to sleep in the trees, and by chance they chose the one used by the northern guards.[7] The Hobbits stayed the night on the guards' *flet*, while the rest of the company slept in a second *flet* nearby.[8] The next day they were guided a short way down the Silverlode and crossed that river on ropes.[9]

Most of the land of Lórien lay east of the Silverlode in the area known as the *Naith* or Gore (a triangle of land). Deep in the woods they came to a great mound, crowned with a double ring of trees: The outer were white; the inner gold. In the center stood a towering mallorn, in which was built a *flet*, once the site of the house of Amroth, the beloved of Nimrodel. The mound was Cerin Amroth, and it was "the heart of the ancient realm as it was long ago."[10] There Arwen and Aragorn had plighted their troth, and after his death it was there she died and was buried.[11]

Caras Galadon

At length the travellers came to Egladil at the heart of Lórien,[12] site of the only city of the realm: a protected city as were all of Tolkien's major settlements, but with variations unique to the Tree-people. The city was on a hill, surrounded by a wall, but the wall was *green*, so it may have been earthen rather than built of stone. Outside the wall was a *fosse*, a ditch or moat, which apparently did not contain water, for it was "lost in soft shadow." A stone path ran in a semicircle from the northern path to a bridge on the south; and where the Great Gates stood, the walls overlapped forming a "deep lane" within.[13]

The most unusual feature of the city was, of course, that there were no buildings and towers; but instead the Elves lived on *flets* (or *talans*) and houses built within the majestic mallorn trees that covered the hill. As the company climbed the winding path to the summit, although they saw no one, they could hear singing and see lights in the trees above.

On the top of the hill was the largest of all the mallorn trees, which held the house of Celeborn and Galadriel. The dwelling was "so large that almost it could have served for a hall of Men upon the earth."[14] The tree has been illustrated as about four hundred feet in height and breadth, which is slightly larger than the tallest redwood,[15] but Tolkien certainly meant the trees to be viewed as immense, saying, "Their height could not be guessed, but they stood up in the twilight like living towers."[16] Up the wide trunk was a ladder, which passed by *flets* "some on one side, some on another, and some set about the bole of the tree," until it came at last to the house that held the oval chamber of Celeborn.[17]

Below the great mallorn was a green lawn on which the Elves set a pavilion for the travellers. Nearby stood a shimmering fountain that fell into a basin, then hurried down the hill.[18] Far down the south slope the stream flowed through a treeless hollow: Galadriel's garden. One could cross through a hedge and descend a long flight of stairs to the lowest point of the dell, where the water ran near another basin and thus provided water for the Mirror of Galadriel.[19]

After visiting the garden with Galadriel, the company stayed one more day, then departed, going southeast from the gate to the confluence of the Anduin and the Silverlode. The path passed through a wall to a grassy lawn, and slightly upstream was a *hythe* (a small harbor)[20] where their boats were moored.[21]

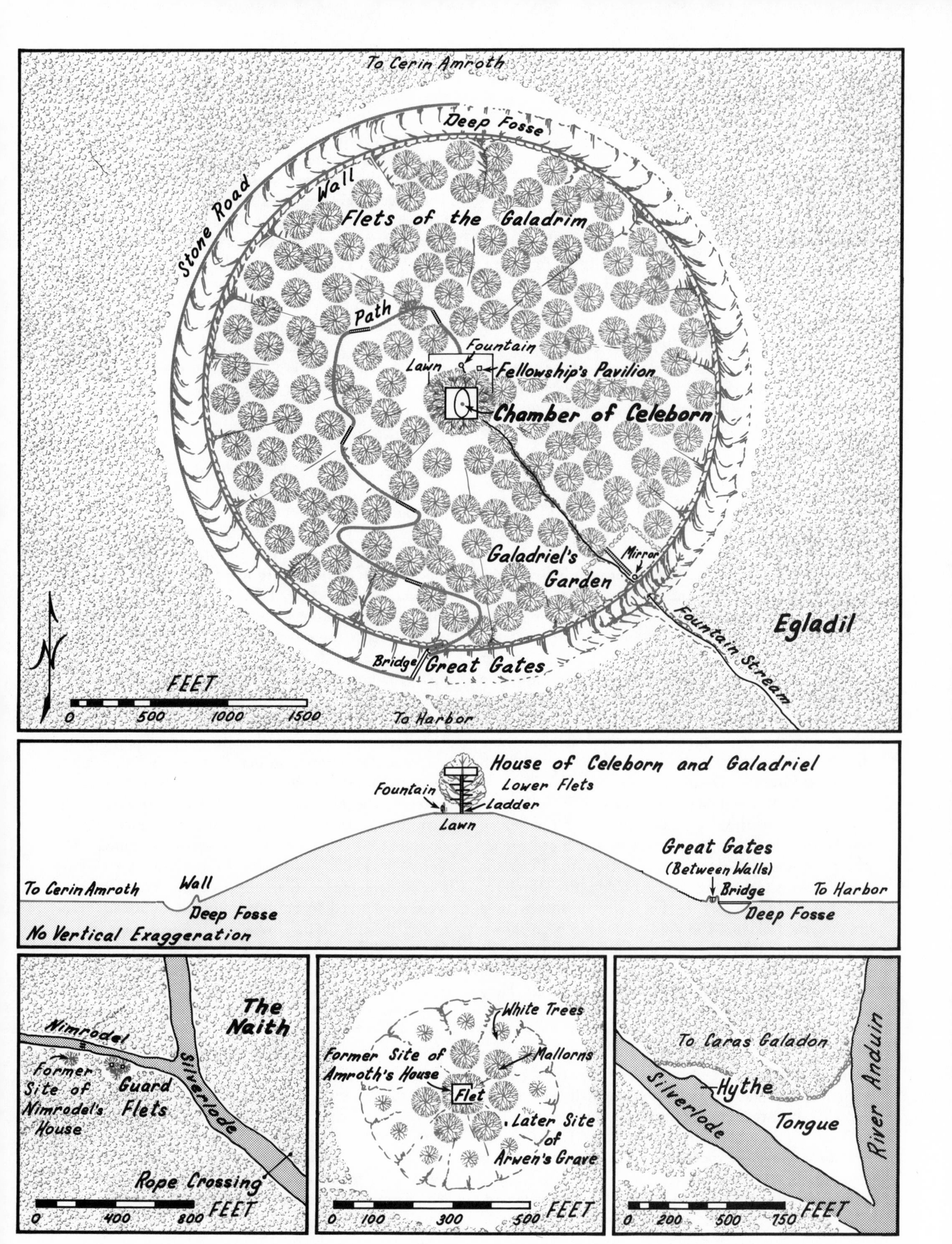

Upper: CARAS GALADON Cross Section: NORTH–SOUTH Lower Left: NIMRODEL
Lower Center: CERIN AMROTH Lower Right: THE CONFLUENCE

Helm's Deep

IN THE FIRST DAYS after Gondor was established the Dúnedain fortified the valley leading from Aglarond, the Glittering Caves.[1] When the land was ceded to the Éothéod, they took over its fortresses as well; and in T.A. 2758 when Rohan was overrun by Easterlings and Dunlendings, Helm Hammerhand retreated to that refuge, and many of his people stayed there through the siege and the Long Winter that followed. Helm's desperate deeds during that time made him one of the most famous of Rohan's kings, and the refuge was named in his honor: Helm's Deep.[2]

The Deep

The entire refuge was often called Helm's Deep, but in the strictest sense the title referred only to the narrow gorge cut by the Deeping Stream between the mouth of the Aglarond and the Hornrock. The presence of caves coupled with a very defensible valley made the Deep ideal for fortification. The caverns were "vast and beautiful . . . [with] chamber after chamber . . . and still the winding paths lead on into the mountains' heart."[3] Water from the pools eventually must have found its way out into the Deeping Stream, which near the cave's mouth cut The Narrows where the Orcs were trapped the first time they crept through the culvert into the Deep.[4]

Away from the caves the ravine was somewhat wider, and after the stream wound around the foot of the Hornrock the valley became much more broad. The point where the stream passed from the Deep was called Helm's Gate,[5] and was blocked by the Hornburg and the Deeping Wall — both clearly shown in a drawing by Tolkien.[6] The Wall, which has been shown as two hundred fifty feet long, would have been well-manned with Théoden's two thousand troops, who fought upon the Wall and in the Hornburg.[7] They were too few, however, to man Helm's Dike, which lay only a quarter mile below the Burg, yet stretched a mile or more across the swiftly widening Deeping Coomb. Although the Dike has been described as "an ancient trench and rampart," it was actually envisioned as a cliff, twenty feet high in places, curving from face to face of the steep mountain wall. The Deeping Stream fell into the coomb below, and the road ran in a cutting beside the stream.[8]

Between the Dike and the Deep lay a greensward, site of the burial mounds of the Eastfold and Westfold riders who fell in the ensuing battle.[9] Although Helm's Deep was described as winding from the north, it apparently ran somewhat eastward, for two of Tolkien's maps showed the vale running from the northeast, and the Hornrock was part of the *northern* cliff.[10] The "evermounting hills" which edged the Deeping Coomb "were too steep to climb on the east, but were long, low slopes on the west.[11] Saruman's troops were trapped between the steep hills on the east, Gandalf from the west, Théoden from the Dike, and the Huorns farther down the valley. Thus, they fell, and the heaps of carrion were later laid in one mass grave delved by the Huorns a mile below the Dike: the Death Down. The Dunlendings were buried more honorably, in a separate mound below the Dike.[12]

The Hornburg

Although the destruction of Saruman's forces came in the Coomb, the primary struggle had occurred during the night at the major battlement: the Hornburg and the Deeping Wall. The Wall stretched from the outer wall of the Hornburg, over the stream, then on across the gorge. It stood twenty feet high, was wide enough for four men abreast, leaned out like a "sea-delved cliff," and was topped by a parapet. It had a wide culvert across the stream, its own tower, three flights of steps leading down to the Deep, and another going up to the outer court of the Hornburg.[13]

The Hornburg was constructed atop the Hornrock, a "heel of rock thrust outward by the northern cliff."[14] The Rock was no more than forty feet high, and required only a ramp, rather than a winding road to reach from the causeway across the stream to the Great Gates.[15] The Hornburg consisted of two stout walls surrounding the outer court, the inner court, and the central tower (which was sometimes called "the Burg").[16] These walls have been shown as slightly thicker and higher than the Deeping Wall, for they were considered to be more difficult to attack.[17] The tower, though "lofty," was much lower than that of Minas Tirith.[18] The outer wall of the Hornburg had three entrances: the Great Gates; the Postern Door next to the cliff, through which Aragorn and Éomer passed to defend the main gates;[19] and the Rear-gate, through which Aragorn and Legolas escaped the Orcs in the Deep.[20] The stairway from the Deeping Wall probably also could be closed off. The Great Gates were topped by a stone arch that apparently had a walkway at the rear, for Aragorn stood above the gates watching the sunrise. A moment later the gates were blasted open, and Aragorn joined Théoden's guard (who were mounting their horses in the inner court where they were stabled), then charged through the rubble to do battle.[21]

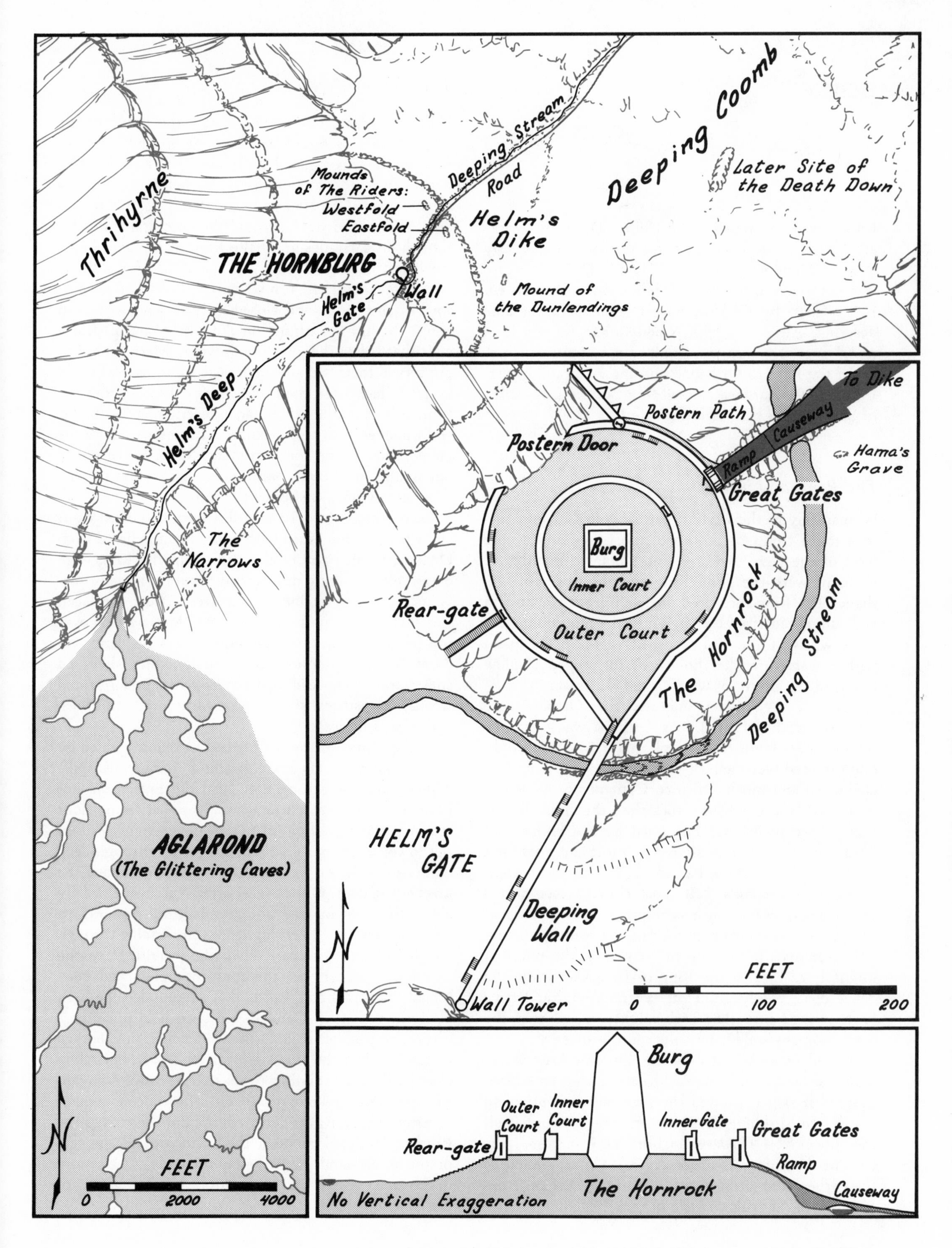
Thrihyrne
THE HORNBURG
Deeping Stream
Road
Deeping Coomb
Mounds
of The Riders:
Westfold
Eastfold
Helm's
Dike
Later Site of
the Death Down
Helm's
Gate
Wall
Mound of
the Dunlendings
Helm's Deep
The
Narrows
AGLAROND
(The Glittering Caves)
FEET
0
2000
4000
To Dike
Postern Path
Causeway
Ramp
Postern Door
Hama's
Grave
Great Gates
Burg
Inner Court
Rear-gate
Outer Court
The Hornrock
Deeping Stream
HELM'S
GATE
Deeping
Wall
Wall Tower
FEET
0
100
200
Burg
Outer
Court
Inner
Court
Inner Gate
Great Gates
Rear-gate
Ramp
The Hornrock
Causeway
No Vertical Exaggeration

Upper: HELM'S DEEP *Center:* THE HORNBURG *Lower:* CROSS SECTION

Isengard

LIKE THE FORTIFICATIONS of Helm's Deep, the works at Isengard were made by the Dúnedain in the early days of Gondor;[1] but unlike Helm's Deep, Isengard was not given to the Éothéod when Rohan was ceded. It was kept by Gondor, but at some point became deserted. After T.A. 2758, when Rohan was overrun and Isengard seized by Dunlendings, Saruman was given the keys to Orthanc,[2] and the great valley surrounding Isengard was named *Nan Curunír,* the Valley of Saruman — the Wizard's Vale.[3]

The Ring and Tower

Isengard lay in the western part of Nan Curunír, sixteen miles from the mouth of the valley and a mile west of the Isen.[4] The two most notable features of Isengard were the outer Ring and the tower of Orthanc. The Ring measured one mile from rim to rim and "stood out from the shelter of the mountain-side, from which it ran and returned again."[5] The plain within was somewhat hollowed, forming a shallow basin, in the center of which stood the tower.[6]

Drawings by Tolkien indicated that Orthanc rose high above the rimwall.[7] As Orthanc was over five hundred feet high, the rimwall might have been only one hundred feet high, or perhaps less: The Ents leveled it without much difficulty. Orthanc was evidently of a much more resistant rock than the rimwall. Although the tower was fashioned by the builders of Númenor, they merely altered it; for it appeared "not made by craft of Men but riven . . . in the ancient torment of the hills."[8] It most closely resembled a volcanic plug or neck such as Shiprock, in New Mexico. If the less resistant outer rock of the cone were partially removed by erosion or quarrying, the remnant might have formed the Ring of Isengard; while the dense black basalts from the central vent could have been formed into the "four mighty piers" that the Númenóreans welded into the central tower.[9]

In Tolkien's earliest drawings Orthanc was clearly manmade — a multi-tiered structure atop an island. The latest sketch showed the eventual conception, in which "the [island] 'rock' of Orthanc becomes itself the 'tower.' "[10] However, a brief note indicated the true final vision was never drawn: a combination of the earliest and latest views, explaining Orthanc's description as "a peak *and* isle of rock."[11]

The Fortification

Until T.A. 2953, twelve years after the Battle of the Five Armies, Isengard had been green and pleasant, with many groves, shaded avenues, and a pool fed by waters from the mountains; but when Saruman fortified Isengard (in rivalry to the newly rebuilt Barad-dûr), the groves were cut and the pool drained.[12] Although an early design of the Ring of Isengard had a small northern gate, this was abandoned for a single entrance: an arched tunnel bored through the rock-wall in the south and closed on each end with iron gates. Within the tunnel on the left (going in) was a stair that led to the guardroom where Merry and Pippin served their friends lunch. The room seemed fairly large: It had more than one window looking into the tunnel, held a long table, had a hearth, and (in the far wall) opened into two separate storerooms where the Hobbits had found the provender. In the far corner of one of the storerooms was a stair that wound its way to a narrow opening above the tunnel.[13]

Inside the basin a Tolkien illustration showed eight stone paths (some lined with pillars) that radiated from Orthanc to all parts of the Ring.[14] In the Ring were delved all the living quarters of Saruman's many servants, including stables for wolves. Thus, the basin was surrounded by thousands of windows peering over the plain. Between the radiating roads the land was dotted with numerous stone domes, which sheltered shafts and vents leading from the vast underground works: "treasuries, store-houses, armouries, smithies, and great furnaces."[15]

In the center of the plain stood Orthanc, welded by some unknown craft into a gleaming many-sided spike of black rock so strong that even the Ents could not harm it.[16] Its only entrance was an east-facing door reached by a high flight of twenty-seven steps. Within the tower were many windows, peering through deep embrasures. Most were shown by Tolkien above the level of the door. One large shuttered archway directly above the door opened onto the balcony from which Saruman spoke.[17] Even higher was a window through which Wormtongue cast down the palantír.[18] At the pinnacle of the tower the four rock piers had been honed into individual horns that surrounded the high platform on which Gandalf had been held prisoner.[19] These sharp spikes gave Orthanc its name, the "Forked Height";[20] and the symmetry of the tower, encircling courtyard, and radiating roads gave fortified Isengard the appearance of one of Tolkien's heraldic devices.[21]

After Saruman was defeated, the Ents destroyed the Ring of Isengard, flooded the basin around the feet of the tower, and planted new orchards. Once more it became green and pleasant: the Treegarth of Orthanc.[22]

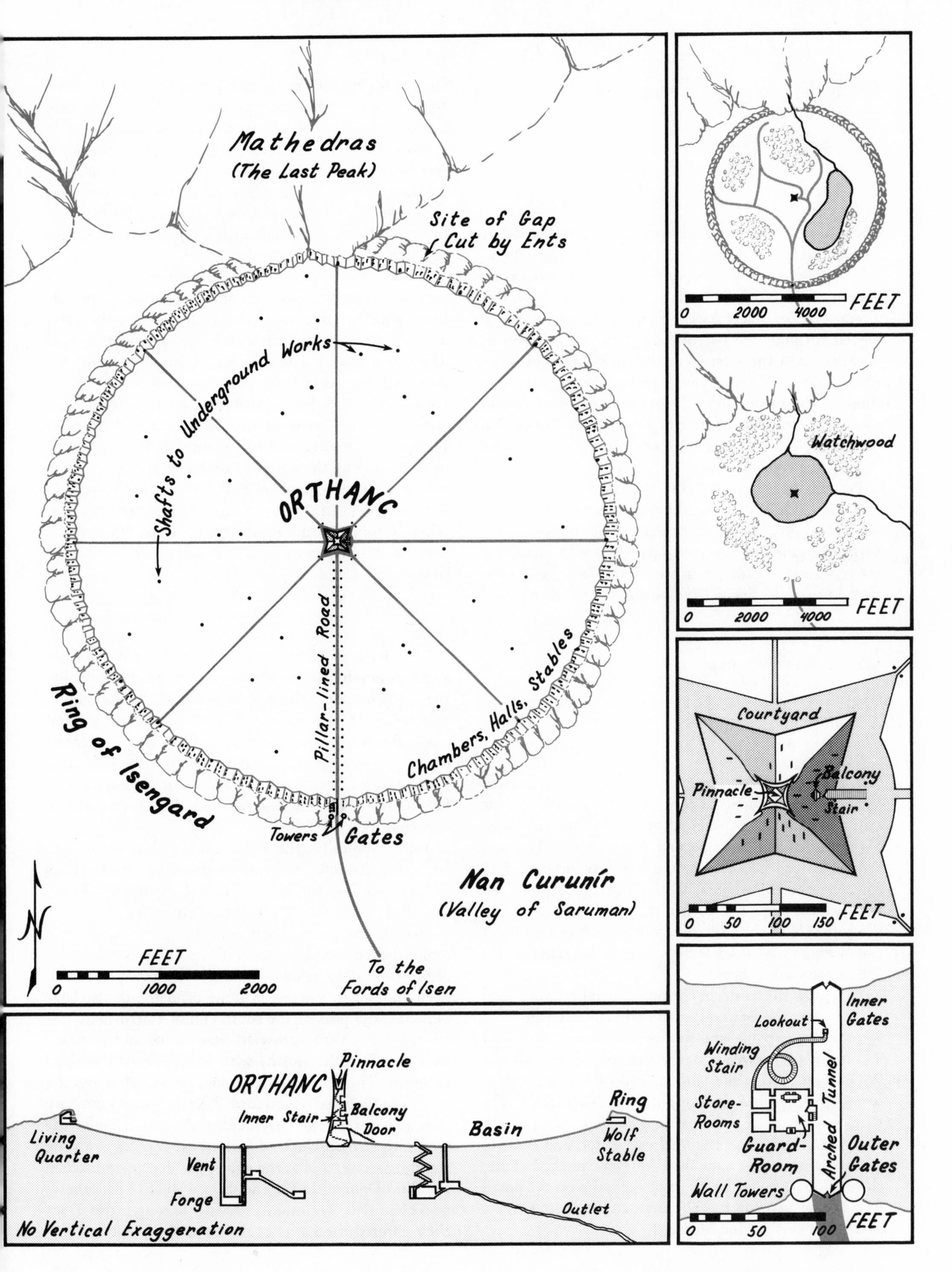

Left: FORTIFIED ISENGARD Cross Section: WEST–EAST Right, Top to Bottom: ORIGINAL ISENGARD, THE TREEGARTH, ORTHANC, THE GATES

Edoras

On a lonely foothill that stood out from the White Mountains "like a sentinel" was raised the city of Edoras, "the Courts."[1] From the west or north a traveller was required to ford the Snowbourn and ride along a rutted road. As the road neared the gates, it passed through the Barrowfield with its two lines of barrows.[2] On the west were the nine tombs of kings of the first line: Eorl through Helm. On the east were those of the second line: the seven barrows of Fréalof through Thengel; and after the War of the Rings, that of Théoden.[3] The oldest of each line was probably nearest the hill.

Past the barrows were the dike and wall that encircled the city. The size of the wall was not stated, but it was "mighty" and was topped by "a thorny fence."[4] Inside the gates a broad paved pathway with occasional stairs wound up to the crown of the hill. Beside the path in a stone channel bubbled a stream that issued from a spring and basin just below the Hall.[5] Where the stream left the city was not told, but it was most likely through a culvert near the Snowbourn.

Atop the hill stood the great house of the king, completed by Brego in T.A. 2969: Meduseld, the Golden Hall.[6] It was surrounded by a green lawn that sloped away from the platform on which the hall was built. Up through the lawn cut a high, broad stair, the top step of which was wide enough to hold benches.[7] The north-facing doors swung inward into a long, wide hall with many pillars. In the center was a hearth, from which smoke could rise to louvers in the gable above.[8] At the far south end was a dais that held Théoden's chair.[9] The hall was apparently multipurpose, serving as a feast room as well as an official reception hall;[10] but it seemed not to be used as a sleeping area,[11] as were the early medieval keeps of Europe.[12] Although the hall seemed to fill the house, as evidenced by the windows on its outer walls,[13] there may have been chambers built into corner towers, at least one for Théoden, one for Éowyn, and the one where Gríma Wormtongue kept his chest.[14] Functions such as the armoury may have been in a building nearby.[15]

Dunharrow

Some miles upstream from Edoras an upland field stood "some hundreds of feet above the valley."[16] This area was known as the Hold of Dunharrow: a refuge developed in the early Second Age.[17] When Théoden returned from Helm's Deep, the Riders entered Harrowdale, the Snowbourn valley, through a gorge on the western slope and forded the river at its feet. On the east side of the valley bottom (which at that point was a half mile wide) were some of the tents of his Riders, as well as horses.[18]

To reach the eastern clifftop a winding road had been hewn: the Stair of the Hold.[19] Viewed in cross section, the step-like appearance was more evident. At each turn of the road Merry saw the statues of the Púkel-men. When the path turned east at the top, it went up through a cutting onto the Firienfeld.[20] The path led on across the upland, edged by standing stones. On the south the field was wider, and most of the tents of Riders and families were pitched there, close to the cliff. In the midst of the camp on the north was a large pavilion for Théoden, and near its entry a small tent was set for Merry.[21]

The vision of Dunharrow changed both historically and topographically as the story evolved. Historically, the semicircular upland field was merely the grassy 'lap' before the stronghold.[22] The Hold was the natural amphitheater beyond the field, with its complement of caverns — including one large enough to serve as a Feast-hall for 500 Riders of Rohan or a meeting hall for 3000.[23] The site was ancient, but held nothing supernatural.[24]

Topographically, the Firienfeld was known as "the lap of Dunharrow" and was described at various times as "set back into the side . . . on the mountain's knee" and that "arms of the mountain embraced it."[25] The source of the Snowbourn was the slopes above the amphitheater, and the stream flowed over the field and fell to the valley below, where it was already wide and deep enough to warrant a stone bridge.[26] In the later versions, the peak at the south end of Harrowdale was altered from Dunharrow to Starkhorn, and Irensaga was added to the north, with the Firienfeld wedged between. The Snowbourn no longer flowed across the field, and required only a ford.[27] As the Grey Company rode east across the Firienfeld, they passed under the Dimholt, a small wood of dark trees; past the warning standing stone; and at the end of the deep glen reached the Dark Door, a cleft in the sheer wall of Dwimorberg, the Haunted Mountain. Passing through the Door they entered the Paths of the Dead.[28]

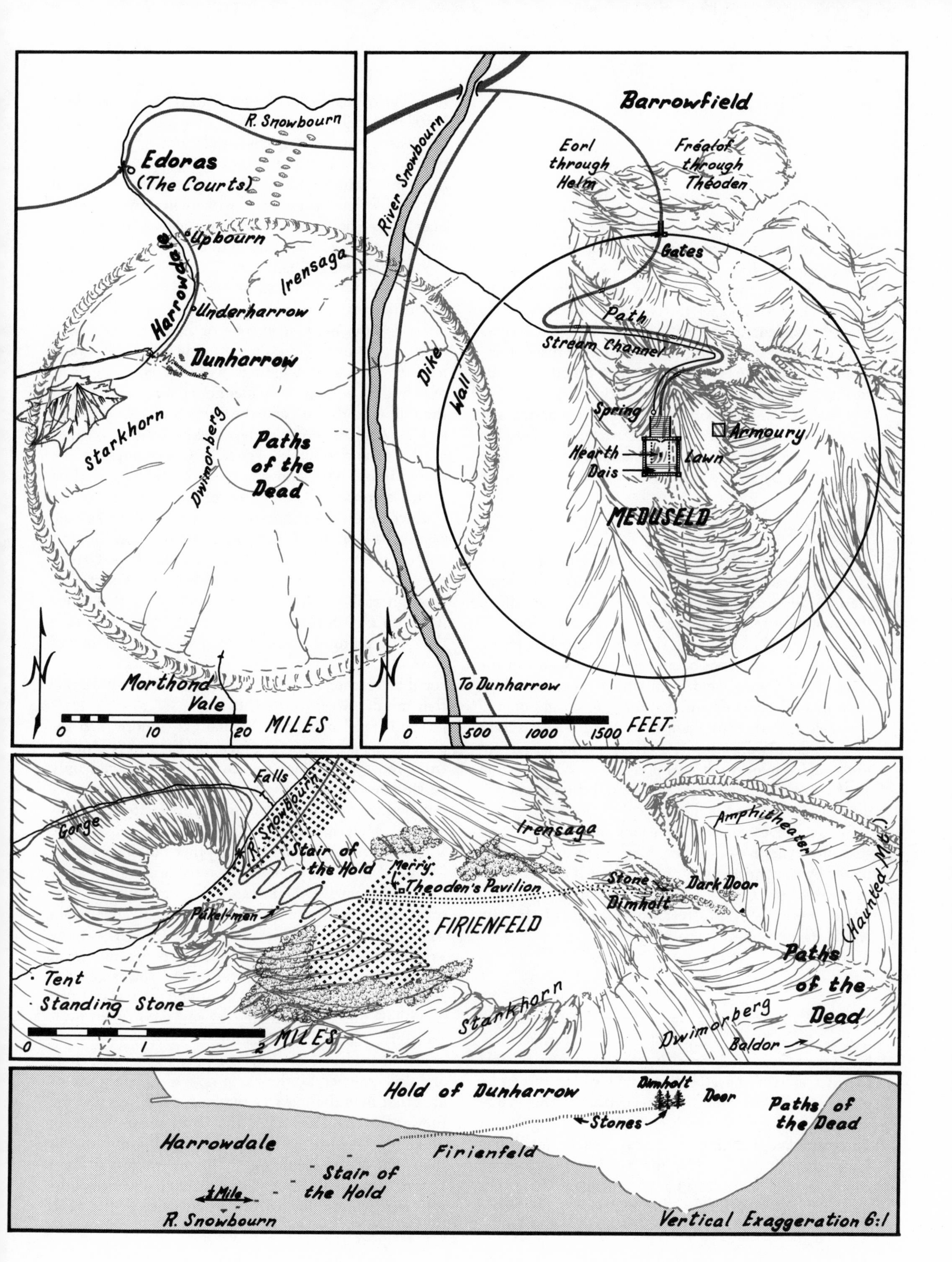

Upper Left: HARROWDALE TO MORTHOND VALE Upper Right: EDORAS
Center: DUNHARROW Cross Section: WEST–EAST

Minas Tirith

In the early years of Gondor the fortress of Minas Anor, "Tower of the Setting Sun," was built to guard against the wild men of the dales of the White Mountains.[1] The city and its tower were reconstructed as need demanded, so the walls and buildings described were certainly not all originals raised over three thousand years before by Anárion.[2] The function of the city had also altered during that period: from outpost fortress to summer king's residence to permanent king's house to capital city.[3] Even the name was changed, for after the fall of Minas Ithil in T.A. 2002, Minas Anor became Minas Tirith, "Tower of Guard."[4]

The Hill of Guard

Tolkien mapped the Hill of Guard as being an almost circular ellipse.[5] Only two features broke the symmetry: the narrow shoulder which joined the Hill to the mountain mass, and the spectacular towering bastion of stone: ". . . its edge sharp as a ship-keel facing east," which rose from behind the Great Gates to the level of the Citadel, and from which "one could look from its peak sheer down upon the gate seven hundred feet below."[6] As this distinctive feature was absent from Tolkien's drawings, its effect on the pattern of the walls can only be surmised.[7] The cross section shows a position midway between the text and the drawings to adjust for this difficulty.

Tolkien revealed no dimensions of the hill except that of elevation — 700 feet;[8] but they may be estimated by comparing two drawings, one of Minas Tirith and one of the Citadel.[9] If the diameter of the White Tower were about 150 feet, the breadth of the city would have averaged 3100 feet.[10]

The City of Stone

The task of excavating and building the walls and towers, homes and hallows, of this almost impenetrable fortress was itself epic. It was "so strong and old that it seemed to have been not builded but carven by giants out of the bones of the earth."[11] The White Tower of Ecthelion rose higher than the highest of European keeps, although it was two hundred feet lower than Orthanc.[12] Not the usual two, but seven, concentric city walls defied any challenger. These facts indicated that the dimensions of those walls would have been at least as large as any we paltry relatives have built,[13] as well as larger than those at the lesser fortress of Helm's Deep.[14] The outer wall of the shoulder was lifted as ramparts: walls atop great earthen embankments, and the outer city wall was crafted of the same impenetrable black rock as the Tower of Orthanc.[15] The seven walls with their towers totaled over forty thousand linear feet and would have required more than two million tons of stone.[16] It makes one think, with Ghân-Buri-Ghân, that the Stonehouse-folk indeed "ate stone for food."[17]

The circles, as drawn by Tolkien, allowed ample room for the main road, one or more smaller lanes (such as the one where Pippin found Merry),[18] and at least two rows of buildings within each circle. The only buildings specifically mentioned were: the stables, the Old Guesthouse, and the Houses of Healing. The stables were in the sixth level, close by the lodgings of the errand riders.[19] The Old Guesthouse, where Pippin found Beregond's son, was in the first level on Rath Celerdain.[20] The Houses of Healing were in the sixth circle on the southern wall, yet were far enough east to be near the Citadel gate and to allow Faramir and Éowyn to look northeast toward the Black Gate of Mordor.[21] The main road wound from the Great Gate through each level, passing through gates that alternated on the southeast and northeast. After each turn the path plunged through an arched tunnel delved through the east-thrusting spur. The seventh gate could be reached only by climbing up a lamp-lit tunnel that ran due west to the Citadel.[22]

The Citadel held many buildings — more than appear on the accompanying map, for they were omitted from most of Tolkien's sketches and received only passing reference in the text.[23] The arrangement resembled western European castles built after the Crusades.[24] Merethrond (the Great Hall of Feasts), the King's House, apartments, and other buildings of unidentified function were all clustered around the Place of the Fountain. Others may have been built into the walls, such as the one in which Gandalf and Pippin were housed.[25] In the center of the Citadel was the White Tower. The tower held storerooms and small dining halls in the lowest level for the tower guard,[26] smaller conference chambers around and above the great hall, and hidden under the summit of the tower, the secret room of the Palantir.[27]

The shoulder of the hill rose only to the fifth circle and was crowned by the Hallows, a completely walled area that held the massive tombs of the Kings and the Stewards. The Houses of the Dead were shown in Tolkien's drawing with domes only slightly smaller than that of the Pantheon.[28] The only access to Rath Dínen, "the Silent Street," was through a walled pathway that wound down from an entrance in the sixth circle: Fen Hollen, "the Closed Door."[29]

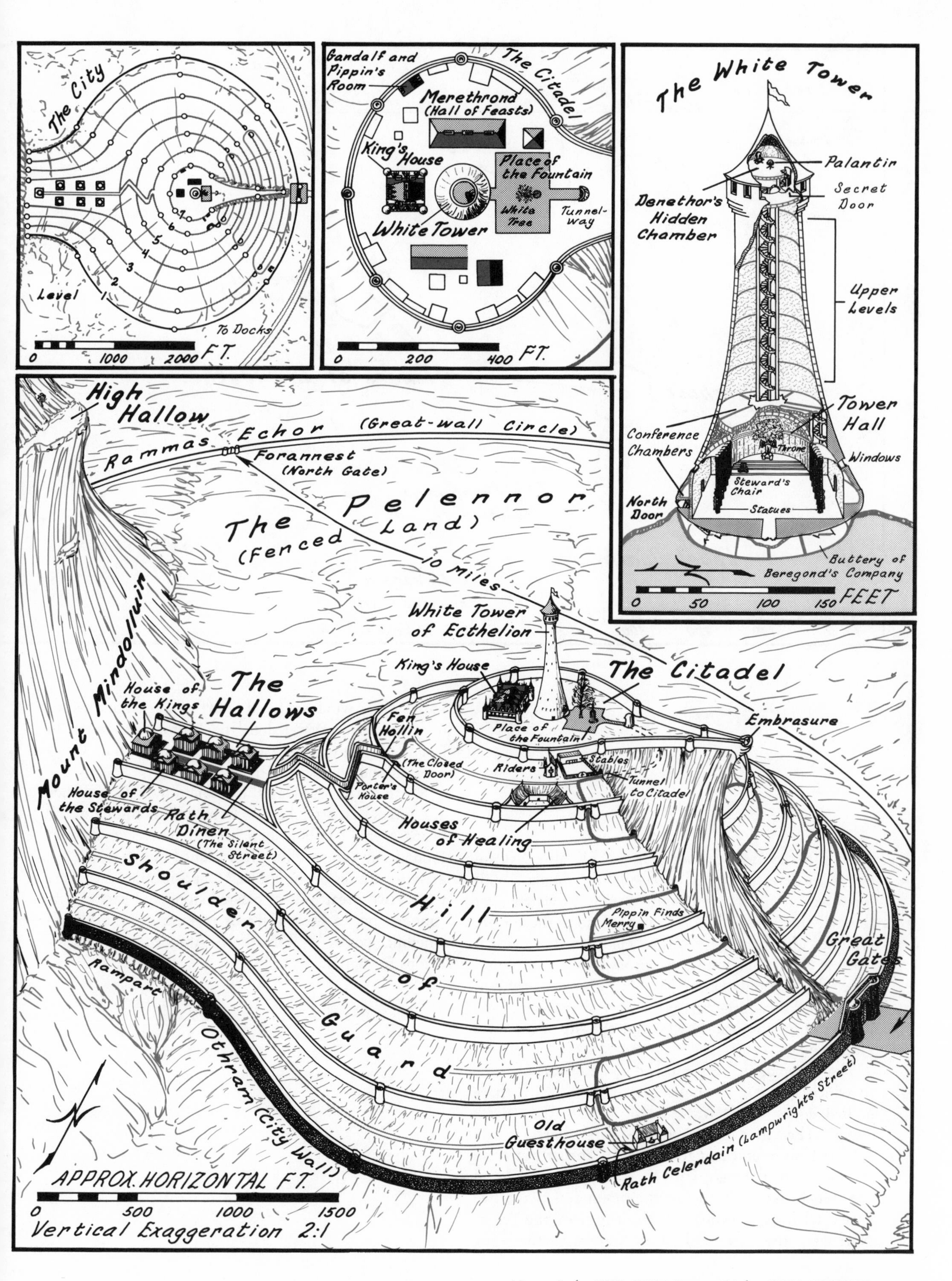
The City
Level
1
2
3
4
5
6
7
To Docks
0
1000
2000
FT.
Gandalf and Pippin's Room
The Citadel
Merethrond (Hall of Feasts)
King's House
Place of the Fountain
White Tree
Tunnel-way
White Tower
0
200
400
FT.
The White Tower
Palantir
Secret Door
Denethor's Hidden Chamber
Upper Levels
Tower Hall
Conference Chambers
Throne
Windows
Steward's Chair
North Door
Statues
Buttery of Beregond's Company
0
50
100
150
FEET
High Hallow
Rammas Echor (Great-wall Circle)
Forannest (North Gate)
The Pelennor (Fenced Land)
10 Miles
White Tower of Ecthelion
King's House
The Citadel
Mount Mindolluin
House of the Kings
The Hallows
Fen Hollin
(The Closed Door)
Porter's House
Place of the Fountain
Embrasure
Riders
Stables
Tunnel to Citadel
House of the Stewards
Rath Dinen (The Silent Street)
Houses of Healing
Shoulder
Hill
of
Guard
Pippin Finds Merry
Great Gates
Rampart
Othram (City Wall)
Old Guesthouse
Rath Celerdain (Lampwrights' Street)
APPROX. HORIZONTAL FT.
0
500
1000
1500
Vertical Exaggeration 2:1

Upper Left: THE CITY Center Right: THE CITADEL
Upper Right: THE WHITE TOWER Lower: THE TOWER OF GUARD

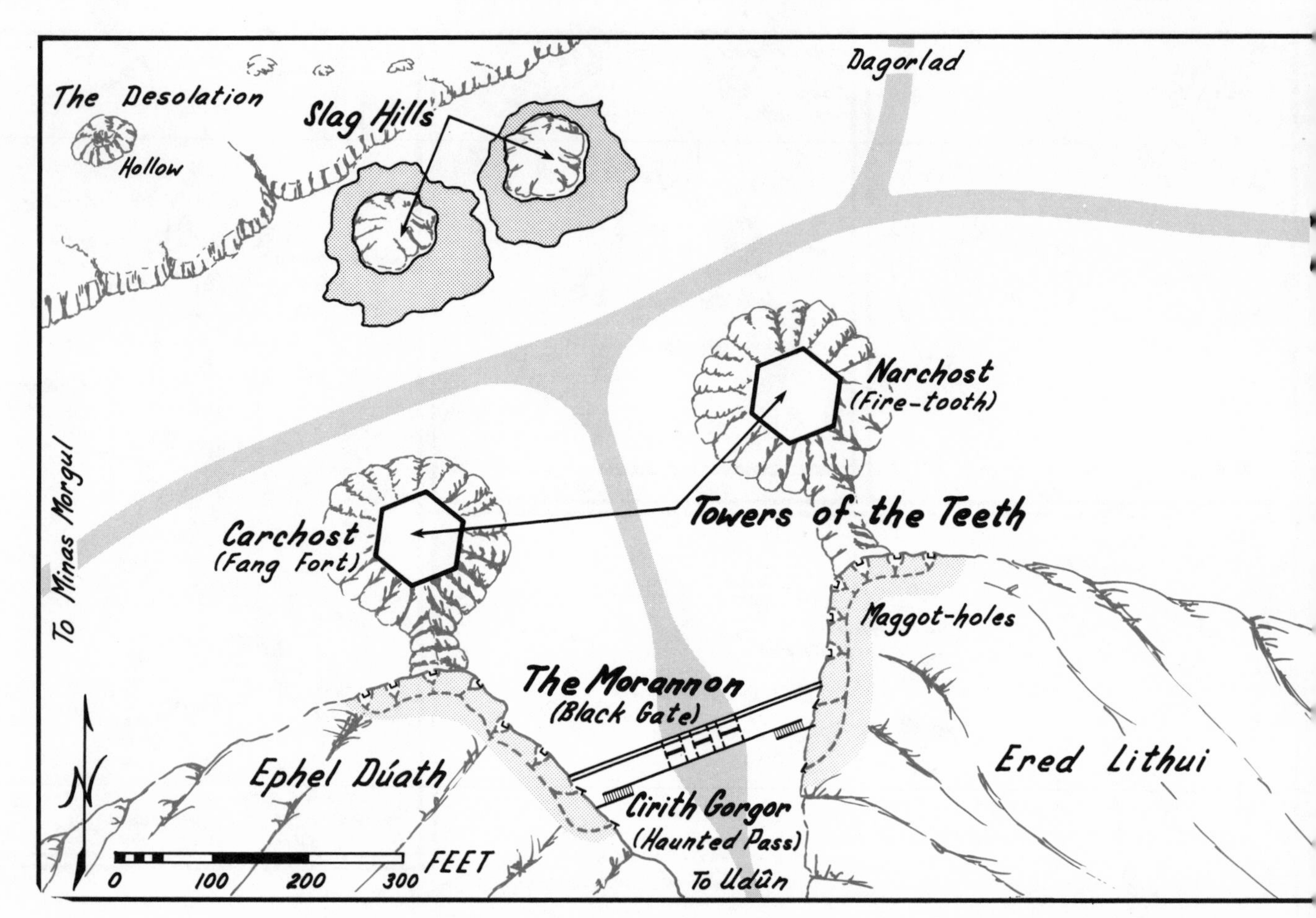

THE MORANNON

The Morannon

At the beginning of the Third Age, after Sauron had been defeated by the Last Alliance, Gondor built fortresses along the fences of Mordor to watch over the evil creatures within.[1] Primary among these were the ones at Cirith Gorgor, the "Haunted Pass," for it was the easiest of all the exits through the mountains.[2] After the depopulation of Gondor during the time of the Great Plague, the fortresses were abandoned,[3] and upon Sauron's return they became the site of ceaseless vigilance.[4]

The "deep defile" was blocked by a rampart of stone in which was cut "a single gate of iron" with three arched doors.[5] This was the Morannon, the "Black Gate." The cliffs on either side were "bored into a hundred caves and maggot-holes."[6] Thrust out from the mouth of the pass, with their feet in the midst of the trench-like valley below the mountains, were two bare black hills, crowned with the Towers of the Teeth: Narchost, the Fire-tooth; and Carchost, the Fang Fort.[7] Their windows faced "north and east and west" over the roads that led to the Morannon: north to Dagorlad, east to Rhûn; and west, then south to Minas Morgul and beyond to Harad.[8]

North of the roads lay the desolation of slag mounds and mires that stretched away for miles. In one of the heaps a small hollow had been delved, and from it Frodo, Sam, and Gollum had peeped out to watch the arriving armies of the south.[9] Opposite the Black Gate were "two great hills of blasted stone and earth" surrounded by "a great mire of reeking mud and foul-smelling pools."[10] On these Aragorn arrayed his troops for battle.

Henneth Annûn

After Sauron took Minas Ithil in T.A. 2901, Gondor built refuges for its troops so a foothold could be kept in Ithilien.[1] The largest and longest used was Henneth Annûn, the "Window of the Sunset."[2] The refuge was beneath a stream that ran from the Ephel Dúath to the River Anduin near Cair Andros. Sam and Frodo had washed at a pool on the stream's upper reaches near the Road.[3] Henneth Annûn lay ten miles west according to Faramir[4] (a figure that agreed with Tolkien's map location[5]); yet Henneth Annûn was supposed to have been so near the Field of Cormallen on the banks of the Anduin that the noise of the waters rushing through the *gate* upstream could be heard.[6]

The Refuge

The last mile of the path to Henneth Annûn was only guessed by Frodo: The river was always on the right and was increasingly loud. Near the end "They climbed upwards a little . . . were picked up and carried down, down many steps, and round a corner." When unblindfolded Frodo stood on the *doorstep* of the cave: a ledge of stone thrust out from the cave's mouth to the streaming waterfall. Behind the step was a low rough arch through which the stream had once poured.[7] The arch was not the entrance to the refuge, however. Instead, the steps had been hewn into the rock and reached the cave via a door in the side-wall.[8]

The cave was "wide and rough, with an uneven stooping roof." Although it was not "kingly," it was large enough to hold the two hundred men who had fought in the battle, as well as sufficient food supplies and tables.[9] In the rear the workmen must have sealed off the old channel that had carved the grotto, for the cave was more narrow there and a recess was partly curtained off, giving Faramir and his guests some privacy.[10]

The Basin

The workmen had directed the stream in a channel that had probably been its original course before the waters cut the cave. Thus, instead of disappearing underground and reappearing in low falls, the stream rushed through a deepening gorge, bubbled over terraces, around a race, and plunged over the cliff in falls double the original height.[11] They were "fairest of all the falls of Ithilien,"[12] so they may have been the largest as well. The length of the turret-like steps, the insecurity of the high ledge above the falls, the danger to anyone diving from the cave-mouth, and the deep scouring of the basin at the falls' foot all combined to give the impression of height estimated as approximately eighty feet.[13]

Part way up the entry stair was a landing below a deep shaft. From the landing a second stair led off to the left, winding "like a turret-stair."[14] The main stair continued up to the cave entrance at the top of the southern bank, and from there Frodo was led west along the bank, with a steep drop on his right. Although he was careful, the bank slope must have descended rapidly, yet smoothly, for no steps or winding paths were necessary to reach the far end of the basin, where he found Gollum.[15]

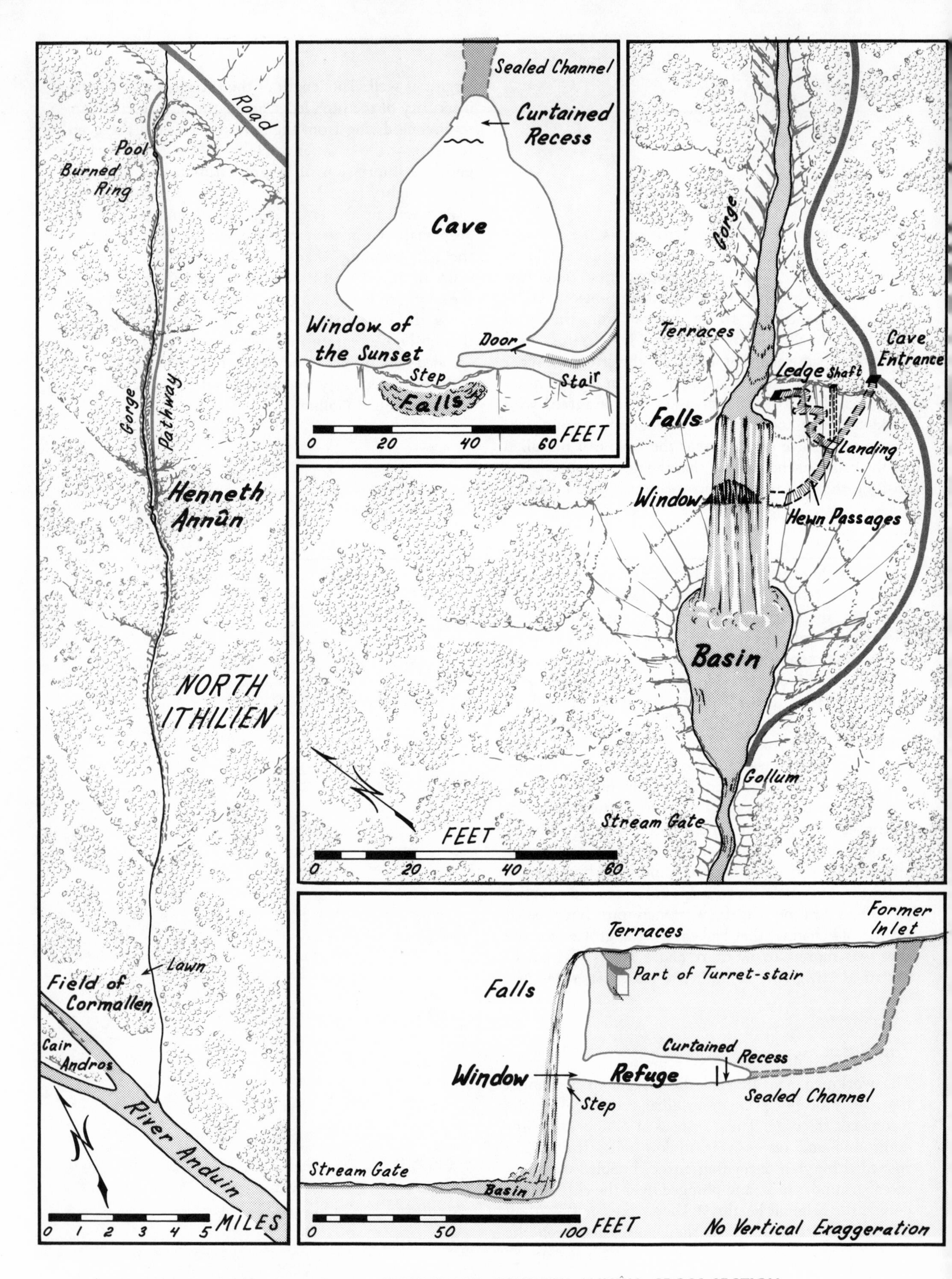

Left: THE STREAM Right, Top to Bottom: THE REFUGE, HENNETH ANNÛN, CROSS SECTION

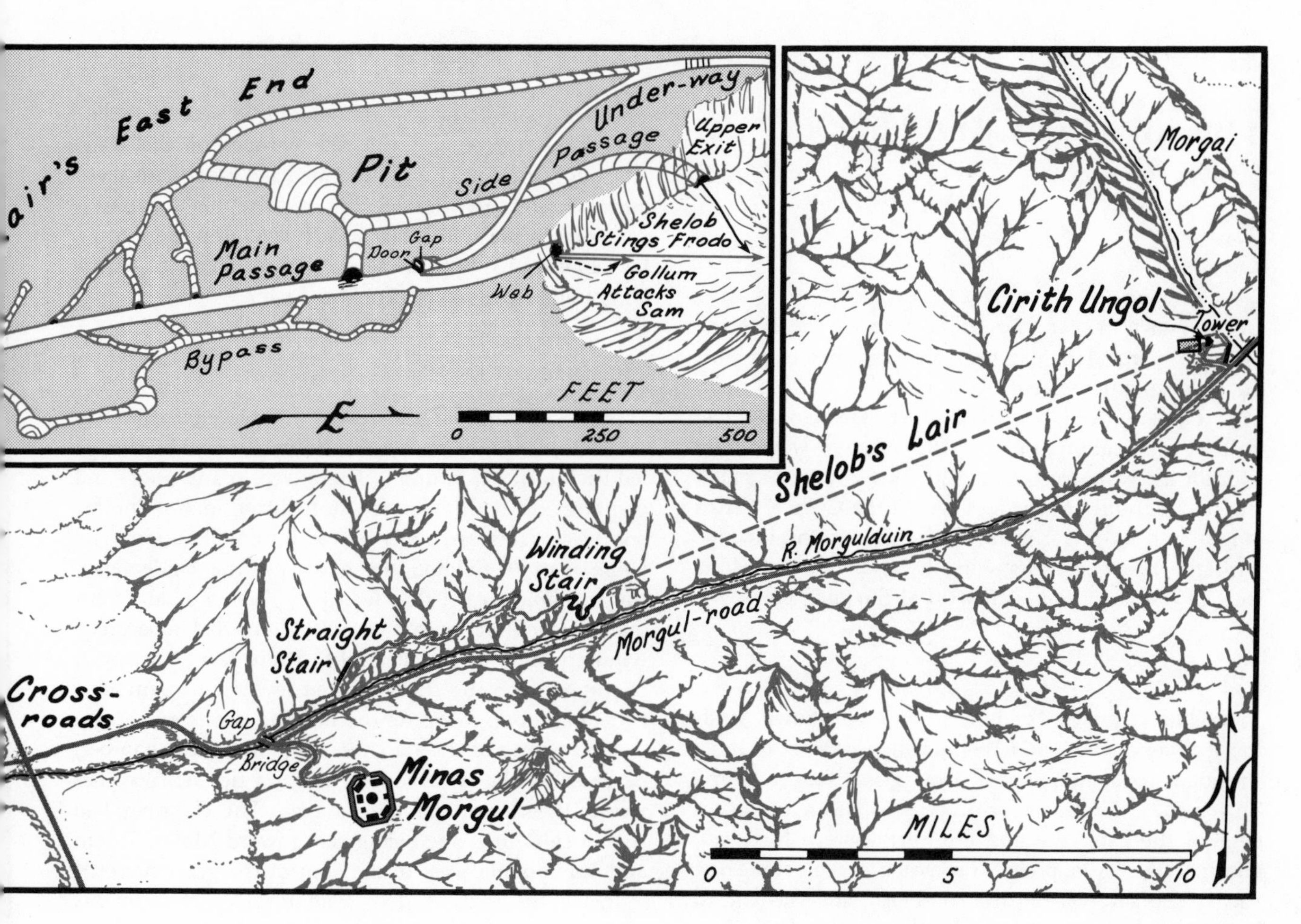

THE PATH Inset: LAIR'S EAST END

The Path to Cirith Ungol

Near the foot of the bridge west of Minas Morgul Gollum turned aside from the Morgul-road, passed through a gap in the wall, and entered the path leading to Cirith Ungol: the "Pass of the Spider."[1] The trail at first led along the northern side of the valley of the Morgulduin, but when it was opposite the north-facing gate of Minas Morgul it turned left along a narrow ledge beside a tributary valley[2] and began to climb the Straight Stair. The Stair was protected on each side by sheer walls of increasing height, yet was so long that the Hobbits began to fear the fall behind them.[3] Had it been even 600 feet in a direct line, it might have measured 900 from bottom to top!

After the Straight Stair the path continued up a rough, but less steep, slope that "seemed to go on for miles," until it ended on a wide shelf with a sheer drop on the right.[4] Beyond was the Winding Stair, which coiled along the face of a reclining cliff. At one point Frodo could see the Morgul-road in a ravine far below.[5]

Originally Cirith Ungol was envisioned as the home for many spiders, and the lair lay between the two stairs. In the writing process Tolkien reversed the order to its final position, apparently without even realizing he had done so until afterward.[6]

Only a mile beyond the end of this second stair was the entrance to Torech Ungol: "Shelob's Lair." The wide arching tunnel was straight and even, climbing at a steep slope. Its length was not stated, but it has been shown as about twelve miles. Tolkien's drawings seemed to indicate the passage was far shorter, but the chronology required the distance; and even to Sam "time and distance soon passed out of his reckoning. . . . how many hours had they passed in this lightless hole? Hours — days, weeks rather."[7]

There were many passages leading away on both sides, but the Hobbits seem to have traversed most of the distance before coming to a wide opening on the left — the way to the spider's pit.[8] Not far beyond, the tunnel forked: A door blocked the left passage, which wound its way to the Under-gate at the guard-tower; the right tunnel led to the primary (but not only) exit. Beyond the exit about 600 feet steps climbed to the Cleft — Cirith Ungol.[9] It was about 3000 feet high,[10] and on the far side of the road leaped down past the Tower to rejoin the Morgul-road.[11]

The Tower of Cirith Ungol

UPON FIRST SEEING the full extent of the infacing Tower of Cirith Ungol, Sam realized it "had been built not to keep enemies out of Mordor, but to keep them in." It was, indeed, one of the fortresses Gondor had built at the beginning of the Third Age to watch over Mordor after Sauron's fall.[1] The Tower leaned against the steep mountain face just east of the Cleft of Cirith Ungol, and its turret jutted above the mountain ridge with the torch near its window visible to travellers west of the pass, and even west of Shelob's Lair.[2]

The Tower

In an illustration by Tolkien the path was shown winding its way down a slope behind the fortress "to meet the main road under the frowning walls close to the Tower-gate."[3] A sheer brink plunged from the outer edge of the gate-road and the northeastern fort wall, eliminating any approach or escape except along the road.[4] The gate was on the southeast, and was barred by no visible door but only by the malice of the Two Watchers.[5] Inside, a "narrow court" surrounded the tower except on the west and has been drawn fifty feet across. It was edged by a wall thirty feet high that leaned out at the top "like inverted steps."[6] On Tolkien's sketch the wall was topped by a parapet shaped like a fence of giant spearheads.

The tower was composed of three great tiers, each smaller and farther back than the one below.[7] The flat roof of the third tier stood just below the ridgecrest, and slightly above the cleft of the pass (200 feet above the gate).[8] Above it rose a turret with a pinnacle so steep that from a distance it appeared as the horn of a mountain.[9] Tolkien's only drawing of the Tower showed four tiers plus the turret (later reduced to three) and the walls appeared to be round; yet from the beginning the text stated that "it jutted out in pointed bastions . . . with sheer sides . . . that looked north-east and south-east."[10] The accompanying map has been made to agree with the text in this respect. The proportionate heights and widths of the tiers were based only upon Tolkien's sketch, but they closely match the final dimensions stated in the manuscript.[11]

	Height	*Depth (Top View)*
1st Level	100 Feet	40 Yards
2nd Level	75 Feet	30 Yards
3rd Level	50 Feet	20 Yards

The flat roof of the top tier measured sixty feet between the turret and the low parapet of the wall. Although the turret was described as "great," and was large enough in diameter to require halls running across from the spiral stair at each level, it had a 'horn'-like appearance both as seen from the path to Cirith Ungol and in the sketch of the Tower.[12]

The Interior

When Sam entered the tower, he passed through a door that faced the main gate. Beyond it a wide passage led back to the mountain. There were many doors and openings on both sides of the hallway, and at the far end was a great archway barred by double doors: the Under-gate.[13] Beyond the gate was the Under-way, the winding tunnel that led up to Shelob's Lair.[14] An opening not far from the great doors led to a steep winding stairway on the right. There were occasional openings from the stair to other levels, but Sam continued climbing until he reached the stair's end.[15]

At the head of the stair was a small domed chamber, perched on the wide roof of the top tier halfway between the turret and the parapet. The chamber had two open doors: one facing east toward Mount Doom and one looking west to the door of the great turret.[16]

Inside the turret's door Sam found a stair on his right, winding counterclockwise up the inside of the round walls. The stair had passed halfway around the turret before arriving at a door leading into the interior. Opposite the door was the west-facing window through which Frodo had seen the red torchlight. Climbing another half-circle brought Sam to the second floor, with its east-facing window. There the steps stopped, so he turned through the open door leading into the central passage. He soon found it was a dead end, with locked doors both right and left. Frodo was overhead in a chamber that could be reached only through a trap-door.[17]

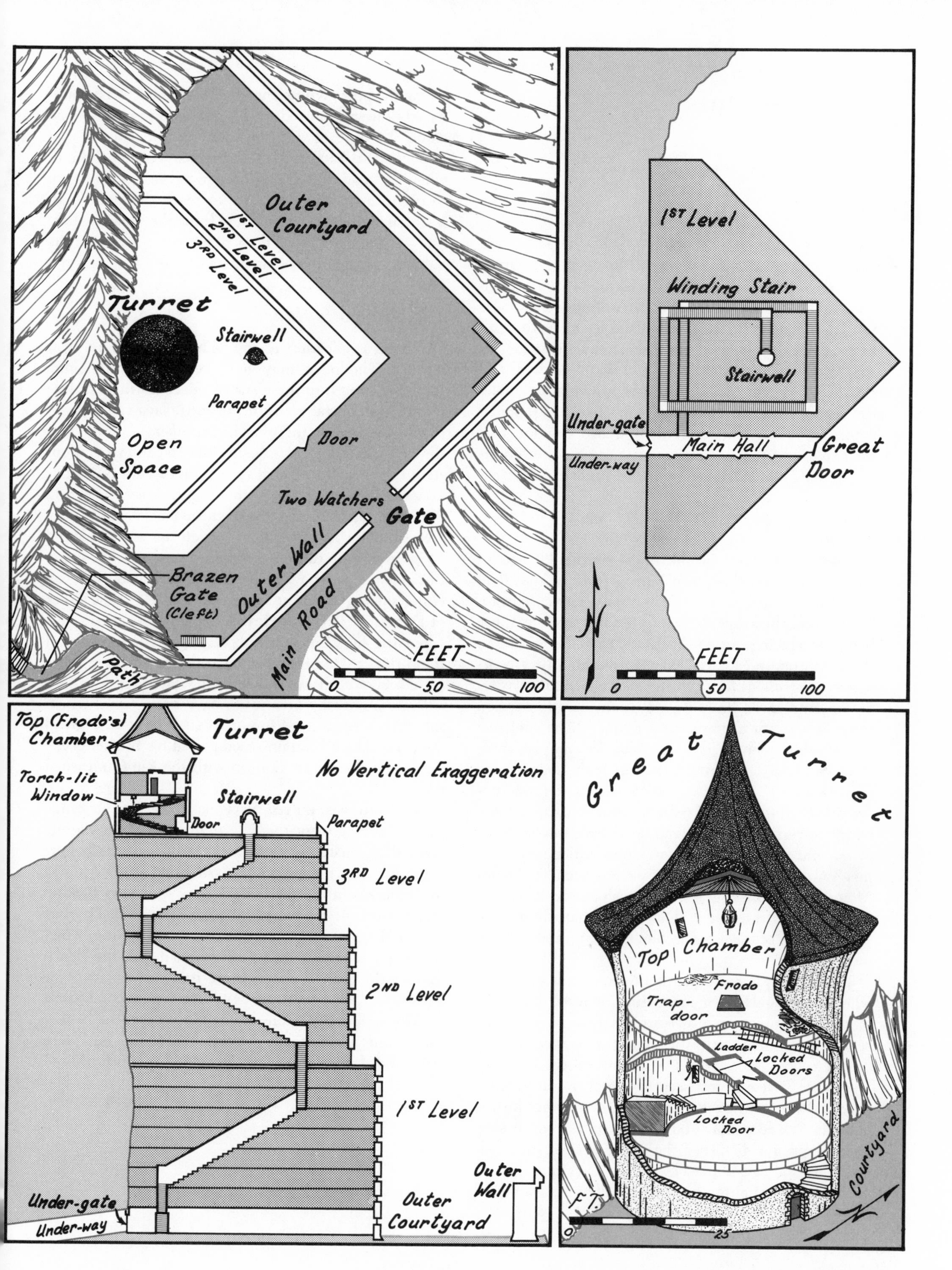

THE FORT Cross Section: WEST–EAST Upper Right: TOWER PASSAGES
Lower Right: TURRET PASSAGES

Mount Doom

SAURON SETTLED IN MORDOR about S.A. 1000,[1] and in that fenced land he found the ultimate forge: Orodruin, the "Mountain of Blazing Fire."[2] In its molten lava he made the One Ring, which no other flame was hot enough to melt; so there it had to be destroyed.[3] Sauron apparently used the fires frequently, for his road up the Mountain was always "repaired and cleared."[4] Whenever Sauron was growing in power the eruptions began anew, and it was in S.A. 3429, just before his attack on the newly founded Gondor, that the explosions caused the Dúnedain to give the Mountain a new name: Amon Amarth, Mount Doom.[5]

The Mountain

Mount Doom stood in the midst of the Plateau of Gorgoroth in northwestern Mordor; yet in that land of vulcanism it seemed to be the only active volcano. There were, however, steaming fissures such as those between which Sauron's Road ran from Barad-dûr to the Mountain.[6] Mount Doom was evidently a *composite* or *strato-volcano,* formed of alternating layers of ash and lava. Both its elevation and description prove it was not a simple cinder cone: "The confused and tumbled shoulders . . . rose for maybe three thousand feet . . . and . . . half as high again its tall central cone."[7] Still, its 4500-foot elevation was not remarkably high[8] — far short of Mount Etna, in Italy, which towers 11,000 feet and has a base ninety miles in circumference (about twenty-nine miles in diameter).[9] A seven-mile-diameter base has been shown for Mount Doom, making its average slope a very typical 20° (although the reader should note that the vertical exaggeration of the cross section makes it appear much more steep).[10]

The slope was more gentle on the north and west, where Frodo and Sam made their climb until they came to the northern sweep of Sauron's Road.[11] The road reportedly climbed onto the Mountain via a causeway on the eastern side, then wound around the base like a snake.[12] Three gaping fissures, roughly south, west, and east, vented the central cone.[13] Fortunately for the Hobbits, the recent lava flows were on the south side, and so had not disturbed the upper part of the road. As Frodo and Sam walked east along the climbing path they came to a hairpin turn, where they were attacked by Gollum. This turn was shown clearly in two sketches by Tolkien, on which it appeared to be just below the point where the slope steepened.[14] The published drawing showed the original location of the road along the base of the central cone, but another (yet unpublished) included the corrected version.[15] In it, when the road turned east once more, it was necessary to cut into the rock in order to reach the goal "high in the upper cone, but still far from the reeking summit" — the east-facing door of Sauron's fire-well, the Sammath Naur, the "Chambers of Fire."[16]

The Sammath Naur

The exact application of the "Chambers of Fire" was unclear. The term may have referred to: the long tunnel leading into the heart of the cone; the Crack of Doom; the central vent; or the entire lava vent system (hence the use of the plural, *Chambers*). It has been shown here in the core, using the last interpretation. As such it may have been synonymous with Gandalf's usage of the *Cracks* of Doom — several fissures within the Mountain.[17] Only one of those cracks was readily accessible, for as Sam crept through the door he found "a long cave or tunnel that bored into . . . the cone. But only a short way ahead, its floor and walls on either side were cloven by a great fissure . . . the Crack of Doom."[18] This was clearly not the central core, for when the fiery magma bubbled up, it lit the *roof* of the tunnel.[19] Had Frodo stood at the central vent there would have been *sky* above. Still, the abyss was deep and wide, and the lava must have been very high in the chambers to have produced such light so high in the cone. The mountain stood poised for further eruptions, and the fall of Gollum with the Ring unleashed the largest.

Orodruin was, indeed, very explosive; and its eruptions probably were the *Vulcanian* type, with viscous lavas that crusted over between eruptions, each new explosion emitting ash and "ash-laden gases . . . to form dark cauliflower-like clouds."[20] These reeking clouds were most widespread on the Dawnless Day but appeared again after the destruction of the Ring, when the cone was rent asunder, ash rained down, and "black against the pall of cloud, there rose a huge shape of shadow . . . filling all the sky," seen even as far away as Minas Tirith.[21] Sam and Frodo escaped to "a low ashen hill piled at the Mountain's foot," but were surrounded by molten lava and could go no farther.[22]

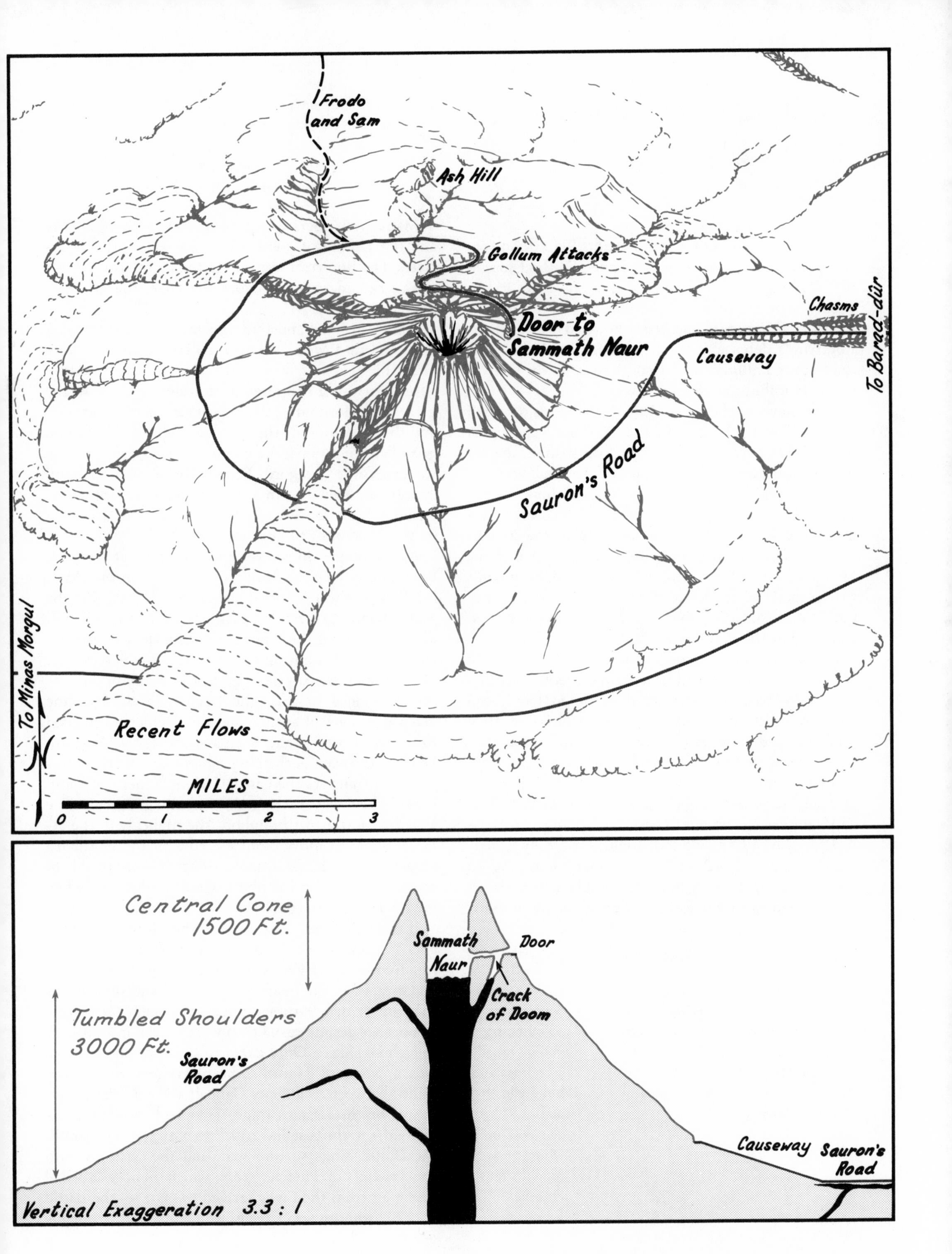

MOUNT DOOM *Cross Section:* WEST–EAST

The Battle of the Hornburg

March 3–4, T.A. 3019

Saruman first sent forces against Rohan on February 25, 3019, and the men of the Westfold fought the First Battle of the Fords of Isen and held off the enemy; but on March 2 the wizard emptied all his forces from Isengard and after they had scattered the Rohirrim's defense at the Second Battle of the Ford, the Orcs and hillmen moved south to assail the fortress of the Hornburg at Helm's Deep.[1]

After news of the First Battle of the Fords, Gandalf advised Théoden to lead the Riders of the Rohan west to ward off new attacks.[2] More than a thousand set out toward the Fords of Isen[3] but turned aside to Helm's Deep after hearing of the disastrous Second Battle of the Fords, while Gandalf galloped off to regroup the scattered Rohirrim and to gain the support of the Ents he knew to be at Isengard.[4] By chance the Ents had arrived at Isengard just before Saruman's troops marched forth, so Merry had seen the enemy go: "'of all sorts together, there must have been ten thousand at the very least.'"[5]

In contrast, Erkenbrand had left Helm's Deep with "'Maybe . . . a thousand fit to fight on foot,'" though they were older or younger than would have been best.[6] Added to the thousand riders of Théoden, they totaled "enough to man both the burg and the barrier wall," yet were too few to defend the dike;[7] and were at best outnumbered five to one. Their end would probably have been noble but unsuccessful had Gandalf's efforts not brought assistance. Riding swiftly he had gathered a thousand foot-soldiers led in by Erkenbrand,[8] and a wood of Huorns that (according to Merry) numbered "'hundreds and hundreds.'"[9] These, then, were the estimated troops at the Battle:

Captain	*Arrived From*	*Troops*
I. Rohan and Allies		
Théoden/Éomer	Edoras	1000 cavalry[10]
Gambling the Old	Helm's Deep	1000 infantry[11]
Erkenbrand	Fords of Isen	1000 infantry[12]
Ents (Huorns)	Fangorn via Isengard	"Hundreds and hundreds"[13]
TOTAL March 3		2000
TOTAL March 4		Est. 3800 (of whom 2700 fought), plus Huorns

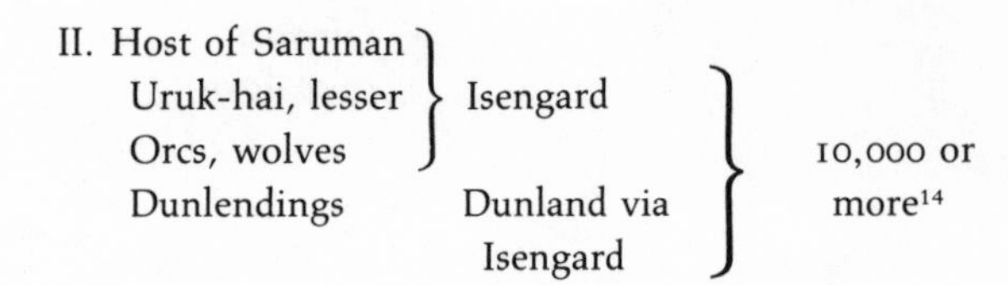

II. Host of Saruman: Uruk-hai, lesser Orcs, wolves	Isengard	10,000 or more[14]
Dunlendings	Dunland via Isengard	

Many wolf-riders were already in the Westfold Dale and the Deeping Coomb when Théoden's Riders arrived. The Rohirrim went up to the Hornburg.[15] After the rearguard retreated from the Dike, the attackers poured through.

Éomer arrayed most of the men on the Deeping Wall and its tower, "where the defense seemed more doubtful."[16] After volleys of arrows, the attackers surged forward in an attempt to scale the Wall. At the gate of the Hornburg "the hugest Orcs were mustered, and the wild men of the Dunland fells."[17] Using two great battering rams, the enemies were splintering the wooden doors. Aragorn, Éomer, Gimli, and a handful of warriors exited from a postern-door and threw the enemies from the Rock; then they instead directed a barricade be built to hold the gate.[18]

As Saruman's forces were unsuccessful at the gate, they quietly crept in through the culvert in the Deeping Wall but were spotted and slain or driven into the gorge, falling to defenders farther up the Deep.[19] Gimli directed some of the men in blocking the culvert; but later, when the fight on the Wall was the fiercest, the Orcs blasted the culvert open just as many other enemies managed to scale the Deeping Wall. All "the defense was swept away," and the defenders retreated to the fastnesses of the Burg and the caves: Aragorn, Legolas, the Men of the king's guard, and many others gained entrance to the Citadel, while Éomer and Gimli fought their way back to the Glittering Caves.[20] The assaults continued throughout the night, with the attackers able to move from all sides of the Hornburg except next to the mountain. Still they were unable to break through the Hornburg Gate until dawn, when they blasted an opening.[21]

Instead of Orcs pouring into the Hornburg, however, Théoden led forth his Riders, perhaps nine hundred or so if about half the surviving defenders had escaped to the caves. So powerful and sudden was their onset that Saruman's forces (though far greater in number despite casualties) were driven in rout back to Helm's Dike.[22] Only a quarter mile beyond the dike was a wood of Huorn's, however, and the enemy milled between. Suddenly Gandalf and Erkenbrand appeared on the western ridge. Trapped between unscalable cliffs to the east and attackers both west and south, the Dunlendings surrendered, and the Orcs ran into the "wood" of Huorns from which none escaped.[23] The men from the caves arrived too late — the Battle of the Hornburg was already won and all of Saruman's great host destroyed.[24]

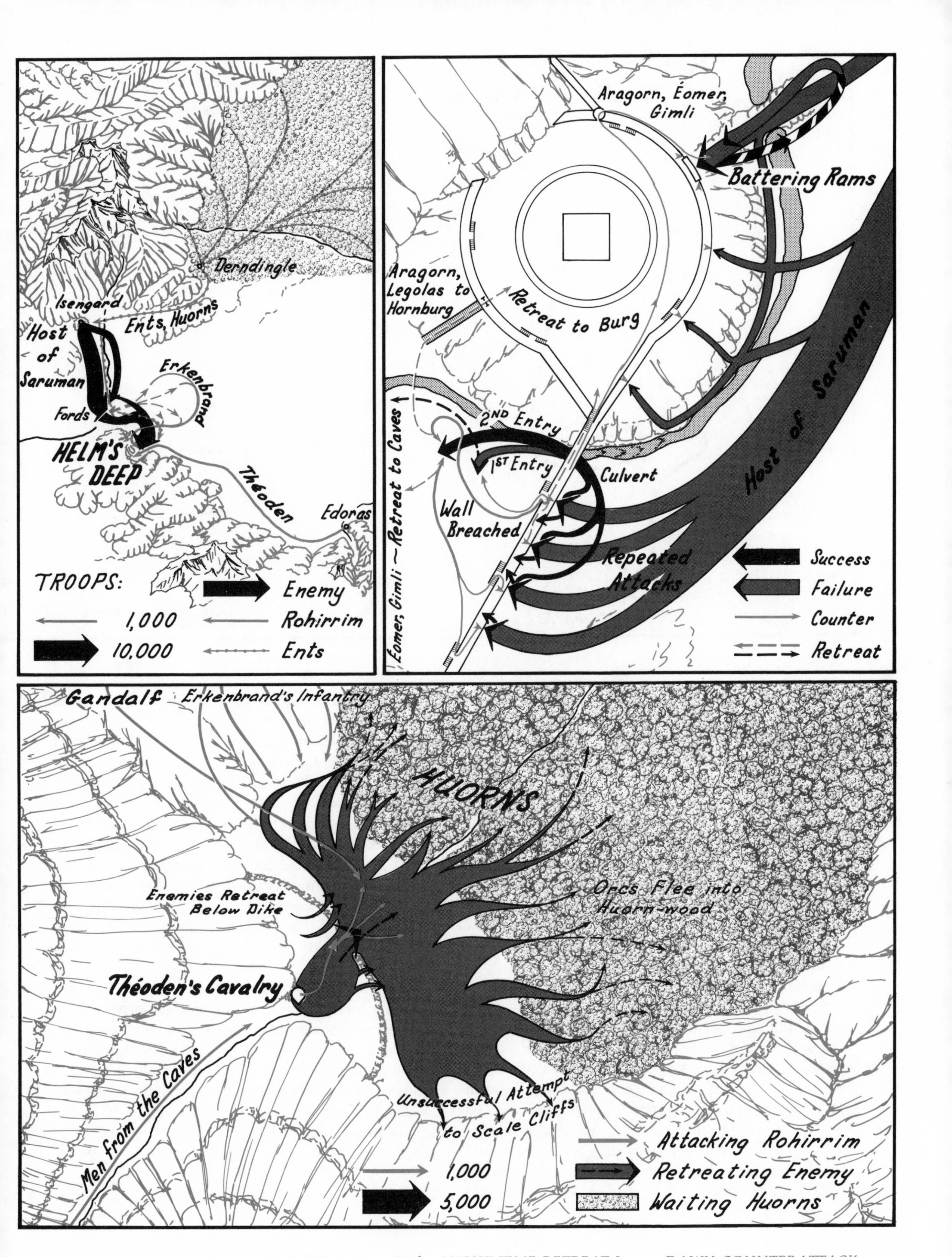

Upper Left: TO THE BATTLE Upper Right: NIGHT TIME RETREAT Lower: DAWN COUNTERATTACK

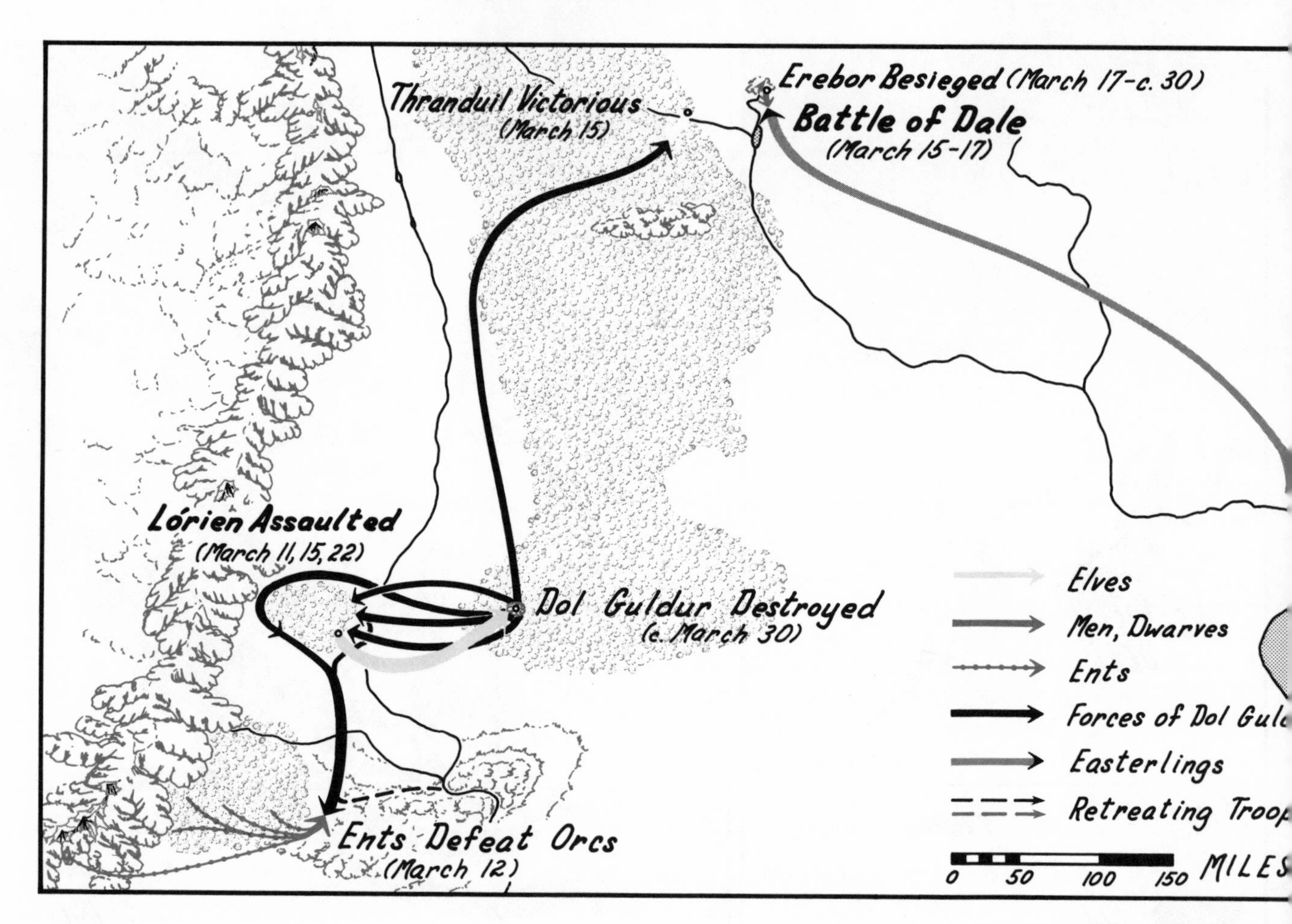

NORTHERN BATTLES

Battles in the North

March 11–30, T.A. 3019

On March 6, when Aragorn revealed himself to Sauron,[1] the Enemy hurriedly initiated the various assaults he had planned. The greatest was against Minas Tirith, utilizing his southern armies; but he also had forces in Dol Guldur and allies in Rhûn who were ever at his call. Simultaneous with the departure from Mordor on March 10, these northern troops must have sallied forth against their appointed targets.[2]

The first to reach their goal were the troops from Dol Guldur who assailed nearby Lórien.[3] Being unsuccessful, many passed around the border of the woods and entered the Wold of Rohan. On March 12 they were surprised by Ents sent east from Fangorn and Isengard, and were routed.[4] Lórien was attacked twice more, on March 15 and 22, but was never entered. Forces from Dol Guldur also went north and battled King Thranduil under the trees of Mirkwood. There, too, the main battle was on March 15; and after "long battle . . . and great ruin of fire," Thranduil emerged the victor.[5]

Eastern allies of Sauron, presumably from Rhûn, crossed the River Carnen and marched against the men of Dale and the Dwarves of Erebor.[6] Once more the battle was joined on that important date of March 15, although this Battle of Dale was no one-day struggle, but lasted instead for three days.[7] On March 17 King Brand fell before the Gate of Erebor, and King Dáin Ironfoot fought mightily over Brand's body before he, too, was slain. Then both Men and Dwarves were forced to retreat into the fastness of Lonely Mountain and were besieged, but the Easterlings could not win past the Gate.[8]

After the Ring was destroyed on March 25, when Sauron's servants were bereft of their driving force, all those who had been assaulted came forth and routed the remaining troops: Celeborn and Thranduil to Dol Guldur; and the besieged in Erebor against the Easterlings.[9] So the North was saved by their valor — and as Gandalf said, "'Think of what might have been . . . savage swords in Eriador, night in Rivendell.'"[10]

The Battle of the Pelennor Fields

March, 15 T.A. 3019

ALTHOUGH SAURON'S MALICE was not directed solely toward Gondor, it was against Minas Tirith that the chief thrust was made. Miraculously, the city did not fall. Faramir was "ten times outnumbered" at the Causeway forts,[1] and the Rohirrim "at their onset were thrice outnumbered by the Haradrim alone."[2] Even a very conservative estimate would indicate that the forces of Mordor overwhelmed those of Gondor by at least four to one. Added to the Orcs of Mordor were allies from Near and Far Harad, Khand, and Rhûn,[3] most of whom had gone to the Morannon for the muster and issued forth with the main army.[4] Nowhere was there a count given for the teaming masses, except that the Haradrim were thrice the Rohirrim (who numbered six thousand).[5] Yet several references attested to the Enemies' enormous numbers: The Morgul-host was greater than any army that had issued "from that vale since the days of Isildur's might; . . . and yet it was but one and not the greatest of the hosts that Mordor now sent forth."[6] The Mordor-host from the Black Gate included "battalions of Orcs of the Eye, and countless companies of Men of a new sort."[7] The Enemy was so great that many were merely held in reserve for the anticipated sacking of the City.[8] Faramir commented that "we may make the Enemy pay ten times our loss at the passage and yet rue the exchange."[9]

Gondor's forces might have been more, but fearing the Corsairs of Umbar, the populous southern fiefs held back all but "a tithe of their strength."[10]

The outcompanies of Gondor totaled "less than three thousands,"[11] and the Tower Guard had at least three companies (possibly of 400 to 500 troops each), plus an out-garrison.[12] All told, probably fewer than five thousand faced the oncoming Black Tide. These were the estimated forces on the field of battle:

Captain	*Arrived from*	*Troops*
I. Gondor and Allies		
Southern Fiefs[13]		
Forlong	Lossarnach	200 "well-armed"
Dervorin	Ringló Vale	300
Duinhir	Morthond	500 "bowmen"
Golasgil	Anfalas	150 (est.) "scantily equipped"
——	Larnedon	50 (est.) "hillmen"
——	Ethir Anduin	100 "fisher-folk"
Hirluin	Pinnath Gelin	300
Imrahil	Dol Amroth	1200 (est.) (700 plus "a company" on horse)
Guard of Minas Tirith		
Denethor	Minas Tirith	2000 (est.)
Rohirrim		
Théoden/Éomer	Rohan	6000 cavalry[14]
Aragorn		
Dúnedain	The North	30[15]
——	Southern Fiefs	1000 (est.)[16]
TOTAL ESTIMATED FORCES OF GONDOR		11,250
II. Mordor and Allies		
Mordor and Morgul-host		
Angmar/ Gothmog	Barad-dûr, Minas Morgul	20,000 (est.)
Allies		
Haradrim	Near and Far Harad	18,000[17]
Others	Rhûn, Khand	7000 (est.)
TOTAL ESTIMATED FORCES OF MORDOR		Minimum 45,000

Having taken East Osgiliath the previous June, Sauron's workers had prepared many barges for the crossing, and on March 12 the vanguard of the Morgul-host swarmed over Anduin.[18] Faramir retreated from Osgiliath to the forts on the Rammas Echor, where he held out for a day, until the Enemy had bridged the river and poured across.[19] Meanwhile, the army from the Black Gate had taken Cair Andros on March 10 and arrived from the northeast, and between the two hosts the Rammas was breached both north and east and the Pelennor overrun.[20] Faramir spent the afternoon in an organized retreat from the Causeway Forts; but when he was only a quarter mile from the city gates, the Nazgûl swooped down, driving both men and horses into disorder. The Haradrim nearby were attacking as well, and Faramir was struck by a Southron arrow.[21] Only the ride of Prince Imrahil, leading all the city's mounted men, saved Faramir and his troops.[22] The sortie was soon recalled, however, and the Gates were shut. All the Pelennor was abandoned to the Enemy, who quickly dug trenches and filled them with fire. The closest was just outside of bowshot from the city walls, and there were placed the catapults and siege-towers.[23] From fire, battle, and horror of the Ring-wraiths, the valor of the besieged was beaten down. During the second night, that of March 14,

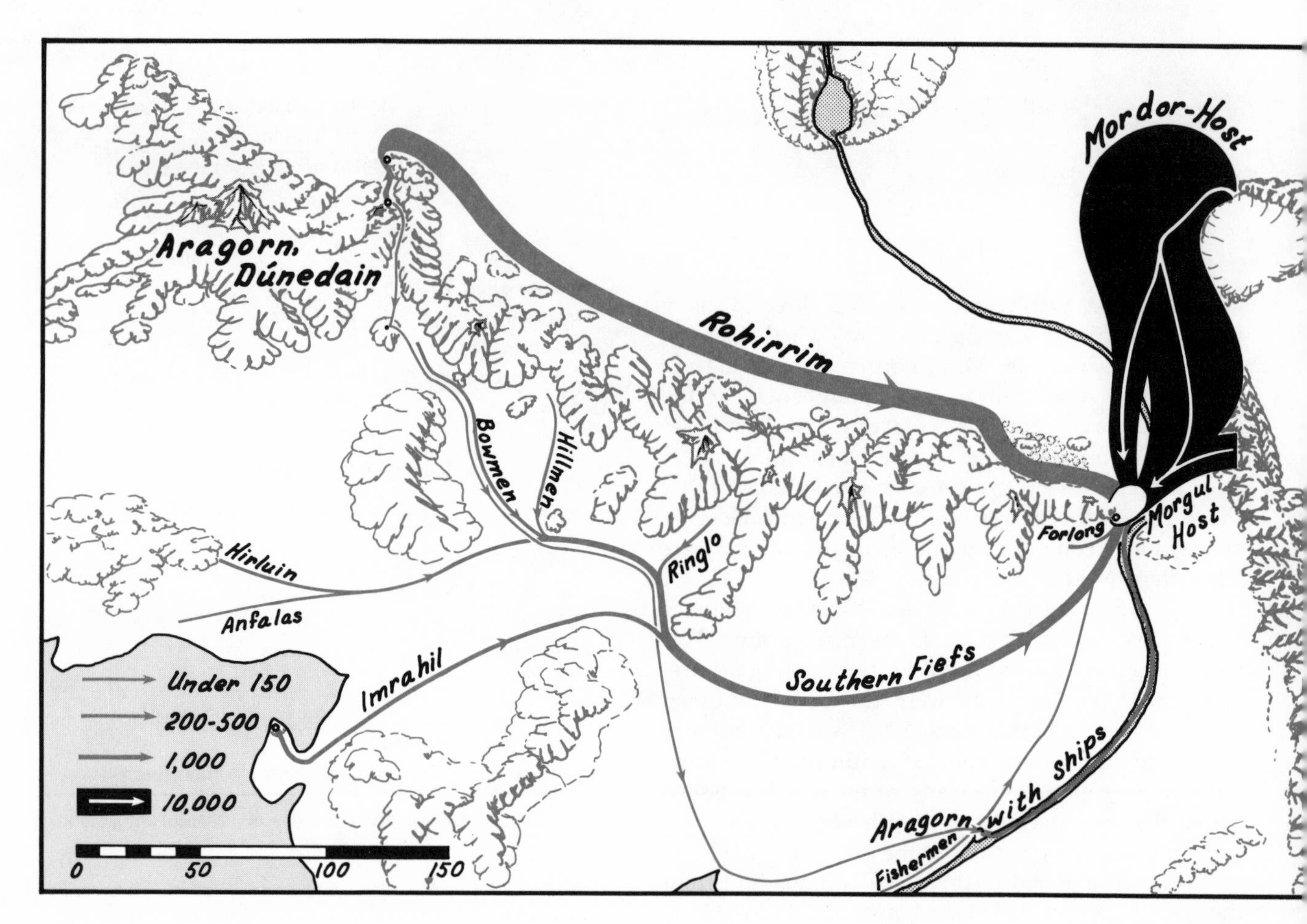

TO THE BATTLE

troops moved against the wall in their siege-towers, and Angmar called for the great battering ram: Grond.[24] Just before dawn the Great Gates were shattered, and Gandalf stood alone, defying the Chief Nazgûl; but from afar the horns of Rohan blew wildly, and the Battle was joined.[25]

When the Rohirrim reached the north gate of the Rammas, they scattered the few Orcs and poured through the breaches. Théoden sent Elfhelm to the right toward the siege-towers, Grimbold to the left, and Éomer's company straight ahead; but the King outran them all, galloping into the midst of the foes. Most of the forces of Mordor were probably encamped near the City, and the Rohirrim overran the northern half of the Pelennor with relative ease.[26] Théoden was first to reach the road to the river, about a mile east of the city gates. The Haradrim were south of the road, and their captain led his cavalry toward the King, but Théoden and his guard countered and were the victors when suddenly the horses went wild because of the approach of Angmar, Chief of the Nazgûl.[27]

The tragic scene found by Éomer spurred the Rohirrim to new feats. On through the cavalry and the ranks of marching Haradrim Éomer charged, but the horses swerved away from the *mûmakil.* Meanwhile, Prince Imrahil had led forth all the forces in the City, but was unable to reach Éomer; and the reserve forces of Mordor had been sent across the river.[28] By midmorning the troops of Gondor were once more badly outmanned, and the battle had become grim. Éomer was engulfed atop a hillock only a mile from the landings at Harlond when Aragorn's ships arrived. When Éomer attacked anew from the north, Imrahil from the west, and Aragorn from the south, the "great press of foes" between were "caught between the hammer and the anvil." The forces of Gondor, though still outnumbered, continued the struggle throughout the day and won the victory.[29]

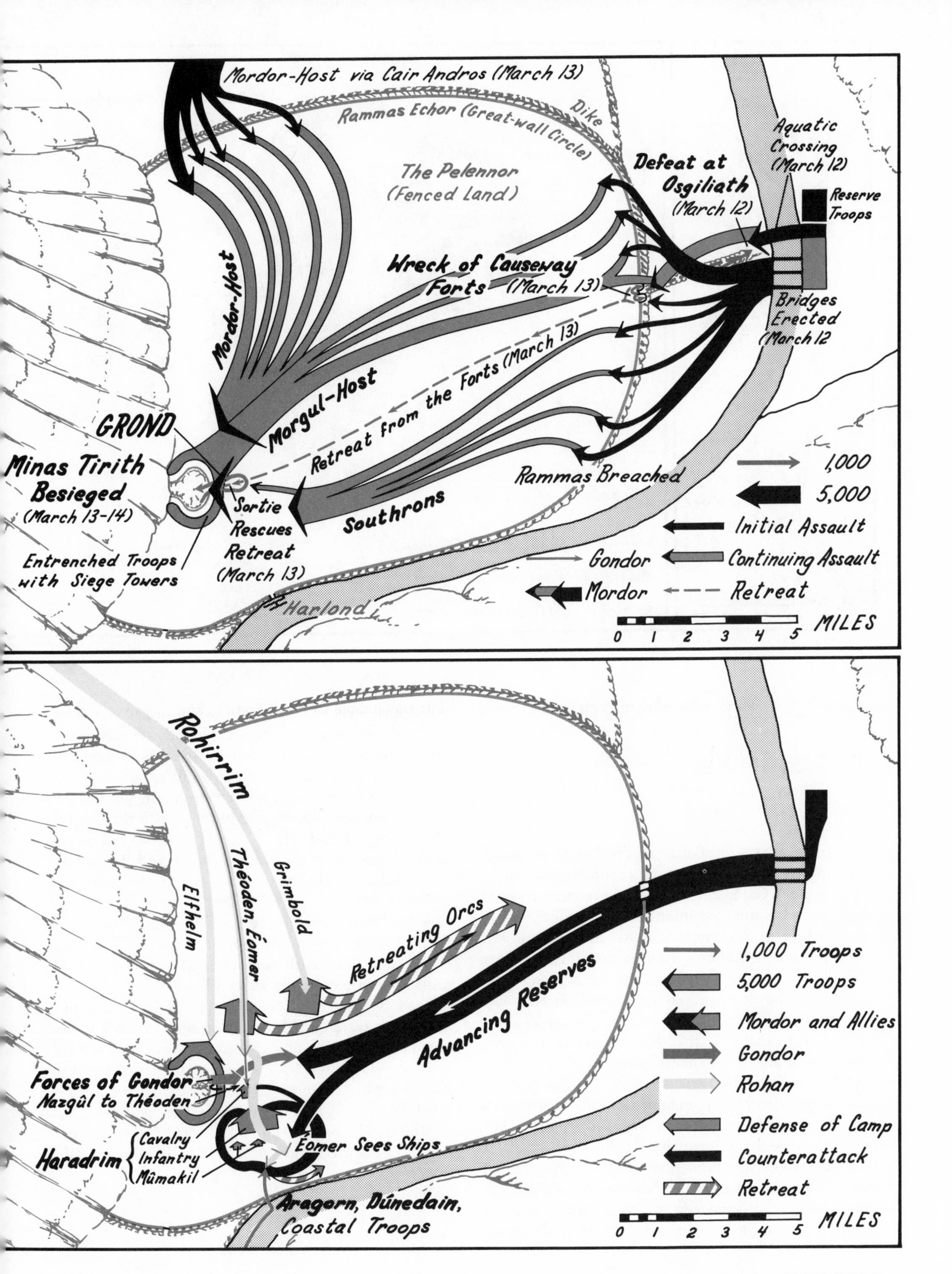

Mordor-Host via Cair Andros (March 13)
Rammas Echor (Great-wall Circle)
Dike
The Pelennor
(Fenced Land)
Aquatic Crossing (March 12)
Defeat at Osgiliath (March 12)
Reserve Troops
Wreck of Causeway Forts (March 13)
Bridges Erected (March 12
Mordor-Host
Retreat from the Forts (March 13)
Morgul-Host
GROND
Minas Tirith Besieged (March 13-14)
Sortie Rescues Retreat (March 13)
Southrons
Rammas Breached
Entrenched Troops with Siege Towers
Harlond
1,000
5,000
Initial Assault
Gondor
Continuing Assault
Mordor
Retreat
0 1 2 3 4 5 MILES
Rohirrim
Elfhelm
Théoden, Éomer
Grimbold
Retreating Orcs
Advancing Reserves
Forces of Gondor
Nazgûl to Théoden
Haradrim
Cavalry
Infantry
Mûmakil
Éomer Sees Ships
Aragorn, Dúnedain, Coastal Troops
1,000 Troops
5,000 Troops
Mordor and Allies
Gondor
Rohan
Defense of Camp
Counterattack
Retreat
0 1 2 3 4 5 MILES

Upper: THE SIEGE Lower: THE BATTLE

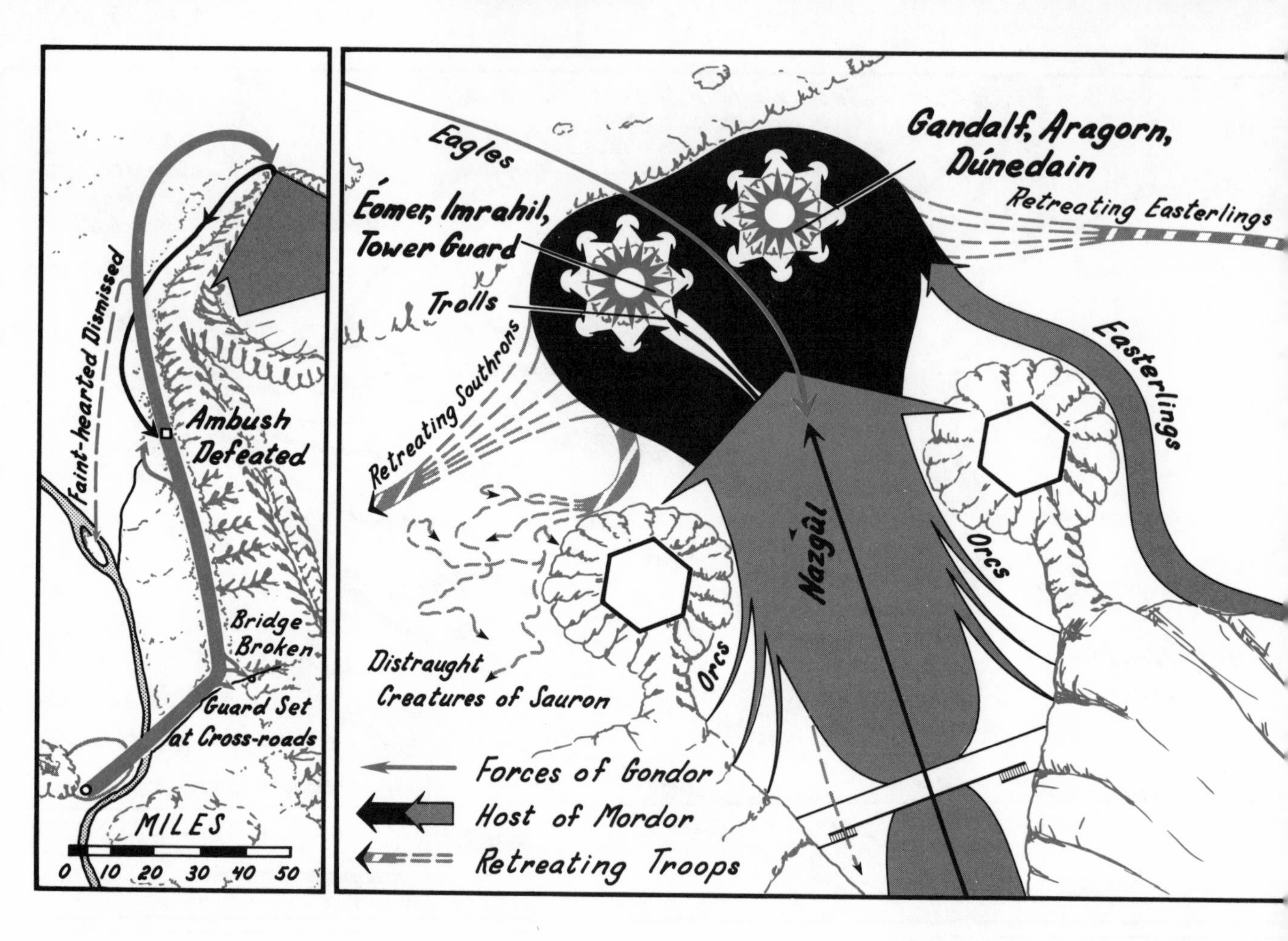

Left: TO THE BATTLE Right: THE BATTLE

The Battle of the Morannon

March 25, T.A. 3019

TWO DAYS AFTER the Battle of the Pelennor Fields, Aragorn led forth an army to challenge Sauron at his own Black Gate. The numbers were clearly stated as 1000 cavalry and 6000 infantry.[1] On the long march Aragorn burned the bridge to Minas Morgul, and left a strong guard at the Cross-roads in case enemies came through the Morgul Pass or up the south road.[2] Two days march north there was an ambush at the very spot where Faramir had trapped the Haradrim, but Aragorn's scouts forewarned him; and he sent horsemen west to attack the enemy flank.[3]

Upon reaching the desolation of the Morannon, some of the Men became so faint-hearted that Aragorn sent them southwest to recapture Cair Andros. Between these and the forces left at the Cross-roads, a thousand troops had been removed from the original 7000.[4] After the departure of the emissary at the Black Gate, the host of Gondor faced "forces ten times, and more than ten times their match."[5] In a desperate attempt to meet the onslaught, Aragorn had placed his troops in rings around two great hills of rubble opposite the gate.[6] On the left he stood with Gandalf, with the sons of Elrond and the Dúnedain on the front line where the thrust would be strongest. On the hill to his right were Éomer and Imrahil, with the knights of Dol Amroth and picked Men of the Tower of Guard in the front. With them stood Pippin and Beregond.[7]

Enemies quickly surrounded them: A great host issued from the Morannon, Orcs streamed down from hills on each side of the rampart, and Easterlings marched from beyond the northern tower where they had hidden next to the mountain slopes. The first to cross the moat-like mire were Hill-trolls, one of whom injured Beregond and was in turn slain by Pippin.[8] The Trolls were quickly followed and Gondor's forces surrounded when eagles appeared and swooped toward the Nazgûl; but the Nazgûl fled toward Mt. Doom and disappeared in the ensuing holocaust.[9] Then Sauron's creatures destroyed themselves, leaving only the Men of Rhûn and Harad to do battle. Most fled or surrendered, but some fought on, and finally all were subdued.[10]

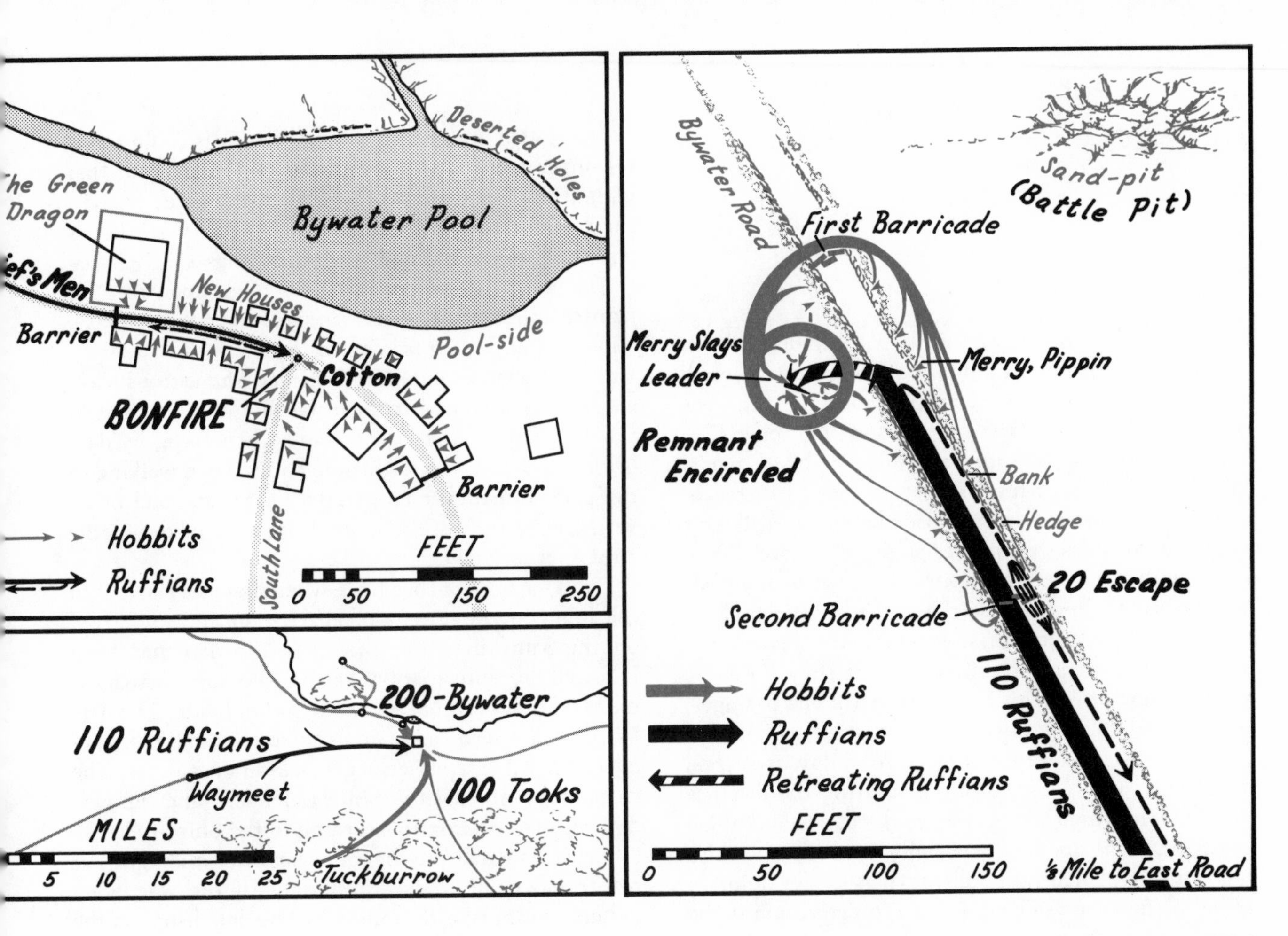

Upper Left: THE SKIRMISH *Lower Left:* TO THE BATTLE *Right:* THE BATTLE

The Battle of Bywater

November 3, T.A. 3019

UPON RETURNING TO THE SHIRE and discovering the changes that had occurred during their absence, the four friends decided to raise the Shire and rid the Hobbits of the ruffian Men who were doing Sharkey's bidding. They arrived in Bywater the afternoon of November 2, and a brief skirmish ensued against the Chief's Men from Bag End. Merry's horncall attracted about two hundred sturdy Hobbits, who hid between (and possibly in) buildings all along the main road through town. At the intersection of the road with South Lane, a bonfire was lit, behind which Tom Cotton stood waiting. At each end of town a barrier was placed across the road, and when some twenty Men trooped in from Hobbiton, the western barrier was opened. Once inside, the ruffians found themselves surrounded. Several tried to escape back west, but when the leader was shot, the rest surrendered.[1]

The next morning shortly after ten, the main Battle of Bywater was fought. Messages had been sent the day before to the large group of ruffians quartered at Waymeet, and they were marching east, joined by others along the way. There were more than one hundred; but for once the enemy was outnumbered, for in addition to the Hobbits who had gathered the previous evening in Bywater, Pippin led in another hundred from Tookland. Merry had chosen an advantageous site where the Bywater Road cut through high banks topped by hedges. A barricade of overturned carts blocked the far end; and after the ruffians entered the cutting, more carts were quickly placed behind them. Once more the Hobbits surrounded the enemies. This time, however, about twenty Men managed to escape back over the second barricade, and many of the rest scaled the western bank. With all the force thrown against one spot, the Hobbits on that side were giving way, until Merry and Pippin brought reinforcements from the east bank. Merry slew the leader, then drew his archers into a wide circle around the remnant. During the attempted escape, seventy of the ruffians were killed and afterward were buried in a nearby sand-pit: the Battle Pit.[2] Thus ended the last battle of the War of the Rings.

Pathways

IN *The Lord of the Rings,* unlike *The Hobbit,* Tolkien gave considerable information about distances covered, time spent in travel, and campsite locations. Hundreds of clues gleaned from the story and the appendices provided the data for not only these pathway maps, but also the base maps themselves. Stated distances occasionally differed from those shown on Tolkien's maps, so the maps were altered slightly to more closely agree with the text. Complete agreement was not always possible, however, so the distances shown along pathways may sometimes not measure exactly the same on the accompanying scale; but they do agree with the text or with estimates made from its passages, using three miles per league as suggested by Tolkien.[1]

When mileages were not listed for a day or several days, they were estimated by measuring the distance on Tolkien's map along the route between known campsites, and dividing it equally between the days (allowing for stated variations, such as longer hours in travel or faster or slower speed). To determine if the various estimates seemed reasonable in relation to each other and to the Primary World, a table was compiled to allow comparison. Although a few of the rates of travel seemed unusually fast or slow (for reasons explained with the related maps), most appeared to be fairly consistent when allowing for such variables as rugged terrain, need for haste, and physical or psychological hindrances. When one day's journey had distinct stages these were listed individually. Most of the journeys were on foot, with occasional rides on boats or horses. The range of speeds in general were:

Walking — Most commonly, about 2.0 to 2.5 mph (24 to 30 minutes per mile) was maintained, but rose to 3.0 mph (20 minutes per mile) run by the Orcs and their pursuers: Aragorn, Gimli, and Legolas.

Riding — Ponies: 3.4 mph, jogging (17.6 minutes per mile). Horses of Rohan: 6.7 mph, galloping (9.0 minutes per mile). Horses of the Dúnedain: 7.0 mph, galloping (8.6 minutes per mile). Shadowfax: 20 mph, galloping (3.0 minutes per mile).

Boating — Small boats with the current: drifting, 2.8 mph (21.4 minutes per mile); paddling, 4.1 mph (14.6 minutes per mile). Ships against the current: rowing, 4.7 mph (12.8 minutes per mile); sailing, 7.2 mph (8.3 minutes per mile).

It was also interesting to note that Ents could travel ten miles per hour (six minutes per mile); and that while the Orcs were no faster than the three friends, their endurance was phenomenal — fifty-six hours with only one camp and two other stops!

The hours listed were calculated based upon a 7 A.M. sunrise and a 5 P.M. sunset in December and January, and a 6 A.M. to 6 P.M. day in September and March. Unless otherwise stated in the story, the various travellers were assumed to have taken full advantage of the dawn-to-dusk sunlight hours when going by day, or the dusk-to-dawn nighttime hours when walking in the dark. Whenever late starts, long rests, and other variations occurred, the hours were reduced or lengthened appropriately.

Dates gave some confusion when marches lasted into the following day, or two separate journeys occurred on the same day. On the table the date has been followed by information relating to any march or marches that began at any time on that date. The date listed beside each campsite denoted the time the travellers finally stopped at a given location to rest. The chronology utilized the Shire Calendar,[2] and the new day began at midnight according to the Shire-folk;[3] so a few times when the march began after midnight but before dawn, or (more commonly) if the wanderers did not rest until after midnight, the date listed on the table or map, respectively, was that of the new day, which had not yet dawned in the western lands.

The History of Middle-earth is fascinating in its revelations of the evolution of the tale, and Tolkien's meticulous calculations and rewritings make the chronology accurate. Nevertheless, here as elsewhere in the *Atlas,* with few exceptions, the pathway table and maps are based on "The Tale of Years," for that was the final authority, synchronized with the published tale.[4]

Only Tolkien's tremendous attention to detail made it possible to trace the pathways so closely; yet as with other maps, assumptions and estimates had to be made, and those judgments are certainly open to interpretation. The following table, therefore, has been put forth not as a statement of absolutes, but merely as a composite listing of the calculations used to produce the accompanying maps.

PATHWAY TABLE

(T.A. September 3018 through March 3019)

DATE	HOURS TRAVELLED	MILEAGE	MILES PER HOUR	COMMENTS	CAMPSITE
Bag End to Rivendell					
S.23	5	18	3.6	Evening march.	Green Hill Country
S.24	8	28	3.5	Black Riders, Elves.	West of Woodhall
S.25	5.5,1,1	17,7,3	3.1,7,3	Marish, Maggot's wagon, Buckland.	Crickhollow
S.26	10.5	25	2.4	On ponies. Knoll, Old Man Willow.	Bombadil's House
S.27	——	——	——	Rain.	Bombadil's House
S.28	5	17	3.4	Ponies. Sleep afternoon, captured in evening.	Barrow
S.29	6	20	3.3	Ponies. Start after lunch.	Bree
S.30	7.5	10–12	1.5	Joined by Strider. Depart 10 A.M. Wandering course.	Western Chetwood
O.1	11	16	1.5	Turn due east.	Eastern Chetwood
O.2	11	16	1.5		Midgewater Marshes
O.3	11	15	1.4	See flashes from Weathertop.	East edge of Marshes
O.4	11	17	1.5		Stream from Hills
O.5	11.5	18	1.6		Weather Hills
O.6	4	12	3.0	Climb hill at noon. Attacked at moonrise.	Dell by Weathertop
O.7	11	19	1.7	Frodo on pony.	Thickets south of Road
O.8	11	19	1.7	Frodo on pony.	Thickets south of Road
O.9	11	19	1.7	Frodo on pony.	Thickets south of Road
O.10	11	19	1.7	Frodo on pony.	Thickets south of Road
O.11	11	19	1.7	Frodo on pony.	Thickets south of Road
O.12	11	19	1.7	Frodo on pony.	SW of Last Bridge
O.13	11	6–10	.5–.9	Cross Bridge, leave Road.	Western Trollshaws
O.14	11	6–10	.5–.9		Western Trollshaws
O.15	11	6–10	.5–.9		Western Trollshaws
O.16	11	6–10	.5–.9	Turn more north.	Shallow Cave
O.17	6	4–6	.6–1.0	Turn southeast.	Top of Ridge
O.18	21	34–21	1.6–1.0	Find Trolls. Meet Glorfindel, march until dawn.	——
O.19	9	20–15	2.2–1.4	Frodo on horse.	Central Trollshaws
O.20	9?	18	2.0?	March to Ford. Attack by Black Riders.	Rivendell
Rivendell to Lórien					
D.25	14	22	1.6	Dusk to dawn march. Turn south at Ford.	——
D.26–J.6	14	15–20	1.1–1.4	Rugged terrain.	West of mountains
J.7	14	15–20	1.1–1.4		Hollin Ridge (J.8)
J.8	14	16	1.1	Turn SE toward Pass, strike road.	NW of Redhorn (J.9)
J.9	14	17	1.2		NW of Redhorn (J.10)

J.10	14	17	1.2		Foot of Redhorn (J.11)
J.11	6	8	1.3	Climb until midnight. Snow.	Redhorn Pass (J.12 A.M.)
J.12	8	28	3.5	March late morning to dusk. Wolf attack at night.	Knoll (J.12 P.M.)
J.13	10,7.5	20, 20	2.0,2.7	Dawn to dusk outside; dusk to after midnight inside Moria.	Guardroom (J.14 A.M.)
J.14	8	20+	2.5	Mid-morning to evening march.	Hall Twenty-one
J.15	1.5,6.5	1.5, 16	1.0,2.5	Attack in Moria. Escape.	Flets by Nimrodel
J.16	8	32	4.0	Smooth paths.	Central Lórien
J.17	8	32	4.0	Cerin Amroth at noon; City after dusk.	Caras Galadon

Lórien to Rauros

F.16	4,7.5	10, 25	2.5,3.3	Walk to river; boat afternoon into night.	Woods on west bank
F.17	13	40	3.1		West bank
F.18	13	40	3.1		Flats north of Celebrant
F.19	13	40	3.1		Opposite Brown Lands
F.20	13	55	4.1	Paddle all day.	Near gravel shoals
F.21	13	55	4.1	Paddle long spells.	Eyot
F.22	18	70	3.7	Change to night journey.	Rugged country (F.23)
F.23	4	12	3.0	Escape rapids and Orcs.	Bay .5 mile N of rapids
F.24	——	1.8(thrice)	——	Portage.	Foot of rapids
F.25	11	40	3.6	Argonath at midafternoon.	Parth Galen
F.26	BREAKING OF THE FELLOWSHIP				

Rauros to Isengard — Merry and Pippin

F.26	5,6	12,15	2.5	Captured at noon. Skirmish in valley at dusk. No camp.	——
F.27	28	84	3.0	Midnight to dusk.	South edge of Downs
F.28	18	54	3.0	Rohirrim surround.	Edge of Fangorn
F.29	2,10	5, 100	2.5,10	Escape before dawn; meet Treebeard.	Wellinghall
F.30	2.5	25	10	Entmoot.	Near Derndingle
M.1	——	——	——	Entmoot.	Near Derndingle
M.2	6	60	10	Entmoot ends in late afternoon; reach gates at midnight.	Isengard
M.3,M.4	——	——	——		Isengard

Rauros to Isengard — Aragorn, Legolas, Gimli

F.26–27	14,12	27,36	1.9,3.0	Late afternoon to dusk of next day. Hills, then plain.	Halfway to Entwash
F.28	12	36	3.0		South of Downs
F.29	12	36	3.0	Reach Downs about 11 A.M.	North end of Downs
F.30	5.5	30	5.5	Afternoon on horseback.	Edge of Fangorn

M.1	2,13	5,100	2.5,7.6	Meet Gandalf. Ride afternoon and most of night.	Part way to Edoras (M.2 A.M.)
M.2	3.3,5	25,37	7.6,7.4	Reach Edoras at dawn; leave at 1 P.M.	Part way to Helm's Deep
M.3	13	96	7.4	Battle of Helm's Deep.	Helm's Deep
M.4	8	40	5.0	4 P.M. to midnight, ride swiftly.	15 miles N of Fords of Isen
M.5	7,5.5	16,17	2.3,3.1	Ride slowly to Isengard and back. Break camp after Nazgûl comes.	Dol Baran

Isengard to Minas Tirith — Gandalf and Pippin

M.5	7	140	20	Late night to dawn, "terrible speed."	Edoras (M.6)
M.6	12	120	10	Travel dusk to dawn.	Firien Wood (M.7)
M.7	12	120	10		Erelas Beacon (M.8)
M.8	12	120	10	Reach Rammas Echor at dawn of M.9.	Minas Tirith (M.9)

Isengard to Minas Tirith — Merry, Rohirrim

M.5	6.5	41	6.3	Late night to dawn ride.	Helm's Deep (M.6 A.M.)
M.6	5	20	4.0	Set out at 1 P.M.	White Mountains
M.7	12	40	3.3	Mountain paths.	White Mountains
M.8	12	40	3.3		Pass in White Mountains
M.9	12	40	3.3		Dunharrow
M.10	3.5,5.5	20,36	5.7,6.5	The Dawnless Day. Leave Dunharrow at 9 A.M.; muster in Edoras at noon.	Willow Wood
M.11	12	80	6.7	Ride dawn to dusk.	Firien Wood
M.12	12	80	6.7	Dawn to dusk.	Minrimmon
M.13	12	80	6.7	Dawn to dusk.	Druadan Forest
M.14	10	50	5.0	Stonewain Valley.	Grey Wood
M.15	3.5	24.5	7.0	Reach Rammas at dawn. Battle of the Pelennor.	Minas Tirith

Isengard to Minas Tirith — Aragorn, Legolas, Gimli, Dúnedain

M.5	6.5	41	6.3	Late night to dawn. Dúnedain join at Fords.	Helm's Deep (M.6 A.M.)
M.6	10	75	7.5	2 P.M. to midnight. Main road.	Halfway to Edoras
M.7	12	85	7.1	Dawn to dusk ride.	Dunharrow
M.8	10.5,7.5	30,30	2.9,4	Dawn to 4:30 P.M., Paths of the Dead; reach Erech at midnight.	Erech
M.9	16	110	7.0		Calembal
M.10	13	90	7.0	The Dawnless Day.	Ringló
M.11	10	70	7.0	Battle at Linhir.	Lebennin
M.12	10	70	7.0	Drove enemy.	SW of Pelargir
M.13	5	35	7.0	Battle. Readied ships.	Pelargir

M.14	18	85	4.7	Rowed.	On Anduin
M.15	9	65	7.2	Sailed midnight to 9 A.M. Battle of the Pelennor.	Minas Tirith

Minas Tirith to the Morannon

M.16–17	——	——	——	Host musters.	Minas Tirith
M.18	6.5 (Pippin)	18	2.7	Infantry.	5 miles E of Osgiliath
	8 (Others)	33	4.0	Cavalry.	Cross-roads
M.19	6 (Pippin)	15	2.5	Infantry joins cavalry.	Cross-roads
M.20	10	25	2.5		Ithilien
M.21	8	20	2.5	Battle in afternoon.	East of Henneth Annûn
M.22	10	22	2.2		Northern Ithilien
M.23	10	18	1.8	Faint-hearted dismissed. Army leaves road.	South edge of Desolat
M.24	10	15	1.5	Go slowly.	Northwest of Morannon
M.25	——	——	——	Battle of the Morannon.	

Journey of Frodo and Sam

F.26	5	10	2.0	1 P.M. to dusk.	Central Eastern Emyn Muil
F.27	12	20	1.7	Dawn to dusk.	Cliff
F.28	12	20	1.7	Dawn to dusk.	Hollow
F.29	13	24	1.8	Dawn to evening.	Feet of Emyn Muil
	5	10	2.0	Capture Gollum. Brief rest, then walk moonset to dawn.	Gully (F.30 A.M.)
F.30	16	25	1.6	Dusk to 10 A.M. M. 1	Northern Dead Marshes (M.1)
M.1	10	15	1.5	Dusk to dawn. Stopped for Nazgûl.	SE Dead Marshes (M.2)
M.2	12	15	1.3	Dusk to dawn.	Noman-lands (M.3)
M.3	12	15	1.3	Dusk to dawn.	Edge of Desolation (M.4)
M.4	8	12	1.5	Dusk to pre-dawn.	One mile from Morannon (M.5)
M.5	12	24	2.0	Dusk to dawn.	North of Ithilien (M.6)
M.6	12	24	2.0	Dusk to dawn M.7	Near pool (M.7 A.M.)
M.7	2.5	10	4.0	Late afternoon to dusk.	Henneth Annûn
M.8	12	22	1.8	Dawn to dusk.	Halfway to Morgul-road
M.9	12	22	1.8	Dawn to dusk.	Morgul-road
M.10	6	10	1.7	Midnight to dawn in rough terrain. The Dawnless Day.	Just west of Cross-roads
	14	12	.9	4 P.M. to dusk (Cross-roads; and all night. Saw Morgul-host.	——
M.11	——	——	——	Slept all day and night.	Top of Winding Stair
M.12	24–30?	14	.5?	Day and night of M.12, and day of M.13.	Shelob's Lair
M.13	——	——	——	Capture by Orcs at dusk.	Frodo — Tower of Cirith Ungol Sam — Under-way

M.14	——	——	——		Tower of Cirith Ungol
M.15	13	15	1.2	Escape from Tower. Walk 5 A.M. to dusk, several halts.	Foot of ravine in Morgai
M.16	12,12	6,21	.5,1.8	Climb Morgai in day; walk in valley all night. Brief rest.	Central valley (M.17)
M.17	12	25	2.1	Dusk to dawn.	North end of valley (M.18)
M.18	6,3	12,8	2.0,2.7	Overtaken by Orcs on road.	Near Isenmouthe (M.19 A.M.)
M.19	11	10	.9	Return to road. Walk early morning to past dusk.	Near road
M.20	12	15	1.3	Dawn to dusk.	Near road
M.21	12	15	1.3	Last cistern.	Near road
M.22	12	15	1.3	Turn south from road. The Dreadful Nightfall.	South of road
M.23	12	10	.8		Gorgoroth
M.24	12	10	.8		Feet of Mount Doom
M.25	2	4	2.0	Ring destroyed.	

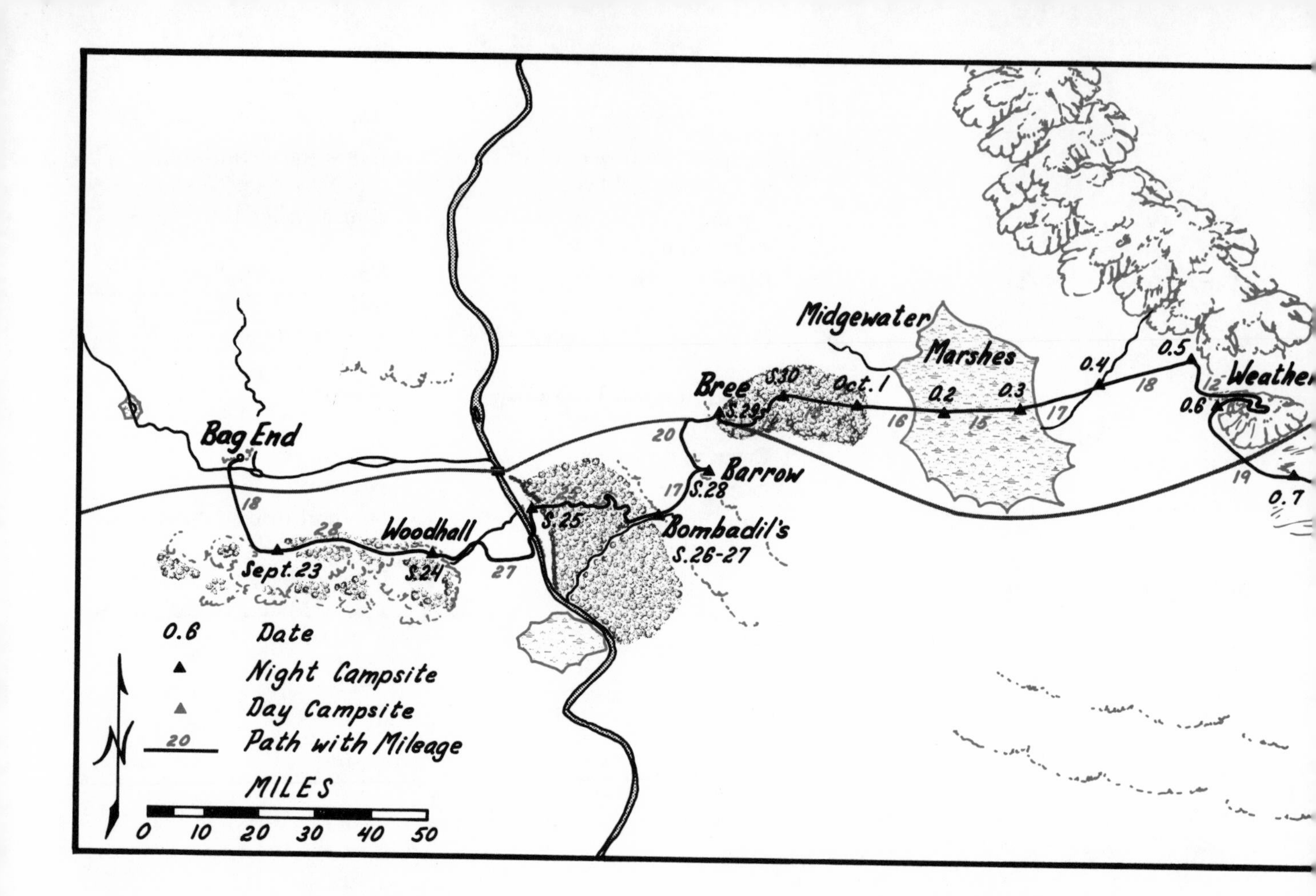

Bag End to Rivendell

The Hobbits hiked out from Bag End at dusk on September 23. They headed toward the Green Hill Country, walking for about three hours. After they ate they continued until they were very tired. The next day they started after 10 A.M. About an hour after dusk, while the Hobbits were hiding from a Black Rider, Elves appeared and led the Hobbits "some miles" to the ridge overlooking Woodhall. The next day the Hobbits went cross-country to Farmer Maggot's, then rode in his wagon to the ferry. They reached Crickhollow in the evening of September 25.[1]

To put off pursuit by the Black Riders the Hobbits cut through the Old Forest. In spite of rugged terrain and capture by Old Man Willow, they managed to reach Bombadil's house at twilight the same day. They stayed all the next day, as well, and on September 28 headed north toward the Great East Road.[2] Tom had told them to stay on the western skirts of the Barrow-downs, but the Hobbits unintentionally turned slightly east. After their unplanned afternoon sleep, dark fell and they were captured by a Barrow-wight. They were freed by Bombadil the next morning, but it was probably almost noon before they set out. Near dusk they reached the Road, and "plodded slowly" the last four miles to Bree.[3]

The attack on the inn delayed the Company's departure until ten the next morning. Strider led them north through the Chetwood toward Archet, taking many turnings to confuse the trail. October 1 they steered east, and on the second they left the Chetwood and by nightfall were into the western part of the Midgewater Marshes. The next day was all spent in the Marshes, and it was not until the morning of the fourth that the fens were left behind. That night they camped by a stream that ran from the Weather Hills. Strider estimated they could reach the Hills by noon of the next day (October 5), but the walk actually took until evening.[4] The morning of October 6 they headed south along a path that "ran cunningly" to the northern slope of Weathertop. After reaching the hill about noon, Strider led Frodo and Merry on the half-hour climb to the summit. It was probably only a mile or two, though Weathertop's size has been exaggerated on the map, making it appear longer. After spotting Black Riders on the Road below, the travellers re-

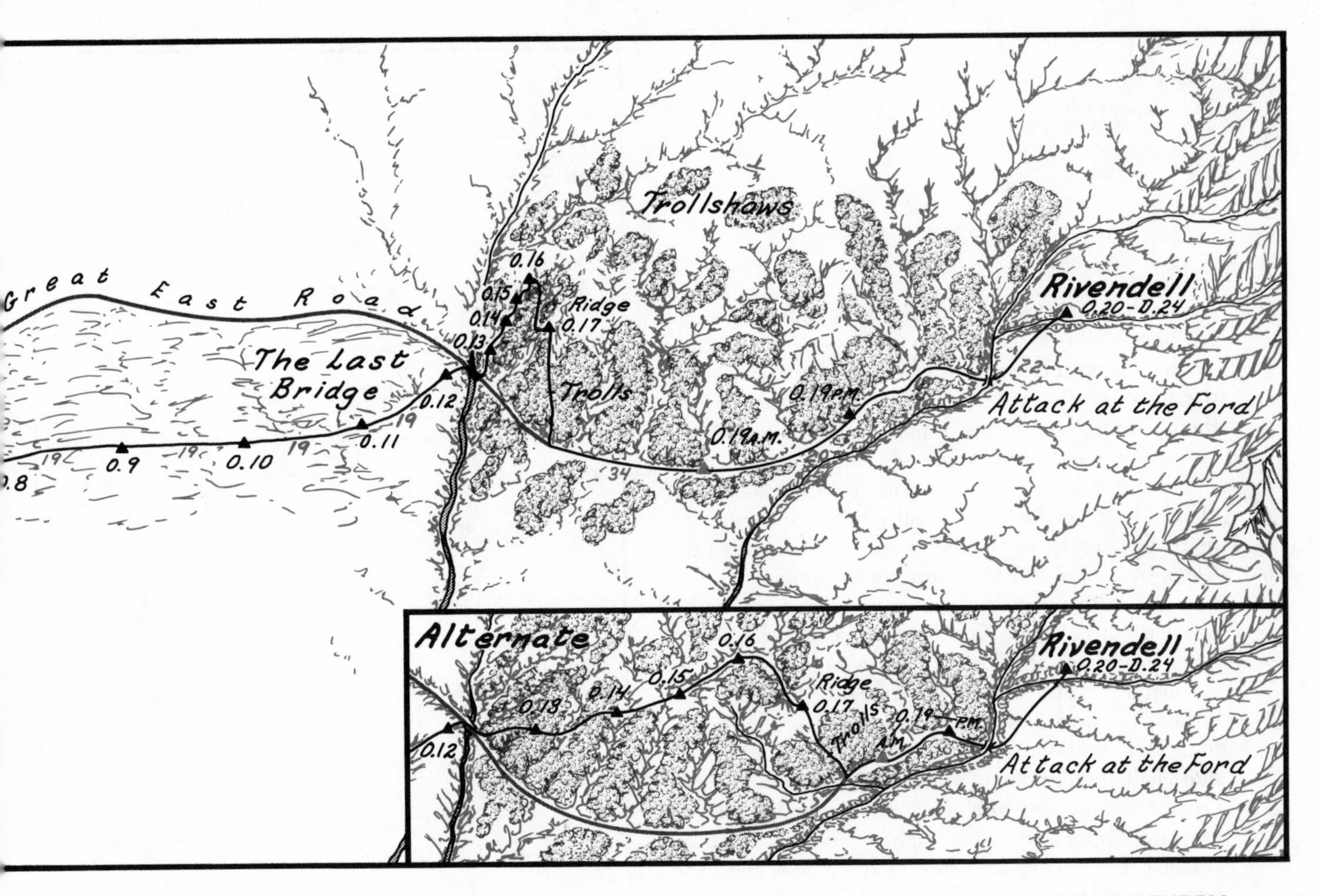

mained in the dell west of Weathertop for the rest of the day, and the night as well.[5]

At moonrise the Riders attacked, and Frodo was injured; so it was necessary to divide the stores among the hikers to allow Frodo to ride the pack-pony. As soon as day was full, on October 7, the Company crossed the Road and entered the thickets on the south. The land was "wild and pathless," and "their journey was slow." Still, they marched more quickly than they had in the woods, marshes, and hill-lands west of Weathertop. In little more than five days they covered the 120 miles to the Last Bridge.[6]

A mile east of the Bridge, they turned up a narrow ravine that led north. Here again, as in *The Hobbit* pathways map, two variations have been shown in the Trollshaws: the original map, based on the 1965 edition of *The Hobbit* in which the Trolls' camp seemed to be near the Last Bridge, and the revised map, placing the campsite near a lesser stream closer to the Bruinen.[7] With either, the reader can at least gain a visual impression of the number of days spent off the Road, and of the relative directions followed through the rugged lands. The walkers "had to pick their way . . . encumbered by fallen trees and tumbled rocks."[8] The weather was rainy, and Frodo's wound was worsening. After following the ravine north they probably attempted to go east, but on October 16 were "forced to turn northwards out of their course."[9] The next day they started late and headed southeast, but once more were blocked by a ridge where they were forced to spend the night. On October 18 they found a path leading southeast to the Road, and at mid-day discovered Bilbo's Stone-trolls.

In the afternoon they reached the Road, and went along it as swiftly as possible. The road in the Trollshaws has been corrected, as was the course of the Bruinen (Loudwater), to agree with Tolkien's original conception: running along the edge of the hills, yet *near* the course of the Bruinen for much of the distance "the Road turned away from the river . . . clung close to the feet of the hills, rolling and winding northward among woods and heather-covered slopes . . ."[10]

At dusk they were ready to rest, but when Glorfindel arrived he led them on until dawn of October 19.[11] Less than five hours later they continued, and "covered almost twenty miles before nightfall."[12] They were still "many miles" from the Ford of Bruinen, but they hobbled on and reached it in the late afternoon — only to be attacked once more.[13] After the Black Riders had been swept away by the flood, the Company carried Frodo slowly on toward Rivendell, reaching it in the deep night. The first stage of the journey was over.

Rivendell to Lórien

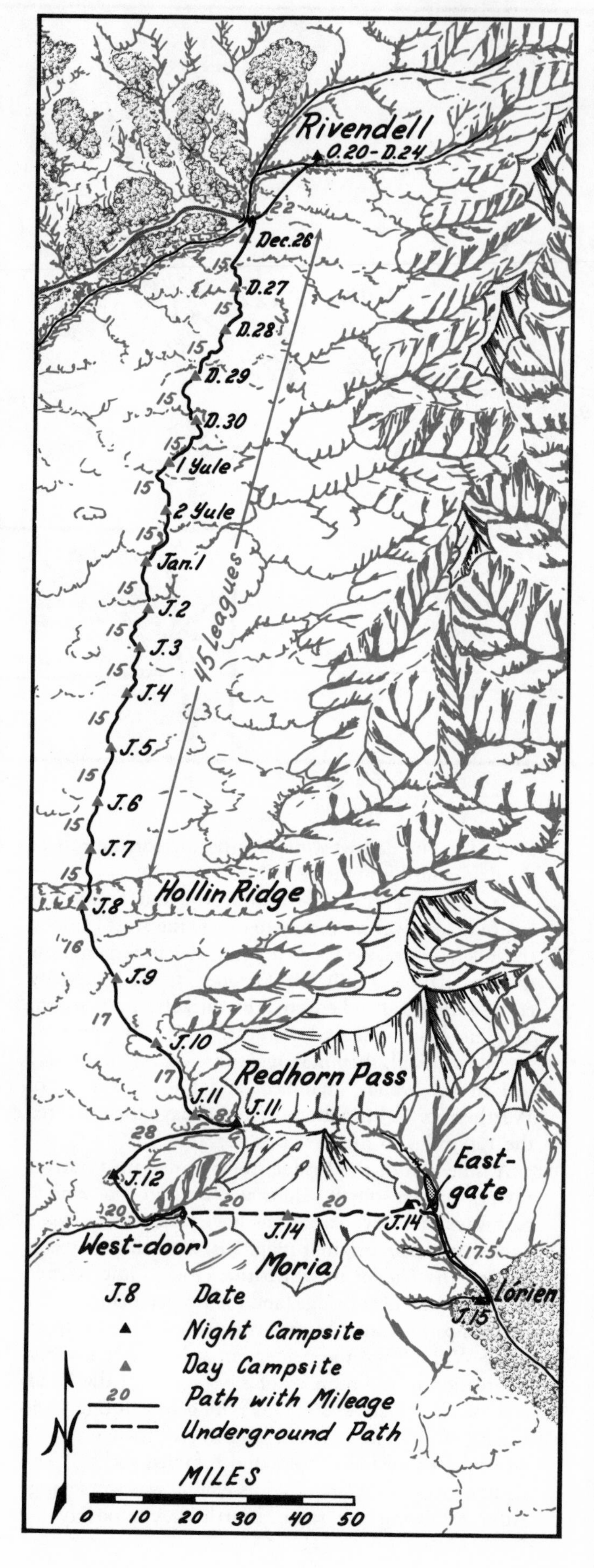

At dusk on December 25 the Fellowship departed, reaching Hollin Ridge at dawn January 8.[1] On January 11 they camped at the foot of the Redhorn and began the ascent in the dark.[2] By only midnight snow forced them to stop,[3] and the next morning they retreated — only to be attacked by wolves that night.

The West-door of Moria was fifteen miles *southwest* of the Pass; yet from the knoll where they spent the night of January 12 Gandalf pointed *southeast* to the Walls of Moria. All the morning of January 13 was required to find the road next to the Sirannon, and it was past dusk when they finally reached the Door.[4] After Frodo was attacked, all "were willing . . . to go on marching still for several hours."[5] Gandalf had estimated it was more than forty miles; yet by sometime after midnight they had apparently covered almost half the distance. From the Guardroom Gandalf decided it was time to climb,[6] and climb they did — for eight hours. By that night (January 14) they reached the Twenty-first Hall of the North End. The next day they were attacked and managed to escape the mile to the first Deep; but there Gandalf fell.[7] The travellers fled from Moria at 1 P.M., and by early evening had reached Nimrodel — "little more than five leagues from the Gates" (about fifteen miles).[8] For the next two days Elves led them through Lórien, and they entered Caras Galadon after dusk on January 17.[9]

On the morning of February 16 the Fellowship departed, and after hiking ten miles to the Anduin, they paddled out.[10] Aragorn insisted they start early each morning and journey far into the dark; yet for the first three days they merely drifted with the current.[11] On February 19 they passed downs on their west, and wolds on their east. The following days the lands seemed so sinister that they paddled for long periods and changed from day to night journeys.[12] Thus, they found themselves unexpectedly at Sarn Gebir about midnight of February 23. Paddling hard, they escaped both the rapids and the Orcs, and during the next day they portaged the few miles to the foot of the rapids. On the morning of February 25 they paddled south again, and by evening they had reached the lawn of Parth Galen.[13]

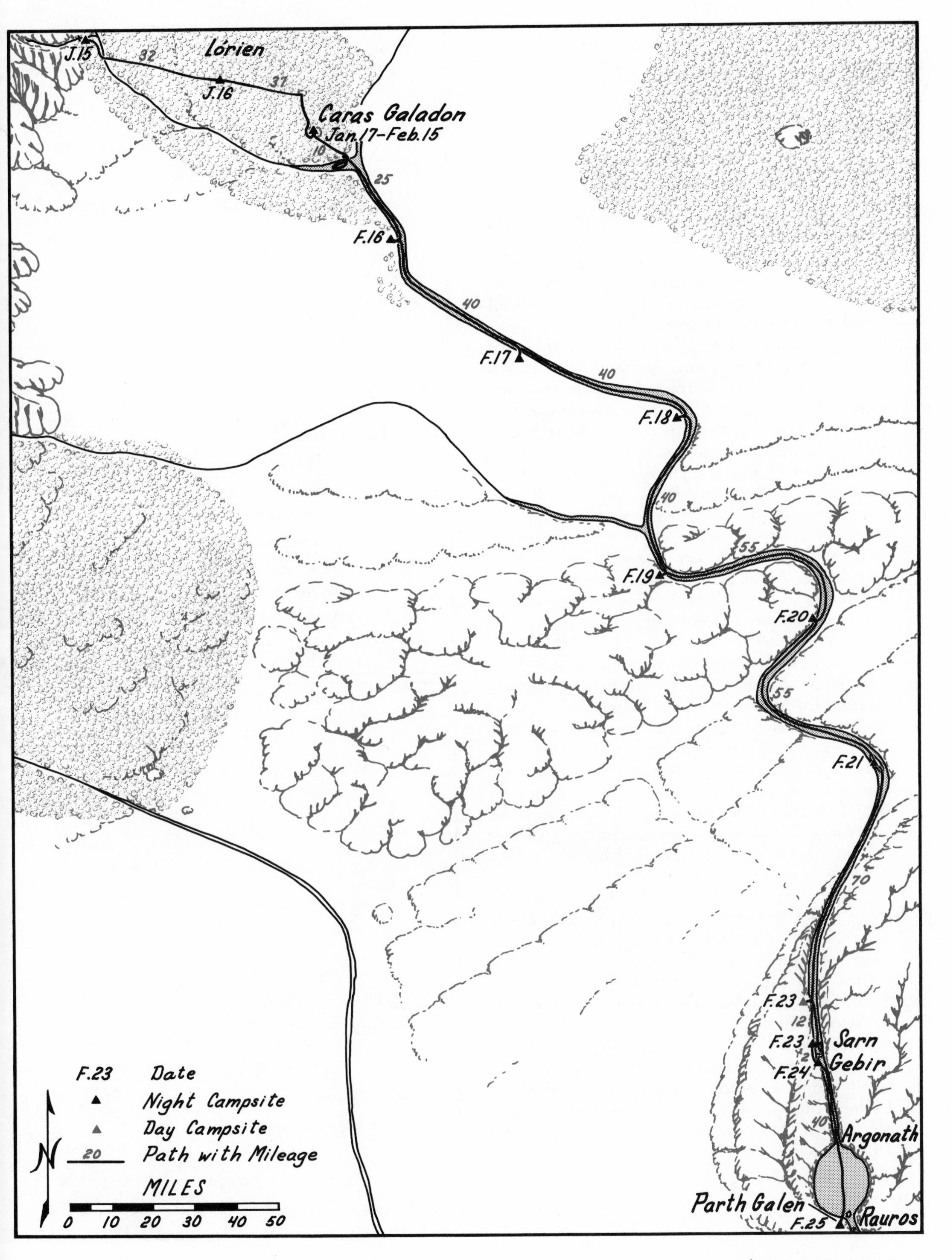
Lórien
J.15
32
J.16
37
Caras Galadon
Jan.17–Feb.15
10
25
F.16
40
F.17
40
F.18
40
55
F.19
F.20
55
F.21
70
F.23
12
F.23
Sarn
Gebir
F.24
40
Argonath
Parth Galen
F.25
Rauros
F.23 Date
Night Campsite
Day Campsite
20 Path with Mileage
MILES
0 10 20 30 40 50

LÓRIEN TO RAUROS

Rauros to Dunharrow

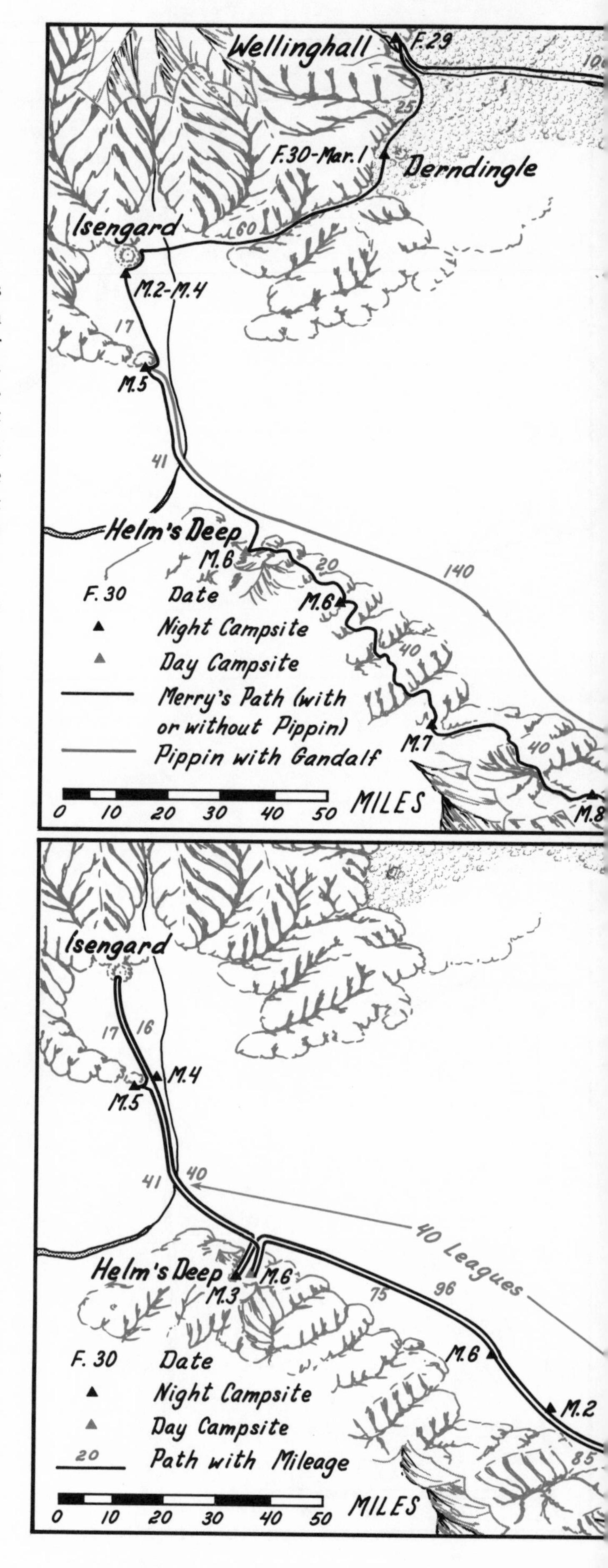

AT NOON ON FEBRUARY 26 the Fellowship was broken: Frodo and Sam fled; Boromir was slain; and Orcs carried Merry and Pippin toward Isengard.[1] Afternoon was fading as Aragorn, Gimli, and Legolas began their chase. The trail went west to the Entwash, then followed the valley to Fangorn.[2] The Orcs' five-hour lead widened to thirty-six,[3] for in the entire distance of some 165 miles they apparently camped only once in sixty hours[4] until they reached Fangorn and were trapped.[5] In contrast the three friends spent one night and three days of running, plus half a day riding, to reach Fangorn. The friends ran forty-five leagues (135 miles), covering twelve leagues each day on the plains; and (as Éomer acknowledged) that was no small feat![6]

The chase of the three friends ended without a reunion, however, for Merry and Pippin had managed to escape the previous dawn (February 29) and had met Treebeard. The old Ent had carried them to Wellinghall by dusk — "seventy thousand ent-strides" (100 miles at seven and one-half feet per stride).[7] On March 1 the Hobbits had already been at Derndingle a day and a half by the time Aragorn came to Treebeard's Hill and met Gandalf.[8] In the late morning Gandalf led the way toward Edoras, which they reached at dawn, March 2. Early that afternoon they rode west, and at dusk on March 3 they turned south toward Helm's Deep and an all-night battle.[9] After the enemy was defeated Gandalf led a small company toward Isengard.[10] They camped at the mouth of Nan Curunír on March 3, and the next morning covered the last sixteen miles to Isengard;[11] but the Hobbits were there before them.[12]

After talking with Saruman, Gandalf collected the Hobbits and the company retraced its path to the mouth of the valley. They camped at Dol Baran; but when a Nazgûl flew over they departed as quickly as possible and sped on through the night.[13] By dawn Gandalf and Pippin had reached Edoras, and the rest of the company returned to Helm's Deep.[14] Then all roads headed east. Gandalf raced toward Minas Tirith, arriving at dawn, on March 9. Aragorn, Legolas, Gimli, and the Dúnedain galloped along the highway, reaching Dunharrow at dusk on March 7. Théoden, Merry, and the Rohirrim took mountain paths and arrived at sunset on March 9.[15]

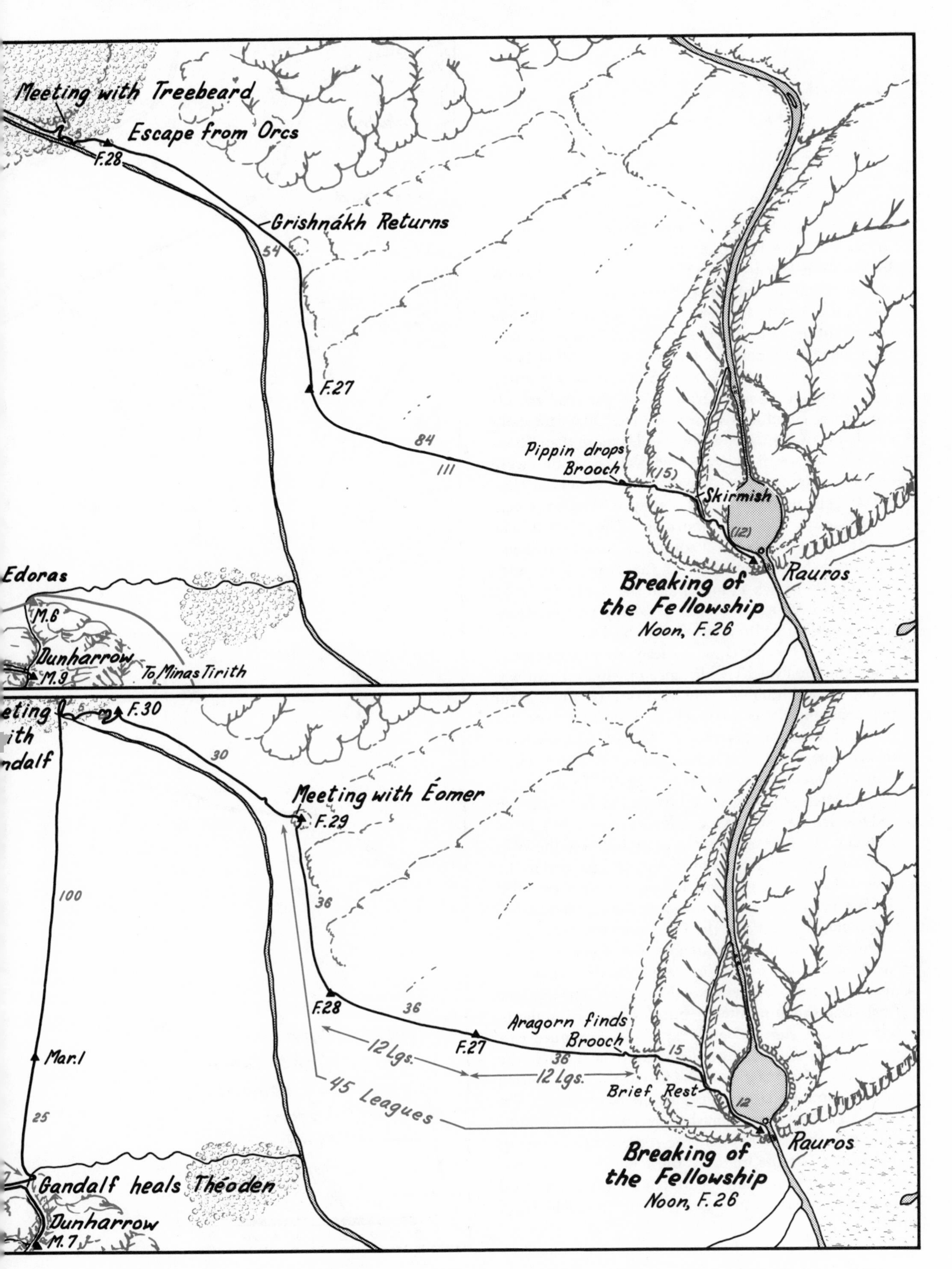

RAUROS TO DUNHARROW *Upper:* MERRY AND PIPPIN *Lower:* ARAGORN, LEGOLAS, AND GIMLI

Dunharrow to the Morannon

Now all the forces of the West were called to Minas Tirith for battle. At dawn on March 8 Aragorn led the Dúnedain deep into the glen behind Dunharrow and they entered the Paths of the Dead.[1] Summoning the Oathbreakers, he went on and at "two hours ere sunset" of the same day they reached Morthond Vale,[2] then rode "like hunters," arriving at the Hill of Erech just before midnight.[3] From Erech it was "ninety leagues and three to Pelargir,"[4] but the road ran almost three hundred sixty miles. The Dúnedain daily covered between ten and thirty miles more than Théoden's riders until they neared the coast and were obliged to fight.[5] After defeating the Corsairs of Umbar at Pelargir on March 13, they readied ships and rowed north the next morning. The current was strong, but at midnight a southerly wind sped them. They sailed the remainder of the distance by mid-morning on March 15 and joined the Battle.[6]

On the evening of March 9, Merry reached Dunharrow with the Rohirrim.[7] On the Dawnless Day, March 10, Théoden chose to lead his Riders swiftly along the highway. The distance to Minas Tirith was stated as one hundred two leagues (306 miles), but this apparently was a straight-line measurement, for the road was about 360 miles. The Rohirrim set forth from Edoras just after noon and camped that night some twelve leagues (36 miles) east.[8] Three nights later, March 13, they were bivouacked near Eilenach in Druadan Forest, having ridden about eighty miles each day. Seeking secrecy, the army followed the Wild Men through the Stonewain Valley and camped in the Grey Wood. Before dawn, March 15, they travelled the last seven leagues (21 miles) to the Rammas Echor and began the Battle of the Pelennor Fields.[9]

On the morning of March 18 the troops set forth for Mordor. With Aragorn went all the remaining members of the Fellowship except Merry. The infantry (including Pippin) halted five miles east of Osgiliath, but Aragorn and the mounted troops continued east to the Cross-roads and were joined by the infantry the next day.[10] On March 20 the Host of the West started north "some hundred miles" to the Morannon.[11] On March 21 they were ambushed near Henneth Annûn; and on March 23 they left the road, lengthening the distance.[12] Off the highway the going was slow, but at last on the morning of March 25 the Host stood among the slag heaps, facing the impassable Black Gate.[13]

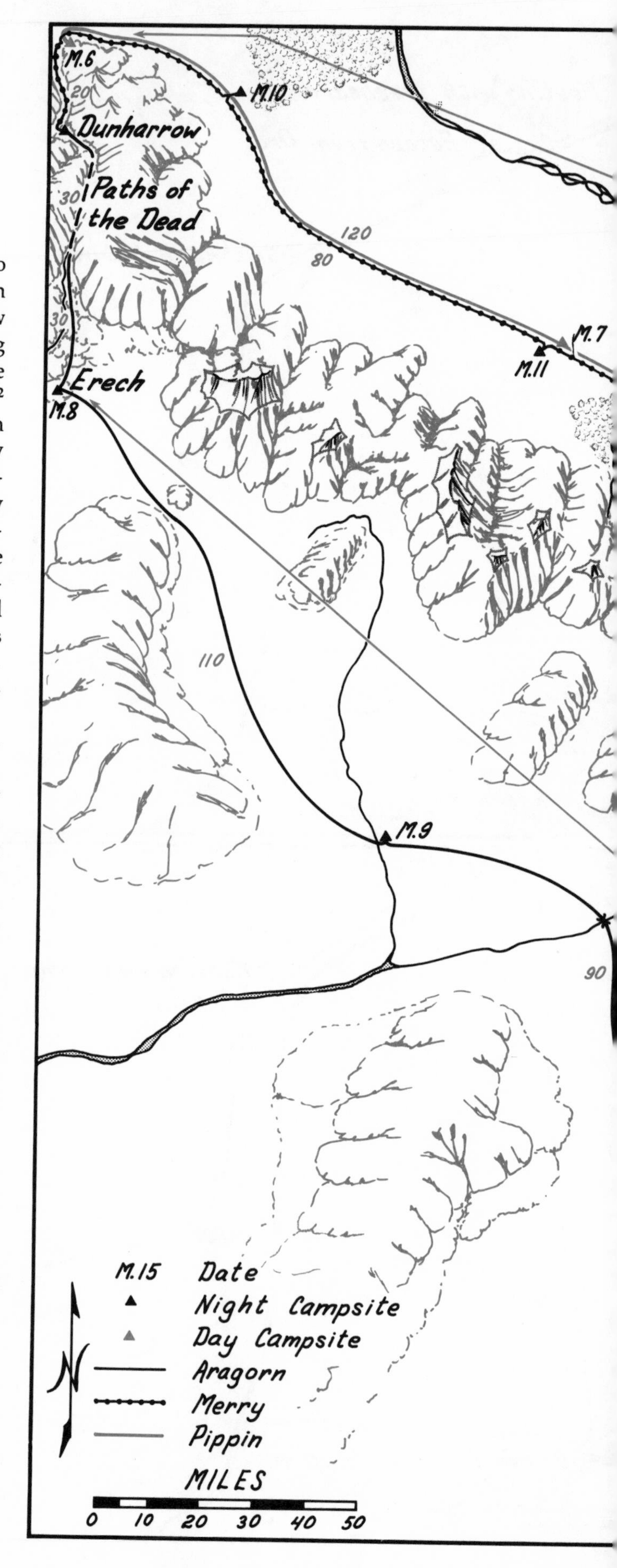

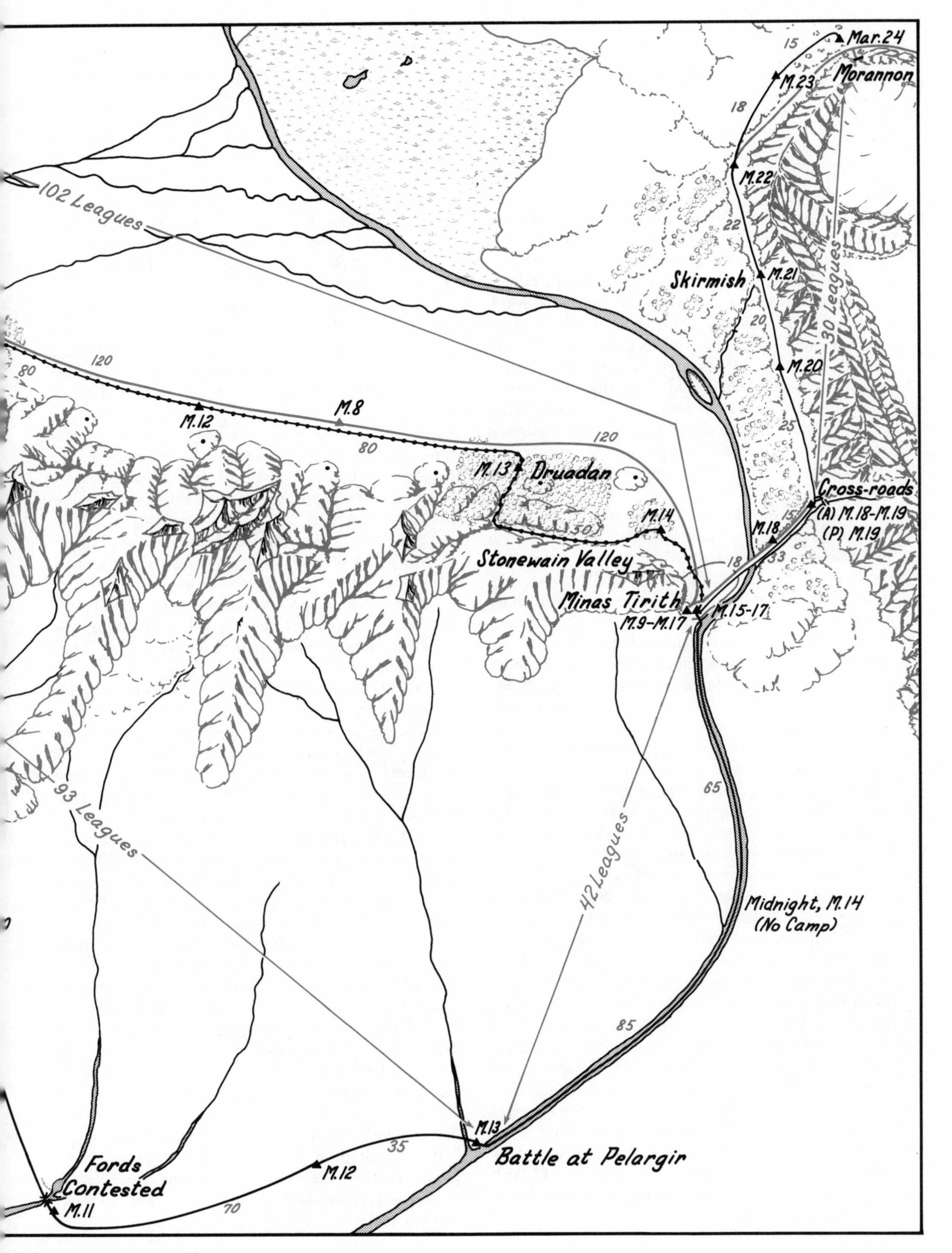

DUNHARROW TO THE MORANNON

The Journey of Frodo and Sam

SHORTLY AFTER NOON ON FEBRUARY 26, the day the Fellowship was broken, Frodo and Sam paddled across Nen Hithoel and beached the boat on the south side of Amon Lhaw.[1] During the afternoon and the following three days they toiled in the eastern Emyn Muil. As the cliffwall overlooking the Dead Marshes was too steep in the south, they worked their way along it.[2] On the afternoon of February 29 they crept down a ravine and finally managed to escape the hills.[3] A brief time later they saw and heard Gollum creeping down the very spot they had descended, and they thought it was best to capture him. Frodo decided to trust Gollum as guide, and upon his advice set out again after moonset the same night.[4]

Gollum led the Hobbits into the nearby gully, and they crept along the stream inside. The gully went south and east toward the Dead Marshes, and after walking the rest of that night and all of the next, they reached the fens at dawn on March 1.[5] They apparently were entering the northern edge, for the marshes stretched west back to the cliffwall, and Dagorlad was only "back a little, and round a little," to the north and east.[6]After only a brief rest Gollum led them into the marshes, and, "when the sun was riding high" they stopped. Before dusk they went on, and in the dark evening they were slogging through the very heart of the marshes, surrounded by lights of the Dead. Continuing, they managed to reach firmer ground. When a Nazgûl flew over they stopped for two hours, then tramped on, and by dawn (March 2) they were near the southeastern edge.[7]

Beyond the marshes lay formless slopes, the arid moors of the Noman-lands; and after struggling through this pathless land for two nights, the Hobbits came to the beginnings of the slag heaps piled for twelve nights between there and the Morannon.[8] During that night's march they stopped twice when a Nazgûl was overhead, but before March 5 they stood a mile away from the western Tower of the Teeth.[9] After Gollum persuaded Frodo to go thirty leagues (90 miles) south to the Pass of Cirith Ungol, they set out after dusk. They crept along just west of the highway heading southwest. By dawn they had covered eight leagues (24 miles) and finally turned the corner of the mountains.[10] During the next night's march they passed into northern Ithilien, and by daylight of March 7 they had reached the swift stream that ran southwest past Henneth Annûn.

When Sam's fire revealed their camp to Faramir, two Men of Gondor stayed with them during the skirmish with the Haradrim. Between late afternoon and sunset they quickly crossed the "somewhat less than ten miles" downstream to Henneth Annûn.[11] At that refuge they spent the night, and at dawn they went south through the wood. Faramir thought it safe: "you may walk under daylight . . . The land dreams in a false peace."[12] They kept well west of the road and after two marches came to the valley of the Morgulduin in which ran the road from Osgiliath. They hid in an oak to rest, and at midnight they headed east.[13] The land was broken and steeply pitching, and the going was slow. As night ended they sheltered under the east bank of a hogback, but there was no sunrise; for during the dark hours Sauron's vapors had blown even as far west as Rohan. It was March 10: the Dawnless Day.[14] Before "tea-time" (about 4 P.M.) Gollum returned and led them south over the broken slope for about an hour, then east to the Southward Road.[15] They crept along and reached the Cross-roads just as the sun was setting.[16]

Turning east, they climbed the Morgul-road to the bridge, which was not far within the valley's mouth. Sam guided his stumbling master to the north where the path left the main road. Slowly they toiled up the winding path, and just opposite the north-facing gate of Minas Morgul, Frodo stopped, and saw the Morgul-host ride forth.[17]

On Tolkien's map the width of the Ephel Dúath was little more than twenty miles, probably no more than a day's journey or so; but three nights and days actually passed. It was the evening of March 10 when the Hobbits had reached the trail, and during the rest of that night they ascended the Straight Stair, then went along a passage that "seemed to go on for miles." They finally came to the top of the Winding Stair, where they stopped at dawn to rest (March 11).[18] They apparently slept twenty-four hours or more, for when Gollum found them asleep "hours later" he said it was "tomorrow," and it was again daytime.[19] Gollum led them a mile up the ravine to the entrance to Shelob's Lair.[20] The travellers entered the passage on March 12 and did not escape the east end until late afternoon of March 13. The discrepancy can apparently be explained by Tolkien's continuing struggle in synchronizing the chronologies of four different simultaneous paths. In his notes he wrote, "It might be a good thing to increase the reckoning of the time that Frodo, Sam, and Gollum took to climb Kirith Ungol by a day . . ." And in the "Tale of Years," the dates agree with those given here; but for once Tolkien seems to have not completely clarified the change in the final text.[21] As a result, it appeared they had spent at least 30 hours in that dark hole!

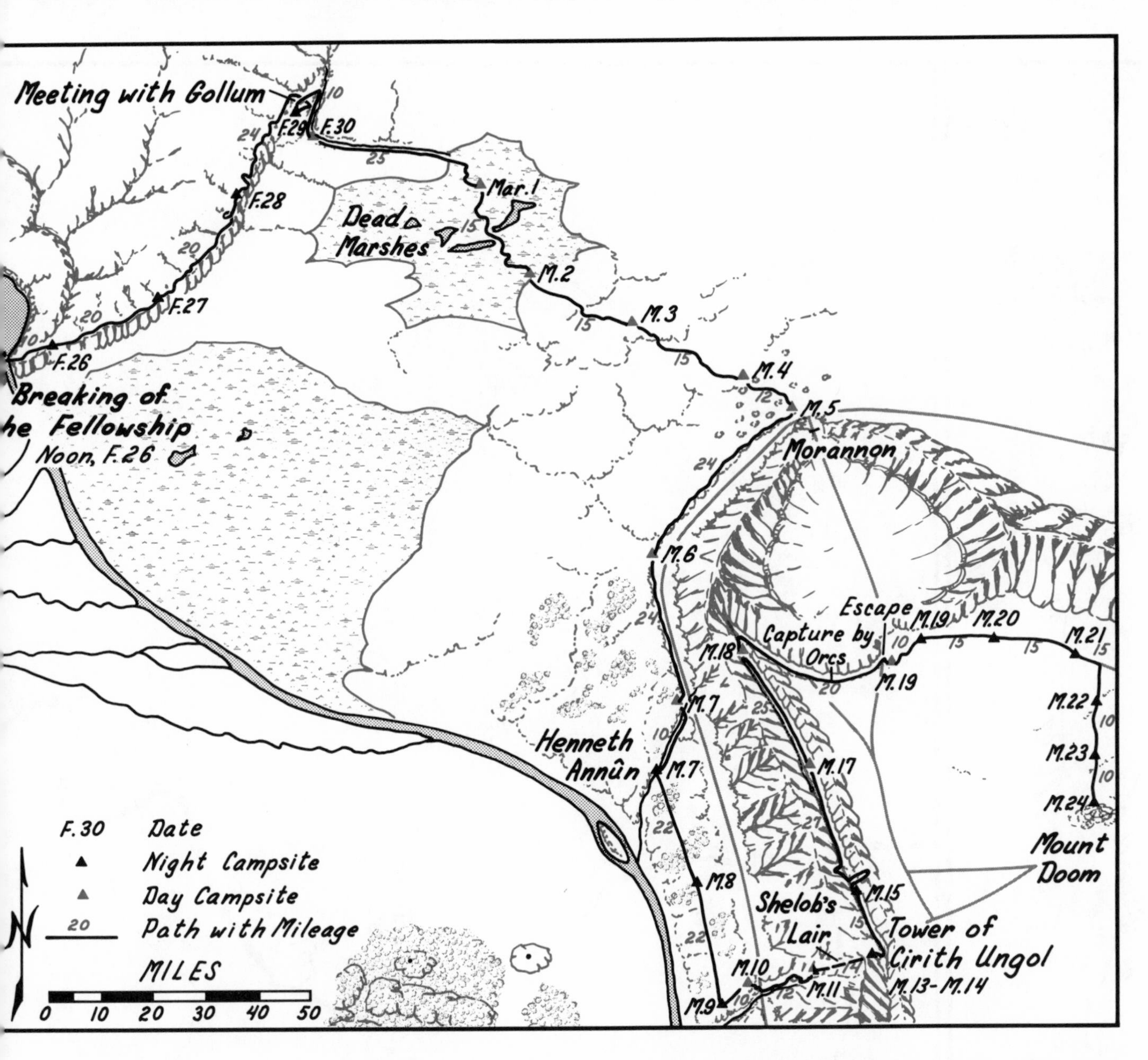

THE JOURNEY OF FRODO AND SAM

Beyond Shelob's Lair Frodo was stung, then captured by Orcs and taken to the Tower. Sam uselessly threw himself against the Under-gate,[22] and when he awoke, it was noon March 14. By the time Sam again reached the exit from Shelob's Lair, it was dusk.[23] Before dawn on March 15 the Hobbits escaped from the Tower and jumped into the ravine west of the Morgai.[24] They plodded north along the valley road until late afternoon, then crossed the valley and slept.[25] The next day they attempted to climb the Morgai, but were directly above a large camp and had to retrace their steps. Turning north again, they trudged on until past dawn of March 17. They had gone "about twelve leagues north from the bridge" (36 miles).[26] During the next night they reached the north end of the valley, and at dusk on March 18 set out on the road that ran to the Isenmouthe. Twelve miles later they were overtaken by an Orc troop and were forced to go at a "brisk trot" the remaining eight miles.[27] After escaping near the Isenmouthe, they slept until early morning (March 19).

The remainder of the journey was made in the daytime, for Sauron's troops moved mostly at night. Rising later on March 19 the Hobbits covered only "a few weary miles" in the rugged terrain until Sam led Frodo back to the causeway.[28] Even on the road they walked only forty miles in slightly less than three marches. During March 22, the fourth day from the Isenmouthe, they drew even with Mount Doom and turned south.[29] After two more days of torment they had crept to the Mountain's foot, and during the morning of March 25 they reached the Crack of Doom and the Ring was destroyed.[30]

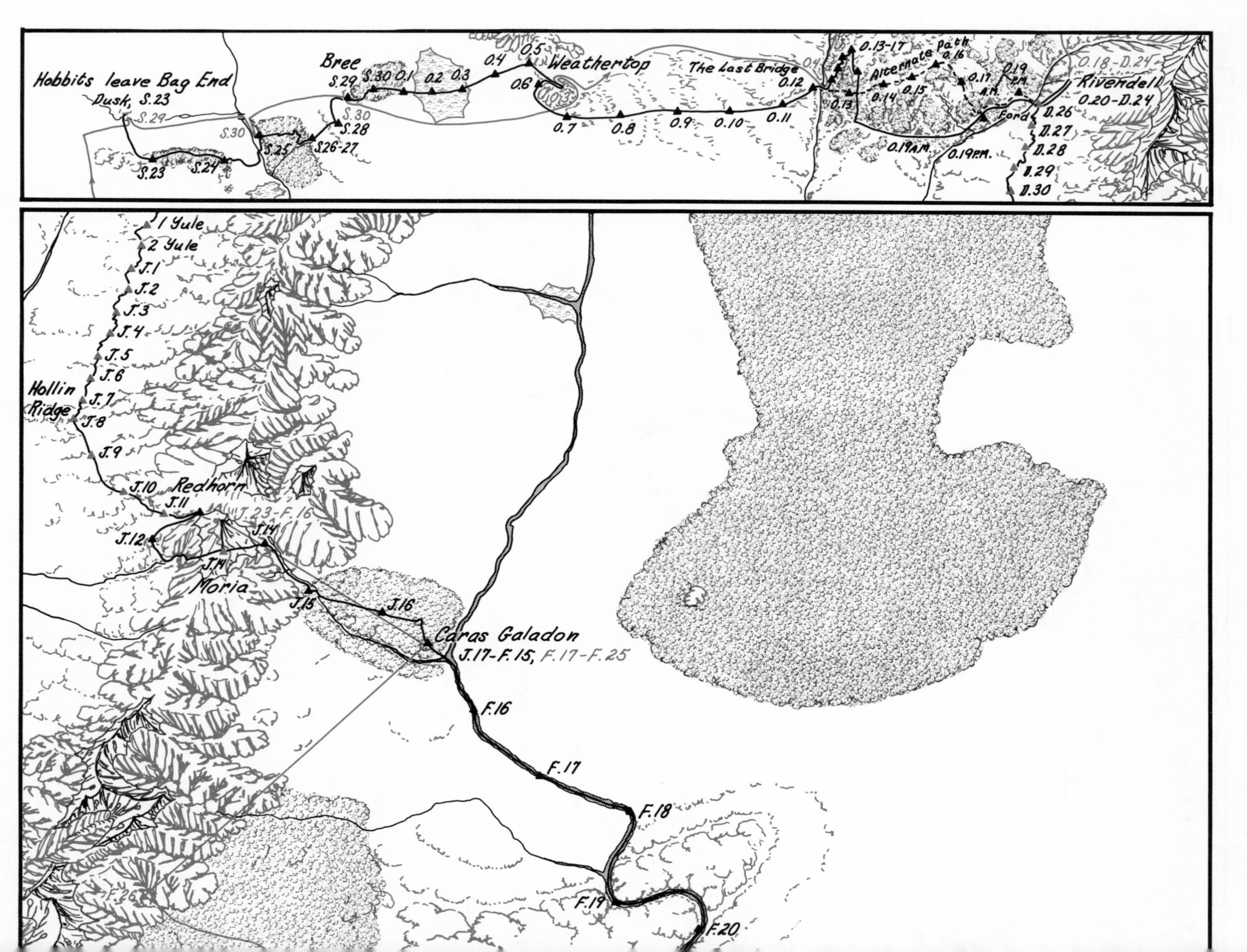
Hobbits leave Bag End
Dusk, S.23
S.29
S.30
S.23
S.24
S.25
S.26-27
S.28
S.30
Bree
S.29
S.30
O.1
O.2
O.3
O.4
O.5
Weathertop
O.6
O.7
O.8
O.9
O.10
O.11
The Last Bridge
O.12
O.13
O.13-17
Alternate path
O.14
O.15
O.16
O.17
A.M.
O.19
P.M.
O.19 A.M.
O.19 P.M.
Ford
O.18-D.24
Rivendell
O.20-D.24
D.26
D.27
D.28
D.29
D.30
1 Yule
2 Yule
J.1
J.2
J.3
J.4
J.5
J.6
J.7
J.8
Hollin Ridge
J.9
J.10
J.11
Redhorn
J.23-F.16
J.12
J.14
J.14
Moria
J.15
J.16
Caras Galadon
J.17-F.15, F.17-F.25
F.16
F.17
F.18
F.19
F.20
F.26

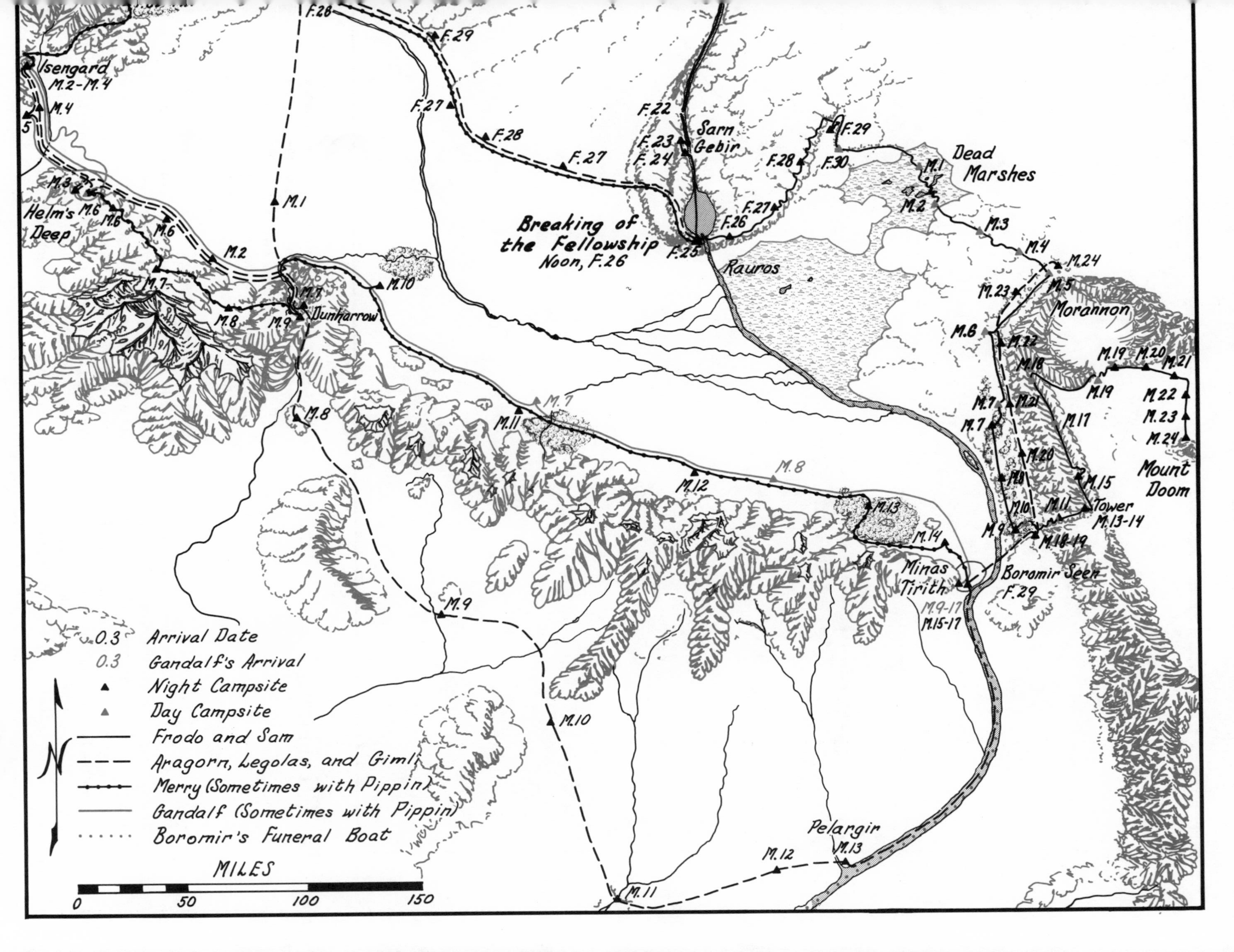
Isengard
Helm's Deep
Dunharrow
Breaking of the Fellowship
Noon, F.26
Sarn Gebir
Rauros
Dead Marshes
Morannon
Mount Doom
Tower
Minas Tirith
Boromir Seen
F.29
Pelargir
0.3 Arrival Date
0.3 Gandalf's Arrival
Night Campsite
Day Campsite
Frodo and Sam
Aragorn, Legolas, and Gimli
Merry (Sometimes with Pippin)
Gandalf (Sometimes with Pippin)
Boromir's Funeral Boat
MILES
0
50
100
150

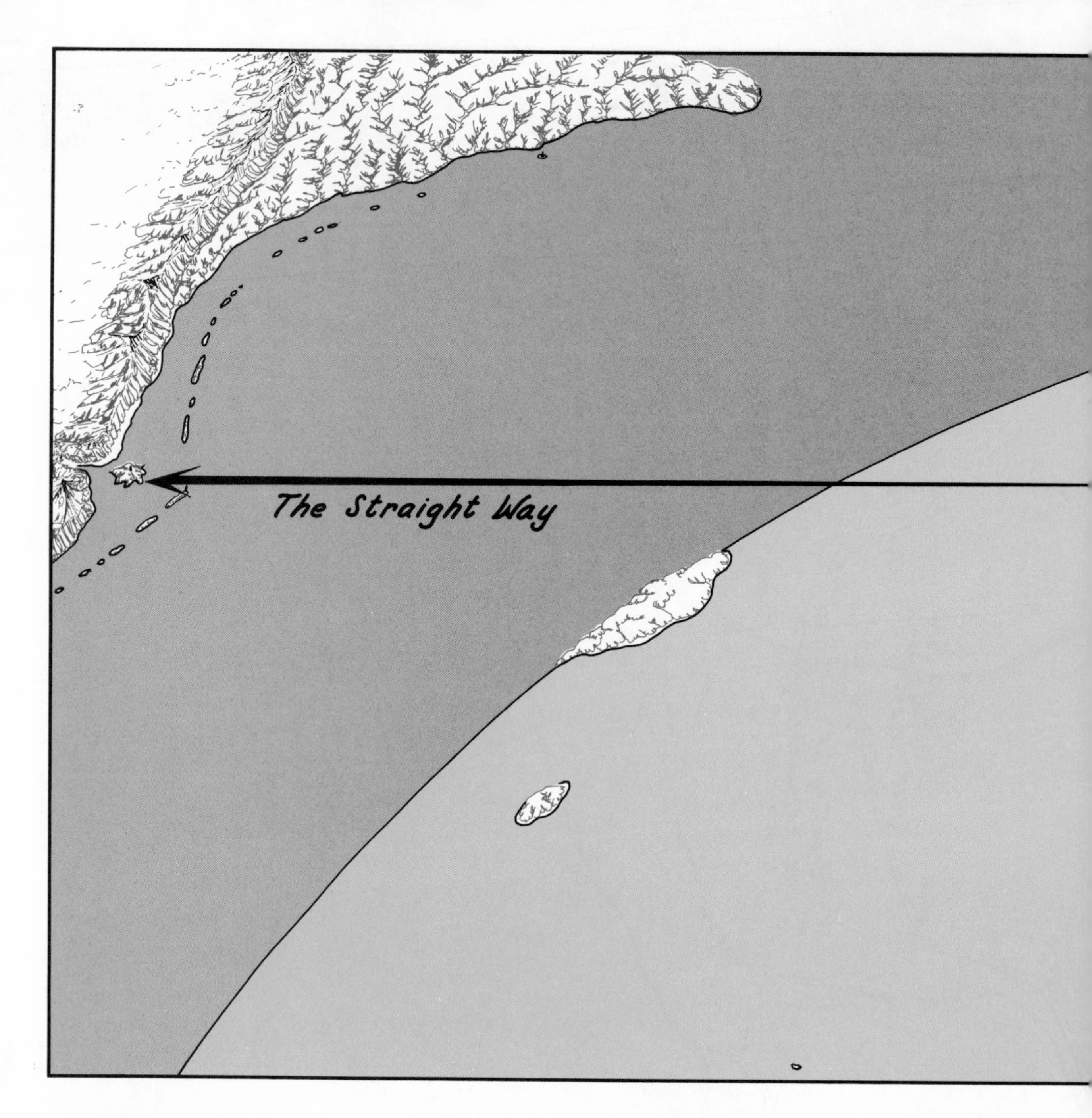

The Road Home

THROUGH THE EARLY SUMMER the travellers remained in Minas Tirith, loathe to dissolve their Fellowship; but after the wedding of Aragorn and Arwen, the time of parting drew near. On July 19 an escort left for Rohan with the bier of King Théoden. Going without haste, they reached Edoras on August 7; and it was not until August 14 that they set out for Helm's Deep. After two days there, they rode north to Isengard, arriving on August 22. On that day the members of the Fellowship separated, with Legolas and Gimli going through Fangorn, Aragorn returning to Minas Tirith, and Gandalf and the Hobbits continuing north toward Rivendell.[1]

Six days later, on August 28, they met Saruman in Dunland. The company continued north; but Saruman turned toward the Shire, planning evil while the Hobbits were "riding round twice as far."[2] On September 6 they stopped west of Moria, and after a week Celeborn and Galadriel departed for Lórien; while Elrond's people, Gandalf, and the Hobbits went on to Rivendell, which they reached on September 21. There they vis-

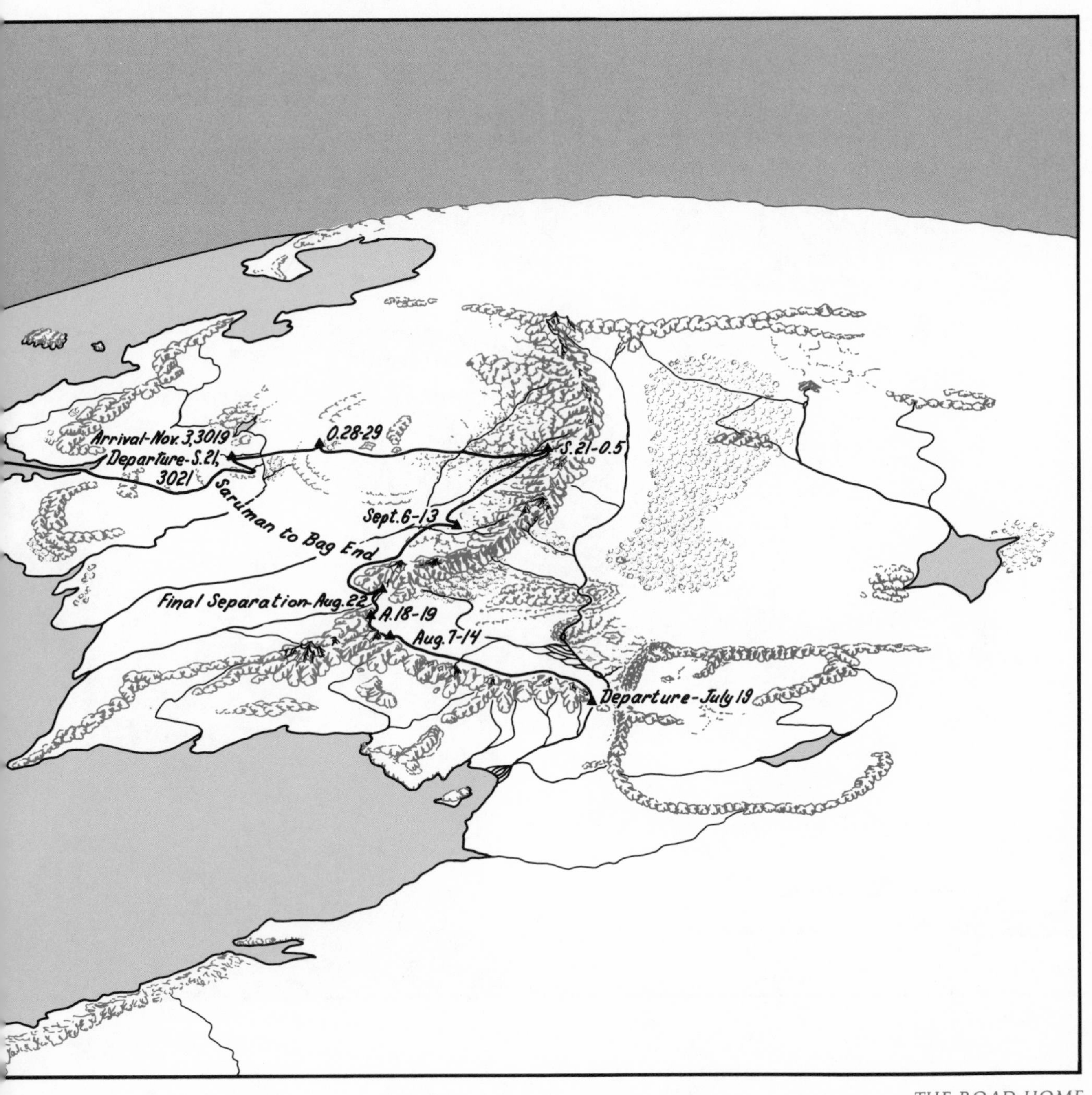

THE ROAD HOME

ited Bilbo for almost a fortnight, until October 5, when they left on the last leg. The next day they crossed the Ford of Bruinen, and (going slightly faster in the worsening weather) they came to Bree the evening of October 28.[3] After visiting for a day with Butterbur they headed out for the one day's ride to the Shire. Gandalf turned aside to visit Bombadil, and the Hobbits hurried on, reaching the Brandywine Bridge in the evening. Seeing the situation of their homeland, they rode straight for Bag End. On November 1 they covered the twenty-two miles to Frogmorton; and the next day they continued to Bywater (with a shiriff-escort for much of the way).[4] After the skirmish that evening and the Battle of Bywater the next morning, they arrived at Bag End in the afternoon of November 3, only to be confronted by Saruman himself. In the ensuing action, Saruman was slain, and with his death came the end of the War of the Rings.[5]

Over the next two years, the Hobbits reordered the Shire, and their own lives; but Frodo was never again wholly free of pain. On September 21 of F.O. 1 (T.A. 3021 by the old reckoning), he set out with Sam for the Grey Havens. Going south to Woody End he met Elrond, Galadriel, and Bilbo; and on September 29 they came to the firth of Lune. There Gandalf awaited them; and as Sam returned to the Shire with Merry and Pippin, the ship crossed the Straight Road into the West.[6]

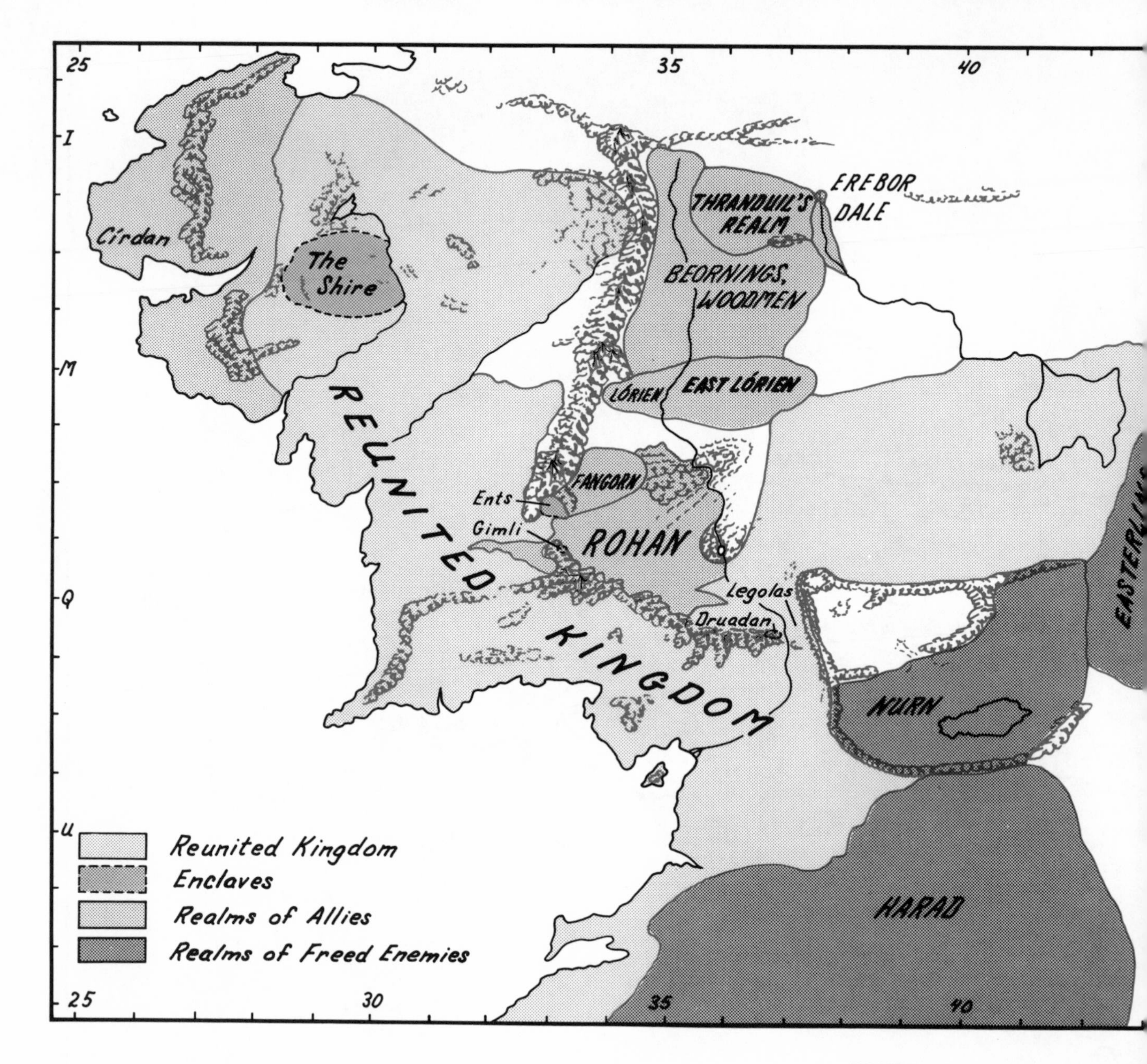

FOURTH AGE OF ARDA

The Fourth Age

After the departure of Elrond, the Fourth Age began. Aragorn reclaimed all the lands of Gondor and Arnor as they had been at the greatest extent (excluding only Rohan) and formed the Reunited Kingdom.[1] Within the borders of the realm were several peoples who were considered part of the kingdom, yet were allowed complete self-governance: the Hobbits of the Shire, the "Wild Men" of Druádan Forest, the Ents at Isengard, Gimli's Dwarves of the Glittering Caves, and the Elves from Greenwood with Legolas and Ithilien. The Shire and the Forest of Druádan were even forbidden entry by any folk other than their own.[2] Nurn was given to the slaves of Mordor, and peace was made with the Haradrim and the Easterlings.[3]

North of the Reunited Kingdom, Mirkwood had been freed. Thranduil added the lands north of the Mountains to his kingdom, and the middle portion was given to the Beornings and the Woodmen. Celeborn claimed the section south of The Narrows, calling it "East Lórien," but after Celeborn's departure "in Lórien there lingered sadly only a few of its former people."[4]

Thematic Maps

Introduction

Tolkien stated in "On Fairy-Stories" that "*Faerie* . . . holds the seas, the sun, the moon, the sky; and the earth, and all the things that are in it: tree and bird, water and stone, wine and bread, and ourselves, mortal men, when we are enchanted."[1] True to this concept, Tolkien included, in varying degrees, every major component of our Primary World: landforms, minerals, weather and climate, natural vegetation, agriculture, political units, population distribution, races, languages, transportation routes — even house types. He did more than merely describe these individual components, however, which would have been tedious and artificial. Instead, by carefully intermingling each element, he produced the very quality he believed so essential to credibility of an imaginary setting: "the inner consistency of reality."[2] So successful was his imagery that his landscape seems to have become a living world in which we could walk bodily, breathing with Frodo and Sam the fresh fragrant air of Ithilien, if we could but find the way.

Although part of a unified system, each of the components is worth evaluating in its own right. Landforms provided more than just the stage on which the story was played. These physical features were the visible results of the struggle between good and evil, the Valar and Melkor and Sauron.[3] They were the battle wounds of the earth. The hills and mountains, valleys and plains, seemed almost animate in their ability to hinder or help the journeys of the various travellers. From the first Elves blocked in their westward migration by the towering Mountains of Mist, to the Fellowship of the Rings struggling to the knees of Caradhras thousands of years later, mountains daunted those who dared to challenge their supremacy.[4]

Climate, and especially weather, were very important in Tolkien's tales. Snows drove Beren from Dorthonion and the Fellowship from the Redhorn Pass. Thunderstorms frightened the Orcs who had captured Túrin, and forced Thorin and Company to take shelter. Fog hid the lands west of the Grinding Ice, lost the Hobbits on the Barrow-downs, and covered the portaging by Sarn Gebir. In a land of prevailing Westerlies, Sauron's fume-filled east winds bit the eastern Emyn Muil and sent storms travelling in an abnormal direction.[5]

Vegetation was essential not only in enhancing the setting, but also in providing yet another medium through which the forces of good and evil, joy and fear, could reach out to the travellers. Although Tolkien included a complete range of flora, from the short, dry grasses of the Downs to the majestically towering mallorns of Lórien, his love and knowledge of trees was evident in the importance he placed on forests. He stated this love clearly through Yavanna: "'All have their worth . . . [but] I hold trees dear.'"[6]

The insertion of living beings completed the imagery, and their distribution told a story in itself. With rare exceptions the evil ones seemed able to produce seas of enemies — from Morgoth's Orcs, Balrogs, and dragons, who had grown so numerous that the whole plain of Anfauglith could not contain them,[7] to Sauron's army in the War of the Rings, great enough to send huge forces against Minas Tirith, Lórien, Thranduil's Realm, Dale, and Erebor, and still be left overwhelming numbers with which to fight at the Black Gate. Against them the forces of good could sometimes gain the mastery by having greater will than the thralls they faced, but they seldom were more numerous than their foes.

Battles were not the only way in which people were important, however. Middle-earth seemed tremendously underpopulated in the western lands, and this increased the sense of loneliness and isolation the travellers must have had while struggling through rugged terrain, far from friends, without allies against the evil beings who pursued them. How satisfying it was to reach a haven where one could have some semblance of familiar comforts. As Frodo and Sam found at Henneth Annûn, how good it seemed after "days spent in the lonely wild . . . to drink pale yellow wine . . . eat bread and butter, salted meats, and dried fruits, and good red cheese, with clean hands and clean knives and plates."[8]

The following maps attempt, in a much more mundane way, to trace individually the patterns of five important elements that Tolkien included in his world: landforms, climate, vegetation, population, and Tolkien's beloved languages. In viewing the maps the reader should keep in mind that in spite of numerous passages providing information, not every region was equally covered by Tolkien. For those that were discussed in his stories, the map could be no more accurate than the cartographer's interpretation of the data. On these maps more than anywhere else in this atlas, it was essential to accept Middle-earth's normal patterns and processes as synonymous with those of our Primary World unless powers of the Secondary World (be they good or evil) were affecting change.

Landforms

THE DETAILED REFERENCES and evaluations for the major landform features have been given with the various regional maps of Valinor, Númenor, Beleriand, and the other known lands of Middle-earth.[1] The accompanying map is merely a composite diagram. Tolkien's maps included all the mountain ranges except the Pelóri and the Iron Mountains, as well as hills. There were many undulating areas, however, and even some rather rugged terrain not included due to cartographic difficulties in showing such low relief. Broadly speaking, it was assumed that the closer land was to mountains, the more rugged it became; and truly flat lands were found only where there were marshes or alluvial plains.

Mountains

The two greatest mountain ranges were never mapped by Tolkien: the Pelóri and the Iron Mountains (Ered Engrin). Each of these has been illustrated as extremely high and broad. The Pelóri were described by Tolkien as having a sheer fault-like seaward escarpment and more gentle western slopes, lending maximum protection against the outer world.[2] The Iron Mountains were shown similarly, but with south-facing cliffs.

The central highlands south of the Iron Mountains and north of Beleriand seemed to be plateaus, yet were edged by mountains.[3] The Echoriath and the Ered Gorgoroth on the southern face of Dorthonion were the highest of these. Of the mountains that were mapped east of Beleriand, the Misty and White Mountains were shown as the highest, for they were snowcapped and seemed to have created the greatest barriers to both climate and travels through the ages.[4] The Mountains of Mordor, though they had only three passes (Cirith Gorgor, Cirith Ungol, and the Morgul Pass) were evidently not snowcapped, and thus, were lower.[5]

Hills and Plateaus

Foothills were probably found adjacent to all the mountain ranges, but where travellers passed through them verification was given. In the rolling hills of Lindon west of the Blue Mountains, Finrod discovered Mortal Men.[6] Tuor passed through "tumbled hills" at the feet of the Echoriath.[7] West of the Misty Mountains rugged lands extended from the Ettenmoors south through Dunland. The Trollshaws were very tortuous.[8] Near Rivendell there seemed almost a plateau, for the moors rose in "one vast slope,"[9] yet were scored by deep ravines. South of Rivendell the lands were more eroded. This topography extended through Dunland, and probably all the way to the Gap of Rohan.[10] North of the White Mountains the beacon-hills huddled close to the northern cliffs; while hills south of the range extended far south of the main range, even forming the rugged coast near Dol Amroth.

The only plateau other than those in Beleriand and near Rivendell was the lava plateau of Gorgoroth in northwestern Mordor.[11] As with the moors near Rivendell, the initial impression of smoothness was deceptive: Gorgoroth's "wide and featureless flats were in fact all broken and tumbled."[12]

Eroding away from the various mountains and from other more broadly folded areas, sedimentary rock layers produced alternating ridges and lowlands. The most obvious hills were those known as *downs,* and were found in Númenor, in Eriador, and around the Wold. The *hogback* climbed by the Hobbits in North Ithilien was produced by the same erosional process, but was more steeply pitching than the downs.[13] Two ridges in Beleriand may also have been erosional: the outcrop extending from the moors near amon Rûdh to the falls of the Esgalduin, and Andram, the Long Wall.[14] Both were south-facing, and thus were not eroding away from the Central Highlands.

Plains and Undulating Lowlands

Flat lowlands develop where there is a weak rock stratum or where nearby mountains provide alluvial materials that wash over the lands near their feet. Tolkien specifically described several plains areas: Ard-galen and Lothlann at the feet of the Iron Mountains; north of the Andram at the Twilight Meres; the plains of Rohan and Rhovanion; Dagorlad, the hard plain of battle; and Lithlad, the ash plain.[15] Unless coastal cliffs appeared on Tolkien's maps (such as those in Nevrast, Númenor, and near Dol Amroth)[16] the shores were considered to be flat coastal plain.

Away from these specifically mentioned plains the land was probably more undulating, for it would have been subject to more stream-cutting action, rather than receiving alluvial fill. In some areas of the north, however, especially in northern Wilderland, the land appeared to have been covered by continental glaciation and may have had depositional hills as well as erosional ones.[17] Much of the travel was in these rolling lands. The gentle topography should have sped the travellers along; yet even in these less rugged areas, other factors could slow or speed their progress.

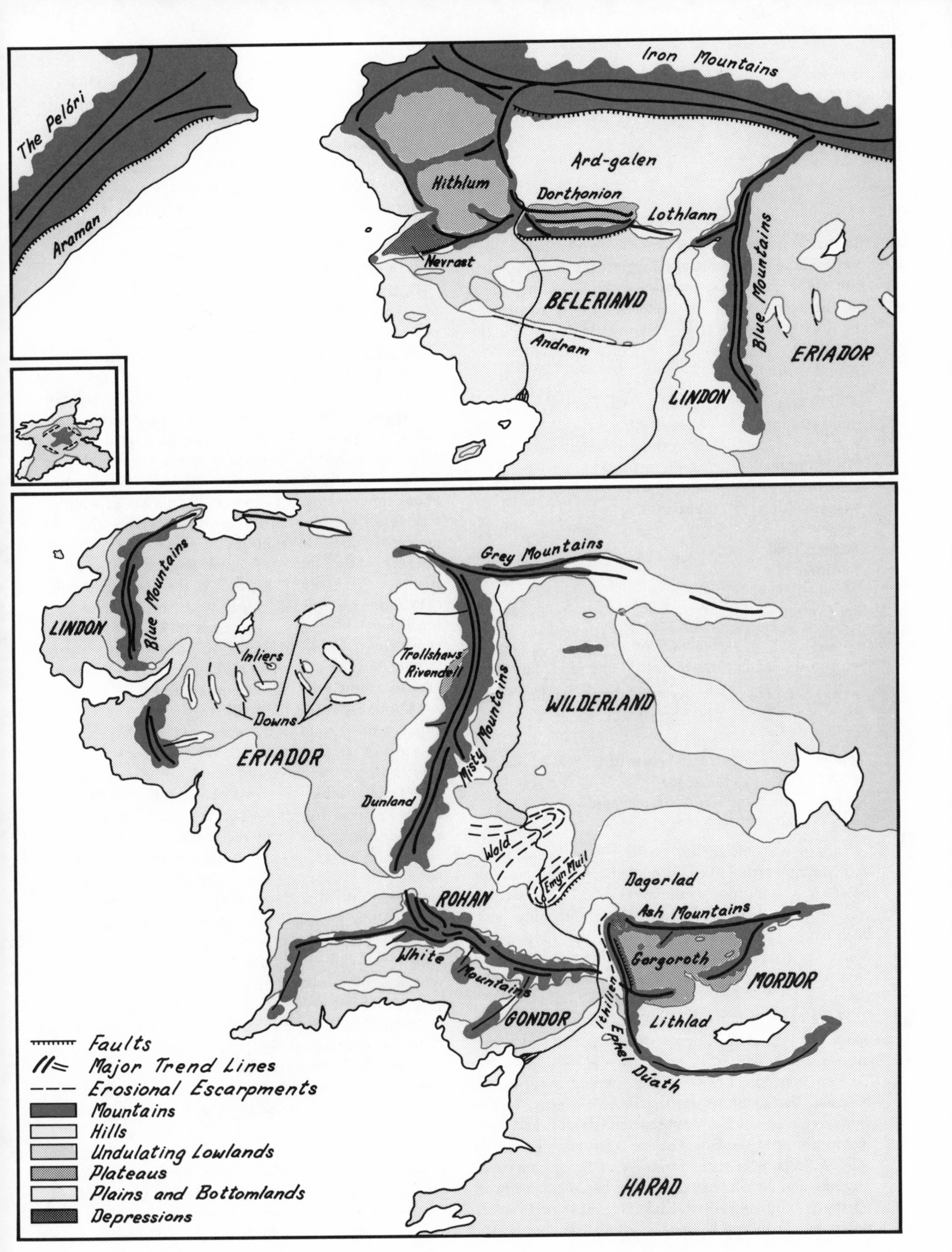

LANDFORMS *Upper:* FIRST AGE *Inset:* SECOND AGE *Lower:* THIRD AGE

Climate

BROAD CLIMATIC REGIONS can be defined based upon both annual and seasonal temperatures and precipitation.[1] The reader may more easily envision the classes on the climate map of Middle-earth by comparing them with examples in our own world.

Humid Climates

Mild winter, mild summer	England, North Central Europe, Western Oregon
Mild winter, hot dry summer	Mediterranean Sea area, Southern California
Mild winter, warm summer; to severe winter, cool summer	Eastern Europe, Arkansas to Wisconsin

Dry Climates

Arid	Arabia, Western Arizona, Nevada
Semi-arid	Iran, Great Plains (e.g., Eastern Colorado)

Polar Climates

Tundra	North coasts of USSR, Alaska, Canada
Ice cap	Central Greenland

Valinor was not subject to the physical controls as was Middle-earth.[2] Even without the ethereal powers, however, the latitude of the areas near Tirion (which was near the Girdle of Arda[3]) would probably have been warm year round. In the north the coast of Araman was cold and Oiomüre was subject to heavy fog from the contact between the warm seawater and the Grinding Ice.[4]

The Known Lands of Middle-earth were probably about the latitude of Europe, for Europe lies in a belt of prevailing westerly winds, as did Middle-earth. Tolkien mentioned west winds numerous times: in Nevrast, in the Shire, on the Barrow-downs, in the Trollshaws, at Lonely Mountain, in Gondor, and even in Mordor after the Battle of the Pelennor.[5] Thus, the mild yet relatively cool *Marine West Coast* climate of England and North Central Europe has been shown in northern Númenor, Beleriand, and most of Eriador. Beleriand, including Nevrast, had mild winters before Morgoth's power increased.[6] The Central Highlands were colder, not only due to their higher elevations but also because they received the full brunt of Morgoth's icy north winds during the winter. Himring was the "Ever-cold," and through the Pass of Aglon "a bitter wind blew."[7] Hithlum "was cool and winter there was cold."[8] The highlands also blocked southerly winds, reducing rainfall, so both Ard-galen and Lothlann were grasslands.[9]

During the Second and Third Ages, after the submergence of Beleriand, the effect of the marine winds probably shifted farther into Eriador. The Blue Mountains would have captured some of the moisture, feeding the forests on their western slopes; yet the gap at the Gulf of Lune and the long coast on the southwest of Eriador could have counteracted the mountain effect, giving the Shire the climate of England. Only 100 leagues north, however, around the Ice Bay of Forochel, Morgoth's cold lingered and was worsened at one time by frosts of Angmar.[10] This was apparently true in all the Northern Wastes, so nearing the cold area the winters were no doubt more severe. East of the Misty Mountains the moderating marine influence was lost. As Aragorn said during the boat trip south: "[We] are far from the sea. Here the world is cold until the sudden spring."[11] Even in Rohan there was snow cover from November to March in the Long Winter,[12] although it was normally mild, as Aragorn, Legolas, and Gimli found it in late February.[13]

Mountains often produce steppe, or even desert, climates on their leeward sides; yet this was not the case of either the Misty or White Mountains. The grasslands of Rohan could have resulted from this *rain-shadow* effect, but east of the Misty Mountains lay widespread forests — perhaps due to less evaporation in the cooler air of the north.

The only arid lands specifically mentioned were the Noman-lands near the Black Gate.[14] The aridity may have been due to noxious fumes rather than to lack of precipitation.[15] Still, dry summers are the rule around the Mediterranean Sea, and steppe and desert lands lie both south and east of the Mediterranean; so it was possible that Tolkien envisioned the same pattern around the Bay of Belfalas. The bitterness of the Sea of Nurnen and the description of Dagorlad as a stony plain (possibly a *pediment*,[16] which can occur only in arid climates) reinforce the probability of Mordor's being climatically arid as well as chemically denuded.

Mid-latitude climates are the battlefield between cold polar and warm tropical air masses, producing a belt of *cyclones* that move from west to east across the lands. With these go the familiar fronts: *Cold Fronts*, with associated thunderstorms and driving rain; *Warm Fronts*, with gentle warm summer rains; and *Occluded Fronts*, with all-day winter drizzles. These were the

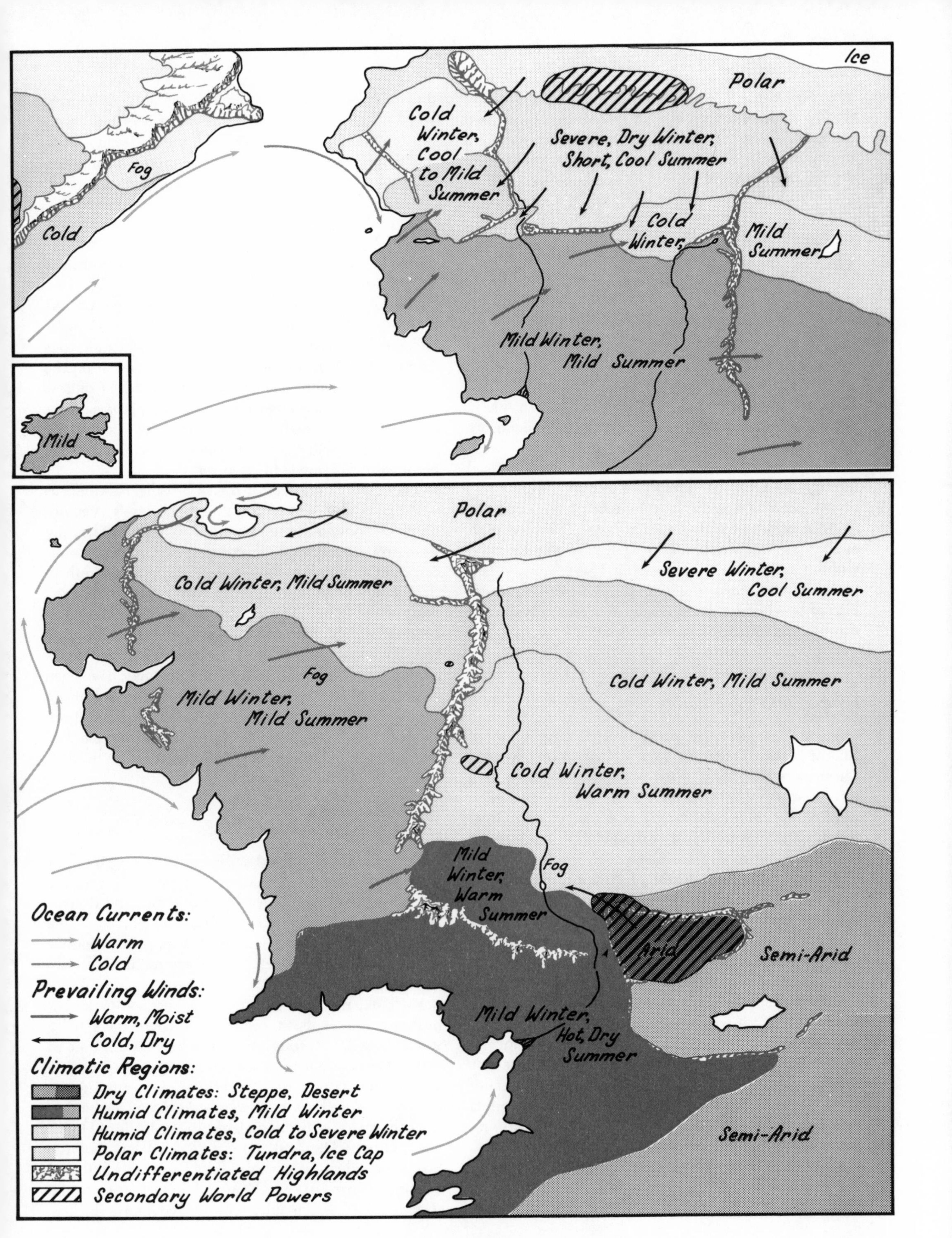
Ice
Polar
Cold Winter, Cool to Mild Summer
Severe, Dry Winter, Short, Cool Summer
Fog
Cold
Cold Winter, Mild Summer
Mild Winter, Mild Summer
Mild
Polar
Severe Winter, Cool Summer
Cold Winter, Mild Summer
Fog
Mild Winter, Mild Summer
Cold Winter, Mild Summer
Cold Winter, Warm Summer
Mild Winter, Warm Summer
Fog
Arid
Semi-Arid
Mild Winter, Hot, Dry Summer
Semi-Arid
Ocean Currents:
Warm
Cold
Prevailing Winds:
Warm, Moist
Cold, Dry
Climatic Regions:
Dry Climates: Steppe, Desert
Humid Climates, Mild Winter
Humid Climates, Cold to Severe Winter
Polar Climates: Tundra, Ice Cap
Undifferentiated Highlands
Secondary World Powers

CLIMATE Upper: FIRST AGE Inset: SECOND AGE Lower: THIRD AGE

most familiar of Tolkien's devices, with weather closely associated with the story-telling. He utilized the normal weather, adding supernatural strength and timing. Whole climates were even superimposed by the Secondary World powers — good powers living in unusually warm, gentle climates (notably in Valinor and Lórien[17]); and the evil powers of Morgoth, Sauron, and Angmar producing cold, bitter climates.[18] In this way Tolkien once again demonstrated his mastery of utilizing the natural to emphasize the supernatural.

Vegetation

Tolkien mapped the major vegetative features, but the accompanying map has attempted to delineate the previously unmapped vegetative regions as well. It has been assumed that if any traveller crossed through an area and no specific features were mentioned, there was probably a mixture of, for example, fields or meadows with scattered trees. The vegetation of the First Age was probably what naturally occurred without interference. That of the Third Age resulted from having been overgrazed, cut-over, burned, blasted by war and bitter winds, and generally abused through millennia.

Forests and Woodlands

Originally, a primeval forest covered large areas of Middle-earth. Treebeard said it had once extended "from here [Fangorn] to the Mountains of Lune, and this was just the East End."[1] The forests also grew west of the Blue Mountains and east of the Great River. There were great variations of tree-species within this broad expanse of forest.[2] Southern Mirkwood was "clad in a forest of dark fir;"[3] yet near Thranduil's caverns were solid stands of oak and beech.[4] Fangorn and the Old Forest, though "dark and tangled,"[5] were apparently less dense than Taur-im-Duinath, the Forest between the Rivers in south Beleriand, which was so wild that even the Elves rarely attempted to penetrate its eaves.[6] Doriath's trees were so distinct that it was broken into at least three parts: Nivrim, oaks; Neldoreth, beeches; and Region, a denser and more mixed forest.[7] It was significant that the trees opposite the doors of Menegroth and those at Thranduil's caverns were beeches, for pure stands appeared as green cathedrals, with the boles forming smooth gray pillars above a carpet of grass.[8] This description was very similar to the setting of Lórien, and *mallorns* were very like the less magical beeches, although *mallorn* leaves were larger.[9] Indeed, *malinornélion* (as Treebeard referred to Lórien) translated as "gold beech tree."[10]

Almost absent from Middle-earth were the coniferous forests that occupy vast areas of Alaska, Canada, and northern Asia.[11] Apparently the only coniferous forest other than southern Mirkwood was that on the northern and western edges of Dorthonion.[12] Coniferous trees were scattered elsewhere in appropriate locations, such as high in the valley of Rivendell and east of the Goblins' tunnels where Thorin and Company were surrounded by wolves.[13]

There were broadleaf or mixed broadleaf/coniferous woodlands also scattered through the lands, yet not mapped. Some of these were quite extensive. They lay in mountain valleys, notably: west of the Blue Mountains in Ossiriand, south and east of the Ered Wethrin of Hithlum on both sides of the Misty Mountains, and west of the Ephel Dúath in Ithilien.[14] Hilly areas also retained woods: Taur-en-Faroth above Nargothrond,[15] the Chetwood east of Bree,[16] and the Trollshaws.[17] The woods east of the Blue Mountains may have been remnants of the primeval stand, for by the end of the Second Age most of the original forest had been cleared.[18] Although much of this cut-over land had been abandoned as the population decreased, the forests had not been reestablished.

Grasslands and Wastelands

Some areas could support only stunted tree growth or none at all. The most pleasant of these lands were the tall grass prairies of Ard-galen, Lothlann, and Rohan. All of these provided rich pasturage for horses.[19] The Hills of Himring, the various Downs, the Weather Hills, and the Wold were more barren, covered only with short grasses.[20]

Wide expanses of land could support some stunted bushes and trees, but those that survived were usually scattered widely through the bleak landscape. Some of this wasteland occurred naturally, but more was caused by the evil power of Morgoth or Sauron. Thorny thickets replaced the pine-woods north of Dorthonion after the Battle of Sudden Flame.[21] The lands of Hollin and southern Dunland, once green and fair, became wasteland when Sauron destroyed Ost-en-Edhil and Saruman turned to evil.[22] Twisted birches clung to the rocks in the eastern Emyn Muil, and thorn thickets

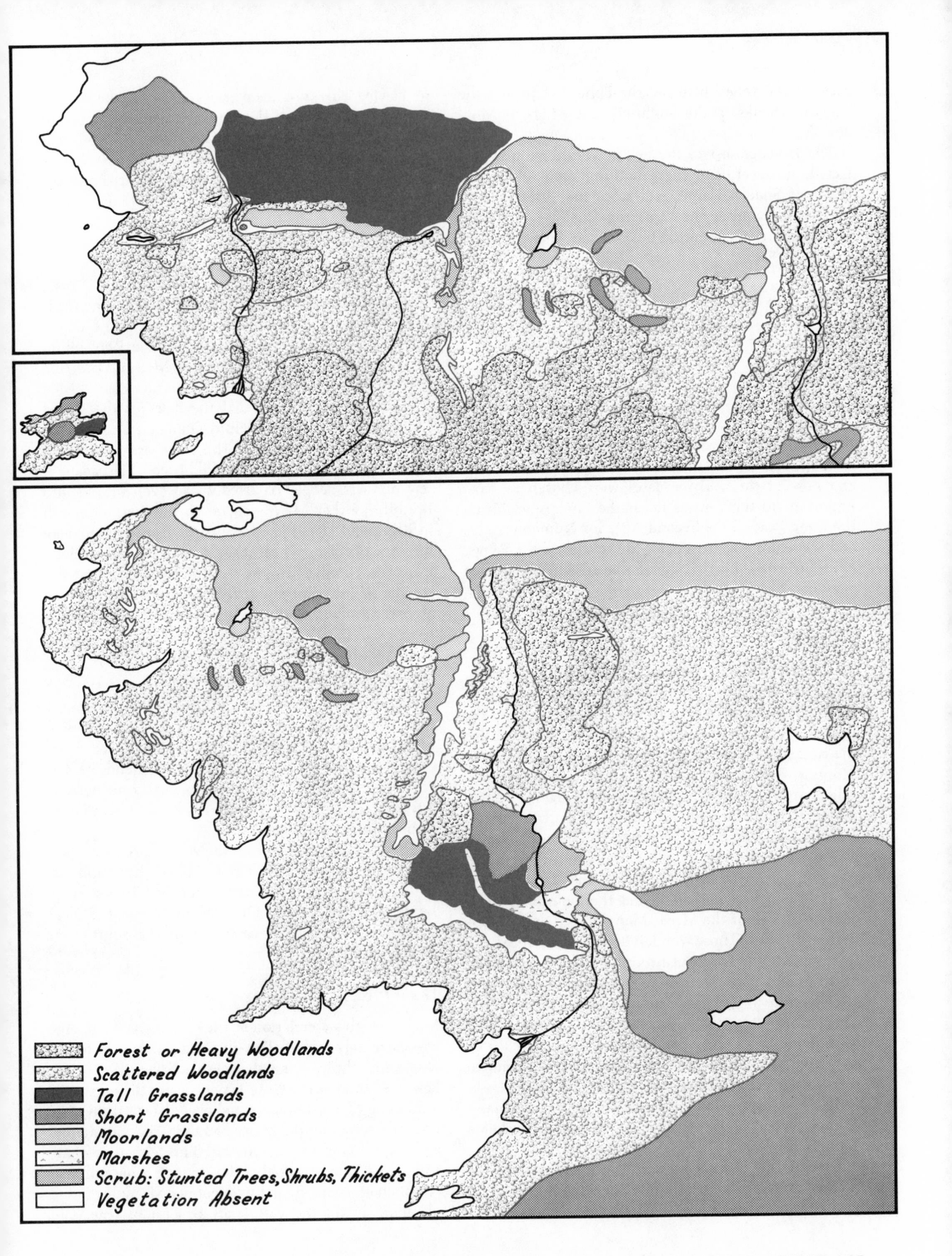

VEGETATION Upper: FIRST AGE Inset: SECOND AGE Lower: THIRD AGE

grew in the valley between the Ephel Dúath and the Morgai, thanks to the blighting east winds of Mordor.[23]

The lands closest to the evil powers were most effected, however, and there nothing grew. After the Battle of Sudden Flame, Ard-galen the "green plain" became Anfauglith the "Gasping Dust" — a barren sandy desert.[24] The fertile fields of the Entwives were so blasted that not even grass grew in the Brown Lands.[25] There were desolate areas at the doors of Angband, at Lonely Mountain when Smaug was present, and at the Black Gate of Mordor.[26] Before the gates of the Dark Tower of Barad-dûr, however, lay the most barren land of all — a seething volcanic desert.[27]

Population

As WITH POPULATIONS in our Primary World, Tolkien's Free Peoples spread and retreated with the ebb and flow of time. Three dates were chosen as most important to the various tales: the First Age, during the Long Peace;[1] the Second Age, for Númenor only; and the Third Age, just prior to the War of the Rings. With little data given, only relative densities have been shown.

The First Age

When the Noldor returned suddenly from Valinor they found most of Beleriand already occupied by people far more numerous than they:[2] the Sindar and the Green-elves of Ossiriand. The Noldor therefore settled the rugged highlands north of Beleriand, beleaguering Morgoth.[3] A few areas were empty: Lammoth, Ard-galen, and Lothlann; Nevrast, after Turgon's people moved to Gondolin; rugged highlands, such as central Dorthonion; Dimbar; the Valley of Dreadful Death, where Ungoliant dwelt; marshlands; and the tangled forest Taur-im-Duinath.[4] During the Long Peace, Mortal Men first appeared, and their numbers were added to those of the Elves. Many stayed east of Doriath at Estolad. Those who left settled in northeastern Dorthonion, the Forest of Brethil, and both south and north of the Ered Wethrin.[5] Two other Free Peoples also lived in the western lands — Dwarves and Ents. The Dwarves mined in the eastern side of the Blue Mountains, with their two large delvings at Belegost and Nogrod.[6] Although they came into Beleriand to work, their presence was transitory.[7] Ents apparently walked the forests, for Treebeard's song spoke of many of the woods,[8] and Ents slew the Dwarves who killed Thingol.[9]

East of the Blue Mountains Dark Elves and Ents roamed the vast forests, while Men made their way into the more open areas. As the forefathers of the Edain had migrated west, some settled along the road: east of Mirkwood, in the vale of Anduin, and in Eriador. They became the ancestors of the Rhovanion, the Wood-men, the Beornings, the Men of Dale, and the Men met by Aldarion in the Second Age.[10] Men of separate origin populated the dales of the White Mountains, moved north into Dunland, and even as far as Bree.[11] In some of the same areas lived the Drúedain, forefathers of the Wild Men of Druadan. A few of their people reportedly had even moved into Brethil.[12] Other Men lived far to the east and south in Rhûn and Harad.[13] Men had even made their way into the icy lands near the Iron Mountains. These were the Forodwaith, the "north-people." Their descendants, the Lossoth, stayed in that cold region even after the sinking of the western lands.[14]

The Second Age

On Númenor the transplanted Edain spread through their new land, and their numbers increased many times by the end of the Age. The most heavily populated area was Arandor, the "Kingsland," which included the cities of Armenelos and Rómenna.[15] The port of Andunië had also been large early in the Age, but was gradually abandoned as the Edain became estranged from the Elves.[16]

There were other ports on the west shore and fisher-villages in the south, but the bulk of the island was rural, with a substantial population of farmers, shepherds, and woodsmen. Only Meneltarma, the bleak northern hills, and the marshes of the south were completely empty.[17]

The Third Age

Middle-earth's population at the end of the Third Age was extremely sparse. The Elves had continued to sail west until those in northeastern Mirkwood, Lórien, Rivendell, and at the Grey Havens were the only ones remaining.[18] The Dwarves had been driven from their homes throughout the Misty and the Grey Mountains, and were found mainly in the Blue Mountains, the Iron Hills, and at Lonely Mountain.[19] The realm of Arnor had been virtually depopulated by war and plague.[20] In all the vast lands of Eriador, the only

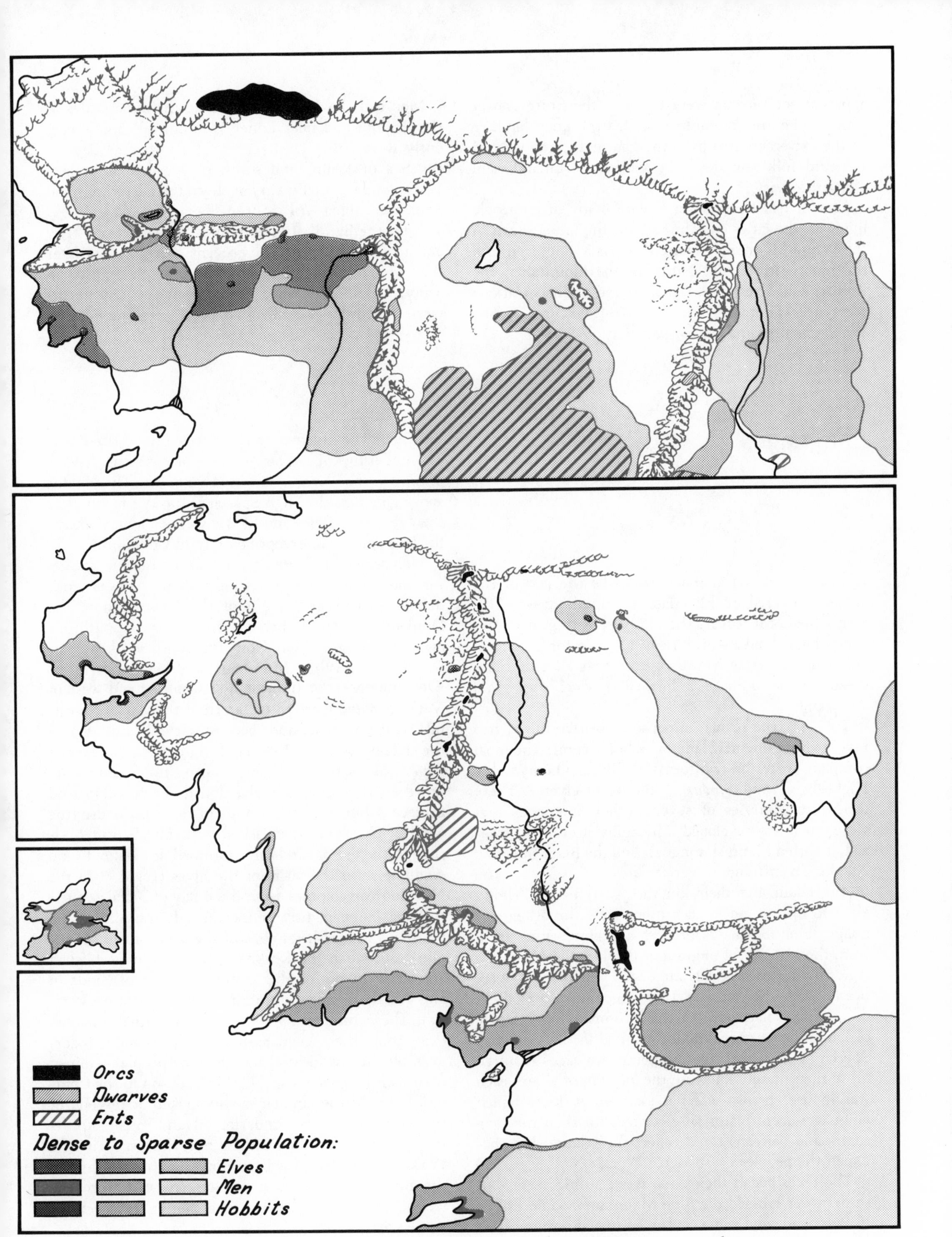

POPULATION *Upper:* FIRST AGE *Inset:* SECOND AGE *Lower:* THIRD AGE

apparent settlements were those in the Shire and at Bree — the area beyond was called the Lone-lands.[21] In the extreme north lived the Lammoth, and west of Isengard folk still dwelt in southern Dunland, and along the coast.[22]

Gondor had fared better,[23] with many of its people living in the cities and throughout the lands south of the White Mountains, along the coasts, and even into the mountain vales.[24] North of the mountains, the Rohirrim had settled.[25] Their greatest concentrations were near Edoras and in the Westfold Vale.[26] The Wold was used mainly for pasturage.[27]

Men had slowly increased along the upper vales of the Anduin and near Lonely Mountain[28] and apparently were still present east of Mirkwood.[29] Beyond the Sea of Rhûn, and south of Mordor in Khand, Harad, and especially Umbar, lived the Easterlings and Southrons allied with Sauron.[30]

After the Battle of Five Armies Orcs had been "few and terrified;"[31] yet only seventy-seven years later they were multiplying again.[32] Saruman had raised an army,[33] Dol Guldur had been reoccupied, and northwestern Mordor was filled with vast, seething hosts.[34]

Languages

It is appropriate that languages be the last of the subjects covered in this atlas, for philology was Tolkien's field. Moreover, the idea of creating an entire mythology "had its origins in his taste for inventing languages . . . He had discovered that . . . he must create for the languages a 'history' in which they could develop."[1]

Tolkien, true to his immensely creative mind, had invented not one new language, but several. The most complete were the two forms of Elvish: *Quenya*, the High-elven; and *Sindarin*, the Grey-elven.[2] There were also glimpses of several other languages that were much less developed: Silvan Elvish, Entish, Khazâd, assorted Mannish tongues, and the Black Speech.[3] All the Elven-tongues were related,[4] as well as those of the Edain and their kin the Northmen.[5] Wholly alien to Elvish and to each other were the other languages mentioned. Differences and similarities arose from the patterns of migration. By the end of the First Age all of the original languages and dialects were present. The Second and Third Ages were periods of decreasing isolation, with the accompanying mixture of languages that eventually resulted in the Common Speech of the Third Age. Mapping languages required more than merely knowing the location of where each was in use. It also was necessary to evaluate which languages were historically related, for then the map colors and patterns could reflect the relationships between the peoples of Tolkien's World.

The Elves began their great western migration, but some never crossed the Blue Mountains; some stayed in Beleriand; and some continued to Valinor and later returned. The Elven-tongues reflected these three major sunderings. The Dark-elves spoke various dialects of *Silvan*. The Grey-elves used *Sindarin*. The Noldor spoke *Quenya*, the High Speech of the West; but after their return to Beleriand its use was abandoned except for lore and song, except possibly in Gondolin.[6]

Men seemed to have no original common language, for some tongues were wholly alien. At least four distinct groups arose: kin of the Edain, kin of the Dunlendings, the Drúedain, and assorted Southrons and Easterlings.[7] Men from the south worked their way into the White Mountains and beyond as far as Bree. The Men of the north settled east and west of Mirkwood and were sundered from those who continued west into Beleriand, becoming the Edain.[8] While the Edain were in Beleriand they used *Sindarin*.[9] When they settled Númenor during the Second Age, however, they gradually abandoned Elvish and instead utilized Adûnaic — the tongue of the third house (the Men of Dor-lómin), enriched with Elvish terms, although the use of Sindarin continued in Eldalondë and Andúnië until the visits of the Elves ceased.[10] In the Númenórean colonies around the Bay of Belfalas, their Adûnaic language became increasingly mixed with the Southern Mannish tongues of the Men of the Mountains. So, when the Realms in Exile were established and grew in power this conglomeration of Sindarin and Northern and Southern Mannish became *Westron*, the "Common Speech." It was eventually spoken throughout the ancient borders of Arnor and Gondor, even by the enemies; although some peoples retained their own languages as well.[11] In addition to the Common Speech, the languages still spoken at the end of the Third Age were: Sindarin, Silvan, Entish, Rohirric, the tongues of the Dunlendings, the Drúedain (the Woses of Druadan), the Easterlings and the Southrons, the multitude of Orkish dialects (twisted from the languages of other peoples), and the Black Speech invented by Sauron.

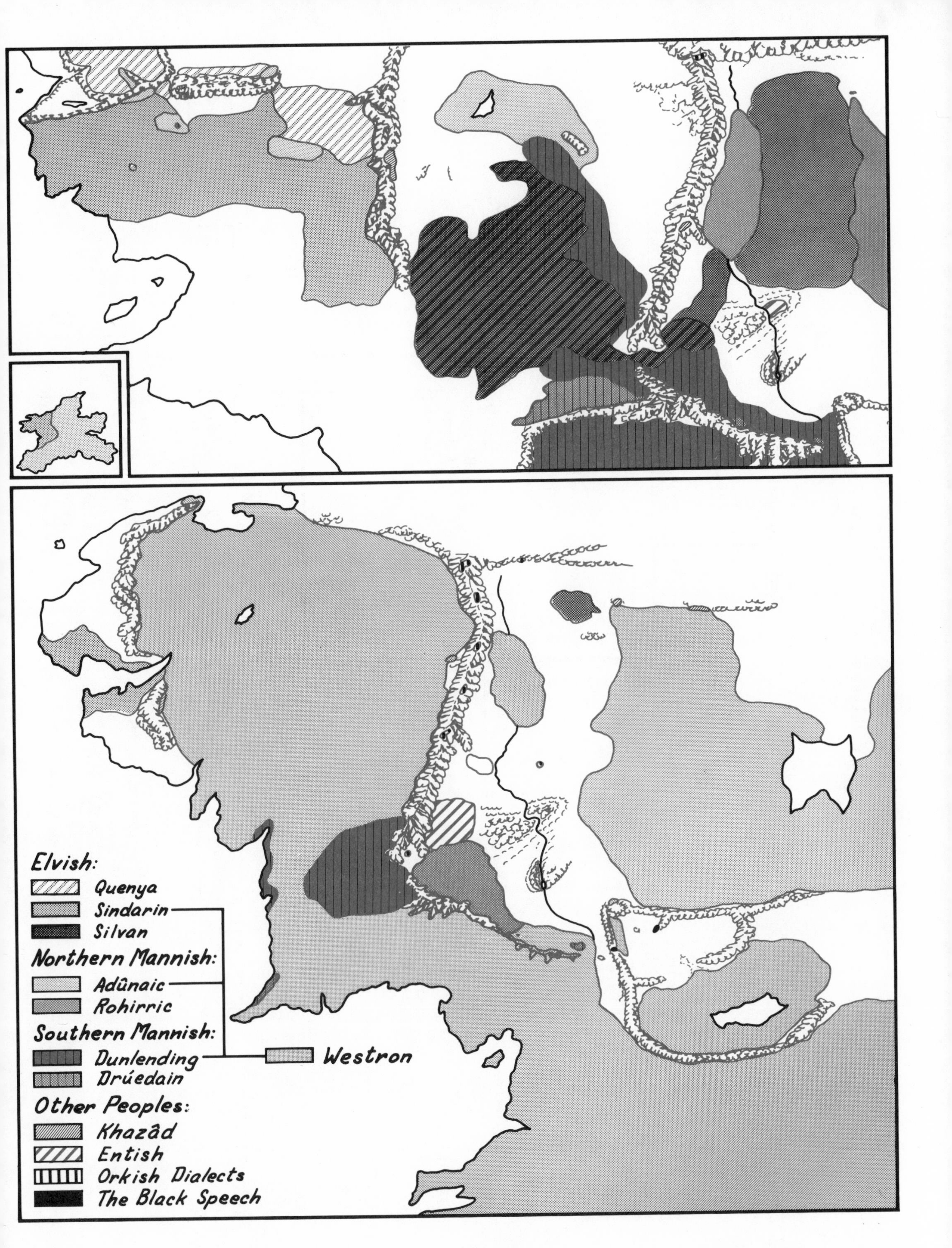

LANGUAGES Upper: FIRST AGE Inset: SECOND AGE Lower: THIRD AGE

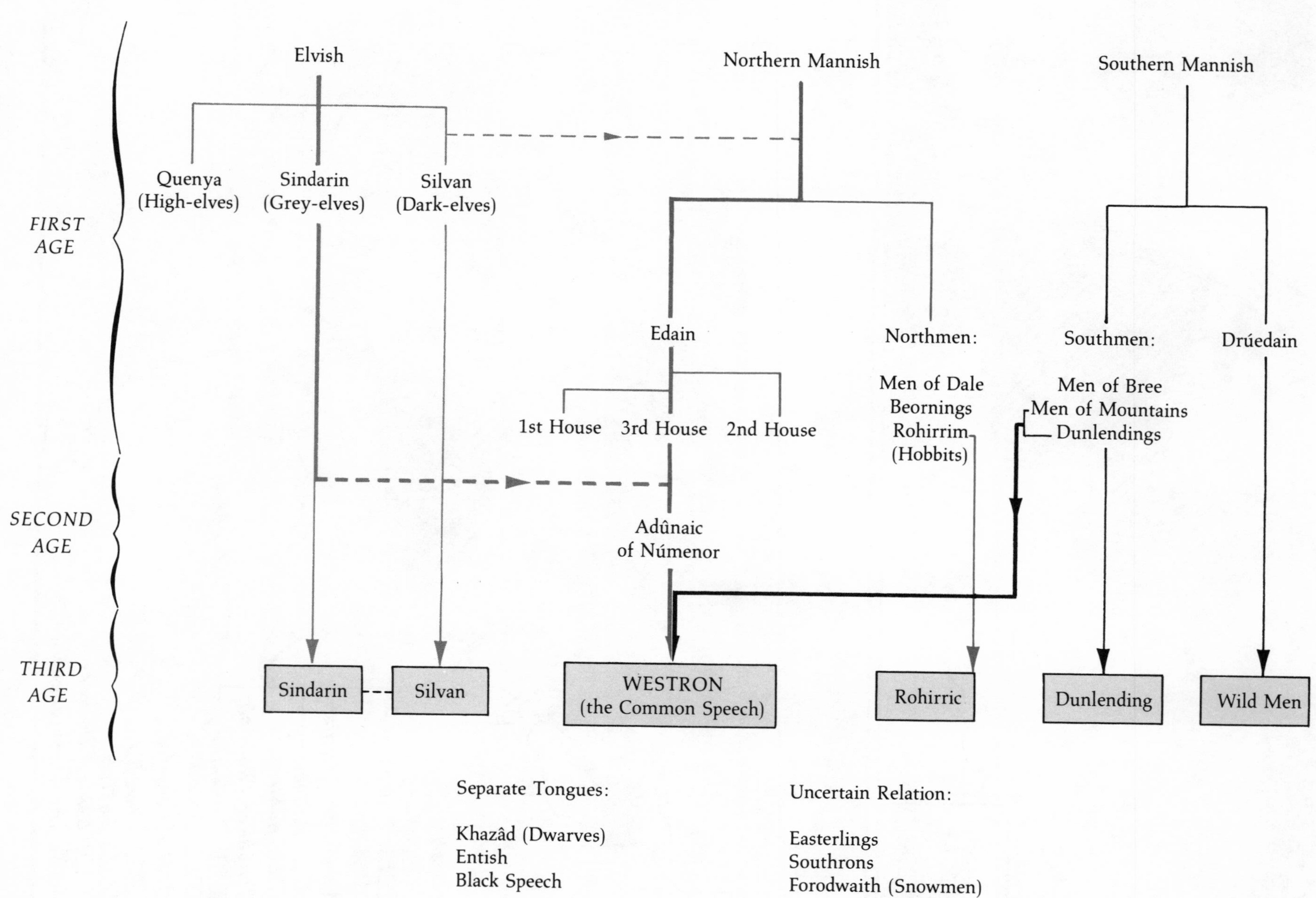
EVOLUTION OF LANGUAGES
FIRST AGE
SECOND AGE
THIRD AGE
Elvish
Northern Mannish
Southern Mannish
Quenya (High-elves)
Sindarin (Grey-elves)
Silvan (Dark-elves)
Edain
Northmen:
Southmen:
Drúedain
1st House
3rd House
2nd House
Men of Dale
Beornings
Rohirrim
(Hobbits)
Men of Bree
Men of Mountains
Dunlendings
Adûnaic of Númenor
Sindarin
Silvan
WESTRON (the Common Speech)
Rohirric
Dunlending
Wild Men
Separate Tongues:
Khazâd (Dwarves)
Entish
Black Speech
Uncertain Relation:
Easterlings
Southrons
Forodwaith (Snowmen)

Appendix

The following tables were compiled using measurements taken from the appropriate regional maps and/or political maps.

Mountain Chains

RANGE		LENGTH IN MILES
Iron Mountains		Unknown
The Pelóri		Unknown
Mountains of Mordor		1282
Ash Mountains	498	
Southern Ephel Dúath	501	
Western Ephel Dúath	283	
White Mountains		852
Misty Mountains (including the Mountains of Angmar)		702
Grey Mountains		580
Blue Mountains (1st Age)		928
Blue Mountains (3rd Age)		559
Northern	389	
Southern	170	

Inland Water Bodies

LAKE OR SEA	SIZE IN SQUARE MILES
Inland Sea of Helcar	1,025,000
Sea of Rhûn	17,898
Sea of Nurnen	5,718
Lake Nenuial	639
Lake Linaewen	407
Lake Mithrim	256
Nen Hithoel	244
Lake Helevorn	105
Long Lake	93

Rivers

RIVER(S)	LENGTH IN MILES
Anduin the Great	1,388
Forest River / River Running	835
Gelion	780
Hoarwell / Greyflood	689
Brandywine	573
Isen	395
Sirion	390
Lefnui	382
Lune	307

Political Decisions

COUNTRY		SIZE IN SQUARE MILES
Reunited Kingdom (4th Age)		909,510
Gondor (greatest extent):		716,426
South Kingdom (including Harondor)	471,158	
Eastern Territories	206,511	
Umbar	38,757	
Harad		486,776
Arnor		245,847
Arthedain	113,957	
Cardolan	83,299	
Rhudaur	48,880	
Númenor		167,961
Rohan		52,763
The Shire		21,400

Notes

For Tolkien's works the following abbreviations have been used. Note that these refer to the Houghton Mifflin editions unless otherwise specified.

S — The Silmarillion
H — The Hobbit
FR — The Fellowship of the Rings
TT — The Two Towers
RK — The Return of the King
P — Pictures by J. R. R. Tolkien
UT — Unfinished Tales
TL — Tree and Leaf

History of Middle-earth series:

I — The Book of Lost Tales, Part One
II — The Book of Lost Tales, Part Two
III — The Lays of Beleriand
IV — The Shaping of Middle-earth
V — The Lost Road
VI — The Return of the Shadow
VII — The Treason of Isengard
VIII — The War of the Ring
IX — Sauron Defeated (Typescript)

The page numbers listed for the Houghton Mifflin editions can be converted to those for the Ballantine editions using the following formulae:

HM PAGE	SUBTRACT	DIVIDE BY	ADD
FR 10 to 423	9	.818	18
TT 15 to 352	14	.778	16
RK 19 to 311	18	.797	18
RK313 to 416	312	.781	386
H 9 to 317	8	1.140	14
S 15 to 365	14	.773	2

Note: The History of Middle-earth volume IX, *Sauron Defeated,* was only available in a typescript copy at the time of this revision, so the pages listed will not agree with the published volume.

FOREWORD
(p. x)

1 Although an interesting tale of Númenor is included in IX.
2 VI, 6; IX, i. One exception is VI, 86 which briefly relates the Gollum/Bilbo encounter as published until 1951.
3 VI, 6, 7.
4 VI, 3.
5 RK, 363.

INTRODUCTION
(pp. xi–xiv)

1 TL, 19.
2 I, 7.
3 TL, 48.
4 TL, 49.
5 Resnick, 41.
6 Carpenter, 89.
7 Kocher, 13.
8 S, 281.
9 S, 253, 265.
10 S, 187.
11 Robinson and Sale, 6.
12 RK, 401.
13 IV, 243, 245.
14 S, 17.
15 Resnick, 41.
16 Kilby, 51.
17 V, 408–411; VI, 297, 300. Although the grid line, letter, and number placements on Tolkien's maps do not quite align with each other or with the *Atlas.*
18 Webster, 480.
19 UT, 285.
20 Noel, Mythology, 45; Howes, 14.
21 V, 25.

The First Age

THE SPRING OF ARDA AND THE ELDER DAYS
(pp. 1–3)

1 S, 35.
2 S, 35, 49.
3 S, 118.
4 S, 118.
5 S, 36.
6 S, 35–37.
7 IV, 149. The archipelagos change several times (IV, 257).
8 FR, 247.
9 S, 37.
10 S, 37.
11 Accounts of the history of Utumno and Angband are contradictory (IV, 259, 260).
12 S, 54.
13 S, 48, 49.
14 S, 49; IV, 249, 251.
15 S, 51.
16 IV, 251.
17 IV, 258.
18 IV, 259.
19 S, 51.
20 FR, 141, 278; TT, 71, 72.
21 S, 54.
22 S, 94.
23 S, 54.
24 S, 57.
25 S, 59. Although originally it was envisioned as standing much farther offshore (I, 84, 120).
26 S, 102.
27 S, 103.
28 S, 104.
29 VII, 302.
30 V, 408–411.
31 S, 96.
32 S, 119.
33 S, 215.
34 S, 122.
35 S, 121.
36 S, 120.
37 S, 120.
38 S, 123.
39 S, 123.

VALINOR
(p. 6)

1 S, 74.
2 S, 73.
3 S, 80.
4 S, 59.
5 S, 86.
6 S, 74; I, 82.
7 S, 74.
8 I, 73–76.
9 S, 38.
10 S, 251.
11 S, 39, 48.
12 S, 71.
13 S, 74.
14 S, 28; I, 77.
15 S, 28.
16 S, 36; I, 73.
17 S, 61; I, 25.
18 S, 59.
19 S, 70.
20 S, 82, 83.
21 S, 61.
22 S, 260.

BELERIAND AND THE LANDS TO THE NORTH
(pp. 9–11)

1 S, 109.
2 S, 118.
3 S, 36.
4 S, 118.
5 S, 96.
6 S, 107, 190.
7 P, 36.
8 S, 100, 108.
9 S, 107.
10 S, 191.
11 S, 111.
12 S, Map; IV, 221; V, 408–411.
13 S, 96; V, 272.
14 V, 271, 409, 412.
15 V, 270, 271.
16 S, 80.
17 S, 109.
18 S, 115.
19 S, 151.
20 S, 81.
21 S, 118.
22 I, 70.
23 S, 179.
24 P, 36.
25 IV, 101.
26 S, 116.
27 V, 270, 271.
28 S, 80.
29 S, 112.
30 S, 207.
31 S, 51.
32 S, 119.
33 S, 118.
34 S, 164.
35 S, 123.
36 Bodman.
37 S, 155.
38 S, 119.
39 Chorley, 192; Meland; Monkhouse, 312.
40 S, 155.
41 S, 119.
42 UT, 43.
43 UT, 68.
44 IV, 230.
45 S, 119; IV, 216. Based on the coast of Cornwall (IV, 214).
46 S, 220, 221.
47 S, 185.
48 S, 203.
49 Refer to *Atlas,* p. 20.
50 S, 122.
51 S, 122.
52 Lobeck, 148.
53 Chorley, 116.
54 S, 92. VII, 302 showed Belegost in this southern location, and IV, 220 indicated two alternate Dwarf-road routes; so the southern placement was shown in spite of IV, 232 and 335 which explained the editorial change on S, Map placing the cities further north.
55 S, 124.
56 S, 140.

THE GREAT MARCH
(pp. 16–17)

1 S, 51.
2 S, 52, 53.
3 S, 53.
4 S, 54.
5 S, 54.
6 S, 57.
7 S, 54, 55.
8 Foster, 358.
9 S, 94.
10 H, 178; Foster, 458.
11 FR, 357.
12 S, 94.
13 S, 96.
14 I, 118.
15 I, 134.
16 S, 55.
17 S, 57, 58.
18 S, 91.
19 S, 59.
20 S, 61.

THE FLIGHT OF THE NOLDOR
(p. 18)

1 S, 75.
2 S, 83-85.
3 S, 87.
4 S, 89, 90.
5 S, 107.
6 S, 100.
7 S, 108, 109.

REALMS — BEFORE THE GREAT DEFEAT
(p. 19)

1 S, 97.
2 S, 111.
3 S, 119.
4 S, 120.
5 S, 123.
6 S, 115, 124.
7 S, 124.
8 S, 124, 142.
9 S, 114.
10 Foster, 561.
11 Foster, 562, 563.

MENEGROTH
(p. 20)

1 S, 93.
2 S, 93.
3 S, 172.
4 Beckett, 50.
5 Collingwood, 128.
6 S, 93.
7 S, 93, 166.
8 S, 233.
9 S, 234.
10 Foster, 563.
11 S, 234, 235.
12 S, 236, 237.

NARGOTHROND
(p. 21)

1 S, 114.
2 Refer to *Atlas*, p. 10.
3 Thornbury, 326.
4 S, 204.
5 S, 230.
6 S, 114; III, 247.
7 Lobeck, 140.
8 S, 114.
9 S, 170; III, 68, 69.
10 S, 173.
11 S, 215.
12 P, 33, 34, 38.
13 S, 169, 211, 213, 217, 230.
14 S, 213.
15 S, 217.
16 S, 169.
17 Foster, 563.

GONDOLIN
(p. 22)

1 S, 125.
2 S, 115.
3 S, 125. IV, 192 explains these dates were an editorial change as the original founding was much later and was never rewritten by Tolkien.
4 Refer to *Atlas*, p. 23.
5 Curran, 44.
6 S, 243.
7 II, 156, 157.
8 Foster, 561.
9 S, 136, 137; UT, 46–49.
10 S, 237.
11 P, 35.
12 S, 138.
13 II, 164, 172, 180, 183, 186.
14 II, 176.
15 II, 176.
16 S, 125.
17 P, 35.
18 Curran, 44.
19 S, 241.
20 S, 241, 242.

THANGORODRIM AND ANGBAND
(p. 22)

1 S, 47, 118. Accounts of the history of Utumno and Angband are contradictory (IV, 259, 260).
2 S, 118.
3 Foster, 483.
4 S, 118.
5 S, 108.
6 S, 197.
7 IV, 22, 101.
8 V, 409. The mountains were still not shown.
9 P, 36.
10 S, 107.
11 S, 179.
12 McWhirter, 253.
13 Refer to *Atlas*, p. 12, 14.
14 Mt. Everest is 29, 028 (Espenshade, 228).
15 III, 282.
16 S, 180; III, 282, 283, 294–296.

COMING OF MEN
(p. 24)

1 S, 103.
2 S, 140.
3 S, 142, 143. It is said on UT, 377–378, that a few Wild Men moved into Beleriand with the Haladin, and there they were eventually named the *Drúedain*.
4 S, 142; Foster, 562.
5 S, 143.
6 S, 145.
7 S, 145.
8 S, 144.
9 S, 143, 148.
10 S, 143, 147.
11 S, 145–147.
12 Foster, 562.
13 S, 157.
14 S, 195.

TRAVELS OF BEREN AND LÚTHIEN
(p. 25)

1 S, 170, 176, 183; Foster, 563.
2 S, 163, 164.
3 S, 144, 164.
4 S, 167.
5 II, 3–68; IV, 150–308, 331–363.
6 S, 168.
7 S, 152.
8 S, 170.
9 S, 173.
10 S, 174. In the Lay the encounter occurs at various times (III, 263, 273).
11 S, 177.
12 S, 178.
13 S, 179–184.
14 S, 184–188. The original version places them instead in the Hunter's Wold near Nargothrond (IV, 223).

TRAVELS OF TÚRIN AND NIENOR
(p. 26)

1 S, 197.
2 Foster, 562, 563.
3 S, 198, 199.
4 S, 200–205.
5 S, 206–208.
6 S, 209.
7 S, 211.
8 S, 214.
9 S, 215, 216.
10 S, 217–219.
11 S, 221, 222.
12 S, 223.
13 UT, 143–145, 149.
14 S, 224–226.

THE BATTLES OF BELERIAND
(pp. 28, 30, 32)

1 Foster, 564.
2 S, 96.
3 S, 106.
4 Foster, 561.
5 S, 115.
6 S, 96, 97.
7 S, 116, 117.
8 S, 150.
9 S, 151.
10 S, 151.
11 S, 153.
12 S, 152.
13 S, 153.
14 S, 152.
15 S, 152.
16 S, 153, 154.
17 S, 188.
18 S, 188, 189. IV, 324 points out that the Havens of the Falas had reportedly been 'ruined' prior to this time.
19 S, 190.
20 S, 192.
21 S, 192.
22 S, 190.
23 Foster, 562–564.
24 S, 251.
25 S, 252.

The Second Age

INTRODUCTION
(p. 37)

1 I, 209, 224; V, 243.
2 S, 285.
3 RK, 259.
4 S, 230.
5 UT, 13, 14; IV, 159, 199; VII, 302; S, 285.
6 UT, 13; VI, 302, 303.
7 IV, 251; *Atlas*, p. 3.
8 RK, 364.
9 S, 261.
10 S, 261.
11 IV, 410 states some go to

THE LAST ALLIANCE
(p. 47)

1 III, 365.
2 S, 293.
3 S, 293.
4 S, 294.
5 II, 75.
6 III, 365.
7 I, 197.
8 III, 365.
9 S, 294; UT, 258.
10 S, 293; I, 256.
11 II, 235.
12 III, 365.
13 I, 256.
14 S, 294; I, 256.

The Third Age

INTRODUCTION
(p. 51)

1 S, 279.
2 S, 281.
3 S, 280; UT, 13, 14.
4 UT, 262.
5 I, 141, 278; II, 71, 72.
6 H, 216.
7 II, 239; III, 375.
8 H, 203.
9 II, 235.
10 S, 299.
11 I, 354, 355, 363; III, 148; UT, 248; Foster, 140.
12 III, 366–370.

KINGDOMS OF THE DÚNEDAIN
(p. 54)

1 III, 330.
2 III, 330; Foster, 32.
3 I, 257; UT, 271, 274.
4 S, 290, 291; III, 320.
5 III, 319, 405.
6 III, 321.
7 III, 320.
8 III, 320.
9 S, 290.
10 I, 257.
11 I, 141.
12 III, 321.
13 I, 158.
14 I, 213.
15 III, 55, 325, 326, 345; UT, 260, 369. Note that the Éothéod did not move into the Vale of Anduin until after the Wainriders attacked, UT, 289.
16 Foster, 127.
17 UT, 369.
18 III, 324.
19 III, 324, 366.
20 III, 326, 344; UT, 288.
21 III, 325.
22 III, 325.

BATTLES (1200–1634) AND THE GREAT PLAGUE
(p. 56)

1 III, 320, 321, 366, 367.
2 III, 326.
3 III, 319, 327.
4 III, 328, 329, 367.
5 III, 328.
6 UT, 289.
7 III, 367.
8 III, 321.
9 III, 367.
10 III, 328; UT, 289; Foster, 227.

WAINRIDERS AND ANGMAR
(p. 58)

1 III, 329, 367.
2 III, 329; UT, 293, 294.
3 III, 320, 321, 366, 367.
4 III, 331.
5 III, 322, 323.
6 III, 321.
7 III, 321, 322.
8 III, 323, 331.
9 III, 331.
10 I, 233; III, 323.

DEEPENING DIFFICULTIES
(pp. 60–61)

1 III, 368–370.
2 III, 332.
3 S, 297.
4 III, 333.
5 S, 300.
6 III, 368.
7 III, 333, 368, 372.
8 III, 334.
9 III, 334.
10 III, 335; UT, 298–300.
11 III, 345.
12 III, 349.
13 H, 26; I, 14; III, 369.
14 III, 346, 347.
15 III, 347.
16 III, 347, 349.
17 III, 348.
18 III, 370.
19 III, 360.
20 Refer to *Atlas*, pp. 65, 110.

MIGRATIONS OF HOBBITS
(p. 64)

1 I, 12.
2 I, 12.
3 II, 163; III, 407, 408.
4 I, 12.
5 III, 366.
6 I, 12.
7 I, 12; III, 366.
8 III, 321, 367.
9 I, 62.
10 I, 13, 161.
11 I, 13.
12 III, 367.
13 I, 162.
14 I, 13; III, 412.

MIGRATIONS OF DWARVES
(p. 65)

1 S, 43, 44; III, 352.
2 S, 289; III, 346, 355.
3 S, 91.
4 III, 353, 368.
5 III, 353, 368.
6 S, 289; III, 353, 357.
7 H, 33; III, 354, 369.
8 III, 355, 369.
9 III, 357, 358.
10 H, 34.
11 I, 254, 337; III, 371.
12 III, 360.

Regional Maps

INTRODUCTION AND THE SHIRE
(p. 69)

1 I, 257; II, 244; Foster, 243, 281.
2 I, 13; III, 345; UT, 305, 306.
3 Although my decisions were independent, the reader may be interested in the discussions of Porteus, and especially Reynolds.
4 I, 14.
5 I, 18; III, 368, 378.
6 The exceptions were Breredon and the Grindwall, mentioned only in *The Adventures of Tom Bombadil*, p. 9.
7 III, 378.
8 III, 381.
9 I, 14; II, 180; III, 292, 295.
10 III, 413.
11 III, 292; UT, 347, 354.
12 II, 217; III, 383.

ERIADOR
(pp. 72–73)

1 III, 319.
2 I, Map.
3 I, 26.
4 Thornbury, 133.
5 I, 197.
6 I, 201.
7 I, 140; Lobeck, 49.
8 I, 146, 147, 149, 150.
9 I, 149.
10 I, 159. Note that this location differs from that on Tolkien's map.
11 I, 54.
12 Meland.
13 I, 82.
14 I, 26.
15 I, 168.
16 I, 119.
17 III, 319.

WILDERLAND
(p. 78)

1 I, Map.
2 H, Map.
3 H, 160.
4 H, 179, 183, 188.
5 II, 152.
6 H, 201.
7 H, 204.
8 H, 204.
9 UT, 288.
10 H, 31, 243.
11 III, 353.
12 Refer to *Atlas*, p. 22.
13 S, Map.
14 I, Map.
15 H, 6; III, 353.
16 H, 293; III, 355.

THE MISTY MOUNTAINS
(pp. 79, 82)

1 Carpenter, 49, 50.
2 S, 54.
3 Espenshade, 164, 229.
4 H, 66.
5 Strahler, 486.
6 I, 212, 278.
7 H, 56.
8 I, 294, 295.
9 III, 261.
10 Strahler, 391–393.
11 I, 296.
12 II, 106.
13 I, 303.
14 I, 349.

DEEPENING DIFFICULTIES
(pp. 60–61)

1 Rk, 368–370.
2 RK, 332.
3 S, 297.
4 RK, 333.
5 S, 300.
6 RK, 368.
7 RK, 333, 368, 372.
8 RK, 334.
9 RK, 334.
10 RK, 335; UT, 298–300.
11 RK, 345.
12 RK, 349.
13 H, 26; FR, 14; RK, 369.
14 RK, 346, 347.
15 RK, 347.
16 RK, 347, 349.
17 RK, 348.
18 RK, 370.
19 RK, 360.
20 Refer to *Atlas*, pp. 65, 110.

MIGRATIONS OF HOBBITS
(p. 64)

1 FR, 12.
2 FR, 12.
3 TT, 163; RK, 407, 408.
4 FR, 12.
5 RK, 366.
6 FR, 12.
7 FR, 12; RK, 366.
8 RK, 321, 367.
9 FR, 62.
10 FR, 13, 161.
11 FR, 13.
12 RK, 367.
13 FR, 162.
14 FR, 13; RK, 412.

MIGRATIONS OF DWARVES
(p. 65)

1 S, 43, 44; RK, 352.
2 S, 289; RK, 346, 355.
3 S, 91.
4 RK, 353, 368.
5 RK, 353, 368.
6 S, 289; RK, 353, 357.
7 H, 33; RK, 354, 369.
8 RK, 355, 369.
9 RK, 357, 358.
10 H, 34.
11 FR, 254, 337; RK, 371.
12 FR, 360.

Regional Maps

INTRODUCTION AND THE SHIRE
(p. 69)

1 FR, 257; TT, 244; Foster, 243, 281.
2 FR, 13; RK, 345; UT, 305, 306.
3 Although my decisions were independent, the reader may be interested in the discussions of Porteus, and especially Reynolds.
4 VI, 300, 302, 305, 309.
5 FR, 14.
6 FR, 18; RK, 368, 378.
7 The exceptions were Brere-don and the Grindwall, mentioned only in *The Adventures of Tom Bombadil*, p. 9
8 RK, 378; S, 292; V, 28–30; VI, 93, 105.
9 RK, 381.
10 FR, 14; TT, 180; RK, 292, 295.
11 RK, 413.
12 VI, 284.
13 RK, 292; UT, 347, 354.
14 TT, 217; RK, 383.

ERIADOR
(pp. 72–73)

1 RK, 319.
2 FR, Map.
3 FR, 26.
4 Thornbury, 133.
5 FR, 197.
6 FR, 201.
7 FR, 140; Lobeck, 49.
8 FR, 146, 147, 149, 150.
9 FR, 149.
10 FR, 159. Note that this location differs from that on Tolkien's map.
11 FR, 54.
12 Meland.
13 FR, 82.
14 FR, 26.
15 FR, 168.
16 FR, 119.
17 VII, 33, 34, 36.
18 RK, 319.

WILDERLAND
(p. 78)

1 FR, Map.
2 H, Map.
3 H, 160.
4 H, 179, 183, 188.
5 TT, 152.
6 H, 201.
7 H, 204.
8 H, 204.
9 UT, 288.
10 H, 31, 243.
11 RK, 353.
12 Refer to *Atlas*, p. 22.
13 S, Map.
14 FR, Map.
15 H, 6; RK, 353.
16 H, 293; RK, 355.

THE MISTY MOUNTAINS
(pp. 79, 82)

1 Carpenter, 49, 50.
2 S, 54.
3 Espenshade, 164, 229.
4 H, 66.
5 Strahler, 486.
6 FR, 212, 278.
7 H, 56.
8 FR, 294, 295.
9 RK, 261.
10 Strahler, 391–393.
11 FR, 296.
12 TT, 106.
13 FR, 303.
14 FR, 349.
15 FR, 347–349.
16 FR, 315.
17 H, 121.
18 H, 118.
19 TT, 32.
20 FR, 225.
21 Foster, 346. Note that the color of the river was included in the original edition (and also in the Ballantine edition, p. 43), while the revised story omitted the color clue (H, 41; VI, 203).
22 FR, 314.
23 FR, 296, 318.
24 FR, 296.
25 FR, 331.
26 Strahler, 486; Riley, 143.
27 Strahler, 278, 279; Juhren, 5.
28 FR, 330.
29 *National Geographic*, 37.
30 VII, 183.
31 Refer to *Atlas*, p. 134.
32 TT, 160.
33 H, 83; FR, 63.
34 H, 107.
35 H, 119.
36 P, 9.
37 VI, 302.
38 VI, 302.
39 VI, 200.
40 VI, 201.

THE BROWN LANDS, THE WORLD, THE DOWNS, AND THE EMYN MUIL
(pp. 83–84)

1 VI, 314.
2 VII, 316, 318, 320, 360, 424.
3 VI, 317, 319.
4 Lobeck, 519.
5 TT, 30.
6 TT, 30.
7 Lobeck, 49.
8 FR, 397.
9 TT, 29.
10 TT, 30.
11 FR, 396.
12 UT, 260, 299.
13 TT, 23.
14 TT, 25.
15 TT, 25.
16 FR, 407.
17 FR, 409.
18 FR, 411, 423.
19 FR, 410, 416.
20 FR, 406.
21 TT, 23.
22 TT, 209.
23 TT, 211.
24 TT, 212.
25 TT, 216.
26 TT, 216.

THE WHITE MOUNTAINS
(pp. 86–87)

1 S, 94.
2 VI, 411.
3 RK, 20, 249; VI, 411; Trewartha, 367.
4 RK, 64.
5 RK, 68.
6 RK, 67.
7 RK, 64, 65.
8 RK, 67.
9 RK, 59.
10 Lobeck, 262.
11 RK, 106.
12 RK, 23.
13 TT, 152.
14 Riley, 292.
15 RK, 60.
16 TT, 110.
17 RK, 59.
18 RK, 24, 96; Lobeck, 669–671.
19 RK, 62.
20 TT, 72.
21 RK, Map.
22 RK, 348.
23 TT, 109.

MORDOR (AND ADJACENT LANDS)
(pp. 90–91)

1 *Niekas*, 39, 40.
2 TT, 258.
3 FR, 390; TT, 212, 239.
4 S, 294; TT, 235.
5 FR, 390; TT, 238, 239. Note that this location differs from that given by Foster, 378.
6 TT, 247.
7 TT, 232; Thornbury, 286, 287.
8 TT, 258.
9 TT, 283.
10 TT, 307.
11 Thornbury, 136.
12 TT, 308.
13 TT, 244.
14 TT, 319.
15 TT, 319.
16 RK, 218.
17 RK, 175, 193.
18 RK, 197.
19 TT, 244.
20 Riley, 506.
21 RK, 218.
22 Riley, 507.
23 TT, 244; RK, 205.
24 RK, 211.
25 TT, 244.
26 Strahler, 496.
27 RK, 201.
28 VII, 309, 414.
29 VIII, 113.
30 FR, Map; RK, Map; VII, 309; IX, 30, 31.
31 VII, 213, 309.
32 VII, 309, 310.

The Hobbit

INTRODUCTION
(pp. 97–99)

1 RK, 384.
2 RK, 389.
3 H, 15, 39; UT, 335.
4 H, 64; RK, 388.
5 FR, 38.
6 H, 40.
7 H, 61.
8 H, 41.
9 H, 42.
10 VI, 204.
11 Strachey, 37.
12 FR, 223, 224; VI, 201.
13 VI, 204.
14 H, 65, 66.
15 H, 107.
16 Harriman.
17 H, 146, 307.
18 FR, 301.
19 H, 153.
20 H, 185.
21 H, 186.
22 H, 212.
23 H, 306.
24 H, 308.

OVER HILL AND UNDER HILL: GOBLIN-TOWN
(p. 102)

1 H, 69, 70.
2 H. 105.
3 H, 106.
4 H, 69.
5 H, 71.
6 H, 71.
7 H, 72.
8 H, 76.
9 H, 78.
10 H, 81, 82.
11 H, 96.
12 FR, 63.
13 H, 83, 92.
14 H, 96.
15 H, 98.
16 H, 100.

OUT OF THE FRYING PAN
(p. 104)

1 H, 100, 101.
2 H, 108, 112, 120, Map.
3 H, 106, 107.
4 H, 108, 109.
5 H, 109.
6 H, 115.
7 H, 114, Map; P, 8.

BEORN'S WIDE WOODEN HALLS
(p. 105)

1 H, 127.
2 H, 127.
3 H, 128.
4 H, 130.
5 H, 136, 138.
6 H, 129.
7 H, 129, 131.

ATTERCOP, ATTERCOP
(p. 106)

1 H, 162.
2 H, 164, 165.
3 H, 166, 178.
4 H, 168.
5 H, 152, 176.
6 H, 175.

THRANDUIL'S CAVERNS
(p. 107)

1 UT, 259.
2 H, 179; TT, 152; Refer to *Atlas*, pp. 20, 21.
3 H, 179, 183, 188.
4 H, 183, 184, 192.
5 H, 180, 185.
6 FR, 268.
7 H, 188, 191, 192.
8 H, 191.
9 H, 197.

LAKE-TOWN
(p. 108)

1 H, 205, 237.
2 H, 202.
3 H, 204.
4 H, 204, 207, 208.
5 H, 209.
6 H, 209, 211, 213, 260.
7 H, 209.
8 H, 261, 262, 267.

LONELY MOUNTAIN
(p. 110)

1 H, 6, 7, Map.
2 Trewartha, 367.
3 The placement of Dale was based on Thror's Map (H, 7), and the description on H, 255, rather than on P, 18.
4 H, 254.
5 H, 215.
6 H, 67, 216.
7 H, 218, 219.
8 H, 218.
9 H, 218, 220.
10 H, 32.
11 H, 227, 253, 272.
12 H, 29.
13 H, 227.
14 H, 225, 228, 233, 239.
15 H, 31, 227.
16 P, 17.
17 H, 250.
18 H, 253.
19 H, 215, 254.
20 H, 257.
21 H, 272.

THE BATTLE OF FIVE ARMIES
(p. 112)

1 H, 292, 293, 302.
2 H, 265-267.
3 H, 271.
4 H, 290, 291.
5 H, 283.
6 H, 294.
7 H, 293.
8 H, 295.
9 H, 296.
10 H, 302.

The Lord of the Rings

INTRODUCTION
(p. 117)

1 RK, 370, 371.
2 FR, 68, 266; TT, 251, 348; RK, 371; UT, 337.
3 FR, 269; RK, 372.
4 FR, 258.
5 UT, 338–341.
6 FR, 270.
7 RK, 372.
8 FR, 275, 276.

HOBBITON AND BAG END
(p. 118)

1 FR, 26; P, I.
2 H, 39; FR, 30, 53.
3 RK, 291, 292, 296.
4 FR, 26.
5 VI, 76.
6 H, 9, 11.
7 FR, 30.
8 FR, 34; RK, 296; P, I.
9 H, 9, 315.
10 H, 12, 21; FR, 78.
11 H, 16; FR, 45.
12 H, 9.
13 VI, 20.
14 H, 9, 19; FR, 33, 47, 48; VI, 235.
15 H, 17, 22, 38; FR, 40.
16 H, 9, 26, 35, 37.
17 IX, 84.
18 RK, 296, 297; IX, 86.
19 RK, 302.

ALONG THE BRANDYWINE
(p. 120)

1 FR, 100.
2 FR, 100, 101, 105; VI, 289.
3 VI, 105.
4 FR, 105.
5 FR, 100; VI, 107, 108. Note (black ink) dotted path: VI, Frontispiece.
6 FR, 108, 109.

7 FR, 108.
8 FR, 110. Originally only one mile: VI, 101.
9 FR, 76, 110.
10 FR, 110.
11 FR, 188.
12 FR, 110; VI, 101.
13 FR, 110, 188.
14 FR, 111.
15 FR, 112.
16 FR, 117.
17 FR, 109, 120.
18 FR, 120–122.

ON THE BARROW-DOWNS
(p. 122)

1 FR, 126, 127, 141.
2 FR, 133, 141; VI, 118.
3 FR, 139, 140.
4 *Atlas*, p. 72.
5 FR, 134, 136.
6 FR, 140.
7 FR, 136.
8 FR, 136, 139.
9 FR, 146.
10 FR, 148.
11 Whybrow, 15, 16.
12 RK, 321.
13 FR, 141, 157; RK, 367.
14 FR, 149–151.
15 FR, 157–159; RK, 320.

AT THE PRANCING PONY
(p. 124)

1 FR, 161.
2 FR, 160, 193. VI, 165, 174, 175 reverse Coombe and Archet.
3 FR, 161; RK, 408.
4 RK, 366.
5 FR, 13, 161. In one stage Bree was considered a Hobbit village: VI, 133, 331.
6 FR, 162.
7 FR, 162; VI, 333.
8 FR, 162, 193.
9 VI, 335, 347.
10 FR, 162.
11 RK, 414.
12 Byrne, 34.
13 FR, 162, 164.
14 FR, 164, 165.
15 FR, 164.
16 FR, 165.
17 FR, 166.
18 FR, 165.
19 FR, 186.
20 FR, 164.
21 VI, 345–347.

WEATHERTOP
(p. 126)

1 S, 315; FR, 195–197.
2 FR, 197.
3 RK, 320.
4 FR, 197, 198; VI, 177.
5 FR, 198–201.
6 FR, 198; VI, 177.
7 FR, 201.
8 FR, 202.
9 FR, 207.

RIVENDELL
(p. 127)

1 S, 288; RK, 364.
2 RK, 321, 323, 365.
3 H, 56; FR, 231, 243; RK, 338.
4 H, 56.
5 H, 57.
6 H, 58, 59; P, 6.
7 H, 56, 59; FR, 252; P, 6. VI, 205 discusses the naming of this river.
8 FR, 237.
9 FR, 238, 242.
10 FR, 293.
11 FR, 231, 238.
12 FR, 250, 285; RK, 264.
13 FR, 238, 252, 267.
14 FR, 238, 252, 284; P, 6.
15 FR, 238, 250, 252.
16 FR, 290.

MORIA
(p. 128)

1 RK, 352.
2 FR, 324.
3 RK, 353, 368.
4 Foster, 285, 351.
5 FR, 296.
6 FR, 295, 331.
7 TT, 105.
8 FR, 296.
9 FR, 301.
10 FR, 347.
11 FR, 301, 307, 311.
12 S, 286; FR, 313.
13 FR, 314; P, 22. Note that P, 24 aligns *exactly* to be the lower part of this drawing, rather than being the "East-gate."
14 FR, 315, 316.
15 FR, 316.
16 FR, 315–319.
17 FR, 323, 324.
18 FR, 324, 325.
19 FR, 326.
20 FR, 327.
21 McWhirter, 284.
22 FR, 328, 329, 337.
23 FR, 332.
24 FR, 333, 336.
25 FR, 338, 340.
26 FR, 340, 341.
27 FR, 341, 342.
28 FR, 343.
29 FR, 342, 345.

LOTHLÓRIEN
(p. 130)

1 Foster, 82. Note that UT, 267, stated the correct spelling as Galadhon.
2 RK, 405.
3 S, 115; RK, 406.
4 UT, 252, and all of Part II, Chapter 4.
5 TT, 70; UT, 168.
6 FR, 352, 353, 355.
7 FR, 356.
8 FR, 358.
9 FR, 361.
10 FR, 364, 365.
11 RK, 341, 344.
12 VII, 288.
13 FR, 368.
14 FR, 369.
15 McWhirter, 120.
16 FR, 368. Note that UT, 167, stated that the mallorns of Númenor were even taller.
17 FR, 369, 383.
18 FR, 369, 372.
19 FR, 376, 377.
20 Murray, 309.
21 FR, 387.

HELM'S DEEP
(p. 132)

1 S, 291.
2 RK, 347. *Letters*, 407 stated they were inspired by the caverns of Cheddar Gorge (in southern England).
3 TT, 152, 153. Although the original name was of the current 'westmarcher': VIII, 8, 9, 23.
4 TT, 141.
5 TT, 133.
6 TT, 136; P, 26. Note that UT, 365, stated the various "Deeping" terms should be hyphenated.
7 TT, 129, 136.
8 TT, 135; VII, 319; VIII, 17, 19, 23. The line of the clifftop is visible in P, 26.
9 RK, 50; VIII, 40.
10 TT, 133; VII, 319; VIII, 269.
11 TT, 146, 147.
12 TT, 158; VIII, 41.
13 TT, 136, 137. Note that Tolkien's drawing showed not one, but four towers (P, 26).
14 TT, 133.
15 TT, 136.
16 TT, 133, 139, 144; RK, 49.
17 TT, 136.
18 TT, 133; RK, 24.
19 TT, 139.
20 TT, 143.
21 TT, 144–146.

ISENGARD
(p. 134)

1 S, 291; TT, 159. Saruman did not build it, as stated in VII, 150.
2 RK, 334.
3 TT, 157, 171.
4 TT, 157, 171.
5 TT, 159.
6 TT, 160.
7 VII, Frontispiece; VIII, 34; IX, 125C ('Orthanc I').
8 TT, 160; VIII, 43, 44, 47.
9 TT, 160.
10 VIII, 34; IX, 125A; P, 27.
11 TT, 160; VIII, 44.
12 TT, 160; RK, 335, 370. According to VIII, 32, 33 the isle stood *in* the pool.
13 TT, 165, 166, 177; VIII, 44.
14 VIII, 34.
15 TT, 160.
16 TT, 160, 182; VII, Frontispiece; VIII, 33, 34; IX, 125A, 125C, 125D ('Orthanc I').
17 TT, 182.
18 TT, 189.
19 FR, 273; VIII, 34.
20 S, 345.
21 P, 46, 47.
22 RK, 257.

EDORAS AND DUNHARROW
(p. 136)

1 TT, 110; Foster, 140.
2 TT, 111.
3 RK, 254, 255.
4 TT, 111.
5 TT, 114.
6 TT, 111; RK, 349.
7 TT, 111, 114.
8 TT, 116; RK, 66.
9 TT, 116.
10 TT, 125; RK, 70.

11 TT, 123.
12 *Encyclopedia Americana*, "Castles."
13 TT, 116.
14 TT, 123; RK, 143.
15 TT, 127.
16 RK, 67.
17 RK, 68.
18 RK, 65–67.
19 RK, 71.
20 RK, 67.
21 RK, 68, 69.
22 VIII, 245, 246.
23 VIII, 238, 245, 248.
24 VIII, 251.
25 VIII, 237, 238.
26 VIII, 238, 240, 245.
27 VIII, 312, 314; IX, 125G.
28 RK, 59.

MINAS TIRITH
(p. 138)

1 S, 291.
2 RK, 365, 372.
3 RK, 36, 324, 365–369.
4 RK, 368.
5 VIII, 290.
6 RK, 24.
7 VIII, 279, 288.
8 RK, 24.
9 VIII, 290; IX, 64; Marquette Archives.
10 If the Tower were wider than 150 feet, it would have appeared stout in spite of its 300-foot height (50 fathoms — RK, 24). Note that the Tower was described as "a spike" — not tiered as shown in VIII, 261; P, 27.
11 RK, 23.
12 TT, 160; *Encyclopedia Americana*, "Castles."
13 *Encyclopedia Americana*, "Castles."
14 TT, 136.
15 RK, 24.
16 "Facts and Figures," 8.
17 RK, 106.
18 RK, 135.
19 RK, 34.
20 RK, 40.
21 RK, 131, 149, 240.
22 RK, 24.
23 RK, 31; VIII, 261; P, 27.
24 *Encyclopedia Americana*, "Castles."
25 RK, 31; IX, 64; Marquette Archives. I originally misread 'King's House' as 'kitchen', but Taum Santoski corrected my error.
26 RK, 35.
27 RK, 84, 94, 95.
28 VIII, 290; *Encyclopaedia Britannica*, 725.
29 RK, 99, 101.

THE MORANNON
(p. 140)

1 RK, 176.
2 TT, 244, 250.
3 RK, 328.
4 TT, 244.
5 TT, 244; RK, 163.
6 TT, 244.
7 S, 357; TT, 247; RK, 176; Foster, 360.
8 TT, 247.
9 TT, 247.
10 RK, 163, 164.

HENNETH ANNÛN
(p. 141)

1 RK, 335, 369.
2 TT, 282; RK, 335.
3 TT, 259.
4 TT, 277.
5 RK, Map.
6 RK, 235.
7 TT, 282, 283.
8 TT, 282, 292.
9 TT, 271.
10 TT, 285.
11 TT, 283, 292.
12 TT, 282.
13 TT, 292, 293, 300.
14 TT, 292.
15 TT, 294, 295.

THE PATH TO CIRITH UNGOL
(p. 143)

1 Foster, 94.
2 TT, 313, 314.
3 TT, 317.
4 TT, 318.
5 TT, 319.
6 VIII, 124, 186, 194, 198, 199.
7 TT, 327. Refer to *Atlas*, p. 170.
8 TT, 327, 328; VIII, Frontispiece 2, 201; P, 28. Note that N and S (north and south) are reversed on the compass on VIII, 201.
9 TT, 342; P. 28.
10 RK, 218.
11 RK, 175, 193.

THE TOWER OF CIRITH UNGOL
(p. 144)

1 RK, 176.
2 TT, 319, 332; RK, 184; IX, 21.
3 RK, 176; IX, 17.
4 RK, 176, 193.
5 RK, 176, 178.
6 RK, 176.
7 RK, 176, 179.
8 RK, 176; VIII, 201.
9 TT, 319; RK, 176.
10 RK, 176; IX, 16–18.
11 IX, 23.
12 RK, 181; VIII, Frontispiece 2; IX, 17.
13 TT, 351; RK, 179, 180.
14 TT, 351.
15 RK, 180.
16 RK, 181.
17 RK, 184–186.

MOUNT DOOM
(p. 146)

1 RK, 364.
2 S, 345.
3 FR, 70.
4 RK, 219.
5 RK, 317, 365.
6 RK, 219.
7 RK, 218; Strahler, 489, 490.
8 RK, 218.
9 Lobeck, 683.
10 Strahler, 490. The side view in P, 30, had even more vertical exaggeration.
11 RK, 218.
12 RK, 219.
13 IX, 1.
14 RK, 220.
15 RK, 222; IX, 37, 39; P, 30; Marquette Archives.
16 RK, 219, 220; IX, 1.
17 FR, 70; IX, 24.
18 RK, 222, 223.
19 RK, 222.
20 Thornbury, 491.
21 RK, 227, 229, 240.
22 RK, 228.

THE BATTLE OF THE HORNBURG
(p. 148)

1 RK, 374.
2 TT, 117, 122.
3 TT, 129.
4 TT, 133.
5 TT, 171.
6 TT, 136.
7 TT, 135, 136.
8 TT, 147.
9 TT, 170, 171.
10 TT, 129.
11 TT, 136.
12 TT, 147.
13 TT, 170, 171.
14 TT, 134, 171.
15 TT, 135.
16 TT, 136.
17 TT, 138.
18 TT, 139.
19 TT, 141.
20 TT, 143, 144.
21 TT, 145.
22 TT, 146.
23 TT, 147.
24 TT, 148.

BATTLES IN THE NORTH
(p. 150)

1 RK, 53, 374, 375.
2 RK, 374.
3 RK, 374, 375.
4 RK, 257, 374.
5 RK, 374, 375.
6 RK, 375, 376.
7 RK, 374, 375.
8 RK, 360, 375.
9 RK, 375.
10 RK, 360.

THE BATTLE OF THE PELENNOR FIELDS
(pp. 151–152)

1 RK, 91.
2 RK, 121.
3 RK, 95, 121.
4 FR, 416, 417; TT, 248, 250, 267, 268.
5 RK, 77, 121.
6 TT, 316.
7 RK, 95.
8 RK, 121.
9 RK, 89.
10 RK, 43.
11 RK, 43, 44.
12 RK, 77.
13 RK, 48.
14 RK, 123.
15 RK, 121.
16 RK, 44.
17 RK, 40, 79; *Encyclopedia Americana*, "Army."
18 FR, 258; RK, 91.
19 RK, 91, 98.
20 RK, 91, 374.
21 RK, 93, 94, 140.
22 RK, 94.
23 RK, 95, 96.
24 RK, 98, 102.
25 RK, 103.
26 RK, 112–114.
27 RK, 114, 115.
28 RK, 118–121.
29 RK, 121–124.

THE BATTLE OF THE MORANNON
(p. 154)

1 RK, 158.
2 RK, 161.
3 RK, 162.
4 RK, 162, 163.
5 RK, 167.
6 RK, 163.
7 RK, 167, 168.
8 RK, 167, 168.
9 RK, 226.
10 RK, 227, 235.

THE BATTLE OF BYWATER
(p. 155)

1 RK, 288–290.
2 RK, 294–295.

PATHWAYS
(pp. 156–161)

1 UT, 285.
2 RK, 376, 389.
3 RK, 32, 386.
4 RK, 363–378.

BAG END TO RIVENDELL
(pp. 162–163)

1 FR, 79–110.
2 FR, 117, 120, 132, 140.
3 FR, 146–159.
4 FR, 193, 197.
5 FR, 197–202.
6 FR, 207, 211–213.
7 Refer to *Atlas*, p. 97, 101.
8 FR, 214.
9 FR, 214.
10 VI, 200–203.
11 FR, 215–223.
12 FR, 224.
13 FR, 224, 225.

RIVENDELL TO LÓRIEN
(p. 164)

1 FR, 294–296.
2 FR, 299, 300.
3 FR, 301, 302.
4 FR, 311, 313–315.
5 FR, 324.
6 FR, 323–328.
7 FR, 329, 337, 341, 345.
8 FR, 346, 352.
9 FR, 364–368.
10 FR, 387.
11 FR, 393, 395, 396.
12 FR, 397–400.
13 FR, 401–403, 407–411.

RAUROS TO DUNHARROW
(p. 166)

1 FR, 418, 423; TT, 16, 47.
2 TT, 21, 30.
3 TT, 23–32.
4 TT, 30, 54.
5 TT, 57.
6 TT, 29, 31, 38, 39.
7 TT, 61, 65, 73. Note that Treebeard's stride measured only a third the length of the Tree-man seen by Sam's cousin Hal on the North Moors (FR, 53).
8 RK, 373.
9 TT, 108–110, 131, 133.
10 TT, 151.
11 TT, 157.
12 TT, 88, 90, 170, 171.
13 TT, 193, 194, 201.
14 RK, 19, 46, 48.
15 RK, 20, 48, 52, 53, 56, 64, 374.

DUNHARROW TO THE MORANNON
(p. 168)

1 RK, 59.
2 RK, 61.
3 RK, 62.
4 RK, 150. This stated distance was irreconcilable with the scale shown on Tolkien's map and with the distance between Edoras and Minas Tirith north of the mountains. It actually measures about 30 miles too long.
5 RK, 151, 152, 374. Although IX, 14 stated that Aragorn took rough paths because the coast road was infested, this idea was clearly later abandoned.
6 RK, 153.
7 RK, 64, 374.
8 RK, 76–78. VIII, 343 stated lesser distance, but VIII, 354 explained that a later map was 40 miles longer — only a difference of 4 miles from the *Atlas*.
9 RK, 104, 108–110.
10 RK, 159–161.
11 RK, 161. Note that the distance shown is 100 miles, but 8 to 10 miles were added by leaving the road. The shorter mileage is a compromise between this quote and the distance of "nearly thirty leagues" (90 miles) given on TT, 256.
12 RK, 162.
13 RK, 163.

THE JOURNEY OF FRODO AND SAM
(pp. 170–171)

1 FR, 423.
2 TT, 209.
3 TT, 211, 212, 217.
4 TT, 218–223.
5 TT, 225–232; RK, 373.
6 TT, 209, 233.
7 TT, 233–238.
8 FR, 390; TT, 239.
9 TT, 242, 244, 247.
10 TT, 256.
11 TT, 265, 277.
12 TT, 304.
13 TT, 306, 307.
14 TT, 308; RK, 374.
15 TT, 310; Magnuson.
16 TT, 310, 311.
17 TT, 312–315
18 TT, 317–319.
19 TT, 323–326. Note that this disagrees with the date on RK, 373.
20 TT, 326.
21 RK, 374; IX, 8, 19.
22 TT, 337, 342, 345, 352.
23 RK, 173, 174.
24 RK, 193, 194, 374.
25 RK, 197, 199.
26 RK, 204.
27 RK, 207, 209.
28 RK, 212.
29 RK, 375.
30 RK, 224.

THE ROAD HOME
(pp. 174–175)

1 RK, 254, 256, 259, 260, 376.
2 RK, 298.
3 RK, 263, 264, 268, 269.
4 RK, 279–283.
5 RK, 298–300.
6 RK, 307–310, 377.

THE FOURTH AGE
(p. 176)

1 RK, 352.
2 RK, 254, 258, 260, 362, 377.
3 RK, 247.
4 RK, 375.

Thematic Maps

INTRODUCTION
(p. 179)

1 TL, 9.
2 TL, 48.
3 S, 37, 51, 54, 252, 279.
4 S, 54; FR, 302, 303.
5 S, 164, 208; H, 66; FR, 149, 302, 405; TT, 212.
6 S, 45.
7 S, 251.
8 TT, 285.

LANDFORMS
(p. 180)

1 Refer to *Atlas*, pp. 6, 9–11, 43, 69–91.
2 S, 74.
3 Refer to *Atlas*, p. 10.
4 Refer to *Atlas*, p. 3.
5 TT, 319; Refer to *Atlas*, p. 90.
6 S, 123, 140.
7 UT, 43.
8 FR, 214.
9 H, 56.
10 FR, 295; RK, 261.
11 RK, Map.
12 RK, 211.
13 TT, 307; Refer to *Atlas*, p. 90.
14 Refer to *Atlas*, p. 11.
15 S, 122, 123; TT, 26, 27, 232, 244; UT, 288.
16 S, 119.
17 Refer to *Atlas*, p. 78.

CLIMATE
(pp. 182, 184)

1 Espenshade, 8, 9; Strahler, 186, 187.
2 S, 74.
3 S, 86.
4 S, 87, 89.
5 H, 66, 289; FR, 81, 146, 147, 214; RK, 200, 217, 268; UT, 24.
6 S, 119, 204.
7 S, 123.
8 S, 118.
9 S, 119, 123.
10 RK, 321, 322.
11 FR, 397.
12 RK, 347.
13 TT, 26.
14 TT, 239.
15 RK, 200, 201.
16 Refer to *Atlas*, p. 90.
17 S, 74; FR, 373, 374.
18 S, 118, 123; FR, 302, 397; TT, 258; RK, 36, 210, 321.

VEGETATION
(pp. 184, 186)

1 TT, 72.
2 See Juhren's excellent study.
3 FR, 366.
4 H, 158, 183.
5 FR, 125; TT, 64.
6 S, 123.
7 S, 121, 122. It is uncertain whether Brethil contained birches (Noel, *Languages*, 120), or beeches (RK, 409).
8 Beckett, 50–52.
9 UT, 167.
10 TT, 70; Noel *(Languages)*, 167.
11 Espenshade, 16, 17.
12 S, 119, 120.
13 H, 108–110; FR, 252.
14 S, 190, 235; H, 108; FR, 12, 252, 395; TT, 258; RK, 261; UT, 36, 53.
15 S, 122.
16 FR, 193, 194.
17 FR, 214, 217.
18 UT, 263.
19 S, 119, 123, 124; TT, 29; UT, 288.
20 S, 123; FR, 147, 196, 397; TT, 29, 30; UT, 166.
21 S, 151, 207.
22 S, 288; FR, 295, 299; RK, 261, 263.
23 TT, 211; RK, 194, 198.
24 S, 151, 191, 207.
25 FR, 396; TT, 79.
26 S, 118; H, 216; TT, 239; RK, 162.
27 RK, 200.

POPULATION
(pp. 186, 188)

1 S, 117.
2 S, 91, 113; RK, 406.
3 S, 111.
4 S, 81, 119–121, 123, 126.
5 S, 143, 144, 147.
6 S, 91.
7 S, 92, 114.
8 TT, 72.
9 S, 235.
10 RK, 407.
11 FR, 161; RK, 407, 408; UT, 214.
12 RK, 407; UT, 383–386.
13 RK, 121, 324.
14 RK, 321; Foster, 195.
15 UT, 165.
16 S, 268; Foster, 15.
17 UT, 166–168.
18 H, 179; FR, 54, 89, 279, 355; RK, 365.
19 RK, 352, 353, 357, 359, 365.
20 RK, 320, 321, 332.
21 H, 40.
22 RK, 261, 321; UT, 262, 387.
23 RK, 24, 328.
24 RK, 43.
25 RK, 345.
26 TT, 111, 135; RK, 76.
27 TT, 39.
28 H, 112; FR, 241.
29 H, 188, 189; FR, 241.
30 RK, 121.
31 H, 307.
32 FR, 53.
33 TT, 171.
34 RK, 200, 205, 375

LANGUAGES
(pp. 188, 190)

1 Carpenter, 89.
2 RK, 405.
3 RK, 406–410.
4 S, 141.
5 RK, 406, 407.
6 S, 129; RK, 405, 406; UT, 55.
7 RK, 406–408; UT, 383, 384, 399.
8 RK, 406–408.
9 S, 147.
10 S, 142, 147, 148; RK, 407; UT, 215.
11 RK, 407.

Selected References

Books

Beckett, Kenneth A. *The Love of Trees.* New York: Crescent Books, 1975.

Byrne, Josepfa. *Mrs. Byrne's Dictionary of Unusual, Obscure, and Preposterous Words.* Secaucus, N.J.: University Books, Inc., 1975.

Carpenter, Humphrey, ed. *The Letters of J. R. R. Tolkien.* Boston: Houghton Mifflin Co., 1981.

Carpenter, Humphrey. *Tolkien: A Biography.* Boston: Houghton Mifflin Co., 1977.

Chorley, Richard J., ed. *Introduction to Fluvial Processes.* London: Methuen and Co. Ltd., 1969.

Collingwood, G. H. *Knowing Your Trees.* Washington, D.C.: The American Forestry Assn., 1945.

Curran, H. Allen, Philip S. Justus, Eldon L. Perdew, and Michael B. Prothero. *Atlas of Landforms,* 2nd ed. New York: John Wiley & Sons, Inc., 1974.

Dury, G. H. *The Face of the Earth.* Baltimore: Penguin Books, 1959.

Encyclopaedia Britannica, Micropaedia, 15th ed. "Pantheon."

Encyclopedia Americana, 1968 ed. S.v. "Army," "Castle," "Fortifications," "Rome," "Columbus, Christopher."

Espenshade, Edward B., ed. *Goode's World Atlas,* 15th ed. Chicago: Rand McNally & Co., 1978.

Foster, Robert. *The Complete Guide to Middle-Earth.* New York: Ballantine Books, 1978.

Ginsburg, Norton, ed. *Aldine University Atlas.* Chicago: Aldine Publishing Co., 1969.

Gottmann, Jean. *A Geography of Europe.* New York: Holt, Rinehart & Winston, 1969.

Helms, Randel. *Tolkien's World.* Boston: Houghton Mifflin Co., 1974.

Kilby, Clyde S. *Tolkien and the Silmarillion.* Wheaton, Ill.: Howard Shaw Publ., 1976.

Kocher, Paul H. *Master of Middle-Earth.* New York: Ballantine Books, 1972.

Lobdell, Jared, ed. *A Tolkien Compass.* LaSalle, Ill.: The Open Court Publishing Co., 1974.

Lobeck, A. K. *Geomorphology: An Introduction to the Study of Landscapes.* New York: McGraw-Hill Book Co., Inc., 1939.

Macaulay, David, *Castle.* Boston: Houghton Mifflin Co., 1977.

Macaulay, David. *Cathedral: The Story of its Construction.* Boston: Houghton Mifflin Co., 1973.

MacKendrick, Paul. *Greece and Rome: Builders of Our World.* Washington: National Geographic Society, 1968.

McWhirter, Norris, ed. *Guinness Book of World Records.* New York: Bantam Books, 1979.

Monkhouse, F. J. *A Dictionary of Geography.* London: Edward Arnold (Publishers) Ltd., 1965.

Murray, James A. H., ed. *A New English Dictionary on Historical Principles,* Vol. H–K. Oxford: Clarendon Press, 1901.

Noel, Ruth. *The Languages of Middle-Earth.* Boston: Houghton Mifflin Co., 1980.

Noel, Ruth. *The Mythology of Middle-Earth.* Boston: Houghton Mifflin Co., 1977.

Raisz, Erwin. *Principles of Cartography.* New York: McGraw-Hill Book Co., 1962.

Riley, Charles M. *Our Mineral Resources.* New York: John Wiley & Sons, Inc., 1959.

Robinson, Arthur H., and Randall D. Sale. *Elements of Cartography,* 3rd ed. New York: John Wiley & Sons, Inc., 1969.

Stamp, Sir Dudley. *A Glossary of Geographical Terms.* New York: John Wiley & Sons, Inc., 1961.

Strahler, Arthur N. *Physical Geography,* 2nd ed. New York: John Wiley & Sons, Inc., 1960.

Thornbury, Wm. D. *Principles of Geomorphology.* New York: John Wiley and Sons, Inc., 1958.

Tolkien, J. R. R. *The Adventures of Tom Bombadil.* Boston: Houghton Mifflin Co., 1978.

———. *The Fellowship of the Ring.* Boston: Houghton Mifflin Co., 1965.

Tolkien, J. R. R. *The History of Middle-earth, Vol. I: The Book of Lost Tales, Part One.* Edited by Christopher Tolkien. Boston: Houghton Mifflin Co., 1983.

———. *The History of Middle-earth, Vol. II: The Book of Lost Tales, Part Two.* Boston: Houghton Mifflin Co., 1984.

———. *The History of Middle-earth, Vol. III: The Lays of Beleriand.* Boston: Houghton Mifflin Co., 1985.

———. *The History of Middle-earth, Vol. IV: The Shaping of Middle-earth.* Boston: Houghton Mifflin Co., 1986.

———. *The History of Middle-earth, Vol. V: The Lost Road.* Boston: Houghton Mifflin Co., 1987.

———. *The History of Middle-earth, Vol. VI: The Return of the Shadow.* Boston: Houghton Mifflin Co., 1988.

———. *The History of Middle-earth, Vol. VII: The Treason of Isengard.* Boston: Houghton Mifflin Co., 1989.

———. *The History of Middle-earth, Vol. VIII: The War of the Ring.* Boston: Houghton Mifflin Co., 1990.

———. *The Hobbit.* Collector's Edition. Boston: Houghton Mifflin Co., 1966.

———. *The Hobbit.* Revised Edition. New York: Ballantine Books, 1966.

———. *Pictures by J. R. R. Tolkien.* Boston: Houghton Mifflin Co., 1979.

———. *The Return of the King.* Boston: Houghton Mifflin Co., 1965.

———. *The Silmarillion.* Boston: Houghton Mifflin Co., 1977.

———. *Tree and Leaf.* Boston: Houghton Mifflin Co., 1965.

———. *The Two Towers.* Boston: Houghton Mifflin Co., 1965.

———. *Unfinished Tales.* Boston: Houghton Mifflin Co., 1980.

——— and Donald Swann. *The Road Goes Ever On: A Song Cycle,* 2nd ed. Boston: Houghton Mifflin Co., 1978.

Trewartha, Glenn. *An Introduction to Climate,* 4th ed. McGraw-Hill Book Co., Inc., 1968.

Webster's Seventh New Collegiate Dictionary. Springfield, Mass.: G. & C. Merriam Co., Pub., 1965.

Whybrow, Charles. *Antiquary's Exmoor: Microstudy C1.* Dulverton, Somerset: The Exmoor Papers, 1970.

Periodicals

Cahill, Tim. "Charting the Splendors of Lechuguilla Cave." *National Geographic,* vol. 179, no. 3 (March 1991), 34–59.

Goodknight, Glen. "A Comparison of Cosmological Geography in the Works of J. R. R. Tolkien, C. S. Lewis, and Charles Williams." *Mythlore,* vol. 1, no. 3 (July 1969), 18–22.

Howes, Margaret M. "The Elder Ages and the Later Glaciations of the Pleistocene Epoch." *Tolkien Journal,* vol. 3, no. 2 (Spring 1968), 3–15.

Juhren, Marcella. "The Ecology of Middle Earth." *Tolkien Journal/Mythlore,* vol. II no. 1 (Winter 1970), 4–6.

Kilby, Clyde, and Richard Plotz. "Many Meetings with Tolkien." *Niekas,* vol. 19 (1968), 39–40.

Mitchison, Naomi, "One Ring to Bind Them." *New Statesman and Nation,* vol. 48 (September 18, 1954), 331.

Niekas, vol. 18 (1968), 39, 40.

Porteus, J. Douglas. "A Preliminary Landscape Analysis of Middle-Earth in Its Third Age." *Landscape,* vol. 19, no. 2 (January 1975), 33–38.

Resnick, Henry. "Interview with Tolkien." *Niekas,* vol. 18 (Late Spring, 1967), 37–43.

Reynolds, Robert C. "The Geomorphology of Middle-Earth." *Swansea Geographer,* vol. 12 (1974), 67–71.

Interviews

Dr. Andrew Bodman, April 10, 1979.

Dr. Neil Harriman, August 3, 1979.

Mrs. Jean Magnuson, October 18, 1979.

Dr. Nils Meland, April 15, 1979.

Miscellaneous Sources

Baynes, Pauline. "A Map of Middle-Earth." London: George Allen & Unwin, Ltd., 1970.

Canada. "Fortress of Louisbourg." Montreal: Parks Canada, Indian and Northern Affairs, c. 1976.

Marquette University, Department of Special Collections and University Archives. "John Ronald Reuel Tolkien Manuscript Collection."

Pioneer Engineering Works. "Facts and Figures." Minneapolis, Minn. PORTEC, 1955.

St. Clair, Gloria S. "Studies in the Sources of J. R. R. Tolkien's Lord of the Rings." Unpublished dissertation. University of Oklahoma, 1970.

Tedhams, Richard Warren. "Tolkien: An Annotated Glossary." Unpublished Master's Thesis. University of Oklahoma, 1967.

Tolkien, Christopher. "Map of Beleriand and the Lands to the North." Boston: Houghton Mifflin Co., 1977.

Index of Place Names

This index includes an alphabetical list of the place names of *Arda* — Tolkien's World. Many of the locales have two or more names, some of which do not appear on any map. The most common form has often been listed in parentheses (without reference to chronology or transliteration). Each name important enough to be found on world and/or regional maps is preceded by a coordinate of the approximate location. Places in *The Shire* are further identified by the appropriate *Farthing* or *March*, abbreviated as:

EF — East Farthing	WF — West Farthing
NF — North Farthing	Bk — Buckland
SF — South Farthing	Wm — Westmarch

All names are followed by the page or pages on which the term (or an alternate form) can be found. The page containing the primary locational reference is shown in italic, while that of the site map is underlined.

The History of Middle-earth has added hundreds of names to those in the previously published works. Many of these were quickly abandoned, and some were later applied to different locations. Only those which were shown as predominant forms in *The History* indexes and others of special interest have been included. These are listed in a separate section to avoid confusion.

Index of Selected Place Names for *The History of Middle-earth*

Each entry is followed by lesser alternates. The primary form found in the main *Atlas* index is listed in parentheses. Terms for which a concept or usage was later abandoned or altered are marked with an asterisk *.